THE HORNS OF AVALON

Book 8 in the Babylon Series

Sam Sisavath

THE HORNS OF AVALON
Copyright © 2016 Sam Sisavath
All rights reserved.

This is a work of fiction. Names, characters, organizations, places, events, and incidents are either products of the author's imagination or are used fictitiously.

No part of this book may be reproduced, or stored in a retrieval system, or transmitted in any form or by any means, electronic, mechanical, photocopying, recording, or otherwise, without express written permission of the publisher.

Published by Road To Babylon Media LLC
www.roadtobabylon.com

Cover Art by Deranged Doctor Design
Editing by Jennifer Jensen and Wendy Chan

ISBN: 0692672400
ISBN-13: 978-0692672402

Some battles are still worth fighting.

Killing has never been something Keo shied away from, but the events of the last year have made him rethink his bloody past. Except nothing lasts forever. Now, Keo has embraced his old ways and set his sights on a new target—and there is nothing more dangerous than a man with nothing to lose.

For Lara and those on the *Trident*, an encounter with a new group of survivors pulls them even further off course. It doesn't seem to matter how hard Lara tries to steer clear of Mercer's war on the ghouls; fate seems intent on drawing her into the conflict.

Meanwhile, the fighting rages in Texas, with Mercer's kill teams roaming the land and collaborators on war footing. Caught in the middle, Danny, Gaby, and Nate are desperate to reach the coast, but find themselves pawns in a nightmarish game of cat and mouse instead.

In this penultimate volume in *The Purge of Babylon* series, loyalties will be tested and destinies embraced, and the road to salvation will finally be revealed to those brave enough to answer the call of the Horns…

PROLOGUE

"FACEBOOK."

"Facebook?"

"Yeah, Facebook. Twitter. Pinterest. Basically, all of social media."

"I never had much use for social media."

"That's because you're old."

"I'm not that old."

"You're pretty old."

He grunted. "Get off my lawn."

She giggled. It was barely audible, and he enjoyed seeing her act like such a kid again, so why did it make him wince just a little bit?

Because there are undead things all around us. Everywhere. They could be hiding under us right this moment.

Great, Riley, freak yourself out some more, why don't ya.

He was glad for the darkness, because it meant Hannah couldn't see the hairs along his arms standing up. After all, he was supposed to be the confident one, the adult that got things done. It wouldn't have benefited either one of them if she saw through that charade over some inane chitchat about what they missed most about the old world.

"What are you going to miss?" she asked.

It was a good question. He hadn't thought much about it; staying alive in the here and now had always been more important. Hannah waited, arms clenched tightly around knees pulled up to her chest, but he could tell his answers were less important to her than the act of (hushed whispers) speaking, their little rebellion against the cold nights and the things that moved within them.

Out there, somewhere...

Always out there...

He fought back another shiver and finally said, "I don't know. I haven't really thought much about it."

"Taco Bell," Hannah said.

"Taco Bell?"

"I love Taco Bell. Their breakfast menu is to die for. Let me guess: You're a McDonald's guy?"

"Neither."

"Neither?"

"Neither."

"That's a first..."

"What's that?"

"I've never met someone who wasn't either a Taco Bell or a McDonald's guy. I did meet this one dude who liked both, but I've never met anyone who didn't like either."

"You need to expand your circle of friends."

"I guess." Then, "Too late for that now."

"Yeah," he said quietly.

He searched out Hannah's form in the blackness but could just barely make out her outline. He only knew where to look because she hadn't moved from the spot she had settled down in, back when there was still light out. This, despite the fact that they were barely five feet apart. There was a time when that distance would be wider, but those nights were long gone. Now, if he didn't reflexively sit down next to her, she would do it.

Strength in numbers.

And dwindling, fast...

"Are they gone?" she whispered, her voice dropping noticeably.

He didn't need to think about the question because there was only one *they* out there, right now...

He nodded before realizing she probably couldn't see despite their close proximity. There was a lonely sliver of moonlight somewhere in the back of the room, but they had made sure to stay away from it. Sometimes the creatures moved across rooftops, and even a small, barely inch-wide hole was too much to risk. After all they'd gone through to survive when so many hadn't, he wasn't going to take any chances now.

Stay alive. Just stay alive...

"I think so," he whispered, matching her pitch.

As soon as the words left his lips, he clutched the shotgun tighter. Two months ago he'd never fired a gun, much less owned one, but now he had three on him. Hannah, meanwhile, carried a small pistol. He had debated about giving a weapon to the sixteen-year-old but eventually caved. She was still uncomfortable around the handgun and rarely drew it, and he never told her it was the same with him.

"I thought they'd never leave," Hannah said. "Do you think they know we're up here? Is that why they were inside the house?"

"I don't know. We were careful..."

"We were really careful."

"We were," he nodded again, hoping that would reassure her. "We'll be fine. We've gotten this far, right?"

"Right," she said softly.

"We just have to stick together."

"Stick together..."

"Hannah..."

"Yeah?"

"I'm a McDonald's breakfast guy. Hotcakes and sausage all the way."

"I knew it," she said, and chuckled softly.

He could just make out the outlines of her shoulders as they drooped slightly, a sign she was finally relaxing after being so tense for much of the night. He had to look around the floor before he could make out the trapdoor about six feet in front of him. The attic was poorly insulated and the outside chill seeped through the boards. It was a good thing they had taken precautions and raided an Archers earlier today for new—thicker—winter clothing.

"Shopping rocks," Hannah had said, and he had beamed because seeing her happy and carefree was such a rare thing these days.

Despite staring at her for the last five minutes, Riley couldn't be sure if she had gone to sleep or was just leaning against the wall to rest. Hannah could sleep anywhere, so he wouldn't have been surprised if it was the former, especially in this attic where they had spent the last three nights huddled inside. Sometimes he wondered if that was a mistake, that maybe the smarter thing was to keep moving.

But go where? There was nowhere to go. Absolutely nowhere.

The city was overrun. The state, too. Maybe even the entire country.

The world...

Jesus, cut it out. Stop filling your head with things you can't change, you idiot.

Concentrate on the now—and right now this little girl is depending on you to keep your head in the present.

His hands had gone numb from gripping the shotgun so tight, and it took some effort for Riley to unclench them. He did it one finger at a time, until he could feel the blood circulating freely through all ten digits again.

Better...

He didn't even know why he was carrying around so many guns. It wasn't like shooting them did any good. The damn things *didn't die* even after you blew their whole head off. He knew because he had done that, and watched with his jaw on the floor as it kept coming like something out of a nightmare. A blood-soaked goddamn nightmare.

When he could hear the telltale signs of Hannah's sleep-induced breathing, Riley allowed himself to finally close his eyes and lean back against the wall. In the first few nights of the end of the world he'd heard a lot of gunfire, sounds of survivors like him and

Hannah fighting back. But then they'd all faded, until there were only the endless silent nights like the one he was listening to right now.

It was hauntingly serene, even soothing, and at the same time terrifying.

THE WELCOMING WARMTH of morning had filled the attic while he had his eyes closed, and his loud yawning woke Hannah, who lay next to him. Her long, dirty hair cascaded over half her face, and she swiped at it before smiling across at him.

"We made it," she said.

"Of course." He smiled back. "I never had any doubts."

"None?"

"Not a one."

Her face darkened a bit. "Was it just me, or did they sounded closer last night?"

They were definitely closer, and they stayed longer than the other times, he thought, but said, "Closer schmoser. It's morning. Let's go enjoy the sunlight."

"My favorite part of every day!" she said, her voice purposefully loud, as if she had been holding the volume back all night—which, he guessed, was true.

He got up and moved around to get the blood flowing to all of his extremities again. The attic was big enough that he could stretch to his full six-one height with plenty of space to spare. Hannah, all five-three of her, never had to worry about cramming into a small corner. He always did his best to find them a hiding place with enough room for both of them to be comfortable, but that wasn't always possible. This attic had been a godsend—not to mention all the supplies packed into the house's pantries underneath it. Still, he couldn't shake the feeling it was a mistake to have stayed here for three straight nights. That was usually one night longer than he was comfortable with.

Stop it. You're alive. Hannah's alive. That's all that matters…

Riley slung his shotgun and walked to the trapdoor. He crouched and eased it open before sticking his head forward and breathing in the fresh air.

"Smell good?" Hannah asked behind him.

"Like a nice Big Breakfast platter at Mickey D's."

"Taco Bell all the way, baby."

"Pfft," he said, exaggerating the smirk before pulling back the collapsible ladder and extending it below. "Ladies first."

"Since when am I a lady?"

"Close enough. Now come on, down you go."

She leaned over the opening and took a long look at the second floor hallway below, just the way they had practiced. The room was lit up by a pool of light that reflected off her slightly grimy face, and Riley wondered what he looked like at the moment. He hadn't showered in…God, he couldn't remember. It didn't help that he had been wearing the same clothes for just as long. The only saving grace was that both he and Hannah had gone smell blind a long time ago.

"Clear?" he asked.

"Looks clear," she said.

"Be certain."

"I'm certain. Pretty certain."

"Pretty certain or just certain?"

She snorted. "Pretty certain, certain."

"Good enough."

He watched the girl climb down, then heard the *thump* as she jumped the last few steps to the hallway below.

"Hey," he called after her.

"What?" she said from below.

"Don't wander off."

"I'm just standing here waiting for you, dude. Can you please hurry it up already?"

He smiled. Hannah had called him *dude* for three weeks after they first met, before one day she started using *Riley*. Now it was back and forth between the two, depending on how annoyed she was with him, like she was now.

He had turned around to position himself on the stairs to follow her down when he heard footsteps below him. "Hannah," he said, slightly alarmed.

"What?" she called back from below.

"Strength in numbers, remember?"

"I'm just going to get my stuff in the bedroom."

"Hannah, wait for me."

She didn't answer, which prompted him to hop the last six feet down the ladder and land in a crouch. Riley had never been particularly athletic, but he'd since discovered some modicum of athleticism he didn't know existed. He wasn't going to take on Michael Jordan at the Y anytime soon, but he was doing things now he never thought he would—or could—do before the world decided to stop making sense.

He was straightening up, hands groping for the shotgun slung over his back, when he looked up the hallway and saw Hannah with one hand on the doorknob of the master bedroom. She had already pushed it open, and he glimpsed pitch darkness on the other side that immediately set alarms off inside his head because *it shouldn't have been that dark in there.*

"Hannah!" he shouted.

She stopped and looked back, and a smile flashed across her face. Even with all that dirt, he thought she looked cherubic—sweet and innocent. Hannah was someone's daughter, someone's sister, and though Riley never had any siblings—

"Hannah—" he said again when he saw the shadows in the master bedroom, barely visible through the small slit in the ajar door, *move.*

She must have either heard or smelled them, because she turned around at almost the exact same moment it reached out—*a deformed hand, bony fingers uncurling*—and grabbed her around the ankle. The acidic stench of searing flesh filled the hallway almost immediately as the exposed part of the creature's skin turned to white ash against the sunlight, and Riley thought he might have heard something that sounded like a squeal of pain from inside the room, but all of that was lost against Hannah's screaming. She might have started out trying to yell his name, but it quickly became lost in a long cry that filled the entire house.

Oh Jesus oh Jesus oh Jesus blurred across his mind as a second hand reached out and long, bony fingers wrapped around Hannah's other ankle. The flesh on the second hand burned off as it made contact with the sunlight, but even as clouds of white-gray ash filled the hallway, both hands tightened their grip around Hannah's legs and the creatures *pulled her in*—

"Hannah!"

It took him less than a couple of seconds to cross the second floor, but even as he launched himself into a run he knew—deep down, he just knew—that it was too late. She was already down, and they were pulling her along the wooden floor. The last he saw of her was Hannah, on her stomach, staring back at him with impossibly wide eyes as she tried in vain to grab the sides of the bedroom door. There was a look on her face, an expression he had first seen during that night when they found each other for the first time as the world died around them.

It had taken him weeks to figure out the story behind it because he didn't want to ask, didn't want to intrude on her innermost thoughts. Finally, one night, he saw it again—just a quick there-and-gone glimpse—but it was long enough for him to understand.

It was sadness.

Hannah was sad. For her loss. For his. For the world's.

She had that same look on her face now as she lost her hold on the doorframe and—

She was gone.

He slid to a stop in front of the open door, sneakers squeaking loudly, but not enough to drown out the pounding in his chest or the constant refrain of *Oh Jesus oh Jesus oh Jesus* running through his head.

They were inside the master bedroom, so many that he couldn't tell where they began and the walls and floor ended. They had covered the windows with bedsheets and blankets, and the small horde of creatures were focused in the very middle, far from the small streaks of sunlight that had managed to badger their way into the room anyway. Their backs were exposed to him, deformed spines prickling against films of flesh that barely resembled skin. The overwhelming stench, like vomit left to roast in the sun, made him gag and take a step back.

But he didn't retreat far enough to avoid seeing one of her legs sticking out of the pile of feeding monsters. She had stopped moving, and the only sound aside from the crash of his runaway heartbeat was the unforgiving *slurp-slurp-slurp*.

He fired the shotgun, racked it, and fired again.

One of them glanced back at him, its hollowed obsidian eyes surrounded by pruned flesh. It looked almost annoyed, the *clump-clump* of coagulated blood dripping out of the hole he had made in its right shoulder.

Then it turned back around and bent its head and resumed feeding.

He racked the shotgun and fired again, this time aiming for the head of the closest one. It flopped forward but picked itself up, moving unsteadily with the top of its head mostly gone. Unlike the previous one, this creature didn't bother to cast him an annoying glance.

Riley stumbled back, back, every step like pedaling through quicksand, the *(Useless. It's useless!)* weapon in his hands impossibly heavy. What good was a gun if it couldn't kill these things? Why did he carry so many on him? Why did he spend so much time arguing with himself about letting her carry a small pistol—

Hannah.

Jesus, Hannah, I'm sorry, I'm so sorry.

He turned, groping the walls for support, and staggered his way down the length of the hallway. There was no railing, or he might have keeled over it and plummeted to his death below. Maybe that would have been the humane thing—the right thing—to do. At least it would prevent him from replaying the look on Hannah's face—that odd expression of sadness—as she realized what was about to happen in the split second before it did.

He fumbled down the stairs, not sure how he was able to keep from falling—clutching to the banister with an iron grip probably helped—while dragging the shotgun behind him, the weapon *clacking* and *thumping* against every carpeted step, still connected to him by the long strap.

The first floor was covered in swaths of sunlight, the air so warm that when it hit him it was like moving through an inferno. There were signs everywhere that they had been inside the house while he and Hannah had hidden in the attic. It was in the air *(The smell. God, the smell!)* and the toppled furniture, the open door, and the broken windows. But they had been here the previous nights, too, and always left. So why didn't they leave this time?

He was blaming them—the creatures—when he should be blaming himself. Because he should have known better than to spend three nights in a row in the same place. He should have known *better.*

I'm sorry, Hannah. I'm sorry…

He was irresistibly drawn to the open door, crashing into furniture and knocking down a vase, though he didn't hear it shatter. His ears rang with the shotgun clattering behind him as the weapon bounced off walls and the legs of a nightstand until it was finally scraping against the concrete driveway outside.

He blinked against the sun, unable to process why it was so bright this morning or why the always-welcoming heat was now trying to suffocate him. Breathing was difficult, and he had the sensation of drowning. He fell to his knees, so numbed that he didn't even feel the impact. He kept blinking, trying to chase the last image of Hannah's face out of his (memories) eyes…

"You okay, son?"

He opened his eyes back up. Someone was standing in front of him.

A man. Tall.

Or maybe not so tall, because Riley was on his knees and his perspective was skewed. The sun hung high behind the man, the flow of light bending around his broad shoulders as if it were afraid to touch him. The brown of his eyes as they looked up at the house, then back at him. There was sadness there, understanding.

This was a man who knew what Riley had been through, who understood Riley's pain.

"Your friend didn't make it," the man said quietly.

Riley shook his head, but when he tried to open his mouth, he only sucked in much-needed oxygen.

"Was she your wife?" the man asked.

He somehow managed to shake his head again.

"Friend," the man said.

Riley nodded.

"I'm sorry about your friend," the man said. "But you're alive. You need to stay that way."

He blinked up at the man. "Why?" he said, the single word coming out almost as a croak.

"Because we're all that's left," the man said. "One of these days we're going to take it all back, but until that day comes, we have to stay alive, whatever it takes."

The man held out his hand. Riley looked at it, then at the man's face. Fifties, at least, almost as old as his father had been when he passed.

"Time to get back up, son," the man said.

Riley reached for the proffered hand and let himself be pulled up. He was very light on his feet for some reason. Either that, or the man was impossibly strong.

"What's your name?" the man asked.

"Riley…"

"Good to meet you, Riley."

The man looked behind him at three others standing on the sidewalk beyond the front yard of the house. Two men and one woman. They were cradling the kind of military rifles Riley had seen in some of the pawn shops around town while he and Hannah were scavenging, but that they'd always been too intimidated by to pick up. A beat-up white truck was parked in the road, the engine still churning.

How was it possible he hadn't seen or heard these people until now? Where had they come from?

"Check the house," the man said to the others. "Kill

everything."

The three didn't hesitate. They jogged up the driveway, passing Riley and the man, and vanished into the house one by one. They moved as if they had been training for this one moment all their lives.

"It's dangerous," Riley said. He wasn't sure if the man had heard him, though, because his own voice sounded lifeless to his own ears. "They're in there. The creatures."

"We know," the man said. "We heard you shooting while we were down the street. Sound travels these days."

"But they don't die," Riley said, trying to get the man to understand. *"They don't die."*

Riley looked back and up at the second floor when he heard the gunshots. Rapid-fire, like how machine guns always sounded in the movies. He flinched when a bullet pierced one of the master-bedroom windows and sent glass plummeting to the driveway in front of him. More rounds punched through the walls and vanished across the street.

The man put a reassuring hand on Riley's arm and led him back to the sidewalk. "Just in case."

"They don't die," he said as he let himself be pulled back.

"There are ways to kill them. I'll teach you."

The shooting had stopped. In fact, it had ended a while ago, and he could hear the three coming back down the stairs. He expected to see just one or maybe two if they were lucky, but instead all three returned. Their eyes searched him out, and Riley saw that they were full of sympathy, especially the woman's.

"Good to go, sir," one of the men said as they passed.

"Well done," the older man said. Then, to Riley, "It's time to go, son."

"Go where?" he asked quietly, the image of Hannah's last expression burned into his mind's eye, replaying over and over and over.

"Away from here," the older man said. "We need time to grow, to train, to prepare. And when we're ready—and only then—we'll finally act."

"Ready?" He looked back at the man, unable to understand what was happening, what he was trying to say. "Ready for what?"

"All that can wait. For now, you should come home with us. There's not a lot of us left anymore and we have to stick together." He pointed at the other three: "That's Benford, Rhett, and Erin."

The two men and the woman nodded back at him, and Riley had never felt more welcomed in his life.

"And you can call me Mercer," the older man said. He squeezed Riley's shoulder and gave him a comforting smile. "We have a lot of work ahead of us, Riley. Are you in? Will you help me take back what belongs to us, whatever it takes?"

"Yes," Riley answered breathlessly.

BOOK ONE
PORT OF CALL

CHAPTER 1
KEO

FIND MERCER. KILL Mercer.

It used to be that he could come up with three goals without having to work all that hard, but these days he was happy with two. These days, things had a way of blowing up in his face. Like with Gillian, like with Jordan...

Jordan...

He wished he could say watching someone he cared for bleeding out was a new thing. Over the years, he'd learned to detach himself, to avoid making friends, and to tune out when they started talking about their families "back home" or their dreams. A nod here, a forced smile there was all it took. Most of them just liked to hear themselves talk anyway, never mind if anyone actually heard them.

There wasn't a whole lot he could do about the last few days of his life. They were done and gone, beyond his reach. All he had left was what was ahead of him: a place in the middle of nowhere called Lochlyn, Texas. Such a minor town that it was barely a blip on the map he carried in one of the pouches around his waist.

What were the chances Mercer was even in Lochlyn? God only knew (not that he believed in God or anything), but it gave him a place to go, a target to focus on. Keo was always at his best when he had someone to go up against. Pollard, Steve, and now Mercer. Men who brought death and misery. It was a good thing he was used to such men. Hell, if you were to ask some of the people he'd known in his life, they would say the same thing about him.

Find Mercer. Kill Mercer.

The former was going to take some doing, but the latter, well, he was an old hand when it came to that. The trick was to find the man first, though. It would have probably helped if he knew what Mercer looked like, but then Keo reasoned a man like that, who controlled an army of fearless killers (and they'd have to be fearless, to bring the battle to the collaborators, to scatter across the Texas countryside in two-men kill teams like they were doing right now) would stand out.

Pollard had. Steve had, too. They all did, if you knew what signs to look for. And Keo did. He had been around enough of them and taken orders from their ilk more times than he could stomach. They were always easy to spot.

The leader. The alpha.

So all he had to do was reach Lochlyn and go from there. No sweat. It was as easy as following the map, using the sun as his compass.

Find Mercer. Kill Mercer.

About four hours before nightfall, there was a noticeable drop in temperature. It had gotten colder these days, but Texas in December was still perversely illogical. Anywhere else and he would be freezing, but here, moving through a field of grass burnt brown by the sun, there was just enough wind against his exposed face to give him a slight chill.

It had taken him too long to get this far. A day now since he had buried Jordan in a nondescript part of the countryside under a grave of rocks to keep the elements (and other dead things) from desecrating her. He wished he could have spent more time, made a better (decent) final tomb, but he'd wanted to flee that place before it was too late.

"Too late" for what, he didn't know, even now. He just had to go.

There wasn't a lot around him now except large patches of untilled fields and the occasional house and accompanying red (always red) barn in the distance. He had lost sight of the highway or anything resembling a paved road about five miles back. Lochlyn was somewhere up ahead of him. Unless, of course, he had gotten lost and didn't know it. That was entirely possible, too. A lot of things were possible these days.

He'd thought about checking the buildings for clues to his exact whereabouts but decided to bypass them. If he was hurting for guns, ammo, or food, he might have taken the time, but he was carrying enough of all three to last for a few weeks if he conserved. So he kept moving. Besides, if he were still running around out here a week from now, that probably meant he hadn't found Mercer. Worse, he had no clue *how* to find Mercer. Either way, if he couldn't locate and kill the man in the next couple of days, then the mission would be a scratch—

A man's deep voice, arriving with a sudden gust of wind from up ahead: "How many?"

"She said three," another voice said. Also male, but younger sounding.

"Shit, we lost *three* so far?" the first one said.

"That we know of."

"More?"

"Maybe."

"Shit." Then, "On the upside, The Ranch's going to be less crowded when we get back."

"Dude…"

"What, too soon?"

Chuckling from both men.

Keo was already on one knee, the unslung AR-15 in his hands. He carefully eased off the rifle's safety while listening to the conversation in front of him. How far? Twenty meters? Thirty?

"You got it?" Deep Voice asked.

"Again?" Younger said.

"I like listening to it."

"You in love with her or something?"

"Or something."

"Don't you think that's kind of weird?"

"What's so weird about it?"

"What if she's fat and ugly?"

"She doesn't sound fat and ugly."

"What does fat and ugly sound like?"

"I don't know, but not like that. Besides, it's better than talking about our MIAs. That shit's just depressing."

A short laugh, followed by a brief moment of silence.

Keo counted one second…five…

…twenty…

What the hell were they doing up there? He hadn't moved since he heard them, but now he let his breath come out in short spurts, in tune to the sporadic gust of wind blowing through the stalks of dying grass around him. It wasn't much cover, but the field did go all the way up to his waist, and on one knee he was almost invisible. Not entirely, but good enough that whoever was up there hadn't spotted him yet. Some of that elusive luck was working in his favor for once, with the men not looking in his direction when he nearly walked right up to them like a blind idiot.

One minute became two, and still nothing.

What the hell are they doing?

He reached down to make sure the handgun was in its holster at his hip before rising back to his feet and, bent forward at almost a seventy-five-degree angle at the waist, took one step and stopped to listen.

Five seconds…ten…

Nothing.

He took a second step, then a third…

There was just the rustling of grass against the wind and the soft *crunch-crunch* of his boots on the sun-hardened ground. Every step sounded like banging drums, and Keo spent just as much time cringing at the noise he was making as he did trying to reassure himself it was just his mind magnifying them, that it was just his imagination on overdrive…

Shit, you almost convinced yourself that time, pal.

The sun was still high in the sky, the warmth giving him just enough assurance to keep moving steadily forward. Nightfall was coming, but it would be a while. He had plenty of time. Plenty of time…

Five meters…

Ten…

Fifteen…

A soft mechanical *click,* very clear against the natural countryside around him, froze him in mid-stride, and Keo went down on one knee for the second time.

"Almost out of batteries," a voice said. Younger. "Did you bring yours?"

"Nah," Deep Voice said. "You're out?"

"Yup."

"Ugh."

"Sucks for you."

A grunt. "You won't believe this, but there was a time when these things could only hold ten songs at a time, and they cost twice as much."

Younger chuckled. "You're right; I don't believe it."

"It's true."

"How long before— What?"

"You smell that?"

"Smell what?"

Keo looked down at his clothes. His *dirty* clothes.

*Sonofa*bitch.

He launched up from the ground and took the remaining ten meters at a dead run, the *crunch-crunch* of his boots exploding loudly under him, and this time he didn't even try to pretend it was just his imagination.

Can you hear me now? he thought, almost laughing out loud.

The first head that popped up in front of him was balding and had what looked like a rash over his right cheek. He was in his forties and wearing nondescript camo clothing, and though Keo couldn't see the rest of his body, the man looked in reasonably good shape. Fading white wires *(earbuds?)* dangled from his ears and connected to a small device in his hand. He turned his head, saw Keo, and his eyes went white and round like baseballs.

Keo snapped off a shot at five meters—close enough that he barely had to aim—and blew the man's brains out.

The gunshot *boomed* and was just starting its echo across the landscape when the second head popped up.

Younger, with some kind of military buzz cut, was in the process of standing up when the older man collapsed next to him. Instead of reaching for his weapon, the man held up his hands and shouted, "Wait—"

But Keo didn't wait. He couldn't, even if he wanted to. He was moving too fast, the surge of adrenaline driving him forward with a full head of steam. He swung the AR-15 and connected solidly with the stock of his rifle. His victim dropped to the ground back onto the already bent stalks of grass where he and his now-dead friend had been sitting.

Keo sucked in a deep breath and spun around in a complete circle, searching for more targets among the wavy blades of grass and the sporadic lines of trees circling him. The gunshot. Someone would have heard that gunshot. It was simply impossible not to these days with the deadness of the world.

So where were they?

Was it possible there were only two in the entire area? Could he be *that* lucky?

First time for everything.

Satisfied there was no one else out there—or at least no one dumb enough to show themselves—Keo dropped down behind the makeshift wall of grass.

Mercer's man—and he had to be one of Mercer's men, because who else would be out here this close to Lochlyn?—was rolling around on the ground, both hands cupping his shattered nose. Blood oozed through his fingers, and the man's eyes, soft blue, blinked erratically up at Keo.

"Relax; you'll make it," Keo said.

The man's eyes dropped down to the holstered sidearm at his hip. It looked like a Sig Sauer, similar to the one Keo was carrying.

"Sure, why not?" Keo said, and grinned at him.

The man stopped rolling and wisely didn't reach for his weapon.

"Are there more of you around?" Keo asked.

The man didn't answer right away. Maybe he was trying to decide how much he should tell, if anything.

"Hey, what's that?" Keo said, and pointed at a random spot on the ground.

The man predictably turned his head to look, and when he did, Keo punched him in the face. Of course, he wasn't instantly knocked unconscious; he simply groaned against Keo's fist, but before he could hold out his hands to ward off further attacks, Keo punched him again, and again…

"WHO ARE YOU? What do you want?" the man asked, though it came out more like "Whaphuduuwhump?" because of the broken nose and busted lip. His face was an odd shade of purple and brown, which was a little hard to see in the darkened second floor of the barn where Keo had brought the man, about a hundred meters (give or take) from the field where they had clashed.

Keo could see the exact spot from one of the open doors; he had been staring at it for the last forty minutes, convinced more of Mercer's men would be responding to the sound of his gunshot. That had been stupid. He'd fired without thinking of the consequences. He couldn't even blame it on the dead man for popping up right in front of him like something out of a bad horror flick. He didn't bother with the lie. He'd shot Deep Voice because he wanted to. After the week he'd had, he just wanted to kill *someone*.

"You got a name?" Keo asked.

"Davis," the man said.
"What about your friend?"
"Butch."

Keo chuckled. Davis and Butch. It sounded like a bad Hollywood Western.

"Where's Mercer, Davis?" Keo asked, looking back at Davis, who was sitting behind him on an old block of hay.

The building around them smelled of year-old animal feces and mold. It was at least ten, maybe twenty times worse than the last barn he had been in *(with Jordan)* in terms of smell, but was still in relatively good shape. This building, along with the farmhouse next door, was going to outlive him; not that that was saying very much.

If it's still here after this week, it might outlast me...

"Mercer?" Davis said.

"Your fearless leader."

"What do you want with him?" Davis was still having difficulty speaking, especially when he had to string more than a few words together. It took Keo a few seconds to understand everything he said.

"Is he in Lochlyn?" Keo asked.

Davis didn't answer. His hands and ankles were presently bound with duct tape, and Keo hadn't been too worried about the man fleeing as they made their way here, then up to the second floor. Davis was in no shape to run, and certainly not while Keo had the AR. Out there, with wide-open spaces for hundreds of meters at a time, there weren't a whole lot of places to hide. That was the only reason Keo felt comfortable enough to stop and wait for Mercer's men.

Or, at least, that's what he told himself.

Give me a break. You're still here because you want *them to show up. You can taste it, can't you? You want this. Admit it.*

Yes, he thought. *I want this. It's what I'm good at...*

When Davis still hadn't answered, Keo said, "Lochlyn. Mercer. Is he there?"

Davis finally shook his head.

"Where is he?" Keo asked.

"I don't know."

Keo casually took his hand off the barrel of the slung rifle and rested it on the butt of the Sig Sauer he'd taken from Davis earlier and had stuffed into his front waistband. Davis's eyes—or his left, anyway, because the right was black and blue and puffy like a blowfish—were drawn to the not-so-subtle movement before snapping back up to Keo's face.

"I don't know where he is," Davis said.

Keo didn't take his hand off the gun. "When was the last time you saw him?"

"Back at The Ranch."

"'The ranch?'" Keo repeated, just in case he hadn't made the words out correctly given Davis's situation. Hadn't the dead Butch said something about a "ranch" too, before Keo shot him?

"Home base," Davis said. "That's what we call it."

"Where is home base?"

Davis shook his head.

"You don't know?" Keo asked.

"I know. I'm just not telling you."

"Are you sure about that?"

Davis nodded with something that could almost be mistaken for conviction, which if true was impressive given his current state. Even though both of them were mostly hidden in the darker corners of the barn, Keo could easily make out Davis's injuries.

"What do you want with him?" Davis asked.

"I want to put a bullet between his eyes."

Keo was watching Davis closely for a reaction, but he had to admit he wasn't quite ready for the grin that broke out across Davis's face.

"That's an interesting response," Keo said.

"You're one of them. Collaborators."

Keo shook his head. "No."

"I don't believe you."

"I couldn't begin to tell you how little that means to me."

Davis snorted. "Then why do you want to kill Mercer?"

"Personal reasons."

The man leaned slightly forward, as if to get a better angle on Keo's face. After the almost hour they had spent together, Keo thought that was another very interesting move from his hostage. At the moment, Davis looked more curious than he was afraid, which wasn't quite what Keo was going for.

"What?" Keo said.

"I'm just trying to see if you look familiar." Davis finally shook his head and sat back. "No. I don't know you. I'd remember that face."

"Scars give a man character."

"So I hear." He paused, then, "What's wrong with your leg?"

"There's nothing wrong with my leg."

"Oh, I don't believe that. You're clearly favoring one side. Old wound?"

Not old enough, Keo thought, but said, "Where's Mercer?"

"I told you, I don't know where he is. The last time I saw him was back at The Ranch."

"And you're not going to tell me where this ranch is?"

"Nope," Davis said, and grinned back at him.

Keo sighed and took his hand away from the gun. He snapped open one of the pockets along his pant leg and pulled something out.

"What the hell is that?" Davis asked, narrowing his eyes at the titanium eating utensil in Keo's hand.

"Spork," Keo said. "Though technically, it's a scork."

"Scork?"

"Spoon, fork, and cork. Get it?"

"Ah," Davis said, though his eyes (or, at least, the good one) never left the object in Keo's hand.

"But the word 'scork' makes me queasy," Keo said. "So I prefer to call it a spork anyway and ignore the whole 'cork' part. Even though, obviously, it's incorrect."

"You're a man of eccentricities."

"No one's ever called me that before."

"So, what are you going to do with that...spork?"

"I'm going to see how much pain you can take." Keo twirled

the utensil between his fingers. "I would have used the Ka-Bar, but it wouldn't hurt nearly as much and you might bleed out too soon. I can't risk that."

Davis stared at the spork, as if mesmerized by its movements. "And that's...not risky?"

"It's a lot harder to cut an artery with this."

Davis swallowed. "I won't tell you where he is."

"You said you didn't know where he is."

"I don't. Not at this very moment."

Keo stopped twirling the spork and pressed his forefinger against the metallic tines. "They're pretty sharp. Not *that* sharp, but pretty sharp. It'll puncture skin, and even bone, if you push hard enough. I saw it go through a forehead once..."

Davis didn't have to say anything, because his tensing body gave it away. The man looked as if he was mentally and physically preparing to spring up to defend himself, but either his bound arms and legs prevented him from taking action at the moment, or he knew it wouldn't do any good. Instead, he remained nervously perched on the bale of hay.

"Tell me where to find Mercer," Keo said. "Is he in Lochlyn?"

"No," Davis said. "I told you. The last time I saw him was back at The Ranch, before all of this. I don't know where he is now."

"And you won't tell me where this Ranch is..."

"No."

Keo sighed and lowered his hand. "All right. This is getting ridiculous. I'm running out of sunlight, and you're just pissing me off now."

He began walking toward Davis.

The man pushed himself up from the haystack and attempted to move toward the stairs, but he predictably tripped on his bound legs and fell with a *thump!* to the debris-strewn floor on his face. He tried to roll over onto his back, but by the time he finally managed it, Keo was already standing over him. Even in this shadowy part of the barn, Keo swore the eating utensil actually gleamed.

"One last chance," Keo said. "Tell me where to find Mercer."

"Jesus, please," Davis said.

Keo grinned. "I've been called a lot of things, but I have to admit I've never been mistaken for our Lord and Savior before. You a religious man, Davis?"

"Yes..."

"Me, I've never had much use for it. More of a hassle in my old line of work. So tell me, Davis. What did you used to do before all of this?"

"I was a teacher..."

"Cool. I killed a teacher once." Keo sat down on Davis's chest, put his hand on the man's forehead, and easily pushed Davis's head back against the rotten floor despite his attempt at resistance. "He screamed and screamed..."

"Oh, God..."

"It took a while, and it was messy..."

"Lochlyn," Davis said, almost spitting the word out.

Keo sat back a bit. "Lochlyn?"

"You can find Mercer through Lochlyn."

"You said he wasn't there."

"He's not, but you can find him *through* there."

Keo let go of Davis's forehead. "Go on..."

"We're using Lochlyn as an FOB. You know—"

"Yeah, I know what FOBs are. Go on."

"The last flight out is tomorrow. Everyone involved in this area is supposed to be back by then. Including Butch and me."

"What were you and the other guy doing out here, anyway?"

"Perimeter security. In case of collaborator counter-attacks."

"What happens when you don't come back?"

"I guess they'll know something happened. They'll be ready for you," Davis said, and Keo thought the other man wanted badly to smile but was doing everything possible to swallow the urge.

"Where's it going?" Keo asked. "The flight?"

"The Ranch. If you want Mercer, he's probably going to be there."

"Probably?"

"I'm a small cog in the machine. I'm not privy to all his movements. But it's your best bet." Davis let out a heavy sigh and closed his one good eye for a moment before opening it again. "If you're going to kill me, just make it fast. I'd like to skip the prolonged pain part if at all possible."

Keo stood up and put the spork away. "See, that wasn't so hard. I knew you'd come around."

"Fuck you."

"Not right now; we both have headaches."

Davis struggled to sit up, pushing against the floor using his elbows. Somehow, he managed it after a few tries.

"I'm curious," Keo said. "What makes someone follow a man like Mercer?"

"You want the truth?"

"That would be nice."

"There are three types of people running around out here. The true believers, the nonbelievers, and everyone else in the middle."

"Which one are you?"

"Everyone else."

"So why do the nonbelievers follow Mercer if they don't buy what he's selling? I don't know if you've noticed, but it's dangerous out there."

Davis shrugged and looked toward the barn doors, as if he didn't want anyone else to hear what he was about to say next. "He saved our lives. Most of us wouldn't be here if not for him. That's the kind of thing that buys a lot of loyalty."

"But you don't believe in his war."

"What we're doing out here..." He focused on Keo again. "You know? About the attacks on the towns?"

Keo nodded.

"I'm just a schoolteacher," Davis continued. "I didn't even know how to fire a gun until the world ended. Butch believed, though. He was one of the true believers. Me, I'm just trying to get by. Mercer saved my life. He saved all of our lives. I owe him..." He shook his head. "But I don't owe him to kill old men and pregnant women and children."

Keo crouched in front of Davis and stared at the man's heavily bruised face.

Davis looked back at him. "I'm telling the truth. All of it."

Keo ignored him and asked instead, "How's the face?"

"It's numb. Everything's numb. I know my right eye is the size of my foot at the moment, but I can't feel it. Or my nose. Or my mouth. I can hear how I sound, but thank God I can't feel the reasons why." He reached up with his bound hands and touched his cheek, wincing at the contact. "Were you really going to do it? Use that spork on me?"

Keo nodded. "Yeah, I was."

"Well, fuck."

"Yeah."

"So, what now?"

"Tell me about Mercer."

"And then?"

"Mercer. What does he look like?"

"And *then?*" Davis pressed.

"Then I move on to Lochlyn, and if Mercer's not there, I go on to this ranch of yours."

"What about me?"

"I don't need you anymore, so you stay here."

"I need a gun. If you're going to leave me behind, I need a gun." He held up his bound hands. "And you have to release me."

"All right."

"You swear."

"Only on Fridays, but never on Sundays."

"Fuck you," Davis said. "I mean it. You swear you're telling the truth."

Keo raised his right hand and smiled at Davis. "Scout's honor."

CHAPTER 2
LARA

"PORT ARTHUR'S A no-go," Danny said through the radio. "It's locked tighter than a virgin's sphincter."

"You know a lot about virgin sphincters, babe?" Carly asked.

"Hey, I hear things."

"I bet you have."

"Any trouble getting from Starch to Port Arthur?" Lara asked, and Carly repeated the question into the microphone.

"Nothing we couldn't handle," Danny said, but didn't expand on his answer.

He was somewhere outside the Texas port city with Gaby and Nate, though he hadn't given any specifics just in case someone was listening in on their frequency. It was a small chance, but these days even the smallest something had the potential to blow up in your face.

Just in case, right, Will?

"What does he think the collaborators are doing in Port Arthur?" Lara asked, directing her question at Carly.

"What am I, your personal parrot?" Carly said, and handed the microphone over to her. "I already spent ten minutes talking to him before you showed up. That's about nine minutes too much with Danny, in case you were wondering."

Lara smiled. That wasn't even close to being true, because she knew for a fact her friend had spent every day Danny was out there worrying about him. That was something they all did a lot of these days. Before Danny, it was her and Will.

Damn you, Will, you promised *me...*

She said into the radio, "Danny, what are they doing in Port Arthur?"

"Your guess is as good as mine," Danny said. "The kid thinks they might be trying to block our path to open waters."

"What do you think?"

"I don't see the point. We're special, yeah—the special-est in my very humble opinion—but we're not worth committing this much manpower to capturing, especially with all the fun and games going on out here right now."

"Mercer..."

"Well, I didn't want to say his name, in case he's like the Candyman or something."

"The what?"

"The Candyman. Clive Barker? Tony Todd? One of the best slasher flicks of the 1990s?"

"Is that like the bogeyman or something?"

Danny sighed loudly through the radio. "You kids and your lack of respect for the classics of cinema..."

She grinned. It wasn't that she was that much younger than Danny, but every now and then it was fun to needle him. She remembered when she used to get the same kind of joy out of doing it to Will.

"Anyway, back to our marvelous road trip," Danny continued. "I figured we'll chug on along south-like, find another part of the coastline to link up with you guys. It's a big state, should be lots of empty beaches for the linking. I'll radio back as soon as we locate one of them, and you can come over and pick us up. Easy as Mother and apple pie."

"Easy, huh?"

"Hey, good things happen to those who think positively, or so I've been told."

"I'll have to give that a try."

"Give it a swing," Danny said. Then, "Carly tells me you guys are doing just fine without us."

"We're getting by. Spend more time worrying about yourself."

"You don't have to tell me twice."

"That's my man," Carly said.

"Speaking of worrying about oneself, where's Keo now?" Danny asked.

"I don't know, out there somewhere," Lara said. "He and Jordan were headed back to one of the towns when I last saw them. T-something."

"They're all T-somethings. Well, if I run across him out here, I'll let you know."

"What about Mercer's people? Any problems with them since Starch?"

"Luckily we've been able to avoid them, too. They seem to be confining their operations further inland. Probably have more FOBs out there all set up and ready even before they launched this little adventure of theirs."

"FOBs?"

"Forward Operating Bases. Places they're using to launch their attacks."

"Like that airport outside of Larkin."

"Exactamundo."

"How many of those do you think they have?"

"As few as one more, as many as a hundred."

"That's…a big number, Danny."

"Mercer's had a year to think this up. The guy's… Well, momma always says not to say anything if you don't have something nice to say."

"That's never stopped you before."

"I'm learning, Lara, I'm learning…"

She smiled. "Good to know. What about this Mason guy?"

"What about him?"

"How useful has he been?"

"Got us around a couple of ambushes, so he's not been a terrible investment in time and duct tape. But I'm thinking I might have to cut him loose real soon the closer we get to a new and less soldier-infested exfil point."

Lara didn't press for details; she didn't want to know. Images of Gage being tossed into the ocean while she slept flashed briefly across her mind. She only needed to know that Danny would do what he had to in order to come back just as she had on the *Trident*. Just as Will had before them...

"How're you guys for fuel?" Danny asked. "You've been doing a lot of running around out there. Did the tank finally get topped off?"

She exchanged a brief look with Blaine standing behind the helm to her left. The fuel. How many times had they discussed the topic? How many times had she stood right here on the bridge and gone through all the scenarios with Carly and Maddie and Bonnie? Too often, and every single time the results were the same.

But Danny didn't need to hear that right now, so she said into the radio, "We're fine, Danny. Concentrate on finding your exit point, and we'll be ready to pick you up."

"Was it my imagination, or did it take you a while to answer that one?" Danny asked.

"It's your imagination," she said, hoping it was at least semi-convincing.

SHE WATCHED THE kids cannonballing off the swimming platform at the back of the *Trident* and into the crystal blue water of the Gulf of Mexico. Most of them were out there—Dwayne, Elise and Vera, and the other kids she had never really made time to get to know. Their energy was boundless, and the cold water didn't seem to have much of an effect on them.

Lara found herself envying their carefree spirit and at the same time was glad they didn't know what was happening in Texas at the moment—with Danny and Gaby, or what Mercer's men were doing to the collaborator towns.

"To let everyone know there's something worse than the ghouls out here," a man named Gregson, one of Mercer's men, had once said to her.

They know now, don't they? They know now...

"Ah, to be young and clueless," a voice said behind her.

Lara looked over as Zoe pushed against the railing next to her. They were on the uppermost deck of the yacht, which gave Lara a great view of her surroundings, including that of the kids jumping into the water in front of her.

"There's definitely something to be said about not knowing too much," Lara said. "Besides, they've seen enough horrors to last a few lifetimes." She paused for a moment. "They deserve this. We all do."

"You partaking?"

"Not in this weather."

"I can't believe they're not freezing to death by now." The doctor tightened her jacket's collar around her neck. "I have a feeling I'm going to get some new patients very soon."

"Do we have flu shots?"

"Fully stocked."

"Good."

"Don't worry, boss, I got the sickbay handled. You just take care of...every single other thing that matters."

Lara smiled and sneaked a look at Zoe. They hadn't known each other all that long, but Zoe had come to her with the best reference—Will's. Over the months she had proven invaluable, and Lara wasn't sure if she'd even have Danny now if it wasn't for Zoe.

We're all doing our part, Will. You'd be proud of us.

"Danny?" Zoe asked.

"Still out there with Gaby and Nate."

"But okay?"

"In one piece," she nodded, and thought, *Thank God, because I'm the one who sent them out there. If anything happens to them, it would be my fault.*

"So are we," Zoe said.

Lara gave her a curious look.

Zoe smiled sheepishly. "We were just talking…"

"Again?"

"We're always talking behind your back, Lara. You should know that by now."

"So what was on the agenda this time?"

"We decided to make it clear to you that we believe in and trust you. That whatever you decide, we're behind you. We know you're going to get us to the Bengal Islands one way or another. We have faith."

"Jesus, how long was this meeting?"

Zoe laughed softly. "And we mean every word of it. We know you've been second-guessing yourself. About Keo, Danny, about everything. And I'm telling you—*we're* telling you—that you don't have to."

"Don't I?"

"No, because none of us could have done a better job. And most importantly, we know it."

"I shouldn't have sent Danny and Gaby out there."

"You made a calculated decision, and Danny agreed."

"If they don't come back, it'll be my fault."

"They'll come back. Danny's an ex-Ranger. He'll make it back."

"I wasted a lot of fuel getting to Sunport…"

"Because Keo called. And Keo is… Keo."

Lara pursed her lips and couldn't help but smile appreciatively back at the other woman. "Question."

"Shoot."

"When do you guys have these chats, and why am I never invited?"

"Because besides talking about you, we do a lot of talking about you."

"Makes sense."

Zoe looked back across the *Trident,* past the kids and at the open waters beyond. "And, oh, we also talked about this Mercer guy. He sounds like real bad news."

"From everything I've heard, he is."

"What do you think's going on out there right now?"

"I try not to think about it too much. Whatever's happening, it's out of our hands. Mercer, the collaborators..." She focused on Elise and Vera, the two girls holding hands as they cannonballed into the water side by side. "This is all that matters. The lives on this boat."

Zoe nodded, and the two of them watched Dwayne landing hard enough into the water that it splashed not just everyone in the area, but also his mother Kendra and Carrie standing on the platform watching them.

"Thanks," Lara said after a while. "For the pep talk."

"Normally we'd let Carly do it, but we thought you might need to hear it from someone else from time to time."

"Who's up next?"

"Bonnie. Then Blaine. And I think Carrie called dibs after him."

"I hope you guys at least wrote down the order."

"Oh, we did. Sarah's in charge of all the paperwork." Zoe turned around. "If you want to talk, about anything, you know where to find me."

"Thanks," Lara nodded and realized she meant it.

"Sure," Zoe said before pushing off the railing. "Now, if you'll excuse me, I have to go tell Bonnie she's up next."

Lara glanced after the doctor before turning back around to look out at the clear blue horizon. The *Trident* was anchored far enough from land that she couldn't make out Texas in the distance, which meant no one along the coastline could see them, either. At least not without high-powered binoculars, and what were the chances someone was scanning the ocean this moment?

Below her, Carrie let out a scream as Kendra grabbed her from behind and pushed her into the water. Carrie went under for a moment before resurfacing, wet clothes and rifle clinging to her.

Lara smiled to herself and thought, *I'll get them to the Bengal Islands, Will. I'll keep them safe. I promise...*

―

"YOU'RE GOING TO catch a cold. Again."

Elise pouted but didn't stop turning around in a circle so Lara could wipe her dry from head to toe. The girl didn't completely stop shivering until she was wrapped in a big, fluffy cotton bath towel that Lara had laid out. She should have been annoyed at the puddles of water the girl had tracked into her cabin, but she was strangely okay with it. Maybe it was because it was Elise, and Lara had forgotten how much she enjoyed these moments.

She sat down on the end of her bed and watched Elise slip out of her bathing suit and into a pair of long pants and a sweater. She was growing up and filling out, and Lara barely recognized the skinny kid she had rescued from Dansby, Texas, nearly a year ago. Elise hadn't gotten any taller—not yet, anyway—but she wasn't as rail thin as before thanks to the plentiful food in the ocean that regularly graced their lunches and dinners.

"You're getting better at swimming," Lara said.

"Practice makes perfect," Elise smiled back.

"You're not there yet."

"Maybe one day."

"Maybe one day," Lara nodded. "Until then, it's going to get colder, so this might be the last time for a while."

"It's not *that* cold."

"Cold enough. Doctor's orders."

"Zoe said so?"

Lara made a face. "Clever."

Elise grinned. "When are Danny and Gaby coming back?"

"Soon."

"I miss them."

"Me too."

"Hey," Elise said suddenly, as if something had just occurred to her.

Lara smiled. The way the girl's thoughts shifted from topic to topic was something to behold. "What?"

"We were outside one night, and we thought we saw something."

"Who is 'we' and when was 'one night?'"

"Me, Vera, and Jenny, and it was last night." Elise's head tilted slightly to one side, a clear indication she was lost in thought.

"What were you guys doing out at night?" Lara asked.

"Jenny said it was a boat," Elise said, ignoring her question.

"*Was* it a boat?"

"I don't know; it was kind of small."

"What color was it?"

"Black, I think?"

"You're not sure?"

Elise shook her head.

"Did you see it again today?" Lara asked.

"Nope."

"And you're sure it was a boat?"

"Maybe…"

"If you see it again—or something like it—you need to come and tell me or one of the adults right away, understand?"

Elise nodded. "Will do, boss."

Lara rolled her eyes. "Not you, too."

"A BOAT?" BLAINE said.

Lara nodded. "She said Jenny thought she saw a boat."

"But she's not sure."

"That's the problem. It could have been a boat. Or it could have been anything. Or nothing."

"Maybe it was Blaine," Carly said. "He's pretty dark."

Blaine smirked. "What does Danny see in you?"

"Must be my winning personality."

"It's not that winning."

"*Personality* is what I call my vagina."

Blaine groaned. "I hate talking to you."

"I love you, too," Carly said, and blew him a kiss.

Lara ignored them, said, "If it *was* something, it was too far for either girls to make out. Who was on watch last night?"

"Carrie," Blaine said. "But she would have said something if she saw a boat out there. The same for Maddie; she relieved me at midnight as usual and was up here until morning."

"Vera didn't mention seeing anything, either," Carly said.

"Elise didn't even want to mention it," Lara said. "I think she just did because it came to her at the moment." She shook her head. "We need to do a better job letting them know to report what they see."

"Could be another body," Blaine said.

He was looking through his binoculars at the surrounding ocean. From up here, on the upper deck of the *Trident*, they had the next best view of the Gulf of Mexico. The only better vantage point was on the roof above them. Lara didn't need binoculars to know there was nothing out there right now. At least, nothing she could see with the naked eye.

But that's the problem, isn't it? It wouldn't be trouble if it didn't sneak up on us.

"We still don't know where that body came from," Carly was saying. "Or what or who put it in the water in the first place."

"There are a lot of things going on out there that we don't know about," Lara said. "For all we know, there's more than one body floating around. It's a big ocean. It was a one in a million chance that one would come close enough for us to see it."

"Like winning the lotto," Carly said, and wrinkled her nose. "A really smelly, bloated lotto."

Blaine let his binoculars hang around his neck and glanced over at her.

"What's wrong?" Lara asked.

"I don't like the idea of another boat out there watching us."

"I don't like the idea of *anything* out there watching us," Carly said, shivering slightly. "Maybe it was a perverted whale."

"And Elise said it was black?" Blaine asked.

"She thinks it was black," Lara nodded.

"That's a good way to blend into the night if you were on a scouting mission. You don't usually find a lot of black-painted boats precisely because you don't want to get run through at night by another vessel."

"You think someone painted their boat black as camouflage?" Carly asked.

Blaine shrugged. "That's what I would do. Not exactly a lot of chances you'd run across another boat all the way out here. So what other reason would there be to paint a boat black?"

No one said anything for a while. Carly looked back out the bridge and Lara joined her.

After a while, Lara said, "Exactly how far are we from land, Blaine?"

"I've kept us steady at twenty miles out," Blaine said. "No one should be able to spot us from the coastline. Especially at night with our lights manually shut off."

"Damn, I wish Danny were here already," Carly said, reflexively crossing her chest with her arms and rubbing her shoulders.

"Who's got guard duty tonight?" Lara asked.

"Gwen," Blaine said.

"Ask for volunteers to join her. I want to double all the sentries until otherwise noted. We'll also need to post someone permanently at the back, too."

"I'll draw straws with whoever doesn't volunteer to back up Gwen tonight," Carly said.

"One last thing," Lara said. "I want all the adults armed again, including Dwayne, even if they're not on guard duty."

"Dwayne too?" Blaine asked.

"He's really good with that bolt-action rifle of his," Carly said. "Scary good, for a thirteen-year-old."

"I thought he was twelve," Lara said.

"He turned thirteen three weeks ago, remember?"

No, she thought, but said, "I guess I forgot."

"Well, you've had a lot on your mind."

Lara nodded and gave her friend an appreciative smile before turning to the big man. "Blaine…"

"I'll bring my cot back up here and tighten the shift between me and Maddie," he said before she could finish. "I'll make sure someone's always up here every hour of the day from now on."

"Maybe bring two cots, one for Sarah," Carly said. "You know, in case you guys want a little late-night boom-boom action."

Blaine groaned. "Please don't ever say 'boom-boom action' ever again."

"Trouble in paradise?"

"Something like that."

"You guys should do what I do. Send one of you out there. Distance makes the heart grow fonder, or some crap like that."

"You get that out of a Hallmark card?" Blaine asked.

Lara stepped closer to the windshield and could barely hear them going back and forth behind her as she looked out at the never-ending expanse of blue ocean outside. Her mind swam with all the potential hidden dangers she hadn't seen—or even tried to look for—before. She had almost convinced herself there was no one out here but them, even though she knew better. There had been the dead body they had fished out of the water off Sunport, and later, that voice on the radio asking her to make contact.

They had been floating around the Gulf of Mexico for so long, safe and sound onboard the *Trident* that she had almost made herself believe they could be safe so long as they stayed far away from Texas. She should have known it wouldn't last forever, and maybe she always did but had just done a very good job of deceiving herself.

The girls could be wrong. There might not have been another boat out there last night watching us.

Yeah, right…

CHAPTER 3
GABY

THIS MUST BE what God feels like.

The man's head drifted slightly left, then right in her rifle's ACOG scope. It had been a while since she found herself in possession of an optic that could shoot long distance, and this one had come courtesy of a dead man.

I can kill him right now. It would be so easy. Just squeeze the trigger...

She did it even as she thought it—tightened her forefinger around the cold steel. All it would take was a little more pressure. Just a little bit more. That was how easy it was to end a life. The Purge might have devastated the planet, but it hadn't changed the way a gun could kill.

"How many?" Nate asked, his voice bringing her out of her own world.

She depressed the trigger and pulled slightly back from the eyepiece, if just to chase away the temptation. "Too many."

"Again."

"Uh huh."

"When has it ever *not* been too many?" he said.

It was a common refrain these days. There were always too many. In the daytime, in the nighttime, there were always too many. Too many dangerous men in the day and too many undead things at night.

Too many. Always too many.

"Are they tracking us?" Nate asked. He sounded run down from the last few days, even a little annoyed, but not scared. Or, at least, she couldn't detect any fear in his voice. "They must be tracking us…"

"I don't know. Maybe."

"First Port Arthur, and now here…" He shook his head. "Gotta be, right?"

"I don't know, Nate."

"Gotta be," he repeated, mostly to himself that time.

She looked over at him lying against the edge of the rooftop next to her. The Mohawk was mostly gone, his hair grown in (out?) around the ridiculous stump in the middle. He had dirt on his cheeks and forehead but didn't seem to notice it. The girl in her spent a moment being self-conscious about her own appearance, but the woman that had emerged easily dismissed the thought without much resistance.

Nate lowered his binoculars and met her gaze. "But why would they be tracking us? For Mason? I thought he was just another grunt these days."

"I don't think he was lying about that part. After Louisiana"— *And Josh and that terrible night on Song Island*—"he's not what he used to be, and I know for a fact he wasn't just another grunt back then."

"Makes no sense," Nate said. "We're not that important, especially with Mercer's people running around blowing up people. The three of us should be at the very bottom of their to-do list."

She nodded because he was right. They weren't important at all. What were three more people when the entire state was on high alert? The collaborators they'd (managed to avoid so far) run across in the last few days were on a war footing; they had their hands full with small teams of hit-and-run…what the hell were they? Rebels?

Insurgents? Or maybe she should just think of them as Mercer's killers, because that was exactly what they were.

Even now, she hadn't dismissed the possibility that either Mercer's men or the collaborators had found Taylor and Alice at their cabin in the woods outside of Larkin. The place had been empty when they showed up to collect the sisters for the trip home like they had promised. The door was open and there were no signs of the girls. More baffling, there was no evidence of a struggle. The sisters had simply...vanished. Nate thought it had to be ghouls, that the girls' luck had finally run out, but she wasn't so sure. Mason, of course, said he didn't know anything about it, but the man was a liar and it was hard to believe anything that came out of his mouth.

In the end, they'd had to move on, with the sisters added to a long list of failures since returning to Texas.

We should have stayed on the Trident. *We should never have come back.*

We should never have come back...

She focused on the present, on the here and now, and looked through her M4's optic again, picking up the same man she'd had in her crosshairs before. He was still leaning against the metal guardrail with his back to her. He had brown hair and spent most of his time working on a thick piece of beef jerky he'd fished out of a see-through bag earlier. He hadn't come alone; his friend had climbed up onto the hood of the Jeep parked between the two highway lanes and was scanning the horizon with a pair of binoculars. They were both wearing black uniforms, and if she squinted, she could almost make out the Texas patch on their shoulders.

What the hell are you guys doing here?

Gallant, Texas, was a small town of about 3,200, surrounded by flat country land almost exactly halfway between Port Arthur and Galveston. The tiny city's one major *(only?)* contribution was the slightly raised I-10 interstate road that joined it with Beaumont and Port Arthur to the east, Baytown to the west, and Galveston somewhere in the southwest.

The soldiers were loitering on that highway right now, looking for…something. They hadn't found this place by accident. She was almost certain of that. So what were they doing here? Could Nate be right? Could these men have been tracking them?

What the hell are the two of you doing here?

She laid the rifle on the rooftop and rolled over onto her back, blinking up at the sun. She didn't have to look at her watch to know they still had hours to go before nightfall. Her body was in tune to her environment and had been since they began picking their way south from Starch, skirting potential ambushes along the way, only to find Port Arthur crawling with collaborators.

"Hey," Nate said.

She glanced over. He was holding a small piece of white paper and handed it to her. It was half the size of a regular writing sheet and was blank on one side. She had to turn it over to see the familiar writing:

JOIN THE FIGHT TO TAKE BACK TEXAS
WAR IS HERE PICK A SIDE
THIS IS ONLY THE BEGINNING

The words were clearly typed on the sheet using a machine, maybe even a computer printer. The idea that someone out there was printing out a bunch of propaganda flyers had been an interesting topic of discussion for a while, but after encountering more of them as they made their way southeast, it had become less interesting.

"First and only one I've seen in Gallant so far," Nate said. "Wondered where it came from."

"Probably from the same batch they dumped over Port Arthur," she said. "It'd make sense for them to bypass the small cities for the bigger ones. Less wasteful that way."

"How many you think have picked a side? Or, I guess, a new side?"

She shook her head. "Who knows? Maybe a lot, maybe very few, or maybe none."

"After all that bombing? I don't know, Gaby. If I were in those towns and I saw what happened to the next town over…"

The memories of what had happened to T29 were burned into her soul. She couldn't forget what she had seen, and God did she want to so badly.

The town, the sisters, all the failures of the last few days…

She closed her eyes. "Can we not talk about this?"

"You okay?"

"Just a headache."

"You should take some of the meds we have in the first-aid kits."

"No."

"That's what they're there for, Gaby."

"They're for emergencies. Besides, it always goes away."

"You sure?" he asked, and she could hear the concern in his voice.

"I'll be fine." She opened her eyes and said, before he could argue the point, "We should head back."

She crumpled up the piece of paper and tossed it, then turned around until she was lying on her stomach again. She picked up the rifle and began crawling backward away from the ledge. The distance between them and the highway was close enough *(Shooting distance, at least with the ACOG)* that she took every precaution. It only added a minute or so to their retreat anyway, and they had minutes to spare at the moment. Nate mirrored her crawl until they were almost on the other side, and only then did they stand up and take the ladder in the back down to the street below.

They had walked over to their position on top of the Waffle House, so that meant walking back to where Danny and Mason were. The area they were in was oddly divided with the stores and restaurants to one side and almost exclusively traveling hotels and inns on the other. The tallest building in the entire place was a Comfort Inn and Suites. The rooftop above the hotel's three stories would have given them a much better spying perch, but the idea of going through those floors just to get to that perfect spot spiked the hairs on the back of her neck even now.

They wound their way through the streets and buildings using the businesses as cover whenever they could. Not that she expected to be spotted from the highway, but again, there was no point in taking unnecessary risks just to shave off a few seconds or minutes. So they took their time and moved along, through, and behind a fast food joint, then a gas station, and a dozen other buildings.

"Wanna get wasted?" Nate asked as they walked past one of the many brick and mortar stores. The sign outside was in gaudy neon, reading "Gallant Liquor Store."

Not very creative, she thought, looking in at the hundreds of bottles still sitting on display shelves. The store was remarkably undisturbed and she couldn't find any signs of ghoul occupation—there were no blankets on the windows or blood smears. Unlike most places they had traveled through, it was rare to find evidence of a ghoul nest in Gallant. It was another reason they had decided to make camp here. That same disregard for the town by the monsters was also why it didn't make any sense for the two collaborators to be lingering around it.

What are you two doing here?

"Let's relive our college years," Nate was saying.

"I never went to college."

"Oh, right. Sometimes I forget how young you are."

"Are you saying I look old?"

"Well, yeah."

"You're lucky I already like you, or else…" She playfully put a hand on the butt of her sidearm.

He raised both hands in surrender and began walking backward, grinning at her. "If you want, we can pretend we're in school. I'll be the big man on campus, and you'll be my cheerleader girlfriend. I bet if we look hard enough we might even be able to find a cheerleader uniform somewhere in this place, maybe at the high school we passed earlier…"

She shook her head but couldn't help herself and smiled anyway. "I have a better idea. Why don't *you* be my cheerleader boyfriend…"

THEY MADE THEIR temporary base about a mile from the Waffle House inside the Gallant First Bank, one of the few buildings that had everything they needed in case they were forced to stay the night in town. Large white GFB letters were easily visible on the rooftop, welded to some kind of scaffolding. It wasn't exactly subtle, but then it fit in with its surroundings, mostly department stores, restaurants, and she guessed the cream of the commercialism crop in Gallant. The bank had security bars over the windows and doors, and when they peeked inside, found it as pristine now as it had been a year ago.

She saw Danny peeking out at them from behind blinders on one of the front windows as they approached, then a few seconds later one of the doors *clicked* opened before they even reached it.

They slipped inside and Danny locked it back up. "What's the word, birdies? Tell me you haven't been giving each other disgusting hickeys out there while I was babysitting in here?"

"A Jeep with two soldiers," Nate said. "They showed up and parked on the I-10 around ten in the morning and haven't moved since. We think they're looking for something."

"Maybe us," Gaby said.

"Has to be, right?"

"Did you go and ask them?" Danny asked.

"Uh, no," Nate said.

"Maybe they're just searching for property to rent or buy. Land's pretty cheap these days, and property's always a good investment. Always has been, always will be."

"We thought they might have been the same two we saw outside of Port Arthur yesterday," Gaby said.

"Were they?"

She shook her head. "Same uniforms but different vehicle, and one of the two from yesterday was blond. These two both had dark hair."

"Dark-haired *muchachos* are seriously the worst."

"Self-loathing?" Nate asked.

"Maybe a tad," Danny said. Then, looking at her, "Why didn't you just shoot them? I gave you that ACOG for a reason, you know."

"It was tempting…" Gaby said.

"Next time when in doubt, shoot."

I almost did, she thought, and tossed her pack on the island counter in the lobby, knocking down a few deposit slips that had been left behind. She unzipped the bag and pulled out a bottle of water and took a drink.

The place was remarkably clean when they had found it, with no evidence of a fight or blood anywhere, and Nate theorized it was closed when the town succumbed to The Purge. Like most small cities around the state, the citizens probably knew something had happened when the big metropolitans like Houston and Dallas went dark. It would have been terrifying as they waited for the second night. She knew the feeling, having lived through it herself a year ago.

There were still piles of money in the registers and safes when they looked around this morning, and the two offices in the back were in immaculate condition. She kept expecting someone to clock in for work whenever she glanced at the counters. There were plenty of lights coming through the closed blinds behind her to see with, but not enough to give their position away to someone passing by, like those two guys…

Maybe Nate's right. Maybe they are following us.

But why?

When she finished drinking and put the bottle away, she looked back at Danny. "Nate is convinced they're tracking us."

"What do you think?" Danny asked her.

"I don't know, maybe. It's just too much coincidence that they—or one of their friends—keep showing up wherever we go."

Danny nodded but didn't say anything. He looked lost in thought, and whenever that happened, he always reminded her so much of Will. They looked nothing alike, of course, but when the usually jovial Danny went still, it was hard to shake the resemblance.

"Where's Mason?" Nate asked.

"Dozing, the last time I saw him," Danny said. "Being a hostage is hard work."

"I should go check on him."

"You think he's going to try something?" she asked.

Nate shrugged as he walked past her. "I just don't like the idea of that guy being somewhere where at least one of us can't see him at all times."

She watched him go into the back hallway, then open the door into one of the two offices and disappear inside. Gaby turned back to Danny, who had returned to looking out the blinders at the street outside.

"Did you talk to the *Trident* yet?" she asked.

"Still waiting to pick us up," Danny said. "All we have to do is get to someplace where they can do exactly that, and then we'll all be on the sundeck drinking piña coladas. Easy breezy."

"Easy breezy, huh?" she said doubtfully.

"Have faith, Gabster. We'll get there. Eventually."

She didn't doubt they would get home—she just hoped they all made it, and in one piece.

"I believe you," she said.

"You should. I'm never wrong."

"Never?"

"Well, mostly never." He glanced up the street in the direction she and Nate had come. "You said two?"

"Two, yeah."

"But one vehicle?"

"That I could see or hear." When he didn't ask or say anything, she continued: "What are you thinking?"

"That if we want to get out of here before nightfall and those two *hombres* are still hanging around on the highway, then we might have a problem."

"Just one?"

"Okay, one of many. The biggest one is the noise factor. As soon as we fire up our ride, they'll know we're here. Then they'll radio their friends, and who knows how many of them are between us and the coastline. We might have to wait them out."

"How long?"

"Hopefully they won't make us wait too long. I'm not a very patient guy when piña coladas are at stake."

"How far is it between Gallant and the coast?"

"Twenty-five miles, give or take. The problem isn't the distance—it's the not knowing how many guys with guns and bad intentions are waiting for us between here and there."

"Captain Optimism," Gaby said.

"That's what Carly said when I told her about our present dilemma."

"They've been out there for a while. What's their fuel situation?"

"I've been told that they're dealing with it."

"Is that good or bad?"

He shrugged. "That's what I said."

She heard voices from the back of the bank and glanced over. Nate had left the office door open, and she could hear him talking with Mason but couldn't quite make out the conversation.

"What about Mason?" she asked.

"What about him?" Danny said.

"Does he know what's waiting for us out there?"

"His knowledge is getting more limited the farther south we get. He only knows what he knew before Starch. Everything after that is all Greek to him."

"Then why are we keeping him around?"

Danny gave her an amused look. "You sick of him already?"

"I've been sick of him since Starch, and I still don't believe he doesn't know anything about what happened to Alice and Taylor. I just don't see any reason to keep dragging him along if he's outlived his usefulness, Danny."

"Wow, talk about breaking my heart," a voice said behind her.

She looked over at Mason coming out of the back hallway with Nate. The collaborator was still wearing the same black uniform they had captured him in back at Starch. His face was grimy with dirt and sweat—which ironically made him perfectly at home among them—and the only thing clean on him was the bandage around his right leg. He walked with a noticeable limp and a grimace, his reward for trying to kill them a few days ago.

"After all we've been through, too," Mason added.

"Give me one reason why we should keep you around," she said.

"Because I'm still more valuable to you alive than dead. You can use me—and I can't believe I'm saying this, but what the hell—as a hostage, if it becomes necessary. And yes, I do think it's going to be necessary."

"Bullshit. You're just trying to talk your way into staying alive. You're not important to them. You never were."

"Then why have they been tracking you all the way from Starch?"

There was just a ghost of a smile on his pale and cracked lips, probably because he knew a full-blown smile would have just pissed her off, and Mason, for all his faults—and the man had many of them—wasn't stupid.

"Good question," Danny said. "So, tell us, ol' popular one, what makes you the bee's knees? And don't say it's because of your stinky armpits, 'cause I'm sure I got you beat on that one."

"It's a secret," Mason said.

"Is that right?"

"You can try to beat it out of me, but I'm still not going to tell you."

"I don't know, I'm pretty good at beating things out of people. Just ask Johnny Paulson back in middle school."

"The difference between me and Johnny Paulson? I know keeping quiet is the only way to stay alive. The second I tell you, I'm a dead man. And I really, *really* like staying alive."

Danny exchanged a look with her, then she did the same with Nate. She wasn't sure if either one of the men believed Mason, but she got the feeling they were like her: They didn't believe a thing that came out of his mouth, but they couldn't disregard it out of hand, either. And that, ultimately, was what Mason was going for.

"You're a tricky little bugger," Danny said, pointing a finger at Mason. "You know what happens to tricky little buggers? They eventually overstay their welcome and end up being stuffed into ventilation shafts. And trust me, buddy, I know my ventilation shafts."

"I don't know what any of that means," Mason said.

"Think about it."

"I'll pass."

"I don't believe you," Gaby said.

The collaborator grinned at her. "Just ask yourself one question, sweetheart: How do you think I've stayed alive this long? It wasn't because of my good looks."

She bristled at the word *sweetheart* but pushed through it. The last thing she wanted was for Mason to see that he had an effect—*any* kind of an effect—on her with his words. It was a weak man's weapon because right now, that was all he had.

Gaby stared at him. "The second you prove you're no longer valuable, I'm going to end you."

"I believe you," Mason said.

"Good. Because when the time comes, you won't be able to say I wasn't honest with you."

He smiled defiantly back at her, but she couldn't help but notice that this time it wasn't nearly as convincing.

CRACK!

Danny, looking down at the well-worn map of Texas spread out on the bank's island counter, snapped a quick glance at the windows that faced the street. He hadn't said anything when two more shots, about three seconds apart, crackled across the city even before the first one had fully faded.

"Same rifle?" Gaby asked.

Danny nodded. "Bolt-action. Heavy caliber."

"What are they shooting at—" Nate said, when the *pop-pop-pop* of an automatic rifle cut him off.

"Someone's shooting back," Gaby said.

"Is that good?" Nate asked.

"Good, bad, as long as they're not shooting at us, that's all that matters," Danny said. He pushed off the counter and moved across the bank lobby to the front windows.

More gunfire washed up and down the street outside. It took her a moment, but there was enough of a sustained volley that Gaby managed to trace its origin back to the highway. Had the two collaborators in the Jeep found someone to shoot at, or had someone found *them?*

"Pack up," Danny said.

Gaby folded up the map and pocketed it. "Are we leaving?"

"I don't think we have a choice, kids. All that racket's doing is drawing a whole lotta attention our way. Pretty soon we'll be up our butts in bad boys in black uniforms, and I don't know about you two, but I'd rather avoid that uncomfortableness."

Gaby exchanged a nod with Nate, and he hurried into the back where they were keeping Mason. She snatched up her rifle leaning against the counter and grabbed her tactical pack from the floor. The weight of the ammo in the bag instantly reassured her.

A soldier who complains about too much ammo is a dead one, right, Will?

Danny was still peeking out the blinds, looking in the direction of the gunfire. The familiar *crack* of the high-powered rifle, followed by the torrent of *pop-pop-pop* of automatic return fire. Someone, somewhere, was wasting a lot of ammo. Will, she thought, would never approve.

"Danny, anything?" she asked.

He shook his head. "Can't see shit, but they're not outside, and that's the good news. The bad news is that I can't see shit from in here. Did I mention that?"

"It sounds like it's coming from the highway. You think it might be Mercer's people?"

"That would be my guess." Danny glanced over as Nate brought Mason out from the back, keeping the shorter man in front of him. "Looks like we might be putting your supposed importance to test sooner than you think, Mason ol' chum."

"Looking forward to it," Mason said.

She looked past the collaborator and at Nate behind him. "Ready?"

"Good to go," Nate nodded.

Nate's pack jutted out from behind his back, making him look like a hunchback. Unlike hers, his was bulkier, because aside from his own ammo, he was also carrying most of their emergency rations. They had more supplies in the truck outside, but they had learned the hard way it was a good idea to carry whatever you could on top of that because you never knew when you might lose your vehicle to an A-10 Warthog on a strafing run.

"Okay," Danny said, "let's blow this three-horse town."

He rushed into the back hallway, Nate and Mason turning and following close behind, while Gaby brought up the rear. She glanced behind her at the closed blinders one last time before crossing the lobby after the others.

Outside the bank the firefight continued, the booming *crack!* of a bolt-action rifle now overlapping with the *pop-pop-pop* of return fire. Whoever was out there, they sounded determined to end one another.

Better them than us.

IT WAS AN older model red Toyota pickup, one that Danny had found in someone's garage after the vehicle they had been using since Starch died on them. The Toyota looked nearly as beat up as the building it was hidden in, but its owner had kept it in good condition and it worked without any trouble once they replaced the battery and fed siphoned fuel into its tank.

It was still parked behind the Gallant First Bank where they had left it, dented cab hood reflecting back the sun. It wasn't exactly the prettiest thing in town, and even before The Purge most thieves wouldn't have looked twice at it.

Nate opened the back door and shoved Mason inside, then slid in beside him. Mason's legs were free, but his wrists were bound with duct tape to keep him from getting any ideas. She kept expecting the man to make a run for it a dozen times since they began their trek, but he seemed oddly content to be their hostage, though she didn't for one second believe that.

Don't trust him. Whatever you do, don't trust him.

Gaby tossed her pack on the floor before climbing into the front passenger seat while Danny settled in behind the wheel. He put the key in the ignition but didn't turn it right away. Instead, he rolled down the window and listened, except there wasn't anything to hear.

It was suddenly very quiet again.

"Sounds like someone finally won the brouhaha," Danny said.

"I don't hear any running vehicles," Gaby said.

"If they called for reinforcements, it would take a while for them to get here," Nate said. "Port Arthur's a long way off."

"Unless they have people closer..."

"There's always that."

She looked over at Danny. "Maybe we should be gone before they show up."

"Works for me," Mason chimed in from the backseat.

"Shut up," Nate said and slapped Mason in the back of the head. "When we wanna hear a peep out of you, we'll ask."

Mason grunted and looked as if he wanted to say something back, but clenched his teeth in silence instead. Gaby smiled. It was a rare thing to see Nate so aggressive, but she couldn't help herself; she liked it when he was.

Danny still hadn't turned the key in the ignition. He continued leaning against the steering wheel and staring out at the empty street in front of them. Until the gunfight a few minutes ago, Gallant was the definition of a dead town. They hadn't found a single soul living here when they arrived, not even an animal or two.

"What are you thinking?" Gaby asked.

"Cheeseburgers," Danny said.

"Cheeseburgers?"

"With chives. And bacon."

"And how does that help us?"

"It doesn't, but you asked what I was thinking, and I was thinking about a nice big juicy cheeseburger."

"With chives and bacon."

"Yup." He sat back, the car's torn upholstery squishing under him. "When this is over, I think I'm going to open a cheeseburger joint. Call it Danny's Cheeseburgers."

"A little on the nose, don't you think?"

"What can I say, I like to make a splash," Danny said just before he turned the key in the ignition.

The truck didn't roar; it meowed to life, but with the absence of any other sounds at the moment, the churning engine might as well be a loud monstrous bellow alerting anyone with ears to not just their existence but their location as well.

"Eyes wide, ears open, and guns hot," Danny said as he put the truck in gear and slowly eased it out from behind the bank, peeking left then right at the empty streets, before turning right and pointing them south.

They hadn't gone more than a mile down the road, passing a series of empty buildings and storefronts to both sides of them, when she heard a new noise and looked at her side mirror and sighed.

"Danny," she said.

"I see them," he said.

"Ah, man," Nate said as he twisted around in his seat and glanced out the rear windshield.

"Better step on it, sport," Mason said, though Gaby didn't hear anything that even resembled triumph in his voice. If anything, he might have sounded a little…anxious?

The pickup gained speed while Gaby put her M4 in her lap and flicked the safety off, then stuck her head out the open window and looked back down the street.

It was the same Jeep from the interstate, she was sure of it, and it was far enough behind them that she couldn't see the driver's face, though she could make out a second figure in the front passenger seat. A part of her knew it was too much to expect they could just exit Gallant the way they had entered it—unnoticed—but she'd clung to the hope anyway.

"Company!" she shouted.

"Tell me something I don't know!" Danny shouted back.

He hadn't even gotten the word *know* out when a second car turned into the street behind the Jeep, and for just a brief second she entertained the possibility that it was going to ram the smaller vehicle in front of it, knock it into one of the buildings, and allow them to escape. Instead the Jeep's passenger waved at the truck, which picked up speed and pulled up alongside it.

"Danny! More company!" she shouted.

"Yee haw! Now it's a party!" he shouted back.

Sunlight bounced off the truck's gleaming dark skin, and it was impossible to miss the machine gun mounted on top of its cab. A man stood behind the weapon, literally clinging to it to prevent the speeding vehicle from shedding him like some unwelcomed pest. He looked like a rag doll back there, and no amount of wishful thinking on her part ended with him flying through the air.

"It's a technical, Danny!" she shouted.

"When it rains, it pours!" Danny said, and she thought he might have been laughing at the same time.

She pulled her head back into the pickup and looked at him. "Can we outrun them?"

"Not in this jalopy," Danny said.

"What, then?"

He glanced over and grinned. "I got a plan."

"A good plan?"

"Call it Plan Z."

She groaned. "We're going to die…"

CHAPTER 4
KEO

HE SPENT THE night in an outside cellar at a farmhouse about half a mile from Lochlyn. You wouldn't know the town even existed if you didn't have a map and someone to point the way. Fortunately, he had the benefit of both. Even so, he ended up stumbling into the south end of the city limits and had to quickly retreat before he was spotted out in the open. If there had been a sniper on duty, he would have been dead. The enemy would be on high alert after Davis and Butch failed to check in, and that made him overly cautious.

Nightfall came quickly, giving him less than an hour to squirrel himself inside the cellar. The door was made of a simple wooden construction, nothing that would stand against a prolonged assault. The room itself was small and damp, and judging by the indentations, once held glass bottles, maybe even spirits. Or moonshine, perhaps. He was in the boondocks of southeast Texas, after all. Who the hell knew what people did down here to pass the time?

There were slits in the door that anyone with eyes (black, blue, or whatever color) could use to look into the cellar, so he grabbed clumps of dirt and plastered them over the vulnerable spots. Fortunately, the earth was wet enough to cling to the wooden slabs. He reinforced the latch on the door with Butch's rifle that he had brought along just in case. It wasn't like the man was going to need it or any of his supplies anytime soon.

The work done, he settled down on the soft ground and rested his back against the sticky wall and took a drink from a canteen. There was something else he had brought along—a small pink iPod barely the size of his thumb that Butch had been listening to when Keo shot him in the fields. The green light flickered when he pushed the on switch, and a voice drifted out of the white earbuds dangling from the device.

Keo placed his AR-15 on the ground and trained his eyes on the cellar door barely ten feet across from him. He had done a pretty good job sealing up the cracks, and the room was almost pitch dark except for a few random strands of inconsequential (fading) sunlight. He had positioned himself in the right spot, which in this case meant staying as far away from the stray slivers as possible.

He was surprised when he slipped one of the buds into his ear—left the other one dangling—and heard her voice. That surprise turned into a grin, because for some reason a part of him expected to see—well, hear, anyway—her again even all the way out here.

"*...the traitors in uniforms that scour the countryside in the daylight for survivors, any bullet will do...*"

Lara's voice, clear as day. He had been on the bridge of the *Trident* when she recorded the message, and he still remembered the lines.

"*...get to a place that is surrounded by bodies of water. Stock up on silver; if you know how, make silver bullets, or any silver-bladed weapons. The daylight is no longer your friend, but don't be discouraged. As long as you're breathing, as long as you are free, there is hope. We will adapt and keep going, because that's what we do. This is Lara, and I'm still fighting alongside you.*"

There was a brief pause before the message repeated itself.

Keo popped the bud out of his ear. Why had Butch and Davis gone through the trouble of recording the message, looping it, then uploading it to an iPod? He would have liked to ask Butch, but that wasn't going to happen. Davis would have had the answer, in all likelihood, but that ship had sailed, too.

He made a mental note to tell Lara when he saw her again. He wasn't sure if she was going to get a kick out of it or find it creepy. How many of Mercer's men were carrying around her message on iPods out there?

Definitely creepy.

He flicked off the on switch and the little green light faded into nothingness, leaving him sitting in the dark all by himself again.

HE DIDN'T GET a whole lot of sleep, not helped by the fact he kept waking up every other hour to throbbing in his legs. Both of them. He didn't know how that was possible and gave up trying to dismiss it as being just figments of imagination after the third time.

He got a total of two hours of shut-eye, spending the rest of the night listening to them moving on the other side of the door. They were going through the farmhouse behind him, racing up and down both stories. There was a barn on the other side of the property, and he heard them raiding it, too.

Did they know he was around? Smell him? *Sense* him somehow? Or maybe it wasn't him. Maybe they were tracking Mercer's men. That was more likely. Mercer's goons might have managed to stay under the radar all this time, setting up their little FOBs around the state before they finally struck, but once the genie was out of the bag…

What were the chances the ghouls were going to get to whoever—and however many—were hiding just outside of Lochlyn at the moment?

He drifted in and out of sleep while waiting for the night to give way to morning, most of it spent staring at the door and listening for the first signs that he had been discovered. He was so used to hearing them out there, skittering across the open, that he found the sound of their movements almost…comforting?

It's official: I've lost my fucking mind.

Around three in the morning, their numbers started to thin out and it became more difficult to pick them up. By four, they were almost completely gone except for the occasional strays that walked or ran or stopped just a little too close to the cellar entrance. He could see their shadowy figures flitting across the small openings, and a few of them paused just a bit too long for his liking.

He kept waiting to hear gunshots, which would be a sign that the creatures had found Mercer's men. But there weren't any. Not at midnight, or at three, or four, or when the first signs of morning finally began filtering through the cellar and the ground under him started warming up. Not a lot, just enough to be noticeable after sitting on the cold, damp earth all night.

The lack of shooting or hints of confrontation between Mercer's men and the ghouls last night was a good sign, because it just meant more men for him to kill.

Yeah, we're officially a little bloodthirsty now, aren't we?

MERCER'S PEOPLE WEREN'T inside Lochlyn itself, of course. They were hunkered down outside the city limits on the north end, hiding (almost) in plain sight, which was ballsy of them, but then again, what wasn't about these people?

Instead of anything that remotely looked like an airfield, there was a two-story house with peeling white paint surrounded by woods. The only thing that made the homestead stand out from the one he had just spent the night in and the dozen others he'd passed while skirting the town proper was the large barn next door and a wide-open clearing.

Keo crouched near the tree line and watched the property for a good ten minutes. Ten became twenty, then a full half hour, and there were still no signs of people anywhere in the open or inside the house or the barn next door. No people, and no movement.

Could Davis have lied to him? Could Mercer's men have left yesterday?

Shit. What if he had come all this way for nothing—

Two figures emerged out of the trees almost half a football field to his left, their movements flickering at the corner of his eye.

Now where had *they* come from?

Keo pressed against a tree trunk and watched the two men, both wearing black and green camo clothing, stride through the overgrown grass toward the main house. Sunlight glinted off the barrel of their rifles, and one of them had a second weapon, some kind of shotgun, slung over his back.

A bit overkill, Keo thought before remembering that he was carrying not just the AR-15 he had taken from Luke, but also Butch's.

What the hell. A little overkill never hurts these days.

He watched the two men—Scouts? Perimeter guards?—bypass the house and continue on to the barn. There was an echoing *click* before a third figure stepped out of the red building, pushing at one of the twin doors. A fourth man soon appeared and helped with the other door. They wore identical black and green clothing, but nothing that looked like an actual uniform or red collar emblazoned with the familiar sun emblems. That didn't really mean anything though; Luke and Bill hadn't been wearing the uniform either, and he was 100% sure they were Mercer's men. The same for Davis and Butch.

The four men exchanged words, but Keo was too far away to hear the conversation. Instead, he sat back and watched the two new arrivals disappear into the barn with the other two before all four returned outside about five minutes later, this time pushing a large, heavy, tarp-covered object out into the morning sunlight with them.

At first Keo thought it was an old tractor, or some kind of farming equipment, given its size. That is, until he stared at it through his binoculars.

It was a helicopter with some kind of heavy netting draped over it. He could make out green metal glinting through the holes in the camouflage, and it was pretty clear the machine had wheels that made it easier to move despite its bulk.

"The last flight out is tomorrow. Everyone involved in this area is supposed to be back by then," Davis had said.

The last flight back to The Ranch…

Four men became six when two more came out of the barn, but none of them were Mercer. Besides the fact everyone was too young to be Mercer, there was no reason for Davis to lie about the man not being here. But while Mercer might not be here right now, these men knew where he was and how to get there, and right now that was good enough for Keo.

Not all six were armed, but at least two of them were. Even if he could take out both of them from this distance, that still left four to make a run for the barn. Once inside, he was pretty sure they wouldn't be unarmed for very long. And how many were inside right now that he couldn't see?

So what, then? Wait for them to climb onboard that helicopter and leave?

No, that wasn't going to work. Not one bit.

Find Mercer. Kill Mercer.

It was a pretty straightforward job. Not a breeze by any means, but he'd had tougher gigs, even if he couldn't think of them right now.

He got up and backtracked into the woods until he couldn't see the helicopter and the men pushing it, then turned and began moving right. He circled the clearing, sticking to the natural camo provided by the thick trees and foliage around him. Keo didn't stop until he was looking out at the rear of the red barn.

He moved back toward the tree line, and crouching, looked out.

The barn was about thirty-five meters in front of him, and from his current angle he couldn't see the front doors or the two-story house on the other side, but he could make out the nose of the helicopter as it was pushed into the wide-open space where it could power up and take off. He hadn't spotted anything that looked like an LZ out there—makeshift or otherwise—but a good pilot probably didn't need one.

He got up and slipped out of the trees and made a straight line for the red building. Closer now, he could hear grunts and voices coming from the other side as the six men put everything they had into pushing the aircraft. Equipped with wheels or not, that thing probably weighed close to 6,000 kilograms or more, not counting however much fuel it still had in the tank. That, he guessed, would depend on how far these men expected it to ferry them.

Keo made the back of the barn without incident but didn't press up against the peeling red paint. Instead, he stopped just short of it and found a small sliver between two boards and looked in, glimpsing a pair of figures moving around on the other side.

So at least two more bodies. Swell. That made a total of eight, which was still less than he had been expecting, unless there were more hiding in the barn or somewhere out there in the woods.

The barn was big enough to have two stories and Keo tried to look up, but there wasn't enough of a crack to see anything past the first floor. He moved along the back, searching for another peephole, but didn't find anything good enough to see through by the time he reached the building's right edge. The good news was, as soon as he rounded the corner, he spotted a side door.

What were the chances it was unlocked?

He put his hand on the rusted-over lever and tested it by pressing cautiously down with his thumb. The latch moved on the other side *(unlocked!)* without any noise, not even a telltale *clack*. He pulled his hand away and craned his head to eavesdrop on the voices coming from the other side of the building, somewhere between the barn and the main house. They weren't really chatting up a storm, but there were a couple of ongoing conversations, though the topics eluded him.

Keo faced the side door again and took a breath.

Eight men that he knew of for sure, maybe *(probably)* more he couldn't see. It wasn't exactly the ideal situation, and God knew the prospect of shooting it out with eight men was intimidating enough that it made all of this seem like one big suicide run. Only an idiot would barge in there in hopes of getting to someone who wasn't even present. Only a damn fool would do exactly what he was about to do against such overwhelming odds.

He almost laughed out loud trying to recall the last time someone had mistaken him for anything other than a damn fool.

Suck it up, pal, and get it done. Mercer's not going to end himself, you know.

He reached for the rusted-over lever a second time, steeling himself for the charge. He'd have to take out the two inside first, then move toward the open front doors and waste the ones pushing the helicopter. Most of them, anyway. He'd need to keep at least one of them alive for interrogation, preferably the pilot. But he wouldn't necessarily know who the pilot was unless the guy was wearing some kind of flight suit, which would be a dead giveaway, but unlikely.

Oh, fuck it. Now you're just stalling.

He sighed, thought, *This one's for you, Jordan*, and pushed his thumb down on the lever a split second before a big chunk of the already rotted wooden door in front of him cratered. Splinters exploded and filled the air *(Gunshot!)*, every single piece seemingly gunning for his face.

Keo's mind screamed, *Gunshot! Where the hell did that gunshot come from?* even as he spun and started dropping to the ground

It was a man, and he was wearing some kind of ghillie suit that would have made him blend effortlessly into his surroundings just beyond the tree line if not for the rifle in his hands. The muzzle was pointed in Keo's direction, and the reason Keo hadn't heard anything resembling a gunshot meant the weapon had a suppressor—

Keo dived left at the last second even as the man fired again, the second round smashing into the wall an inch from his head, so close that the sound of the weapon drilling through the vulnerable wood *(Thwack!)* and disappearing into the barn was the only noise the shot made. He had thrown himself down to avoid the bullet without thinking and had to stick out his hands—with the AR-15 clutched in them—or else he would have smashed face first into the ground.

There was a loud *boom!* from behind him, and Keo didn't have to look back to know someone had just kicked the barn's side door open. Not that he could have looked to be sure, because he was still falling—

He hit the ground, spun onto his back, and grimaced as the second rifle slung over his back dug into his flesh *(Should have left it behind, dammit!)*, but the pain vanished quickly and was replaced by blinding fury when a steel-toed boot slammed into his side. He was pretty sure one of his ribs cracked. If he was really lucky, it would just be one.

He glimpsed figures flashing across his line of vision, blotting out the sun above him, just before the stock of a rifle cracked over his face.

There goes the nose again.

He tasted blood in his mouth and felt his rifle being yanked out of his hands as if he were some old man incapable of holding onto anything, then another boot (or was it the same one?) landing a second kick, but thankfully this time it only glanced off his thigh. It still hurt like a sonofabitch, and it was all he could do to grit his teeth to keep from crying out.

He waited for more, but his punisher had apparently decided that two (Or was that three? Four?) was enough and backed away, leaving Keo to lie on his back staring up at a glowing orange ball. At least it was warm and sunny this morning. He could think of worse ways to go—somewhere cold, for instance.

God bless freaky ass Texas weather, he thought with a wry grin.

"What are you smiling at?" a voice said. Female. Partially amused, but mostly confused. "I don't think you should be smiling right now."

"You sure that's a smile?" a second voice asked. This one was a man and wasn't nearly as pleasant-sounding.

"Looks like a smile."

"Hard to tell with all the blood…"

Keo shifted his sight from the sun to the first silhouetted figure looming over him. For a moment he thought it might have been

Marcy again, but it couldn't have been because she was a collaborator and these were Mercer's men. Or had he stumbled across the wrong group of people? Had Davis lied to him after all and sent him to his death?

Clever, Davis. Real clever, you jackass.

"You missed," the man said. It didn't sound as if he was directing the accusation at Keo. "Twice."

"It's the suppressor," a second male voice said. "Threw off my aim."

"Riiiight."

"I'm serious, man."

A third silhouette flanked the first two, except this one seemed to have the outline of a…bush? No, not a bush. He was looking at a ghillie suit…the guy with the rifle who had taken the shots at him.

"He's seen better days, that's for sure," Ghillie Suit said. "Damn, look at that face."

"That's my bad," the other man said.

"You did that?"

"Had to make sure he stayed down."

"I think you made sure."

"Damn straight." Then, "Is that what I think it is?" The man crouched briefly before straightening back up, this time with a familiar white wire dangling from between his fingers. "Aw, shit, it's Davis's iPod, isn't it? What the fuck's he doing with Davis's iPod?"

"I guess now we know what happened to him and Butch," Ghillie Suit said.

"You think they're dead?"

"I don't think they gave it to him out of the goodness of their hearts."

"Is he alone?" the woman asked.

"As far as I know," Ghillie Suit said. "Could be more hiding in the woods."

"I swore the nightcrawlers found us last night," the other man said. "They might have sent their human lackeys to check. You think he's a collaborator scumbag?"

"Maybe," woman said. "Spread out; make sure he doesn't have any friends hiding out there."

The man who wasn't Ghillie Suit left and Keo heard a radio squawking, but that was quickly drowned out by the sound of a machine roaring to life. First slowly, then gradually gaining speed and power until it was all he could hear and the ground under him began trembling, pebbles dancing near his right eye.

The helicopter. Wait for me, boys!

He must have grinned a second time, because the woman said, "There it is again. What's so funny?"

He thought of a joke Danny had once told him about a priest, a rabbit, and a horse walking into a bar, but when he opened his mouth to tell it, the only sound that came out was a slightly labored wheeze.

"I guess not!" Ghillie Suit said. With the noise continuing to grow in the background, the man had to shout to be heard. "What're we gonna do with him?"

"I don't know yet!" the woman shouted back. She crouched next to Keo and her face slowly came into focus.

Not completely, but enough for him to know she wasn't entirely bad looking.

"What's he doing sneaking around out here by himself?" the woman asked, though Keo wasn't sure if she was asking him or Ghillie Suit, or just talking mostly to herself.

Maybe I should ask her out for drinks. Get to know one another…

"He looks like he's going to be way more trouble than he's worth," Ghillie Suit said.

"Maybe," the woman said, standing back up. "We can always just throw him out of the hatch later if he becomes a pain in the ass."

Or not.

CHAPTER 5
GABY

"READY, KID?"

"No."

"On the count of five…"

"Danny, I'm not ready!"

"One…"

"Not yet!"

"Two…"

"Danny!"

"…four…"

"What happened to three?"

"*Go!*"

She would have cursed him if she had the chance, but by the time his *Go!* echoed in her ears, the pickup's tires were screaming and the smell of burning rubber filled her nostrils as the vehicle slammed to a stop in the middle of the road. She threw her body into the door, one hand jerking at the lever, praying she had timed it just right, because otherwise she was going to go *splat* on the pavement—

The door snapped open, rusted hinges working overtime, but was soon lost against the overwhelming squeal of tires under her and the quickly approaching engines of the two vehicles behind them. Her feet didn't so much as touch the road as they grazed it, and she was racing forward. A sheet of abandoned newspaper crumpled under her boots, the sound like gunshots despite all the other noises swirling around her at the moment.

The road out of Gallant, Texas, was a two-lane street separated by fading yellow lines, and their vehicle had turned slightly left as it skidded to a stop and she lunged out. That pointed her right toward the shoulder and the row of cars on the other side. They hadn't made it very far out of town before Danny came up with his (not so) brilliant plan. She would have argued to keep going and hopefully lose their pursuers among the side streets, but Danny hadn't given her any choice.

Her heartbeat thundered against her chest as she ran for all she was worth, the M4 clutched in her right hand, her left swinging back and forth as if that would somehow make her go faster. She couldn't help herself and tossed a quick look to her right and down the street just as she crossed the shoulder.

They were still coming—both of them. The Jeep that she had seen on the I-10, which may or may not have been tracking them since Port Arthur, and the big black truck with the dark uniformed man perched behind the towering cab. It wasn't the size of the second vehicle that made the pit of her stomach drop. No, it was the mounted machine gun. Gaby had seen what one of those things could do, and the thought of being on the wrong side of it made her run faster and *faster*.

She forced herself to turn forward and focus on the long white metal pole separating the car lot from the street. She reached out with her left hand and leapt over it, her momentum almost sending her right into the grill of a used Ford truck.

She stuck out both hands to protect herself, rifle *clanging* against the parked vehicle, and twisted her body until she slid against the dirt-caked side. She didn't waste any time and leaned against it— ignoring the surprisingly cold contact! She raised the M4 and laid it across the hood and took just a second—maybe even a half-second, just long enough to see the Jeep filling up her ACOG—to aim before she pulled the trigger.

The rifle bucked and empty shell casings *clink-clink-clinked* against the truck and slid down like raindrops to scatter at her feet, but she never released the trigger. Gaby oscillated her fire left and right, sweeping the street as the Jeep swerved about fifty meters away *(Jesus, how did they get so close so fast?)* until it somehow ended up on the northbound lane. That left the southbound wide open and the big truck—a GMC, from the logo up front—taking up the entire lane as it continued barreling in her direction.

She was sending everything she had downrange because it was her job to slow them down (or stop them, but she didn't think that was possible) in order to give Danny and Nate just enough time to—

The *pop-pop-pop* of automatic weapons coming from her right told her she had done her job and given her friends the time they needed. Danny and Nate were pouring it on, and the *ping-ping-ping!* of bullets punching through the truck's body were some of the best sounds she'd ever heard in her life.

She kept shooting, waiting for the GMC to stop under the prolonged assault, but the damn thing *kept coming*. It wouldn't stop or slow down even as bullets raked its front windshield and grill and hood. The pavement around it exploded, chunks of asphalt flickering into the air like missiles.

And then the thing she had been dreading: The ferocious roar of the machine gun finally coming alive, the *brap-brap-brap* of the MG drowning out her shots and Danny's and Nate's—

She ducked as bullets smashed into the other side of the Ford, the *ping! ping! ping!* like bombs going off next to her. It was all she could do to reload the M4, concentrating on getting a solid grip on a fresh magazine from one of her pouches even though her hands were covered in sweat. Every inch of her trembled every time a round slammed into the vehicles and road around her. The damn machine gun never seemed to run out of bullets and continued to rain long after she had finished loading her rifle and pulled back the charging handle.

And then, just like that, nothing.

The suddenness of it froze her in place, still crouched behind the bullet-riddled truck, her breath hammering out of her. It took her three full seconds before she allowed herself to finally believe what her ears were telling her.

It was quiet. Unbelievably quiet.

It took her another five full seconds to will herself to stand up—her legs were wobbly for some reason, and her hands trembling slightly—and look over the hood of the vehicle up the street.

The GMC had come to a stop *(Thank God)* at an odd angle in the middle of the road about twenty meters from the red pickup, its hood facing her end of the street, which allowed her to see the (at least) two dozen or so holes spread out from one side of the windshield to the other. Spilled gasoline tickled at her nostrils, and the painfully gradual *drip-drip-drip* sound of leaking fuel from somewhere at the back of the vehicle was the only thing she could hear other than her own labored breathing.

The enemy truck was so close that she didn't have to look through her weapon's optic to see the smoke coming out of holes along the grill and hood or the driver slouched over the steering wheel, unmoving. The machine gun on the cab was resting on its stock, the muzzle pointed up at the cloudless sky. Sunlight beat down on the shiny black coat of paint as if it had just come off the lot.

She was so focused on the dead-in-the-street truck that it took her a while to recognize the sound of an engine roaring to life. She scanned past the GMC and spotted the Jeep still fifty meters up the road. It was attempting to make a wide U-turn and almost crashed into a stop sign in the process. The driving was erratic, to put it mildly, which made her wonder if the driver was hurt.

Pop! as someone fired at it, the round hitting the back of the Jeep as it completed its desperate U-turn before speeding away. She thought about shooting after it, but it was already too far away and hitting a moving target—even one as big as a car—was never an easy shot, even if her hands weren't shaking.

"Gaby!" a voice shouted. *Danny.*

"Yeah!" she shouted back. She didn't take her eyes off the unmoving technical; a part of her expected it to come back to life as soon as she relaxed, the man in the back rising behind the machine gun like some unkillable monster.

"You good?" Danny asked.

"Yeah! You?"

"Right as rain."

"Now what?"

"Clear the technical!"

She stepped away from the Ford and climbed over the metal pole barrier—keeping her eyes on the target the entire time—before finally moving up the street. The smell of spilled gasoline became more evident as she drew closer, and broken glass *crunched* under her shoes. Her heartbeat had slowed down, her breathing returning to (mostly) normal, and she picked up her pace to cover the remaining distance.

Gaby glimpsed the fading Jeep in the distance just before it vanished completely, taking the sound of its engines with it. With that threat gone, she turned her attention to the technical, her finger testing the M4's trigger, ready to shoot anything that moved. Any goddamn thing at all.

But nothing moved in or around the truck. At least, nothing living.

She kicked empty brass casings around the vehicle before finding the soldier in the truck bed. His hands were clutched around his throat where he'd been shot. By the amount of blood pooled under him, she guessed he had bled out soon after he fell.

There were two more bodies in the truck—the driver and his passenger. They were both wearing black uniforms, and the passenger was crumpled on the floor in an impossible ball shape. For a moment Gaby thought the man was hiding, but no; he was just dead. She made sure by opening the door and nudging him in the shoulder with her rifle's barrel until he toppled sideways in the other direction and didn't move.

"Clear!" she shouted.

She gave the street one last look, listening for the Jeep's engines, and when she didn't see or hear any signs of it, she turned and jogged back to Danny and Nate.

She hadn't seen the pickup earlier because she was so focused on the enemy, but if Danny thought it was a jalopy before, she wondered what he was going to call it now. The side facing her was covered in holes, and like the GMC's, its tank was leaking gasoline. Sheets of glass covered the road and one of the back tires had been shot out, though she didn't remember hearing anything that sounded like a tire blowing. Then again, given how fast she was emptying her rifle, she probably wouldn't have heard a bomb going off next to her at the time.

The truck was there (mostly, anyway), but there were no signs of Danny or Nate. Or Mason, for that matter.

"Danny!" she called.

"Here," Danny said, his voice coming from the other side of the truck.

She jogged the rest of the way and went around the pickup. Danny had his back to her, but she could see that he was crouched next to Nate, who sat with his back against the driver-side door. Their weapons were on the pavement.

"Nate," she said.

He looked past Danny and smiled at her, but it was overly forced and that realization only made her run faster to him. She went around Danny and kneeled on the other side of Nate, her stomach dropping at the sight of blood gathered around his waist.

"How bad?" she asked.

"I'll be okay," Nate said.

She ignored him and fixed on Danny. "How bad?"

"Could have been worse," Danny said. When she gave him a disbelieving look, he added, "He could be dead." Then, "Press here," and pulled his hands from a T-shirt he was holding against Nate's left side.

She replaced his hand with her own, her fingers turning red as soon as she touched the fabric. She looked down at Nate.

He was smiling at her. Or trying to. "I'll be fine. Just a scratch."

"Right. Just a scratch," she said quietly.

Danny had stood up and was looking around them, his rifle back in his blood-covered hands. "He's gone."

"Who?" she said, glancing over.

"Mason."

She looked around them—at the car lots to both sides of the street, then the empty road out of town behind them. "He couldn't have gotten far."

Danny was too busy squinting at the cars in the dealerships to answer, as if he could magically pick up Mason's scent if he made his eyes small enough. Gaby looked back at Nate, keeping her hands on the bloody bundle of clothing pressed against his wound. As much as the idea of Mason escaping made her furious, she found it easy to push it aside to concentrate on keeping Nate from bleeding to death.

"My fault," Nate was saying, his voice so soft she barely heard him. "He was my responsibility. I wasn't paying attention…"

"Shut up, it doesn't matter." She was trying to find the balance between pressing too hard and not hard enough against Nate's side. She couldn't even tell what color the T-shirt used to be anymore. "What about Nate, Danny?"

Danny slung his rifle. "We're going to have to look for the bullet and take it out. Can't leave it in there."

"You've done this before?"

He shrugged.

"Danny," she pressed. "You've done this before?"

"Well, there was that time in a diner, though Willie boy did most of the work. But I think I got the gist of it."

Nate groaned.

Danny grinned at him. "Relax, Nathaniel-san. Back in college they used to call me Danny the Surgeon, and it wasn't because I always wore white surgical gloves around campus, though yes, I could see the confusion. Those things are super soft, you know."

THE PICKUP MAY have been beaten up before it was shot up, but it was a tough old thing. Despite leaking fuel and brandishing new bullet holes along most of one side, once they replaced the blown tire, the truck was still serviceable, and the engine came alive when Danny turned the key.

"I told you I picked a winner," Danny said before he righted the vehicle and pushed them down the street.

She sat in the back with Nate, keeping an eye on his paling face and the bandages around his waist. Like the shirt earlier, the white fabric was already soaked with blood and growing a darker shade of red every second.

She must have grimaced at the sight because Nate made an effort to smile up at her. "It looks worse than it really is."

"Bullshit," she said.

"No, really."

"Stop lying."

"What makes you think I'm lying?"

"Because I know you."

He smiled again. Or tried to again. He was doing a very poor job of it, and she wished he would stop. The effort alone was probably causing him more harm than good.

"You know me too well," he said.

"Not well enough," she said, and kissed him on the forehead.

She kept her arms around his body to keep him from moving around too much. Danny was driving just fast enough to get them as quickly down the street as possible while glancing at the map of Gallant spread out on the front passenger seat next to him. He only swerved once or twice, which was amazing given everything he was multitasking. He was also amazingly calm, but she wondered how much of that was a façade, or maybe she was just projecting her own fears and emotions onto him. Danny was an ex-Ranger, after all. It wasn't as if blood was anything new to him.

"How much farther, Danny?" she asked.

"A mile or two," Danny said. "Can't go too far in this thing, with your boyfriend back there bleeding all over the upholstery."

"Sorry about that," Nate said quietly.

"You'll clean it up later."

"Gotcha."

She put a hand over Nate's mouth to shush him, then said, "How much gas do we have left?"

"Not enough," Danny said.

"Maybe we should have siphoned some from the GMC…"

"Maybe this, maybe that. Maybe it's Maybelline. We'll be fine."

"Will we?"

"You betcha."

He sounded confident, and that more than anything did a lot to ease her mind. This was the new Danny. The leader. Other than Lara, there was no one else Gaby would trust with her life. Except maybe Nate…

"See, we're almost there," Danny said as he slowed down and made a right turn.

The road under them went from smooth asphalt to uneven dirt road. Nate groaned in response.

"Danny," she said.

"I know," Danny said. "We'll be there soon. Better he suffers a little now than die a lot later."

A sheen of sweat had covered Nate's face as he looked back up at her. She smiled at him, then bent down and kissed him softly on the lips. When she pulled back, he was smiling again, and this time it actually looked acceptably convincing.

"Gotta get us our own room on the *Trident*," he said quietly.

She nodded. "Definitely."

"It'll be nice. Our own room. We can sleep in whenever we want. Finally."

"You always want to sleep in."

"Or maybe we won't sleep at all."

"Don't get ahead of yourself, mister."

"It'll be nice," he said again, and closed his eyes.

She fought the urge to tighten her arms around him, to keep his body steady against hers as the truck continued to rumble down the patch of dirt road, but she was afraid even too much additional pressure would just hurt him.

She kissed his unresponsive lips instead.

Stay alive, Nate. Please, stay alive.

I can't bear to lose you too…

GALLANT HAD MORE land than it did people, so the houses on the outskirts of the main commercial area were spread out. The dirt road Danny had turned into eventually became smooth asphalt again, and they passed a series of residential homes with large front and backyards.

Danny finally settled on a house with a dirt driveway and nothing but empty fields behind it. If not for the map, they would have driven right past this part of town and never known people lived here. The house had a white truck parked in the front yard and an unattached garage big enough for two cars, which was good because she didn't think the jalopy was going anywhere after this. If they could even start it again with the drain on its already leaking fuel tank.

She stayed inside the truck with Nate while Danny cleared the house by himself, then did the same to the garage next door. When he came back, they hid the pickup in the garage, then carried Nate inside the house and put him down in the living room. The residence was a single-floor building with burglar bars outside the windows and over the front door. Those security measures were the main reason Danny had chosen it out of all the other houses in the area.

"I'm going to need your help," Danny said as he shrugged off his pack, took out a bottle of water, and poured it over his hands.

"I'm not going anywhere," she said.

Nate lay on the couch with his eyes closed. His hair was soaked in sweat and his entire midsection was covered in blood, as were his pants and what was left of the shirt Danny hadn't already cut away to put on the bandages earlier.

"Tell me you can do this," she said to Danny.

"The first-aid kit has everything we need."

"Danny, tell me you can do this."

He nodded. "I can do this."

She stared at him for a few long seconds before finally nodding. "Okay."

"Let's get to work," Danny said, then handed her another bottle of water to clean her bloody hands with.

"WANT A SOUVENIR?" Danny asked.

She shook her head. "Be my guest."

"Eh, souvenirs are for old people anyway."

Danny flicked the bullet he had dug out of Nate into the bathroom sink. There was just enough light coming from the small rectangular opening behind her to see the 5.56 bullet as it *clinked* around the porcelain bowl before vanishing down the drain.

All that damage, from such a small thing…

Gaby concentrated on rubbing Nate's dried blood off her fingers, but it didn't seem like she was making any real progress. After a while, she gave up and grabbed a blue cotton towel hanging off a rack and forced herself to be satisfied with wiping the sweat off her face.

"He's gonna be out the entire night from the morphine," Danny said, "which means you and I get the privilege of guard duty."

"Yay us."

"What I said. Anyway, we have everything we need to survive the night. Burglar bars over the windows, extra food, and water. All we have to do is stay as quiet as mice and they won't ever know we were here."

"Who are we talking about? Ghouls or humans?"

"Both."

"You think there's more of them out there? Besides the guy in the Jeep?"

"I think that technical was already on its way here before the fun started. Maybe because of whoever they were exchanging fire with earlier."

"It had to be Mercer's people. They're everywhere."

Danny nodded. "Yeah. Mercer's fun boys are becoming a real pain in my ass. Right now, though, I'm more concerned with why those boys in black were here in the first place. That technical came later."

"The Jeep."

"Uh huh."

"What if Nate was right? What if they were tracking us?"

"The question is why."

"Mason?"

"Maybe."

"But you don't believe it."

"No. Something else is going on." He shook his head. "I'd give my left pinky finger to find out what."

Danny seemed to drift off, lost in thought, and Gaby did the same, staring at herself in the mirror above the sink. She was already covered in dirt and sweat, but now she'd added streaks of blood by touching her face with her bloodied hands. A year ago the sight of the girl looking back at her would have horrified her, but these days it barely registered. She wetted the towel with a dab of water from what was left in her bottle and went to work.

"He's still out there," she said after awhile. "Mason."

"Yup," Danny nodded.

"We should have killed him."

"Probably." Then, "Get some rest, kid. It's been a long morning, and it's going to be a long night. We can't travel with Nate in his condition, at least not if you want to keep him alive for cuddling later."

"I'd really like that."

"A little cuddling, a little premarital sex…" Danny said before turning and leaving the bathroom.

She smiled wryly after him before returning to cleaning Nate's blood off her cheeks and forehead. When she was (mostly) done, she tossed the towel into the overflowing trash bin, snatched up her rifle, and went outside to join Danny. She could already feel the temperature starting to drop around her.

It would be dark soon. Very soon…

CHAPTER 6
KEO

WELL, THIS DIDN'T quite go as planned.

Or maybe that wasn't entirely true. The fact of the matter was, he was (somehow, some way) still alive, and more importantly, there was a good chance he was being taken to Mercer. Of course, that was the best-case scenario, and he had a feeling he knew what Danny would say if he ever caught wind of Keo's presently overflowing optimism.

Not that he had much of a choice. It was either focus on the positive or wallow in the pain. Because there was a lot of pain.

His face was on fire, and moving even just a little bit sent jolts of electricity coursing through his body. But it wasn't the type of pain that signaled a broken rib (or two), so that was the good news. The bad was that his captors hadn't bothered to clean up his face, which explained the feeling of sandpaper scraping at his eyeballs. He still had a mouthful of blood, most of it coming from his broken nose. His forehead might have been slightly cut, though that was currently taking a backseat to the pounding originating from between his eyes.

The pain should have been worse with the helicopter pulsing continuously through him as it traveled over the state of Texas, the *whup-whup-whup* of its rotors like sledgehammers pounding nails into his skull. He had no idea where they were or where they were going, only that they were already in the air and moving when he opened his eyes and (discreetly) took stock of his situation.

He was surrounded by the same people he had seen back at the barn—three of them sat across from him while two more flanked him. A sixth, sporting aviator shades, was perched behind a machine gun mounted along the open starboard-side hatch. The weapon looked like an older model M240 with a box magazine; the man behind it pointed the weapon playfully at a flock of birds outside and mimed shooting them. The port-side door was closed and the only thing Keo could see out the windows were empty skies.

Six men and one woman, which probably meant two or three more in the cockpit up front. It wasn't even close to being manageable numbers; not that he had any ideas about escaping anyway, especially with his wrists and ankles duct taped together. Never mind the fact that he had never learned to fly, because going out one of the open doors was probably his only real option at the moment. They had removed everything he had on him, leaving just his clothes and the blood on his face.

He wasn't sure how long the woman had known he was awake; she was watching him with a curious expression on her face. She looked tall even sitting down—maybe just a shade under five-ten, and like most women he had encountered since The Purge, carried very little if any excess pounds on her. She wasn't wearing any makeup, and that made the bags under her eyes more apparent.

Someone hasn't been getting their beauty sleep lately.

She looked tired but was trying to power through the fatigue. He'd seen plenty of guys do that on jobs either with caffeine or pill-sized stimulants. She had short black hair, but he could imagine her with a long, flowing mane just a year ago. The obvious Parisian genes were easy to spot and she reminded him a little of Bonnie, the ex-model whom he had spent a lot of time with back on the *Trident*. Like the men around her, the woman wasn't wearing anything that looked like a uniform or a name tag, which made perfect sense if they were indeed Mercer's men and were out here launching guerilla-style hit-and-run attacks on collaborator positions.

His ruse exposed, Keo gave up pretending to still be asleep and straightened up, or as much as he could manage while restrained. His nose felt as if there were cotton balls jammed into both nostrils, and the hard floor was sticky with fresh mud and dirt and (no doubt his contribution to the mess) blood.

"Where we going?" Keo asked, directing his question at the woman. He had to shout to be heard over the turbine engine that made every inch of the helicopter thrum as if it were going to come unglued at any second.

She didn't answer him, but she didn't take her eyes off him, either. The guy behind the machine gun glanced over at the sound of Keo's voice before returning his gaze out the hatch as the helicopter caught up to another flock of birds.

"Can I get some water?" he asked the woman.

She stared but still didn't say anything.

"Towel?"

Nothing.

"I smell jerky in the air. I wouldn't mind some of that. I'm famished. Haven't eaten all day and most of yesterday."

"Shut up," the man sitting to his left said.

Keo ignored him and said to the woman, "Ever heard the idiom 'You catch more flies with honey?'"

"If I give you some jerky, will you shut up?" the man sitting to the woman's left said.

"Absolutely," Keo said.

"Too bad. I finished it off this morning. Chased it down with some coffee and an oatmeal cookie."

"Sounds like fine dining."

"It ain't the Hilton, but it'll do."

He turned back to the woman. "Maybe you can tell one of these gentlemen to give me some water."

"What makes you think she's in charge?" Beef Jerky Guy asked.

"Oh, come on. It's obvious she wears the pants around here."

Something that looked almost like a smile flickered across the woman's face, but it only lasted for a blink of an eye before vanishing.

"Right?" he said to her.

She ignored him, said instead, "What happened here?" and traced one side of her face with her forefinger. "Looks like it must have hurt."

"It did," Keo said, remembering the cold steel of Pollard's knife as it sliced its way into his flesh. "You should see the other guy."

"Prettier than you?" Beef Jerky Guy said.

"Not even a contest."

"Considering how you look, that's saying something."

"I still have nightmares about it."

"I bet."

"Where we going?" he asked the woman again.

"Don't worry about it," she said.

"Give a guy a hint."

She didn't answer.

"Then can I at least get some water?" Keo asked.

"You already asked that," she said.

"Figured I didn't have anything to lose by asking a second time."

She nodded at the man sitting next to Keo. The guy produced a canteen and leaned over. Keo opened his mouth gratefully and took as much water as he could, then swished it around to wash away the blood clinging to the walls of his mouth before swallowing the whole thing down.

"Thanks," he said to the woman.

"Next thing you know Slaphappy Jerry here'll want a change of clothes," Beef Jerky Guy said.

"I'm Keo," he said to the woman.

"Good for you," she said.

He couldn't help but smile back at her even though doing so

made the entire lower half of his face hurt, as if someone were punching it repeatedly.

"Where we going?" he asked for the third time.

"Ask that again and I'm going to throw you out the hatch," the woman said.

"I'd like to see that," Beef Jerky Guy grinned.

"Only if you buy me dinner first," Keo said.

"Smart guy, huh?"

"It's my disguise. I'm actually very dumb. Hence my current situation."

"Yeah, you really bungled that one, didn't you?" He chortled. "Man, what were you doing showing up by yourself like that?"

Being the world's biggest idiot, or something pretty goddamn close, Keo thought, but said, "You sure you're out of those jerky?"

"Pretty sure," the man said, and smacked his gums for effect.

"Too bad. There's nothing better than two guys bonding over some meat."

Beef Jerky Guy stared at him like he didn't know how to respond to that. The woman next to him, Keo noticed, barely managed to suppress a snort.

―――

A COMBINATION OF pain and lack of sleep took its toll and he dozed off soon after, and didn't wake up a second time until someone was nudging him on the shoulder. A gruff male voice half-shouted, "Wake up, Sleeping Beauty!"

Once the haze cleared, Keo opened his eyes to empty seats in front of him, just before Beef Jerky Guy and a second man yanked him out of his own seat and pushed him toward the open door. He stumbled, expecting to fall on his bound legs, until he noticed he was moving freely again, though he couldn't say the same about his still-bound wrists.

One out of two ain't bad.

"Don't fall, princess," Beef Jerky Guy said. "No one's picking you up. We'll make you crawl the rest of the way."

"Thanks for the warning," Keo said.

"Don't say I never gave you nothin'."

"You're too kind. I would have settled for the jerky breath."

"Heh. Funny guy. You a professional comedian or something?"

"No, but I've been told I can be a pretty stand-up guy."

"Oh, funny," Beef Jerky Guy said. "Now *move*."

A third man was waiting for him outside the open hatch as Keo hopped out of the helicopter. It was a mistake, and he grunted against a sudden surge of pain as he landed in a slight crouch. The still-spinning rotors swarmed the area with cold winds that made every inch of his exposed face sting.

They were in a field surrounded by grass that went up to his knees, but all he had to do was sniff the air to know they were next to the ocean. Keo breathed in the fresh breeze and tried not to think about the last time he was this close to the sea and who he had been with at the time.

One of his captors, maybe Beef Jerky Guy, pushed him in the back, and Keo stumbled forward. He ducked his head reflexively, the way people do without thinking when they exit a helicopter. Of course the rotors didn't come close to slicing off his head, but it made him feel better anyway as he struggled across the hard ground, grass slapping at his legs.

He didn't have to look far to see where the woman and the rest of his traveling companions had gone. They were up ahead, beyond the field and on a long stretch of beach. The men had spread out to stand guard while the woman had a radio to her lips, one hand shielding her eyes as she looked out into the ocean. He wasn't sure what she was looking at because he couldn't see anything out there except blue waters. Given that it was still midday, it didn't take a genius to know he was staring at the Gulf of Mexico.

"Wanna go for a swim?" Beef Jerky Guy asked from behind him. "Wash all that crap off your face?"

"Sure. Maybe you can help me clean it off," Keo said.

"Maybe if you had a pair of tits I might think about it."

"You're all heart, pal."

"I'm not your pal, dude."

"And I was saving up for that friendship bracelet, too."

They were in a very isolated part of the coastline without anything that looked like civilization, much less houses, within sight on either sides of the beach. There were no hints of industry further inland and the beach was littered with seaweed and trash, along with fish carcasses. They were probably the only souls around for miles, which made it a pretty good spot for an extraction point.

The woman glanced over as Keo and his guards reached her. "Keep an eye on him. If he makes one wrong move, shoot him."

Keo stopped next to her, the sunbaked sand sinking under his boots. "Now why would I do a stupid thing like that?"

"We should shoot him now, Erin," Beef Jerky Guy said.

"Don't say that," Keo said. "What about that friendship bracelet we were going to get?"

"Shut up."

"Is that a no?"

"Erin," Beef Jerky Guy said, ignoring Keo. "This guy doesn't know anything. Whoever he is, he probably killed Davis and Butch."

"Not yet," Erin said.

"Give me one reason."

"I don't have to give you a damn thing, Troy," Erin said, and it was hard to miss the finality in her voice.

Troy grunted but didn't press the issue.

Keo suppressed a smile, when the roar of a turbine engine revving up made him look back, just in time to see the helicopter rising slowly into the air. The man with the aviator shades sitting behind the machine gun waved at them, and Erin returned it.

"See you when we see you," Erin said into her radio.

"Have a safe trip," a male voice answered.

It didn't take the helicopter long to turn into a small dot in the sky, and soon Keo could barely hear its *whup-whup-whup*.

"Where's it going?" Keo asked.

Erin ignored him and said, "Looks like we're early."

"That's a first," the man standing next to Troy, whose name Keo had never caught, said.

"ETA twenty minutes. Until then, I want the area secured. The last thing we need is someone sneaking up on us again."

"Definitely wouldn't want that," Troy said. "What about him?"

"He's not going anywhere."

Footsteps faded behind Keo, along with Troy and the second man's presence.

In the next few seconds, Keo ran through all the possible escape scenarios, but each time he always came to the same conclusion: Mercer. Find Mercer. And the only way to do that was to let these people take him to the man.

Should be easy enough…as long as I don't get killed on the way over.

"So who's picking us up?" he asked.

"You'll see," Erin said.

"A boat?"

"Unless you can swim very, very far."

"I happen to be a very good swimmer."

She ignored him, said instead, "What were you doing back at the barn?"

"Hunting game."

"With two semi-automatic rifles," she said. It wasn't a question.

"I was hunting big game."

"There is no big game. Not anymore."

"I'm an eternal optimist."

She smirked, though he couldn't tell if that was amusement or annoyance. Maybe a little of both. "You had Davis's iPod on you."

"There's a lot of iPods just sitting around out there. What makes you think the one I had belonged to this Davis guy?"

She fixed him with a long look, and he was mostly convinced she didn't believe a single thing he was saying. "It doesn't matter if you don't want to tell me now. We have people who are very good at extracting information. You'll be telling me everything anyway, including what you were doing back there."

"I told you—"

"I know, hunting game."

"I get the feeling you don't believe me."

"You know what I think?"

"Do I have a choice?"

"I think you killed Davis and Butch, just like Troy said. Maybe Luke and Bill, too, but that's a bit of a stretch. What I can't figure out is what you were doing out there at the barn. Alone. You had to have seen the others pushing the helicopter. That's six people. And you still moved on us anyway." She squinted her eyes at him. "You're either the dumbest man alive, or you're looking to get yourself killed. So which one is it?"

Can't it be both? he thought, but said with as much conviction as he could muster, "Neither. I was just curious what you guys were doing out there. If I had known people were going to start shooting at me, I would have kept going."

"You're going to stick to that?"

"It's the truth."

"Uh huh," she said before turning back to the endless blue waters in front of them. "Of course, I'm not discounting the possibility you're one of those guys with more balls than brain cells."

"Have you been talking to my old girlfriends?"

She ignored him again, said, "You know how I know you were looking for us?"

"Even though I wasn't?"

"You never asked who we were. That tells me you already knew."

Well, shit, Keo thought, and wondered how long he was going to be able to keep this up before Erin finally agreed with Troy that it wasn't worth taking him with them.

ERIN HAD SAID the ETA was twenty minutes, but it was more like seventeen before the gray dot appeared in the horizon, followed by the slowly growing whine of twin outboard motors.

Keo knew it was some kind of offshore fishing boat before it got big enough for him to make out its V-shaped hull. As soon as the boat appeared, the others began converging back on his and Erin's location.

"Are we all going to fit in there?" Keo asked.

"We'll make do," Erin said. "And if not…"

"I know, I go over the side, right?"

She smiled but didn't confirm or deny.

As the boat neared, Keo counted two guys onboard—one behind the helm and the other squatting at the bow with a rifle. On cue, the radio in Erin's hand squawked and a male voice, almost entirely drowned out by the motors on the other end, shouted, "Any trouble?"

"You're clear," Erin said into the radio.

"Roger that," the man answered.

Erin clipped the radio back to her hip. "I'm surprised you haven't tried anything yet."

Keo held up his bound hands. "Hard to try anything like this."

"Still, knowing what you did, where you're going, and what's going to happen when you get there…"

"Maybe you're assuming too much. Maybe I didn't do the things you think I did, and as a result I have nothing to fear."

"Sure, whatever you say, Keo."

A hand clamped down on Keo's shoulder, and he smelled the familiar odor of beef jerky in the air as Troy said, "Cheer up, buddy. It's a nice, long trip back to The Ranch. Plenty to see and do on the way."

"Hey, as long as you're around I'm sure it'll be a great time, Troy," Keo said.

"That's the spirit."

Keo looked over at Erin, but she was busy watching a couple of the men slinging their weapons and stepping into the lapping waters of the Gulf of Mexico to wait for the boat. Keo focused on the moment—the here and now.

And right now, he was alive.

Hurt, sore, and bleeding, but alive. And as long as he stayed that

way, he could still finish the mission: Find Mercer, then kill him.
Who's Captain Optimism now?
This guy...

CHAPTER 7
LARA

THERE WERE TWO of them, and they were olive drab, not black; though in the darkness of the night, they might as well be black.

"Jon boats," Maddie whispered next to her.

"Jon boats?" Lara repeated.

"That's what those are called. Looks like they have trolling motors in the back, but they're keeping them quiet and rowing the old-fashioned way so they won't make any noise."

The better to sneak up on us, she thought, watching the two crafts as they glided smoothly across the water. If not for the half-moon, she wouldn't have been able to see them at all. It was pretty clear where they were headed—right toward them.

The *Trident* was anchored like it had been the last few days with its lights shut off, which was standard operating procedure, because despite their distance from shore, it wasn't a good idea to be the only lights blinking out here. But SOP or not, they had been spotted and had been since last night, maybe even longer. These men approaching them now knew exactly where they were and how to reach them without being seen or heard.

Or they thought they did, anyway. They were about to get a very rude awakening.

"What are those things made of?" Lara asked.

"Usually aluminum," Maddie said. "Sometimes fiberglass or wood."

"Wood?"

"But usually aluminum."

There were three figures in each boat, with one sitting forward at the bow while the two behind him slowly rowed them forward with paddles. They were likely armed, since you didn't try to sneak up on an anchored yacht in the middle of the ocean in the dead of night without bad intentions.

The radio resting between her and Maddie squawked—it was just a small sound with the volume turned almost all the way down, but it still made enough of an impression that she flinched a little bit.

"Wonder what they're doing all the way out here at this time of the night," Blaine said through the radio. He was somewhere above and to the left of them, hidden by the darkness of the bridge. In case they needed to abandon the charade, she wanted him up there and ready. She wanted everyone ready.

Just in case, right, Will?

"Maybe they just want to borrow some sugar," Bonnie said. She was positioned on the upper deck and tasked with watching the other side of the boat in case there were more surprises coming their way.

"I guess we should greet them all friendly like," Carly said. She was on the main deck behind them, keeping an eye on everyone else. "That would be the Christian thing to do."

"Fuck that," Blaine said.

"Hey, there are children present."

"Oops."

"Sucker," Carly said. "Everyone's locked inside their cabins, snug as bugs." Lara could hear a slight echo from Carly's radio, which meant she was in the hallway outside the rooms, probably pacing nervously back and forth and doing her very best not to let it show in her voice. "Just make sure to keep the collateral damage limited to outside, okay guys?"

"That's going to depend on them," Bonnie said.

"Shoot first and never mind the questions; isn't that the Ranger way?" Blaine asked.

"Sounds familiar," Carly said.

Lara picked up the radio and keyed it. "That's enough chitchat. We're going radio silent from now on. Everyone, wait for my signal."

She had let them go back and forth because they needed it; there was something unnerving about sitting (or standing) around in the dark waiting for men with guns to slowly, oh so slowly, reach you. All that anxiety needed a release, and talking or joking always seemed to do the trick. She'd seen it work for Danny and Will plenty of times.

Next to her, Maddie was peering over the railing. "I still just count six. All armed, probably. I don't know about you, but I don't believe they're coming here to borrow some sugar."

Lara gave her a wry smile, then picked up her M4 and checked that the safety was off for the third time since she arrived at the spot next to Maddie on the boat's port side. They were almost exactly in the middle of the main deck, hidden behind a wall section of the railing that provided plenty of cover in case of a firefight. The better shooting position was on the upper deck, and she already had Bonnie and Benny up there right now.

Maddie fidgeted and switched up her grip on her own carbine. "It's times like these I miss having the Ranger around."

"He'll be back soon enough. Then you'll be complaining about his bad jokes."

"Yeah, probably." She paused for a moment, then, "Too bad Keo didn't come back with you. We could sure use him, too."

She shared Maddie's regret and wondered what Keo was doing right now. The last time she saw him, he and Jordan were on their way back to T18 to get the oft-talked about but never-seen Gillian out of Mercer's destructive path. Had they made it? Where were they now? He knew exactly how to contact her, so why hadn't he?

You still alive out there, Keo?

She pushed the question away and peeked over the railing. Without binoculars, the boats looked more like two long, black shapes bobbing slightly up and down against the ocean currents. They were still far enough away that she couldn't hear the *slosh-slosh* of their paddles moving against the water, but close enough that she noticed a slight pang of anticipation and maybe, just maybe, a little bit of fear, which was something she hadn't felt in a long time since coming out here.

"Who do you think they are?" Maddie whispered.

"I don't know."

"Can't be collaborators…"

"Why not?"

"I've never known those guys to be this subtle. Remember the last time they assaulted Song Island?"

She nodded. How could she forget? That night still haunted her dreams. The blood, the deaths, the piles of bodies, then later the tide of ghouls…

"Maybe they're pirates," Maddie was saying.

"Pirates?"

"Not the Johnny Depp metrosexual type of pirates, but more like those Somali pirates you hear about on the news. They take over boats and hold the crew for ransom." The smaller Texan shrugged. "But that was back when money was still, well, money."

"Pirates," Lara repeated. For some reason, just saying the word made her smile.

"Hey, stranger things have been happening these days. Ghouls, end of the world, blood towns… Why not a little pirate action?"

She looked over the railing at the jon boats again. The six figures inside them still lacked details even though they were closer than before, which probably meant they were all wisely wearing black clothes that helped them blend into their environment.

They had definitely come prepared. The question was: For what?

"BLAINE," SHE SAID into the radio. She wasn't whispering, but it was close. "Call it."

"Forty yards," Blaine said. She couldn't tell if he had changed his voice to match hers or if it was the result of the lowered volume on the two-way. Whatever the reason, she had to strain more than usual to hear him.

Next to her, Maddie shuffled her feet and there was a sharp *click!* as she thumbed her rifle's fire selector off the safety position.

"Thirty-five," Blaine said.

"They're taking their sweet time," Maddie whispered. She couldn't—and maybe wasn't even trying—to hide the anxiety in her voice.

"Thirty," Blaine said. "They're still on course to make contact almost directly below you, Lara."

"Roger that," she said into the radio. "Bonnie, anything on the other side?"

"Still nothing," Bonnie said. She sounded anxious. "Should I go over to Benny's and back him up?"

"Yes."

"Moving!"

Thank God for Blaine, hidden on the bridge, observing as the two jon boats slowly crept toward them; she couldn't see anything now that she was completely hidden behind the thick wall. It went up to three feet along the side of the yacht, and the only way to see over it would be to raise herself and peek. With the men so close, the chances of being spotted were just too good.

Even though she couldn't see them, she could hear the quiet but persistent *slosh-slosh* of their plastic paddles moving against the water as they neared.

"Bonnie, where are you now?" she said into the radio.

"In position!" Bonnie said, her breathing coming through the radio in labored gasps.

"Twenty-five yards," Blaine said.

Lara poised her thumb over the radio's transmit lever and glanced briefly at Maddie. The other woman was watching her back, the M4 rifle gripped tightly in her hands.

"Twenty," Blaine said.

"Cutting it a little close, aren't we," Maddie said. It may or may not have been a question.

"Fifteen," Blaine said.

She keyed the radio and hissed into it, *"Now!"* and stood up.

The lights snapped on around her, the sudden switch from darkness to blinding brightness like sharp knives pricking at the corners of her eyes. This despite the fact she was prepared for it, so the effect on the men in the jon boats would have been even more dramatic.

And it was, she saw as she peered through the iron sights of her carbine at the smaller boats in front, and, as Blaine predicted, right below her. They were caught in the water about ten yards off the side of the yacht, both vessels moving side-by-side and close enough that the two men at the bows could have swapped places by jumping over. The four in the back still had their paddles in their hands and were leaning over their respective sides when the lights hit them in mid-row. They were all wearing black clothes like she had guessed, though she didn't expect their faces to be painted black and green.

The two up front were the real problems, because there was a reason they weren't rowing. It was why she focused on them first and instantly spotted the rifles in their hands, the weapons dangling off their shoulders by straps. Half of the men had one hand shielding their eyes from the bright lights blasting in their faces, but she knew that sudden disorientation wasn't going to last forever.

And it didn't. It took three eternally long seconds for the men to understand what had happened—that they had been caught in an ambush—and for the ones in the back to drop their paddles and reach for their rifles on the floors of the boats. Two of them actually let go of their paddles in mid-row and the plastic devices sank into the water. The two up front were already taking aim, swinging their weapons from side to side and up and down as Lara and Maddie, and Bonnie and Benny above them, then Carrie, Gwen, and Lorelei popped up along the sides of the *Trident*. Lara wondered what they must look like to the men, with the bright spotlights doing a number on their field of vision.

But they had to know, didn't they? It may have just been six against seven, but it was more than that: They were at a great disadvantage on their small boats adrift in the ocean. They had no cover, no room to maneuver, and they were, for all intents and purposes, sitting ducks.

Sitting ducks with rifles.

"Hold your fire!" Lara shouted. "If you open fire, we will kill you!"

They didn't react right away, but they also didn't start shooting, either. Instead, they kept looking left and right, and up and down, maybe counting how many guns were pointed at them, maybe trying to decide if they could make it through this encounter alive. All the lights on the *Trident* weren't turned on the boats, but there were enough to be hazards, and she could see the way the men below her were blinking, trying to focus on what they were facing.

They had to know they didn't have any chance, didn't they? *Didn't they?*

"Put down your weapons!" Lara shouted. "You have ten seconds to comply before we open fire and kill every single one of you!"

Most of the six men began honing in on her voice.

"You now have five seconds!"

They didn't move. A couple of them exchanged looks, the whites of their eyes visible thanks to the black paint covering their faces.

"Four!"

Before she could get to three, one of the men lowered his rifle and said something to the others. The other five didn't seem to react until the man tossed his weapon off the side of the jon boat. It *plopped* into the Gulf of Mexico and sank. Maybe it was the noise, but the men suddenly realized what he had done and began looking at one another. If they were talking, she couldn't hear it over her own racing heartbeat.

"Oh Jesus, come on, guys, come on," Maddie whispered next to her.

Lara didn't take her eyes or her weapon off the small open crafts below her or the men standing unsteadily on them. Maddie, despite her quiet pleading, also didn't relax, and Lara hoped the rest of her people were equally stout right now. One man throwing his gun away didn't mean anything when the other five hadn't followed suit, and so many things could still go so, so wrong in the next few seconds.

"The rest of you!" Lara shouted. "Do it!"

Slowly, one by one, they grudgingly lowered their weapons.

"Thank you, Jesus," Maddie whispered when the men began tossing their rifles into the ocean and raised their hands into the air.

"Your belts, too!" Lara shouted.

They obeyed, even though she kept waiting for at least one of them to rebel, to take his chances rather than be captured. But none of them did, and slowly as the gun belts slipped into the water, she blinked out the sweat in her eyes despite the cold night air. Her shirt under the assault vest was already drenched, though she hadn't noticed it until now.

The man who had surrendered his weapon first had moved to the bow of his boat while the others remained in the back with their hands raised. "What now?" he shouted up at them—at her.

"Pick up your paddles and start rowing toward the back!" she shouted down. "Attempt to go in any other direction, and we will open fire! Do you understand?"

The man turned around and nodded at the others, and they sat back down and picked up their paddles. Or the ones that hadn't dropped theirs into the ocean, anyway.

"Wow," Maddie said breathlessly next to her. "That was too intense."

Lara glanced over at Maddie, who was wiping sweat off her forehead with her shirt's long sleeve. "Head to the back and get them onboard, Maddie."

Maddie nodded and jogged off.

Alone, Lara lowered her rifle and leaned against the railing and wiped at her own dripping sweat. She sighed and willed her heartbeat to slow down, slow down…

Jesus, Will, how did you do this day in and day out?

Jesus, Jesus…

———

THEY PULLED BOTH small boats out of the water and left them in the back, and even as the six men were led through the lower deck (she wanted to keep them as far away from the upper decks and the kids as possible), Blaine powered up the *Trident* and got them moving again, just in case the men had friends who might come looking for them. Lara posted additional sentries on both sides of the yacht and equipped everyone with night-vision binoculars.

With their hands bound with duct tape, the captives were led through the lower deck and placed inside a small room where the boat's crew usually ate their meals. Their ankles were bound, and five of the men sat down while Benny and Maddie stood guard outside the door. The sixth man, the one who had been first to surrender, left with Lara.

She led him, his hands still bound, to one of the crew cabins they had been using as an extra storage room, and closed the door after them. The man sat down on a box of military MREs and looked around him. He was older than the rest—late forties, with gray liberally sprinkled along a military-style haircut. He could have passed for her father, except he was lean and muscular and almost six feet.

It should have been imposing for her to be in a room alone with him, but she wasn't afraid. She didn't know why, exactly, but she wasn't the least bit intimidated. Maybe it was the Glock in her hip holster; or maybe she was just tired of being afraid of people when there were so many other things out there to be scared of.

"You have a name?" she asked.

"Hart," the man said.

"I'm Lara."

"Nice to meet you, Lara."

"Likewise, Hart. How old are you?"

"That's my line," he smiled. "What are you, twenty?"

She smiled back but didn't answer him.

"Twenty-five?" he said.

"You're getting warmer."

"Gotta admit, you're the last person I expected to find in charge of this boat."

"What were you expecting?"

"Older. More male."

"Happy to disappoint you."

He sighed. "I guess we should get on with it, huh? It's late, and I'm sure we're both tired. Especially me. These bones aren't made for sitting on those tiny boats for hours."

"How long were you guys out there?"

"Long enough."

"Where did you come from?"

"I can't tell you that. At least, not yet."

"'Not yet?'"

He gave her a noncommittal shrug.

"You wanted the boat," she said.

He nodded. "We wanted the boat."

"You're not even going to try to lie?"

"No point. You got us by the balls. I figure whether we live or die now depends on what I say next."

"That's a very astute observation."

"I have no idea what that means."

"What?"

"Astute."

"It means you're right. Whether you live or die depends entirely on what you say now, in here."

"Ah," Hart said.

"Were you going to kill us?"

"No."

"Then how were you going to take the boat from us?"

"Hopefully without bloodshed."

"You were pretty heavily armed, if that was your hope."

"The plan was to sneak onboard and take it over with minimal collateral damage. We needed the boat. The weapons were insurance."

"I could have killed you and your men out there."

"I know…"

"If one of your guys had opened fire…"

"I know," Hart said again. "Trust me, I know."

They let a few seconds of silence fall between them.

Five seconds became ten, then fifteen…

He wasn't afraid of her, she could tell that much. Mostly he seemed completely resigned to his fate. She told herself not to believe him, that he wasn't telling her the complete truth, but for whatever reason, she chose to ignore it.

"Where's your base of operations?" she asked. "I know you didn't come all the way from shore. We're too far for that."

"We didn't."

"So where did you come from?"

"I can't tell you. At least, not yet."

"That's the second time you've said that."

"Do you have a pen?"

"What would I need a pen for?"

"I'm going to give you a radio frequency," Hart said. "The guy you'll want to talk to will be on the other end."

"Is he in charge?"

"Yes."

"Why would I want to talk to him?"

"How long have you been on this boat?"

"That's none of your business."

He shrugged slowly, as if just doing that simple move was tiring. "What I'm trying to get at is you're probably running low on fuel and supplies. Am I right?"

She didn't say anything.

"Of course I am," he said. "The collaborators have all the marinas and fueling stations along the coastline on lockdown. The ones they haven't already destroyed, anyway."

"You're not a collaborator…"

"And neither are you, or we wouldn't be having this conversation right now. I'd be fish food at the bottom of the Gulf of Mexico. Which is why I think we can make a deal."

She stared at him but remained silent.

"Call my CO," Hart said. When she still didn't say anything, he leaned slightly forward, his eyes almost pleading with her now. "*Please*. I promise you, you have nothing to lose and everything to gain."

CHAPTER 8
GABY

SHE HATED THE sinking feeling that always came with waiting for night. There was a thickness in the air, as if the molecules that made up the world suddenly doubled in density. Even breathing seemed to get a little harder, and it didn't help that the weather got immeasurably chillier as the sun disappeared. Darkness, unencumbered by artificial lights that once dotted the landscape, fell over everything.

They left the living room windows the way they had found them—dirty linen curtains over the glass panes on the inside, without any extra barriers that hadn't been there when they found the house. Danny had locked the doors because a locked door wasn't obvious like windows that were barricaded with furniture. The ghouls were dead, not stupid, as Will always used to say, and they knew when an environment had been altered. It was instinctive, a level of base intelligence that remained long after their humanity had been stripped away.

Eventually they retreated into the main bedroom in the back.

There was a single window in the room, and thankfully it had blinders that were already closed earlier today. That made perfect sense. The previous owners wouldn't have wanted their neighbors looking in at their bedroom. She and Danny upended the king-size bed and leaned the box spring and mattress against the window, then wedged them into place with a heavy wood armoire.

"Should hold," Danny said.

"You think?" she asked.

He shrugged. "Probably."

"That's not very reassuring, Danny."

"Oh well."

They moved Nate into the master bedroom and placed a mattress from a smaller room on the floor for him to lie on. He hadn't woken up from the morphine, and a part of her was glad he wasn't going to be awake for this. Not just because of the pain, but in case things went from bad to worse. She hated the thought but the possibility was there, especially if the collaborators really had been tracking them since Starch.

What makes us so special? Hopefully we won't have to find out.

They had brought all their supplies and weapons into the house, and while Danny called the *Trident* on the ham radio in the living room, she sat with Nate in the bedroom and watched him sleep. He was covered up with a throw blanket, but every now and then he would still shiver. She knew it wasn't from the slowly building cold outside the house's flimsy walls or from his wounds.

Nate suffered from nightmares where he would relive that night at the pawnshop in Louisiana and the days and nights afterward when she thought he was dead. It had taken a long time before he would confess it to her. She would have held him now, the way she did all those other nights, if not for his wound. She had to be satisfied with stroking his hair, and when that didn't seemed to help, leaned close to him and whispered, "It's okay. I'm here. You're with me now. You're safe, Nate. You're safe. I'll watch over you. I always will..."

His trembling subsided, whether because of her whispers or because the nightmares had run their course she didn't know, and he slowly settled into a peaceful slumber. She kissed his forehead and ran her fingers along the sides of his neck, feeling the very distinct indentations that covered most of his body underneath his clothes. They were teeth marks, a daily reminder of what he had been through and why he was never going to outrun his nightmares.

It was dark enough inside the room that her wristwatch's hands were glowing when Danny came back inside. He walked to the corner and put the radio away.

"How's everyone?" she asked.

"Still waiting to pick us up," Danny said. "Other than that, nothing they couldn't handle."

"Problems?"

"Maybe, maybe not. They'll know for sure tonight."

"That sounds ominous."

"Eh, they'll deal with it like they always do." He sat down and rummaged through his pack. "They're in good hands. I'm more worried about us tonight."

"Did you tell them about Nate? Or why we're not already waiting on a beach for them?"

He shook his head. "I just told them we got delayed. Accident on the road, and everyone's slowing down to take a look. You know, the usual Texas traffic. Besides, nothing good's going to come from them knowing what kind of creek we're up without a paddle."

"That good, huh?"

"Hey, we've been in worse situations. Compared to that whole Larkin snafu, this one's a peach. At least no one's trying to strafe us from above."

"Good point."

"That's why they call me Good Point Danny." He took a drink from a bottle before continuing. "The smart move would have been to *adios* outta here before dark. Take our chances on the road."

"You know we couldn't do that. Not with Nate's situation."

"Nate schmate."

"You don't mean that."

He shrugged. "You might be overestimating my fondness for him."

She didn't believe him for a second. Danny would never leave her or Nate, just as she would never leave the two of them. And Nate...well, she knew Nate would never leave her. He had proven that twice now.

"Maybe it's not too late to find a better hiding spot," she said.

"I'm pretty sure this is as good as it's gonna get. At least, in the time we have left."

"That's disheartening."

"Just have to get through the night; then we're home free." He stood up and walked back over to the door. "If you hear something that sounds like bad news, you know what to do."

"Take Nate into the bathroom."

"I was gonna say run outside and see if I might need some assistance, but sure, do the other thing, too."

Danny stepped outside and closed the door after him.

She looked down at Nate again and brushed specks of dirt out of his hair. Maybe it was the chaos of the day combined with the stress of almost losing him *(again)*, but somewhere between six and seven o'clock she closed her eyes and went to sleep without realizing it.

TAP-TAP.

Her hand was reaching for the M4 leaning against the wall next to her before she had fully opened both eyes. Nate was snoring lightly, the rise and fall of his chest underneath the flimsy throw blanket drawing her attention temporarily.

Tap-tap.

It came from above and slightly in front of her, which made sense because there was nothing behind her except the back of the house. She pulled her eyes away from Nate and turned them upward, trying to pinpoint the exact location—

Tap-tap.

More than one. Two at least, but likely more because where there were two there was usually a horde right behind them. They were moving back and forth on the roof of the residence directly above her. There was no pattern to their movements that she could detect, almost as if they were testing their footing, which didn't make any sense. The creatures were almost reckless when it came to their lives.

She sat perfectly still on the mattress next to Nate, acutely aware of everything about her surroundings, including her own slightly labored breathing, which provided a stark contrast against Nate's slow and steady heartbeat. She located the second rifle—Nate's— nearby and reached for it, then laid it on the floor next to her. The fact that both weapons were loaded with regular bullets made her question why she was even arming herself.

Danny. Where was Danny?

The bedroom door was still closed and she craned her head slightly forward, hoping to hear something from the hallway on the other side, but there was nothing.

Did Danny know they were out (up) there? If she could hear it—if they had been loud enough to wake her up—it would have been impossible for Danny to miss them. Unless he had gone to sleep, too. Was that possible? Could Danny be asleep right this minute, oblivious to what was happening above them?

She started to get up when the door *clicked* open. She lifted the rifle as a silhouetted figure slipped inside and slid the door closed before leaning against it.

Danny.

The whites of his eyes searched her out in the darkness, but if he said anything, she didn't hear it. Gaby finished getting up and tiptoed across the room toward him. Halfway to Danny, she glanced back at the window on the other side of the room. The armoire remained pressed against the bed, which was long enough that it covered up the entire window frame and didn't allow any moonlight to penetrate inside.

She pushed up against the wall next to Danny, whose head was slightly tilted as he listened to the persistent *tap-tap* above them.

"Are they inside?" she whispered.

He shook his head and whispered back, "Not yet."

"How many?"

"Don't know. Dollars to donuts it's a buttload."

She looked back across the room again and could just make out Nate in the pitch darkness. With just his head sticking out from underneath the blanket, he looked like a bodiless head floating in the shadows. They had purposefully put the mattress with him in the corner closer to the bathroom to make moving him in there easier if they had to.

Tap-tap-tap.

She glanced up, drawn irresistibly by the noise. If there had only been a few before, they had just gotten some company. Five? Ten? Not that it mattered—

Tap-tap-tap!

"Danny," she whispered.

"The bathroom," he whispered back.

"And then?"

"We'll cross that bathtub when we get to it."

They hurried across the room to Nate. Gaby slung her rifle, then picked up the spare M4 and added it to her own. She grabbed their backpacks as Danny bent at the knees before standing back up with Nate cradled in his arms. She half-expected Nate to wake up as soon as Danny lifted him, but he remained limp as the ex-Ranger turned and, with some effort, carried him into the bathroom. Gaby hurried over to open the door for him.

"Much appreciated," Danny said, grunting with the strain of Nate's weight.

Danny went into the bathroom first, then gingerly laid Nate down on the small single-size mattress they had inserted into the bathtub earlier. She thought Nate might have groaned as Danny lowered him, or it might have actually been Danny sighing with relief.

"Guy weighs a ton," Danny said. "Time to put him on a diet."

"I'll get on it as soon as we get back to the *Trident*." She looked back at the bedroom. "What—"

A loud *crash!* tore through the house before she could finish. It came from their left and was soon followed by the unmistakable sound of glass breaking. On cue, the *tap-tap* noises above them ceased entirely.

"Danny," she said breathlessly.

"I know, I know," Danny said. "Maybe we should have barricaded those windows after all, huh?"

"Gee, ya think?"

He grinned back at her then nodded at Nate. "Keep an eye on him."

"Where are you going?"

"Be right back."

"Danny," she said, but he had already vanished through the door, the darkness on the other side swallowing him up in a matter of seconds.

She unslung the rifles, laying one across the sink, then spent a few seconds pushing their backpacks and supplies into the crevices around the toilet so she didn't accidentally trip on them if she had to scramble around the tight confines. It was dark enough inside that she couldn't even see her own reflection in the mirror above the sink. She only knew where to find Nate because the white porcelain tub stood out—

Another loud *crash!* and Gaby thought, *There goes the bedroom door...*

She spun toward the open bathroom door at the same time the first gunshot rang out. It was followed by two more shots, both single shots but fired in such quick succession it was easy to mistake them for burst-fire. They seemed to have come from right outside the bathroom, except she didn't see the telltale staccato flash of gunfire, so it couldn't have been that—

The single shots became a volley as the shooter switched from semi-auto to full-auto, the *pop-pop-pop* blowing across the house and she thought, *At least Nate won't be awake to see this.*

She ran back into the master bedroom and immediately made

out a solitary figure *(Danny)* crouched in front of her and firing at where the door had once been. Something had shattered the slab of wood into pieces that were now spread across the room—something either very heavy or very, very strong.

Danny snapped a quick look behind him as he stood up, his hands busy with loading a fresh magazine. "Get back inside! We're fu—"

She was pretty sure she knew what he was going to say but didn't get the chance to, because one second he was standing up in front of her trying desperately to feed a magazine into his rifle, and the next he was on the floor and there was a *ghoul perched on top of him.*

Jesus!

The thing had moved so fast she hadn't even seen it coming through what remained of the door. It was just suddenly *there* and on top of Danny, pinning him to the floor with one hand while ripping the rifle out of his grip and tossing it across the room as if he were a petulant child in need of discipline.

Then it turned its head, and deep, pulsating blue eyes bored into her soul.

"Run!" Danny shouted despite the creature's hand wrapped tightly around his throat.

Run? Run where, Danny? Where can I run that it can't find me?

Of course, she didn't say any of those things out loud. She was too busy backpedaling, moving as fast as she could (though it didn't seem to be nearly fast enough) toward the bathroom door behind her. She lifted her M4 *(Go for the head! Shoot it in the head!),* but before she could pull the trigger, something moved in the corner of her left eye.

She finished the pull anyway, but her aim was off and the round sailed past the creature's head and disappeared into the shadows. She had missed! How the hell had she missed from such a short distance? Or had the thing simply moved its head to avoid her shot? Could it move that fast?

Yes. Yes, it could. She remembered that time at the farmhouse in Louisiana and how fast that blue-eyed monstrosity had been—

It was just a blur, but even before her eyes could report its presence to her brain, it had already reached her and broadsided her. It couldn't have been flesh and blood because the blow was too strong, like being hit with a jackhammer, and it sent her flying across the room and into the armoire. She was still trying to comprehend why she was no longer holding her rifle (or standing) as she was falling and finally slammed into the floor.

She couldn't find the wherewithal to stick her hands out in time to stop her fall, and the face-first blow with the floor sent pain rippling through her entire body. Which was just as well, because most of her bones were still rattling from being slammed into by that semi-trailer *(Anyone get the license plate of that thing?)*, then not even a second later crashing into the armoire.

Which part of her *wasn't* screaming at the moment?

She expected to hear gunshots, something to indicate Danny had gotten the upper hand on the monster that had knocked him to the floor, but there wasn't any. Which were more bad signs. With Danny, silence was never a good thing.

Gaby managed to flatten her palms against the floor and pushed herself up, if just slightly, even as her face throbbed. She turned her head and saw two figures entering the room, stepping over splintered wood sprinkled across the floor. But they moved like men, not ghouls, and were wearing gas masks and carrying rifles.

A pair of bare feet entered her line of vision, blocking her view of the figures in gas masks. The legs in front of her were black but somehow still stood out against the suffocating darkness inside the room. She craned her head, her neck straining with the effort, until she was staring into a pair of blue eyes. They looked like crystal heartbeats hanging in the air, beating slowly. The thing's skin emitted an unnatural combination of cold and heat that had little difficulty piercing through her thermal clothing, making every inch of her shiver uncontrollably.

"So frail," the blue-eyed creature *(hissed)* said. Thin strips of purple lines on the lower part of its face twisted into a grotesque facsimile of what must have been a mocking smile.

She looked past the creature and at Danny, unmoving on the

floor behind it. The blue-eyed ghoul that had been perched on top of him was gone—no, not gone; it had simply abandoned him after Danny was no longer a threat and was now standing over him.

"Danny," she said, his name coming out as barely a whisper.

The creature in front of her bent, grabbed her by the throat, and lifted her up from the floor as if she weighed nothing. It held her effortlessly in the air, and she struggled to breathe even as the toes of her boots scraped the floor, desperately trying to find the solid footing that was no longer possible.

Being in such close proximity to the creature, being *touched* by it, made her almost gag. If not for the pain, she might have lost the battle. Its fingers were more bone than flesh, and she swore she could feel every single joint that made up all five digits. And as hard as it was to fathom, she didn't think it was even using most of its strength, because it looked almost amused by her flailing. Its lips (or what passed for lips) again formed that twisted thing that might have been an attempt at a smile.

"How did you ever survive for so long, little thing?" it asked her, its voice a sharp hiss that left no room for doubt it was no longer human.

Did it expect her to answer? And if so, how? She couldn't reply with its hand around her throat, constricting her ability to do something as simple as breathe, never mind articulating sounds into understandable words.

Behind the creature, the two figures in gas masks had grabbed Danny by the legs and were dragging him out of the room. His body was limp and she couldn't tell if he was even still alive. Had the monster done something to him? And what about her? What were they going to do to her?

She remembered Nate in the bathroom behind her. She thought about the teeth marks that covered his body that he went to great lengths to hide unless he was with her. Maybe they were going to do just that to Danny, use him the way they had poor Nate after the pawnshop. And once they were done with him, she would be next. And there would be nothing she could do about it. Nothing. Not a goddamn thing.

No.

Hell no!

Her fingers brushed against the Glock holstered at her hip as she focused everything she had left on the ghoul in front of her. It seemed content to watch her struggling to breathe, finding some sick amusement in her pain, which it could clearly see on her face. It wasn't as if she were trying to hide it; she couldn't even if she wanted to.

Fuck you.

Fuck you!

The gun slid out easily—

The head!

—and she raised her arm and fired from almost point-blank range—

Shoot it in the head!

Its head seemed to twitch slightly, and the bullet vanished into the wall behind it.

No!

Before she could squeeze the trigger a second time, it casually grabbed the barrel with its other hand and twisted, and she somehow managed a scream despite its fingers wrapped impossibly tight around her throat, constricting everything from breathing to sounds. Or had she screamed at all? Was it all in her head?

It dropped her to the floor as if she were nothing, and Gaby forgot all about the fire burning in her throat because there was fresh, excruciating pain from her right wrist. She scooted back, away from the creature, cradling her hand in her lap, sure that it was broken, or if it wasn't, then *something* was broken *somewhere.*

The second blue-eyed ghoul appeared behind the first (How the hell had it moved so fast?), and it too looked down at her as if she was barely worth its time. The mere presence of two of them in the same place, standing so close to one another, combined to give off an intense cold and heat pulse that threatened to drown her in some thick invisible ocean.

They looked down at her, blue eyes like living orbs against the darkness, but for some reason she didn't think they were really seeing her at all. She had stopped mattering to them; they'd had their fun with her and now she had become…insignificant.

"How long until he comes?" the second one hissed.

"Not long," the first one said. "He spies on us. The clever boy."

"Not clever enough."

"He'll come for them soon."

"Yes."

"And when he does…"

"We'll end him."

"Finally…" the first one hissed, its thin lips worming their way into something that almost—almost—resembled a smile.

CHAPTER 9
FRANK

"WE HAVE HIM."

He didn't need the voice to tell him that. He had seen the black-eyed ghouls swarming on the small Texas town, waiting as the men in gas masks entered the house. He could taste the acrid smell of gunpowder on the tip of his tongue as the creatures swarmed the building only to hang back as the two blue eyes made their entry.

"But you already know, don't you?"

He had hoped they would have made it back to the sea by now. Back to the safety of the ocean, where she waited. From Larkin to Starch and back again. It was risky, but if anyone could do it, it would be them. Danny was well trained, and Gaby had been a quick student. But Port Arthur was a nest of ghouls and collaborators, and they'd been forced to reroute.

"You saw us take him."

The voice wasn't Mabry's. No, Mabry had gone silent these last few days. *(Why? You know why.)* It was someone else drawing him into the river of consciousness that connected the brood, showing him images in the aftermath of the assault on the house. The projection was vivid, which meant they were close, though sometimes distance could be deceptive when he was in the hive mind. They knew he would be listening and watching while hiding along the edges, always beyond their reach.

"And the girl."

It was his fault. He had exposed them to the enemy because of what he had done outside of Larkin. He had revealed himself, but even worse, he had shown them his weaknesses. *(Danny…Gaby…)* He couldn't sever those ties and didn't want to, not if he had any hope of clinging onto what still made him who he was, and without that he might as well be one of the mindless husks that serviced Mabry's will.

"She's a weak one. She won't last very long."

They moved and prodded at the corners of his mind, always threatening to break through his defenses. But it was all a trick, a cheap mirage, because he had learned to camouflage himself from them. It had taken days, weeks, and months, with so many trials and errors and near-misses that nearly cost him everything. There were so many times when they almost had him, when one crucial mistake could have ended everything he was working toward.

"They're both such frail things."

If they only knew where he was now, what he was doing and had been for the last few nights. Moving in silence, sleeping in the day, drawing closer to the beginning and the end, while staying invisible. Always in the shadows. It hadn't been easy, because the chances of being discovered increased exponentially the closer he got…

"It doesn't take much to break them."

Waiting. For him. A small town with a sign at the city limits reading: Gallant, Texas. They had let him see the markers, showed him the way in.

"Don't make us wait very long."

It was a trap. An obvious trap. Even a fool could see it, and he wasn't a fool. He had never been one, and he wasn't one now.

"You know how easily bored we can become."

Danny. Gaby. He should resist and stick to the plan.
Stick to the plan!
But he couldn't.
"Hurry," the voice said inside his mind, *"before it's too late. They're only human, after all."*
Danny. Gaby…

SMOKE AND GUNPOWDER lingered in the air between Houston and Gallant. He recognized signs on overpasses and along the roads, and there were enough landmarks to know he was moving in the right direction.

"Mercer."

The name reverberated inside his head, sometimes screamed out by the many consciousness—both strong and weak—that flowed through it day and night. The creatures knew the name, despised it. He was the cause of their pain, the man who brought fire from the skies and sent the armored machines into their carefully preserved towns. The man who was threatening their food supply, their future.

"Mercer!" they cried. *"Mercer!"*

He saw the evidence of Mercer's victories wherever he went. Towns that once brimmed with life—many of them on the verge of bringing in new life—had been wiped out in torrents of violence. Survivors—and there were always survivors—scattered across other locations, always taking their stories of horror and blood with them.

"Mercer! Find him! Kill him!"

And each time the stories grew. Bigger and bloodier, the exaggerations mixed in with the truth. The fear was spreading among the food supply, taking root in the souls of men and women that had surrendered. They were becoming hesitant, doubts sprouting from their once-contented minds.

"Mercer! Stop him at all costs!"

He had to cross another town, and like the last few, he didn't have to skirt around the edges to keep from being seen, because there was no one left to witness his passing by. It was just debris and the fading stench of smoke and gunpowder now, residues of a bloodbath from two days ago. The bodies were gone, removed to be fed on before the precious liquid in their veins became useless.

"*Mercer!*"

And as Mercer's people rampaged, the agitation grew inside the hive. The brood was restless, the blue eyes swearing retribution, and yet their human collaborators seemed incapable of stopping the chaos. How, they wondered, could so few people cause so much destruction?

"*Humans,*" they said, "*this is what they do.*"

"*This is what they're capable of,*" others agreed.

"*Violence,*" still others chimed in.

"*Destruction.*"

"*They'll slaughter even their own.*"

"*Even the ones bearing children.*"

"*They're indiscriminate.*"

"*Animals.*"

"*Worse than animals.*"

"*Yes.*"

"*This is why we have to show them a better way.*"

"*Our way.*"

"*Yes…*"

He moved along the piles of rubble, making sure not to touch the bullet casings that littered his path. The black eyes were out there (everywhere), watching and listening and feeling for every slight shift in the wind, every out-of-place item. They weren't nearly as intuitive, their senses not nearly as heightened as his, but they made up for what they lacked in ability with sheer number. And there were so, so many of them.

The town receded into the distance behind him, and he circled buildings that once thrived with life. A faded yellow *M* seemed to almost glow in the distance, beckoning him, but he went the other way, avoiding the long, gray concrete highway that connected

Houston to the cities along the coastline.

The voices had stopped calling to him hours ago, but even as he neared his destination, a surge rippled across his skin with the first hint of morning. It was coming, rising in the east as it always did night after night after night...

"Don't make us wait very long," the blue eyes had said. *"You know how easily bored we can become."*

But he didn't hurry. He knew they would wait for him. That was, after all, the whole point of last night. Capturing his friends. Danny and Gaby. And the boy.

What was his name again?

It would come to him, eventually. It always did.

HE SLEPT, AND like all the other nights, he dreamt of her. The crystal blue of her eyes, the golden strands of her hair, the sweet taste of her lips, and most of all, the feel of her skin against his. She would cringe if she could see him now, he was sure of it. He wasn't the man he once was. He wasn't even a man at all.

Lara.

She was out there somewhere, waiting for Danny and Gaby. Maybe even waiting for him. No, not him. She would have given him up for dead long ago. Days ago. Weeks ago. Months *(?)* ago.

How long had it been since he died?

He couldn't remember. The nights were a blur. Not that it mattered, anyway. The past was the past; he had to concentrate on the future. The here and now.

Mabry.

Out there, vulnerable. So, so vulnerable.

He had spent days in the city poking at their defenses, looking for ways in. A small sliver of access, a forgotten point of entry. Anything that would allow him to get close and do what he had to do.

Mabry.

He should have stuck to the plan and not left to come here. But it was Danny. And Gaby. And if he wanted to retain an ounce of his humanity (it was already so difficult; he could feel it slipping every night, every time he had to rest, to heal his wounds), he couldn't leave them in the blue eyes' hands.

"Don't make us wait very long."

He opened his eyes to gunfire in the distance, followed shortly by the very distinctive taste of blood in the air, carried to his position by the wind. He licked his lips, and every inch of him yearned to taste it. How many days had it been since he satiated himself on the raccoon? Too long ago, and it had been such a small creature; he'd been forced to spend so much of his energy on recovering from his wounds.

The gunfire rolled across the world like thunder. Close, but beyond his reach. He could feel the siren of daylight calling to him. He longed to embrace its warmth. It had been so, so long. It wouldn't have taken much, and there was nothing to stop him.

Except her. And the future.

Not for him, no. The future was for her. Everything he did now was for her.

Lara.

He closed his eyes and concentrated on the blue of her eyes, the yellow of her hair, the sweetness of her lips...even as the *pop-pop-pop* echoed, then faded, only to start all over again...

GALLANT, TEXAS.

A nothing city in a nothing part of the state. It was close enough to the ocean that the breeze teased at his skin. He ignored it—easy to do this far from the *(killing)* water—and pressed on through the darkness, moving toward the center of town.

The business district. Shops and glass storefronts. Car dealerships.

They were here somewhere. Danny and Gaby. Like mice, held

against their will to draw him closer.

So he went.

There were nests in the bigger buildings around him. Fresh ones. They had only come here recently and were staying off the streets, though he spied a few of them on the rooftops leaning over the edges, watching and waiting to report in. The black eyes were always smarter when the blue eyes were around to command them.

"He's here," a voice said inside his head.

"Close," another added.

Had they seen him? No. He was too careful, and he wasn't "him" at the moment. Maybe they had sensed him. It was always a challenge to hide from the blue eyes when he was in close proximity, and "close" was a matter of perception. Distance, when connected to the consciousness the way he was right now, was not always easy to pinpoint.

"He's wearing one of them."

"The black eyes."

"Clever boy."

"Not clever enough…"

They knew. *No.*

No, no, *no.*

Hands reached out and grabbed him by the shoulders, and his arms snapped, the *clacking* of bones against loose skin as they converged, coming out of the shadows around him. Fingers groped at his face, slipping into his mouth and eyes for a foothold.

He abandoned the black-eyed ghoul he had been wearing, letting go of the creature's mind and slipping back into the river that all the ghouls were connected to. He floated, spying visions and sounds and smells.

There, another one. It was alone, perched on a rooftop overlooking the center of Gallant. A lookout. He seized its mind, pushing it to the edge of its own existence and assuming command. It resisted, but not for long. Never for long. The black eyes were mere husks, as weak mentally as they were physically.

A horde stormed down the street below him, passing him by. They were searching for him, trying to locate the creature he had jumped into, unaware he was above them, watching—

Hands grabbed both his arms from behind, turned him against his will, and a fist punched through his chest.

Twin blue orbs pulsed in the darkness, surrounded by other blue eyes.

"There you are," the creature said, its voice dripping with triumphant glee. It leaned forward while others held him in place. *"Tell me, where are you hiding?"*

Razor thin lips formed snakelike smiles.

"You're close!"

He pulled back, back...

HE OPENED HIS eyes. His real eyes.

"There you are," the voices said inside his head. More than one, a dozen echoes overlapping, and as loud as if they were standing right next to him. *"You didn't think you could hide forever, did you?"*

Footsteps converging on his location. Dozens? Hundreds?

"Take him!" the voices shouted. *"Take him now!"*

They poured in through the windows and doors, and some battered their way through the thin walls. He abandoned the darkened corner, legs that had been still for hours coming alive and pistoning under him. There was no hiding now. They knew where he was. They *all* knew where he was.

The black eyes were weak, slow things, and he snatched up a piece of metal from the floor and smashed his way through them, and when the floor turned into a writhing black tide of pruned flesh, he went into the air. Hands groped at him, fingers scraped against his arms and legs and sought out desperate pieces of the trench coat that fluttered behind him.

He crashed through the window and into the street. The gray concrete highway gleamed to his left, the city of Gallant to his right. He was close enough that he could smell the rest of the ghoul population moving toward him as one, coming out of the buildings. *All* the buildings.

Hundreds. *Thousands.*

He flung himself onto a car and used it to grab a windowsill and crawled up the side of a bakery. He hadn't had the chance to swing up onto the ledge before there were three—four—*five*—throwing themselves at him.

"*He's ours!*" the voices echoed inside his head. "*There's no escape for him! Not tonight!*"

He shattered a ghoul's skull with his fist and threw two more off the rooftop. The fourth and fifth attempted to wrestle him to the gravel floor by diving at his legs, but he caved in one's chest with his foot, then twisted and decapitated the other one with the edge of his hand.

And he was free again, but not for long. The structure trembled as they raced up the stairs below him while more crawled up all four sides of the building, just as many plummeting back down to the street below when they lost their grip.

The wind whipped at his face as he ran, then leaped, across two rooftops. He sprung back up to his feet as they pulled themselves over the ledges around him. He raced past them and sailed into the air again—

Pop-pop-pop.

The sound of gunfire coming from nearby forced him to twist his body in mid jump until he was moving in that direction.

"*Something's wrong,*" the blue eyes said inside his head.

Was it a trick? Another trap? No, not this time. There was no need because they had him where they wanted him. Here, now, within their grasp.

Pop-pop-pop.

He tasted blood in the air. Not tainted blood like the kind that flowed through his veins. No, fresh blood. *Human* blood.

Pop-pop-pop.

He leaped across rooftops and raced toward the source of gunfire even as they surged around him, clamoring against one another to be the first to reach him. But he was faster and he leaped when he had to, dodged when he could, and bashed a path through flesh and bones when it was the only way left to him.

The night was thick with their number. Ghouls. Black eyes. They had secured all the rooftops as far as he could see, and he was forced to go down. He plummeted, grabbed a windowsill, swung left, then right, and finally caved in the roof of a parked vehicle on the sidewalk.

And they were on him almost immediately. A wave of black flesh slamming into his body from all sides, bony fingers grabbing at the fabric of the trench coat while dead black eyes pooled around him. Jagged yellow and white and brown teeth bit into his arms and legs and neck in an attempt to slow him down, but still he fought.

He couldn't let them stop him. Not here, not now. He fought, for Danny and Gaby. For Lara. For her future.

But there were so many, and they forced him to the cold, hard pavement. Blood gushed from fresh wounds and his legs weakened as they climbed over him, then over each other, their weight doubling, then tripling. And still they grew, until it became impossible to throw them off with mere physical strength.

Then something new and unexpected rippled across the sky, sending a ferocious gust of wind across him and the swarm that blanketed him. It froze them in place for a split second—which turned into a full second, then a full two seconds—as the noise grew and grew until it became unmistakable.

"No!" the voices screamed inside his head.

He managed to look up through a small sliver in the forest of wrinkled flesh just as the belly of the mechanical beast flashed overhead and its roar filled the world, shaking him—and the creatures around him—to the bones.

"No, no, no!"

As he watched it pass overhead, he was reminded that there were still things out there to fear that didn't sleep in the shadows and hide from the sunlight.

Then the beast bellowed, and he might have smiled.

Brooooooooooorrrrttttttttt!

BOOK TWO
ON A PALE HORSE

CHAPTER 10
LARA

"I DON'T WANT bloodshed," the man said. Lara detected what might have been a Southern accent, but those things were tricky over the radio, so she couldn't be absolutely sure. "We can resolve this in a way that avoids that. No one's been hurt yet, and I'd rather keep it that way."

You should have thought of that before you sent them over here, she wanted to say, but resisted.

"Bottom line," the man continued, "we can still come to an arrangement. Nothing's happened yet that makes that impossible."

"What if we had opened fire on your men?" she asked.

"But you didn't."

"I *could* have."

"But you *didn't*," the man insisted. "That's all that matters, and all I want to focus on right now."

She exchanged a look with Carly, who was standing next to her with her hands on her hips, and then with Blaine at his usual spot behind the helm. Morning sunlight slowly filled up the bridge of the *Trident*, pushing away last night's chill. Unlike the last time she was in the room, all three of them were armed and rifles leaned against the walls within easy reach.

It had taken her all of last night to decide whether to take Hart up on his offer. She was still too wary of a possible trick in case Hart and his CO had a backup plan if their boarding went awry and had ordered Blaine to keep moving all night, with a full guard rotation inside and outside the yacht.

"Mighty generous of him," Carly was saying.

"You don't believe him?" she asked.

"If being with Danny's taught me anything, it's that you can't trust anyone who tries to sneak up on you in the middle of the night. It always ends badly—and painfully."

Lara looked to Blaine. "What do you think?"

The big man shook his head. "I guess it depends on what he can offer us in return for sending his guys back. What did Hart say they had over there, wherever there is?"

"Supplies and fuel."

"Like he knew exactly what we needed," Carly said.

"He knew about the fueling stations and marinas being manned by collaborators," Lara said. "They've been out there. They know what's happening back on land."

The bridge's speakers squawked, and they heard the man's voice again: "Are you still there?"

Lara held the microphone up to her lips and *clicked* the transmit button. "I'm still here."

"You're thinking about my offer."

"We're talking about it."

"You're in charge?"

"Yes."

"I'm Riley, by the way," the man said.

"Lara."

"Nice to meet you, Lara. Wish it was under better circumstances."

"The man's a master of understatement," Carly said. "First he spies on us, then tries to board us, and now he's acting all 'Golly gee, I just wanna be friends.'" She rolled her eyes. "Goes to show you guys are as trustworthy as a knife in the back."

"Hey," Blaine said.

"Present company excluded, of course."

"Damn straight."

Riley, of course, hadn't heard any of the back and forth, and he said now, "I assume my man told you about what we can offer?"

Lara pressed the transmit button on the mic. "He did."

"Supplies. Fuel. Guns and ammo too, if you need them, though I get the impression you don't."

"Where do you get your fuel from?"

"Does it matter? The important takeaway for you is that we have what you need."

"Maybe he's living on a big oil tanker," Carly said.

"Oil tankers carry crude oil," Blaine said. "They have to be processed into usable fuel."

"What are you, an expert on oil now?"

"Hey, I get around."

Lara said into the radio, "I need to know your location."

"I'll be happy to give you the coordinates as soon as you tell me we have a deal," Riley said.

"That's the problem. We don't have a deal. Not until you can convince me I can trust you."

Riley didn't answer right away. Next to her, Carly began humming the *Jeopardy* theme song.

"*Can* he convince us of that?" Blaine asked. "After last night?"

"I don't know," Lara said, "but I'd like to see him try. Maybe he'll end up telling me something he doesn't want us to know."

"You sly fox," Carly said.

The speakers squawked again, and Riley finally said, "I think we need to do this face-to-face, Lara. I don't see how this could work any other way."

Carly smirked. "If he thinks we're going to just show up at his front door after what he tried to pull last night, he's got another thing coming."

"You have six of my men," Riley said, almost as if he had heard

Carly, "so I'd say you have a pretty big bargaining chip."

"He's got a point," Blaine said.

"What if he doesn't give a crap about any of them?" Carly asked.

"We might have to take the risk."

"No, we don't."

Blaine sighed. "Yes, we do, Carly." He glanced at his dashboard's readings, then back at them. "We're running out of options here, guys. We need to refuel *soon*."

Carly sighed and turned to Lara. "What about Danny and Gaby?"

"They're not due to radio in for another two hours," Lara said.

"You know Danny can barely tell time."

Lara gave her friend a half-smile. "You think this is a bad idea."

"Depends."

"On?"

"Is your definition of *bad* also *terrible?*"

"We have the upper hand. Once he gives us his location, we'll know where he is. We can show up from any angle and be ready for anything."

"Bonnie's awfully good with that M240," Blaine said.

Lara nodded. "There's that, too."

"I still don't like it," Carly said.

"We'll see what they have to offer. If the terms aren't to our liking, then we'll leave."

"Just like that?"

"Just like that."

"What if they try to stop us? Do I have to keep mentioning last night's shenanigans? We can't *trust* these people."

"They want the *Trident*," Lara said. "Hart made that pretty clear last night. They're not going to risk damaging it now. All we have to do is keep our distance."

Blaine smiled. "I like it. We hold all the cards."

"They could always change their minds about wanting the boat intact," Carly said. "Shoot us with a rocket launcher or something. Plenty of those things just lying around."

"Maybe," Lara said, "but then why bring us over? If they don't need the boat anymore, this seems like a lot of effort to go through. Besides, sinking us means sinking six of their own."

"Again, boss lady, *if* he actually cares about his guys," Carly said.

Lara nodded. "There's that..."

HART LOOKED UP when she stepped inside the room where they had been keeping him and the other five men below deck. The room was small enough that all six squeezed into the same narrow space made for an uncomfortable night, especially with their hands still bound.

"We need to talk," she said to Hart.

"Did you call him?" Hart asked.

She nodded, then turned to Benny, who was standing guard outside the door with Carrie. "Any trouble?"

"Nope," Benny said.

"They haven't tried anything," Carrie added.

Lara turned back to Hart. "Let's go."

He struggled up from the floor using the wall for support. The other five remained where they were, Benny eyeing them like a hawk with his M4 held at the ready in front of him. Lara stepped aside as Hart exited the room, and they closed the door and padlocked it from the hallway.

"Where to?" Hart asked.

"Follow me," she said.

"What did Riley say?"

"He confirmed your story."

She couldn't tell if Hart had breathed a sigh of relief, because it was so loud below deck and she couldn't even hear their footsteps as she led him through the engine room, then out and onto the lower deck of the moving yacht.

Hart blinked up at the clear skies and let out an almost blissful sigh (she heard that, that time), holding his bound hands up to shield his eyes from the sun. Above them, Maddie moved along the railing. Higher up, Bonnie was stationed behind the M240 machine gun that she had spent a lot of hours on, back when Keo and Danny were running all the adults (and Dwayne) through weapons training.

"Keep going," she told Hart, who walked in front of her. She kept just enough distance between them that he couldn't do something stupid like twist and try to grab her, or, more likely, the Glock in her hip holster.

"So what else did Riley say?" Hart asked.

"He gave us his location. We're on our way there now."

"No wonder we're moving." He stopped at the back of the boat when they reached the ladder leading down to the swimming platform below and turned around to face her. "So what are we doing out here, Lara?"

"Tell me about last night."

He pursed his lips at her, and she thought he looked almost embarrassed. Hart didn't have the face of a cold-blooded killer, but she couldn't forget that he was the leader of the group that had tried to sneak up on them last night. That, more than anything, made her extremely cautious of him.

"What about last night?" he finally said.

"Riley sent you to board us."

He nodded. "We couldn't risk you saying no if we showed up and asked to borrow the *Trident*."

"Why?"

"Why?" he repeated.

"Why do you need the *Trident* so badly?"

"You'll have to talk to Riley about that."

She shook her head and drew her Glock, then held the gun nonchalantly at her side. "I want you to tell me now."

Hart looked immediately down at the gun, then back up to her face. He swallowed, and she saw the fear in his eyes and knew he wasn't acting.

But he said anyway, "I can't. I'm sorry, but I can't. If Riley hadn't told you already, then he wouldn't want me to."

"I need you to tell me right now, Hart."

"I can't."

"Yes, you can. You just choose not to."

"You're right. I choose not to."

She clenched and unclenched her grip on the gun. "You see my dilemma, don't you?"

He nodded. "I do."

"You came here last night to take our boat, and now your Mister Riley is telling me he'd be willing to trade fuel and supplies for you and your five friends. You'll forgive me for being cynical, but that doesn't jive."

"It's complicated."

"What isn't these days?"

He smiled, though it came out just a bit too forced. "You have to trust someone sometime, Lara."

"I do. I just don't trust people who try to board my boat in the dead of night."

Hart looked down at the gun hanging at her side again. "Are you going to shoot me?"

"Do you want me to?"

"No. I don't want to die."

"That's the most honest thing you've told me yet."

"Not true. I've been honest with you since last night. I just haven't told you everything you asked, but I haven't lied once."

"That's the problem. I have no idea if you're lying or not because I don't really know you."

"That can change. All you have to do is listen to what Riley has to say."

"He sounds younger than you."

"That's because he is." He glanced down at the gun again. "Are you going to shoot me, Lara? I'd really prefer it if you didn't."

"I haven't decided yet," she said.

IT JUTTED OUT of the ocean like the torso of a mechanical beast, limbs stretching outward in every direction. It was impossible to miss, and she saw it as soon as she stepped back onto the bridge. The *Trident* had powered down, though the waves were still pushing it forward toward the object.

"Holy shit," Lara said.

When Riley had given her the coordinates and Blaine punched it into the yacht's computer, they had theorized what Riley's location could be—an island, a marina, maybe even a fleet of boats—but she had to admit, this was not one of their guesses.

"That's exactly what I said," Carly said. "Blaine was telling me how they got something like that out here in the first place. Educate her, big man."

"They build it along the coastline, then transport it out here before setting it down," Blaine said. "They're essentially self-sustaining cities with a crazy long shelf life. Most of the time they'll still be sitting out here long after the wells they're tapping have dried up."

"Here's a better look," Carly said, handing her a pair of binoculars.

"I did a lot of odd jobs back when I was younger," Blaine said. "One of them was construction; got to work on one of these, though that one was a lot smaller. It takes a huge crew to put them together, but the money was really good. Afterward, I applied to come offshore but didn't get picked."

"Did you tell them you were totally legal?" Carly asked.

Blaine grunted. "It's a tough gig to get, that's all."

"Sure, sure…"

Lara stared through the binoculars and scanned it up and down. The thing was yellow and gray and rested on four massive columns that looked like meaty stumps sticking out of the water. A giant crane extended out of its right side, gray metal sticking out against the soft blue of the cloudless sky.

It was an offshore oil rig sitting in the middle of the ocean.

"You ever seen one in person all the way out here?" Carly was asking Blaine.

"Nah, but one of my uncles did time out here," he said. "He would leave, and I wouldn't see him for months at a time. Most of his work was overseas, but sometimes he'd be sent out to the Gulf."

Lara lowered the binoculars. "How close are we, Blaine?"

"At least a mile," Blaine said. "We're safe. Current's pushing us closer, but nothing to be concerned about yet."

"How far were they from our last position?"

"Ten miles, give or take."

"They rowed those pieces-of-shit boats ten miles to get to us?" Carly said.

"They probably used the trolling motor for most of the trip," Blaine said, "then shut them off when they were close enough and rowed the rest of the way. They could afford to take their time. It wasn't like we were going anywhere."

"What's our situation?" Lara asked.

"Everyone's in position," Carly said. "Like you said, boss lady, if this Riley guy thinks he's going to lure us here and try to board us with our pants down a second time, he has another thing coming. The last time I saw her, Bonnie was literally chomping at the bit to let fly with that M240."

"Champing," Lara said.

"What?"

"It's champing at the bit, not chomping. Common mistake."

Carly sighed. "Have I told you how much I hate you lately?"

Lara smiled, then peered through the binoculars again. She couldn't detect any signs of movement on the platform or along the raised crane. There was a tall tower-shaped object that was red and yellow at the very center of the rig. She knew it was large even if it looked practically quaint next to the towering crane.

"What is that thing in the middle?" Lara asked.

"That's the derrick," Blaine said. "The drill."

"Can they see us yet?" Carly asked.

"If we can see them, it's a good bet they can see us," Blaine said. "Especially if there's someone hanging off that crane."

"I don't see anyone," Lara said.

"Sneaky people are good at being sneaky, remember?" Carly said.

Lara lowered the binoculars and looked at Blaine. "What do you think?"

He thought about it before answering. "Well, no one's shot at us yet."

"Jinx," Carly said.

Lara glanced back at the rig. It looked empty. *Looked*, anyway. But of course she knew better. Riley wouldn't have given her coordinates to an abandoned platform. There would be no point if the man was hoping to convince her to hand his men back to him.

A light flickered on the dashboard and Blaine said, "It's him."

"I guess they can see us after all," Carly said.

Lara nodded, and Blaine pressed a button. Riley's voice echoed through the speakers along the walls of the bridge a second later: "Thanks for coming."

Lara picked up the microphone and pressed the transmit button. "So how is this going to work?"

"I don't suppose you'd take my word that I mean you no harm and send my men back to me?"

"Captain Optimism, this guy," Carly snickered.

Lara said into the microphone, "You supposed correctly."

"Then I guess there's nothing left but for us to talk face-to-face," Riley said.

"Just you and me."

"Yes."

"And your men?"

"Since you're not willing to return them to me yet, the only way I can see this working is for you to hold them onboard while you're over here. Is that acceptable?"

She exchanged a long look with Carly and Blaine.

"I know I haven't told you this recently," Carly said, "but you're worth more than six of them. Let's turn around and leave. Danny's going to radio in at any moment, and we need to be there to pick him up when he does."

"Blaine?" Lara said.

He shook his head. "Carly's right. You're worth more to us than six of them."

She couldn't help but smile back at the two of them. "Stop it, guys, you're making me blush."

"We mean it," Carly said. She was as serious as Lara had ever seen her. "Blaine, me, everyone on this boat—we don't know this Riley from Adam. He may or may not give a crap about Hart and the others. I don't think we should risk it if it means risking you."

"I can go," Blaine said.

"Or me," Carly said. She shrugged, then smiled mischievously. "He doesn't know what you look like."

"He knows what I sound like," Lara said.

"Hey, who sounds like themselves over the radio?"

"She's got a point," Blaine said.

"Gee, thanks, Blaine," Carly said. "I don't know whether to be happy-happy that you're backing me up or kind of pissed off you're willing to risk my life if it means keeping boss lady here."

"I, uh..." Blaine said, but wisely didn't finish.

"*Anyway,*" Carly said, turning back to Lara. "I'll go. We can't afford to lose you. Me, on the other hand..." She let it trail off with a shrug.

"Danny would kill me if I did that," Lara said.

"Yeah, there's *that*," Carly smiled. "But he'll get over it. I mean, look at all the single *and* available ladies on this tub. He'd probably forget about me within a week, that asshole."

"No, he won't," Lara said. "Besides, this is why I get paid the big bucks, remember?"

Carly shook her head. "I don't like it."

"Neither do I, but I don't see any other way unless we want to turn around and leave, and our fuel reserves can't afford that right now."

She looked over at Blaine, as if to ask him, *"Right?"*

He nodded back, even though she could see he didn't want to.

Before Carly could argue, Lara pressed the microphone and said, "Riley."

"I'm still here," Riley answered.

"You've been awfully quiet."

"I assumed you and whoever is on the bridge with you needed time to debate the pros and cons of accepting my offer."

"He can *definitely* see us," Carly said, lowering her voice for some reason while turning to look out the windshield at the oil rig.

"He probably has lookouts on that big ass crane out there," Blaine said. "I would."

"Did you come to a decision?" Riley asked through the speakers.

"One hour," Lara said.

"I'll send a boat to come get you. One man. Unarmed. You're free to bring your weapons."

"One boat, with one man on it. If I see more than one at any time between now and when I return to the *Trident*, the yacht will turn around and leave with or without me onboard. My people will then execute Hart and the others and toss their bodies overboard so you can pick them up. Are we clear?"

"Crystal," Riley said. Then, "Expect my man in one hour."

Lara put the microphone back down on the dashboard. When she looked up, Blaine and Carly were staring at her.

"Tell me you weren't serious," Carly said. When Lara didn't answer right away, she sighed. "God, I don't know whether to be impressed with the new and way more badass Lara, or hate you so much right now for taking this stupid risk."

Lara smiled at her friend. "I love you, too." Then, to both her and Blaine, "Now pay attention; this is how we're going to do this…"

CHAPTER 11
GABY

SHE WOKE UP to gunfire—or, at least, she thought it was gunfire. She couldn't be entirely sure because of the sea of molasses swooshing around inside her head that made every part of her body heavy and at the same time disjointed. How was that even possible? Maybe it had a little something to do with the constant pounding—

"There she is," a voice said. "Good morning, sunshine."

It only took half a second for her to recognize the voice : *Fucking Mason.*

"Back to the land of the living," Mason said. "Well, mostly anyway."

"Fuck you," she said. Or croaked. What mattered was that she got it out.

"Now where'd a pretty little thing like you learn to talk like that?"

She had opened her eyes to Mason's face (*Squirrelly*, as Lara would say) hovering in front of her. He was crouched with his hands draped over his knees, but what she really noticed was the fresh black uniform he had on. The only thing missing was his name on the tag over his breast pocket; there was no cursive stenciling, just the word *Mason* written in what looked like permanent marker.

"Yeah, it's a rental," Mason said when he saw where her eyes were lingering. "Unfortunately, proper uniform distribution's taken a bit of a hit recently. Can't blame them, what with Mercer's goons running around out there."

The *crack!* of a rifle shot echoed in the background. She tried to figure out where it had come from, but it faded too quickly, replaced by the same pervading silence of a dead world that was all too familiar to her.

"Speaking of the devils," Mason said, tilting his head a bit. "They've been at it all morning. Showed up as soon as the sun poked over the city. I guess all that action from yesterday drew them here. What's that saying? Like moths to the flame? Making a real mess out there, too."

They? she thought, but couldn't push the word out this time.

Why was she so tired? She wasn't in pain. Not really, even though her throat felt as if she had a rubber band around it, constricting airflow. She reached up and massaged the area where the creature had grabbed her last night, but it didn't seem to help. She had to use both hands, because her wrists were bound together with plastic zip ties. Her legs were similarly restrained at the ankles. How long had she been like this? Tied up and sitting on the floor against a wall? Probably the entire night.

"I know how you feel," Mason said. "The first time I met one of those things, I almost shat my pants. They still give me the willies."

He shivered, but she couldn't be certain if that was involuntary or for her benefit.

She stared at the man. Mason was short, and while not physically disgusting, he wasn't exactly attractive, either. He had dark eyes and short dark hair, and although he had cleaned himself up since he was Danny's and her prisoner, it hadn't done anything to improve his looks. But why should it? The man was a piece of shit and nothing would change that—

"Oh, come on," Mason said. He was eyeing her closely. "Cut me some slack. I'm just a guy trying to get by is all."

"You're a piece of shit," she said, forcing the words out with some effort.

"But does that make me a bad guy?"

"Yeah, it does."

He glanced to his right. She followed his gaze over to a bundle lying on the floor. She sat up straighter at the sight of Nate. He was swaddled in camping gear with only his head sticking out of the thick fabric. He looked sound asleep, and she breathed a sigh of relief at the sight of his chest rising and falling underneath the sleeping bag.

It took her a few seconds to realize they were back at the Gallant First Bank where she, Danny, and Nate had stayed previously. They were in one of the back rooms—the manager's—with the familiar big oak desk still pushed off to one corner, giving them plenty of space. Except for herself and Nate, only Mason was inside with them. The door to her right was open, which was the only reason there was enough natural light for her to see not just Mason but Nate, since both offices were windowless. She thought she could hear voices drifting from the bank lobby outside, but she didn't quite have the strength to focus on that part of the world.

"So tell me, sweetheart, would a piece of shit save his life?" Mason asked.

She gave him a disbelieving look. "You?"

"Yes, me. Is that so hard to believe?"

"Yes."

He grunted. "They wanted to 'play'"—he did air quotes—"with your boyfriend last night while they were waiting for him to show up. But I convinced them if having two of you as insurance was good, three's even better. Took some convincing, but they bought it."

She glared at him, trying to decide if she could believe this traitor to the human race. He looked back at her, a small smile playing across his lips. Mason was scum, and the idea that he would actually go to bat for Nate seemed absurd.

"I liked him," Mason said, as if he could read the doubt on her face—and maybe he could since she wasn't doing very much to hide it or her dislike for the man. "Most of the time, anyway. He was nicer to me when you and the Ranger weren't around. Mostly when you weren't around. I dunno, but maybe he didn't want you to think he was weak." He shrugged. "He was decent enough to me; I never had to ask him for a drink or some food. So when he wakes up, tell him I paid back my debt."

"You're lying."

"Honest to God."

She stared at him. "I don't believe you."

He sighed, as if he were disappointed with her. "Whatever. Just tell him. He knows the truth."

She looked over at Nate again. If Mason was lying, he was doing a very good job of selling it, because the Nate she knew would absolutely do what Mason was saying, even for someone with Mason's very questionable history. Nate had hardened noticeably since that first meeting in Louisiana, but maybe that was just an act for her benefit because deep down, even after everything he had been through, Nate was still the most decent man she knew.

She turned back to the collaborator. "Why would they listen to you?"

"You mean because I'm just another sack of meat to them?"

"Not the 'sack' I was thinking of."

He chuckled. "Good one. But to answer your question, it's because I'm *not*. Just 'another sack of meat,' I mean."

"I never believed you were anyone important before, and I still don't now."

"The other guys in uniform couldn't care less about what happens to me. But I'm talking about the *real* bosses here. How did you think they found you in the first place? Because Nate was right. They were tracking you—just not in the way you think."

"How?"

"I'm connected to them. Well, one of them."

"'Them?'"

"*Them*," he said, as if she should know—and Gaby guessed that she did. There wasn't a lot of *thems* out there right now. There was only one *them* that mattered.

He's talking about the ghouls.

The blue eyes…

"They have a way of getting into your head and sticking," Mason said. "They've been in my head since the early days of what you call The Purge. After my demotion post-Louisiana debacle, I thought they had cut me loose. Turns out it really is true what they say: Once you go black you can never, ever go back."

She watched his face closely, waiting for him to keep going, but he didn't. Mason seemed to drift off as if all the talk about "them" had gotten him thinking about something else. Something that might not be entirely…pleasant.

When he returned his eyes to her, his mouth turned upward into a forced smile, and he might have been about to say something else—maybe even give her more information on how "they" had used him to track her and Danny all the way from Starch to Gallant—but before he could say a word, the very clear *pop-pop-pop* of automatic gunfire echoed from outside the bank's walls. There was something that sounded like return volley before silence took over again.

"What's happening out there?" she asked.

"Told you, Mercer's men," Mason said. "Turns out there's not that many of them. A few hundred, give or take. But man, they're kicking up one hell of a ruckus."

"A few hundred?" Gaby asked, remembering all those soldiers outside of Larkin when they were captured. It had seemed like more than just "a few hundred" back then. "How do you know there's only a few hundred of them?"

"They got ahold of one of his regulators. The blue eyes, I mean." He tapped his temple. "Got into his head. He didn't have to tell them anything after that." He went quiet for a moment and looked almost…what? Thoughtful? Frightened? "They know everything that poor bastard knew, and as it happens, everything he's ever going to know."

"He's dead…"

"Dead, not dead. Either way, death is a release."

"So why don't you 'release' yourself from them? End it now. That way you won't have to worry about them"—she tapped her own temple with the back of her knuckles—"back in there anymore."

He chortled. "I would, but I like this thing called living too much. What, you thought I was a believer or something? I'm just trying to stay alive here, sweetheart."

She gritted her teeth, wanting badly to tell him to stop calling her *sweetheart*, but she managed to restrain herself. Showing him an emotional outburst would just give him something else to use against her, and the man already had too much ammunition as it was.

"They're like cockroaches, showing up wherever you least expect them," Mason said, taking a moment to listen to the *pop-pop-pop* from outside the building.

Gaby had to fight back the smile. Cockroaches would be exactly how she would describe Mason and his collaborator friends, and it was ironic to hear him referring to someone else as that.

"They're not here to rescue you, in case you were wondering," he said.

"I wasn't," she said.

"Maybe you're smarter than you look, then. Brains and beauty, huh?"

She ignored his comment and said, "Where's Danny?"

"He's around."

"Where is he?"

"Around," Mason said before standing up.

She watched him and saw him grimacing as he stood up on slightly unsteady legs. Gaby took a lot of satisfaction in knowing that she had done that—gave him a lingering pain he wasn't going to get rid of anytime soon.

"No one's going anywhere," he said. "We're all going to camp out here until nightfall."

"Maybe you won't have a choice."

"Cute. You think a couple of shooters are going to force us out?" He shook his head. "No can do, sweetheart. The bosses would have our heads if we abandoned this place. No, it's going to take more than what they got out there right now to send us packing."

"They don't need more than a couple of guys to do that. Are you forgetting what they did outside of Larkin?"

"Oh, I remember. But it's pretty obvious they don't have a lot of planes. Or if they do have more than what they've shown so far, not a lot of pilots. They're picking their targets, hitting some of the denser towns. It's a real bloodbath out there, and the bosses are pissed. I didn't know how much until they brain-jacked into me. They are *really* pissed."

"You're scared of them," she said. It wasn't a question. "The ghouls. You're terrified of them."

"Of course I am," Mason said, staring back at her. "I'd be fucking crazy not to. And after last night, I'd think you would be, too."

WHERE ARE YOU, Danny?

He had to be either in the lobby or in the room next to them, because there wasn't anywhere else to be inside the building. Gallant First Bank was designed to serve a limited client pool, and there was no need for a larger space. So where were they keeping Danny? Were they separating them on purpose?

Without Danny to talk to, and with Mason gone, Gaby was left to watch Nate's sleeping form. He was alive, and that meant everything to her, even if she couldn't stop thinking about what Mason had said.

"They wanted to 'play' with your boyfriend last night while they were waiting for him to show up."

"Him?" Who was the "him" Mason was referring to? And why

were the blue-eyed ghouls waiting for "him?"

Mason had closed the door behind him, but if she pressed her ear against the wall she could just barely make out voices coming from the hallway. She had no trouble hearing the echoes of shooting outside the building, though. They remained sporadic, a series of attacks and returned volleys, followed by long periods of silence. Then they would start all over again, almost as if whoever was exchanging fire out there were constantly on the move. That was the only thing to explain why the shooting seemed to be coming from different directions every time she heard a new exchange.

"They're like cockroaches, showing up wherever you least expect them," Mason had said, referring to Mercer's kill teams that were running around Texas at the moment, making life miserable for the collaborators. She had no doubt whatsoever they weren't here to rescue her, Nate, or Danny, so why were they attacking a town like Gallant at all? There was nothing here that was of any value. No collaborator civilians to murder or resources to ruin.

Or maybe it was even simpler than that. Maybe she was overthinking it. Maybe it really was as basic as the continued presence of Mason and the others drawing them in like, as Mason had said, moths to the flame. They were, after all, called "kill teams." And their goal right now was to kill collaborators.

Great. Trapped between two groups of psychos. This road trip just keeps getting better and better.

She sighed and took a moment to gather her thoughts before finally deciding there was nothing she could do about what was happening out there. Instead of wasting more time on a problem that was beyond her control, she gave up and scooted across the room until she was sitting next to Nate. Thankfully the floor was mostly devoid of debris or anything to get in her way as she clumsily moved sideways, doing her best not to trip over her own bound legs and relying on the wall behind her as much as possible.

Nate was unconscious, but he was breathing normally, which was a very good sign. Just to be sure, she unzipped his sleeping bag to check his wound. Whoever had tended to him since last night had done a very good job; the bandages she and Danny had wrapped around Nate had been replaced, and very recently, from the looks of it. He also wasn't quite as pale as he had been yesterday. If anything, Nate's physical appearance looked better and color had returned to his cheeks and lips.

The sleeping bag kept Nate (mostly) insulated from the cold that had gathered inside the room. She still had her own thermal clothing on underneath her jacket and boots, which was the only thing keeping her from trembling against the chill at the moment.

With the door closed, it was darker now than it had been when she first woke up. She leaned her head against the wall and listened to a new round of automatic gunfire. It had started up again a few minutes ago and hadn't quieted like the last few times. She couldn't quite make out if they were getting closer, though it sounded as if they were.

"They're not here to rescue you, in case you were wondering," Mason had said.

She didn't doubt that whatsoever. Mercer's men had their own agendas. A bloody one. She had seen that for herself outside of Larkin and had witnessed more of it as they picked their way south from Starch. Even now, as she closed her eyes, she could still smell the blood and smoke from T29. It had been a real town once upon a time, with a real name, but it was just T29 now. Or it had just been T29, because it wasn't much of anything anymore…

She must have been more sluggish and tired from last night than she realized, because by the time she snapped her eyes open to the sound of approaching footsteps, the door was already opening and—

Danny entered the room with a collaborator in a black uniform walking behind him.

Danny saw her and smiled. "Hey, kid."

"Hey, Danny," she said, and gave him a half-smile back. It was all she could muster.

He started to sit down next to her when the soldier said, "Not there."

"You said I could sit anywhere," Danny said.

"When did I say that?" the man asked. He was in his thirties, with brown hair. The name stenciled across his name tag read: *Lopez*.

"On the way over here."

"Bullshit. Sit across the room away from them."

Danny got back up, walked across the room, and sat down next to the big desk. "Don't be like that, Lopez. I thought we were becoming friends."

"That's what happens when you assume," Lopez grinned.

"What?"

"What?" Lopez repeated.

"What happens when you assume?"

"You know."

"I don't," Danny said, looking completely serious.

"Fuck off," Lopez said, stepping back through the door and closing it behind him.

She waited to hear the collaborator walking away, but he didn't, which probably meant Lopez had taken up a guard position outside their door. Neither office had locks anymore, but the carbine in Lopez's hands solved that problem.

"How's the Natester?" Danny asked.

"He's better," she said. "Where were you?"

"In the lobby. They had some questions for me."

"About what?"

"This, that, everything in between." He cocked his head when they both heard the sharp *crack!* of a rifle shot outside the walls. "And some of that, too."

"Mercer's men?"

"Yup. They wanted to make sure I didn't know anything about it. I told them maybe."

"But you don't."

"Yeah, but they don't have to know that. Also, I wanted to see how far they'd push with the questioning."

"How far did they push?"

"Not very, as you can see by my still-pretty face."

"Ah."

"I got the sense they were afraid to tune me up. At least, ol' Danzinger was."

"Danzinger?"

"The guy asking the questions. The leader of the pack, from the looks of it. His name sounds like a '70s rock band front man, but the guy looks like an accountant."

"I thought Mason was the leader."

"He's more like a floating consultant. Looks like Danzinger's team just got saddled with him."

"Mason told me he was connected to them. The blue-eyed ghouls. That that was how they always knew where we were. How they tracked us from Starch. Because he told them."

"'Told them?'"

"That's what he said."

"Hunh," Danny said.

"I'm not sure if I believe him. Do you?"

"Will…" Danny started, but didn't finish.

"What about Will?" she pressed.

"Kate used to visit him all the time. In his dreams. They would talk, hold whole conversations. The way he put it, the whole thing was beyond freaky. I'm glad I never slept with that bitch."

"Is that how it works? You have to sleep with them to become—I don't know the word—connected, I guess, to them?"

"Hey, nothing's more powerful than swapping the ol' baby-making spit."

"Gross, Danny."

"It's a medical term. I swear." Then, "Anyway, I hope I never find out. The thought of one of those things crawling around in my head…" He shivered. "Damn. I think I might have wetted myself there. Wait, did I just say that out loud?"

"You think she's still out there? Kate?"

"I hope never to find that out, either."

"What else did they want to know?"

"Nothing worth repeating. Danzinger seemed more annoyed by the constant hit-and-run attacks than anything."

A long series of *pop-pop-pop* crackled, but this time it actually sounded like it was coming from farther away than the last few back-and-forth. It went on for a few seconds, which stretched into a full two minutes before things fell quiet again.

Danny was looking down at his watch. "They're biding their time. I don't think we're going anywhere anytime soon, kid."

"Mason told me they—the blue eyes—are waiting for someone. They're using us as bait to get this person here."

"Our little buddy Mason seems to know more than he's letting on. That sneaky little pussy...cat."

"I told you, we should have killed him back at Starch."

"Yeah, yeah, stop nagging. You're starting to sound like Carly."

"That's a compliment."

"It should be, she's a wildcat in bed." Danny glanced at the door. "Most of them are still in the lobby, including Lopez and Mason. At least eight more running around out there engaging Mercer's boys."

"Twelve in all?"

"Uh huh. That includes the driver of the Jeep that was chasing us earlier."

"Twelve men is a lot of resources, Danny. If Mason's to be believed—and I'm not one-hundred percent buying it—they're here because of the blue eyes, and this person they're trying to lure to Gallant."

"He'll come for them soon," one of the creatures had said last night as it stood over her.

"Yes," the other one had replied.

"And when he does..."

"We'll end him."

"Finally..."

Across from her, Danny was staring at the wall next to the door. She didn't know how long he had been doing that, but it was obvious to her by the look on his face that it wasn't the barren white wall that was on his mind. He was somewhere else...

"Danny," she said.

He shook his head before she could say anything else. "I don't know."

"You don't even know what I was going to ask."

"Yes, I do."

"What was it, then?"

"He," Danny said. "The person all of this is for. The reason we're still alive."

She nodded.

"I don't know," he said again.

"Are you sure?"

"Maybe…"

"Danny, what is it? What's been on your mind since Starch?"

He shook his head, then started to speak, only to stop himself.

"Danny," she pressed. "What is it?"

"The blue-eyed ghoul back in Starch," he finally said. "And at the airport outside of Larkin before that."

"Danny, what are you saying?"

Larkin and Starch were burned into her memory—two nights of confusion that she still struggled to understand even today. She didn't know how she was going to tell Lara and the others about them if she couldn't even make up her own mind what had happened. There was a reason Danny hadn't mentioned all the details to their friends back on the *Trident*. He hadn't known how, either.

"Are they related?" she asked. "What happened outside of Larkin, then in Starch?"

"I don't know," Danny said.

"Danny…"

He shook his head.

"Danny," she said again, unsure if she actually wanted to hear the answer.

"Maybe," he finally said. "Maybe…"

CHAPTER 12
LARA

YOU SHOULD BE here right now, Will, not me. This was never the plan. Why did you have to go and ruin the plan?

The "man" Riley sent over was a girl named Faith, who couldn't have been older than twenty, and arrived alone in a small ten-footer to pick Lara up.

They were halfway to the oil rig when Lara glanced back at the *Trident*. She couldn't see Bonnie on the roof, but she'd be there right now watching her back with binoculars while Blaine kept guard on the other side of the wraparound windshield on the bridge. Carly, Benny, Carrie, Maddie, and everyone else would be at their stations and on full alert until she returned.

This is such a bad idea. You know that, right?

Everything about this was risky, but they were running out of choices. They had already exhausted most of the refueling locations on Gage's list around the area—the ones that hadn't been razed to the ground or occupied by collaborators, anyway. The only other place left to explore was down south along the Mexican coastline, and what were the chances collaborators hadn't either destroyed or taken over those places, too?

Mercer. This was all because of him. Before his attacks on the towns, they hadn't had any difficulty finding abandoned but plentiful fuel.

Mercer…

Even when she did everything possible to steer clear of the man, his war still somehow managed to affect her.

She faced forward and looked past Faith, standing behind the controls in front and slightly to the right of her, and at her destination.

The platform looked bigger and more imposing out here in the open sea. It was at least 500 feet long and probably half as wide, though she couldn't be sure of the latter since she was looking at it from the front. It stood well over a hundred feet above the water and rested on four massive foundations made of solid concrete, the heavy gray color marred by bright yellow stripes.

"How many people are onboard?" she asked Faith, shouting over the roar of the engine to be heard.

"The *Ocean Star*," Faith said.

"What?"

"That's what it's called. The *Ocean Star*."

"They have names?"

"I don't know if all of them do, but this one does. It was designed for about 150 crewmen."

"*Are* there 150 people onboard?"

"Not exactly," Faith said.

From what she could see, the rig consisted of four levels, including the top platform. The lower three were a tangled web of beams and tubing, with rows of yellow guardrails and stairs crisscrossing all four sections from end to end and top to bottom. She paid special attention to the massive crane towering over everything like some kind of metal tentacle rising out of the ocean. She expected to see the snipers that she knew were somewhere up there, but even closer now she still couldn't spot them. Either they were very well hidden, or Riley had taken them down. Maybe that also explained the lack of visible people moving around on the platforms.

"You live here?" Lara asked.

Faith nodded. "We all do."

"I noticed you're not wearing a uniform."

"We're not soldiers," Faith said. She had on khaki cargo pants and a long-sleeve plaid shirt underneath a thick winter coat. Long, stringy black hair poked out from under a hoodie and blew against the cold wind. Unlike Hart and the five with him, the young woman looked nothing like a soldier.

Faith was also not armed when she showed up, and Lara's cursory inspection of the boat—made easier because she was standing at the stern behind Faith—had revealed no weapons, though of course Faith could have hidden something inside the compartment under the vessel's middle console. Lara wore her gun belt, but she hadn't bothered bringing a rifle. If Riley was setting her up for an ambush at the oil rig, whether she came with one M4 or ten wasn't going to make a bit of difference. The logic behind her decision was a no-brainer, but the emotional part was less easy to swallow.

"Don't go onto the bad man's oil rig, Lara," she imagined her mother telling her.

"Listen to your mother," her dad would say.

She crossed her arms over her chest for warmth. It might have been her imagination, but she swore it had gotten noticeably colder since she climbed onto the small boat and began her trek to the oil platform.

"Why did he send you?" she asked the girl.

"I don't know; he didn't tell me why," Faith said. "He asked if I would come get you, and I agreed."

"He asked you," Lara said. It wasn't a question.

"I told you, we're not soldiers, Lara."

Then what are you? she wanted to ask, but didn't. She said instead, "You're survivors."

"Yes." Then, as if sensing her hesitation, the girl said, "Riley's not trying to trick you, Lara. He wouldn't do anything to risk Hart and the others."

"He took plenty of risks when he sent them to take my boat last night."

Faith seemed to hesitate, but Lara couldn't see her face, so she didn't know what the younger woman was thinking.

Finally, Faith said, "He regrets that. I don't think he got any sleep at all last night."

That makes two of us.

The girl slowed down the vessel as the *Ocean Star* loomed in front of them before finally killing the motor completely. She expertly used the boat's forward momentum to ease it underneath the structure until they were alongside one of the docks. Riley may not have needed to order Faith to come get her, but it was pretty obvious the young woman knew her way around a boat.

Two men, both unarmed (at least as far as she could see without telling them to strip off their thick coats), were waiting for them underneath the platform.

"Riley's orders," Faith said, finally looking back at her for the first time since they started away from the *Trident*.

"What's that?" Lara said.

"No one you meet on your way up to see him will be armed, but you're free to keep your weapons on you at all times."

"That's awfully considerate of him."

"He's trying to make up for last night. Please let him, Lara."

The plea caught her by surprise, and Lara didn't answer right away.

Finally, she nodded. "Lead the way."

Faith took her up along the winding stairs while the two men worked to secure the boat behind them. There were a dozen vessels of various models already in the water when they arrived, including a couple of fast boats. She didn't see anything bigger than a fifteen-footer tied to any of the docks and had to wonder if that was the reason they were so desperate to get their hands on the *Trident*—it was easily many times bigger than all the vehicles they had combined.

"Can I ask?" Faith said hesitantly.

"Depends on what you're going to ask," Lara said.

"Our guys. Are they okay?"

"They're all alive, if that's what you mean."

"No, I meant…" She paused, then, "I meant, was there any shooting last night? During the siege?"

"There was no siege. We took them prisoner before they even climbed aboard."

"Oh."

"What did Riley tell you?"

"Not a lot, but I thought something bad might have happened—" She stopped short and shook her head, then glanced over her shoulder with an almost apologetic look. "So there was no shooting? No violence?"

Depends on what you mean by "violence," Lara thought, but said, "No. We took them prisoner and put them in a room all night." She saw the relieved look on the girl's face and said, "Who are you worried about?"

"What do you mean? I'm worried about all of them."

"But there's one in particular, right?"

Faith might have blushed. "My boyfriend. James. Do you know if he's okay?"

"I don't remember talking to anyone named James, but if he's part of the crew, then he's fine. Like I said, we didn't hurt anyone. They were smart and surrendered when we caught them trying to sneak onboard."

"Oh, thank God."

God had nothing to do with it, Lara thought, remembering how close she had come to giving the order to open fire. If Hart hadn't seen how badly out-positioned he had been and told his men to stand down, things might have gotten bad. The six-men-dead-in-the-water kind of bad.

"I guess everyone here knows what happened," Lara said.

Faith nodded. "It's not a very big place and Riley doesn't hide many things from us, especially something this big."

Lara was startled by a flock of birds that appeared out of nowhere and glided in for a landing along the railing next to her.

They were small and purple, and she got the feeling she was more wary of them than they were of her. That is, if they noticed her presence at all.

"Oil rigs are magnets for birds," Faith said, smiling back at her. "We get every kind."

Faith wasn't lying. Lara had seen flocks in the air as they were coming in. At first she thought they were going to swerve around the human-made monstrosity squatting in the middle of the ocean, but instead they honed in on it, landing all along the multiple levels.

"Where do they come from?" Lara asked.

"Everywhere," Faith said. "By the time they reach us out here, they've been flying for so long they just crash. I've never seen anything like it." Then, with a look that Lara wasn't sure was a joke, Faith added, "Bird stew used to be on the menu until we realized how awful it tasted."

They went up another set of stairs before finally reaching the top platform. As they climbed up, she took the opportunity to sneak a look at the ocean behind her before settling on the familiar white shape of the *Trident* about a mile away. From out here, the luxury yacht looked absolutely lonely surrounded by vast open ocean, which was exactly what she was hoping to see. It was going to take a lot *(a miracle)* to sneak up on the yacht's crew. Anything other than a submarine was going to get shredded by gunfire before they even got close.

Seeing the solitary boat in the distance eased her mind tremendously. Even if everything went bad and Riley turned out to be the snake in the grass a part of her expected him to be, at least she could say everyone onboard would be safe. Most of all, she could count on Blaine to put the *Trident* in gear and get out of there at the first sign of trouble. He wouldn't want to do it and there would be all kinds of internal and external conflict, but Blaine would do the right thing. She had made damn sure of that before she left.

"That clearheaded rush you just got?" Faith said in front of her. "That's the altitude. It'll clear up any sinuses you have. That's the good news. The bad news is it's friggin' cold up here, so keep your jacket on at all times or you'll end up in sickbay."

When she turned around again, the first thing she saw—because it was simply impossible to miss—was the giant derrick in the center. It was red and white and looked like a shrunken version of the Eiffel Tower. The only thing taller than the drill was the massive crane to her right. She spent a few seconds looking it up and down but like all the other times, she couldn't make out any figures perched along its many sections. Even so, she didn't believe it was empty for a second. It was simply too perfect a location to not have someone up there, and if her civilian mind knew that, someone like Hart and Riley would, too.

Come out, come out, wherever you are.

"To answer your question, no; we haven't turned the drill back on," a voice said.

She looked over as a tall man walked toward her. He was wearing green cargo pants and, like Faith, wasn't armed in any way that she could see. His jacket's collar stood up against the sides of his neck to protect him from the cold.

"I'm Riley," the man said, sticking out his hand.

"Lara."

"I know," he smiled.

She didn't return it. "Nice place you got here."

"It's got a great view and the rent's cheap," he said before nodding at Faith. "I'll take her from here, Faith; thanks."

"I'll go wait with the boat," Faith said. To Lara: "Please listen to what he has to say."

"That's why I'm here," Lara said. She couldn't decide if she was annoyed or genuinely touched by the girl's earnestness.

"Thank you."

"I'm not promising anything."

"I know," the younger woman said before heading back down the stairs.

Lara turned back to Riley and caught him looking her over.

He recovered quickly and said, "Come on; let's go inside. I should have worn my thermal socks."

"I can't stay long."

"One hour?"

She nodded. "One hour."

"That's more than enough time."

He turned around and started off and she followed, leaving just enough space between them that she could still see every inch of him and the spaces around them at the same time. She had done it unconsciously, and recognizing it, thought, *Is this what it's like to be you all the time, Will? Always on 24/7?*

"I'll be perfectly frank with you, Lara. I'm surprised you came," Riley was saying.

So you agree this is a stupid idea, too?

"But I'm glad you did," he continued. "I know it took a lot of guts after everything that happened. But I wouldn't have expected anything else from *the* Lara."

He had glanced over his shoulder when he said that last part, and she gave him a wry look back.

"When did you figure it out?" she asked.

"That you're the same Lara who sent out those messages over the radio? Not right away. I had to listen to our conversation a few times before it clicked."

"You recorded our conversation?"

"The rig has a pretty impressive comm system. I had our talk recorded just to make sure I didn't miss anything. A lot's riding on this—six lives, for one—and I didn't want to fuck it up the way I did last night."

She smiled to herself because she knew he couldn't see. "It takes a big man to admit when he fucks something up."

"Thank you for not harming Hart and the others."

"How can you be so sure that I didn't?"

"You said you hadn't."

"I might have been lying."

"Are you?"

She didn't answer him.

He looked over his shoulder again. "Are you?"

"No," she said finally.

"So my thank you stands."

"People have gotten killed running around out here believing everything a stranger tells them."

"But you're not just any stranger, Lara. You're *Lara*."

She wasn't entirely sure how to take that. The radio messages were therapy as much as they were an attempt to reach out to other survivors. She had only added her name to it with the second broadcast because, deep down, she still expected Will to be listening. It was stupid and desperate, but at the time she didn't have anything to lose.

Riley led her through the platform and around the large drilling devices that occupied a good portion of the rig. They stepped over pipes of various shapes and sizes, a hard hat that someone had left behind, and passed a bright orange vessel hanging off the side. She guessed it was some kind of emergency raft. They entered a maze of pumps and tanks circling the derrick like army ants, each with their own command unit. She wasn't paying attention to where she was going and almost stumbled into a group of heavy machinery but managed to swerve around them at the last second.

The remnants of spilled liquids—chemicals, additives, and fuel used to keep this place churning night and day back when it was still in operation—filled her nostrils. She could only imagine how loud it would be up here when everything was up and running. Right now she might as well be zigzagging through a museum, a showcase of how mankind once bled the earth for resources.

Riley didn't seem to have the same kind of trouble, but then, he had probably gone through this maze so many times he didn't even have to think about where he was going.

"How do you get around this place?" she asked.

"You get used to it," he said. "We were running into everything the first few weeks. A lot of accidents, bumps, and bruises. But we've cleared up everything that isn't nailed down and even took apart some of those that were. You should have seen it when we first got here. About fifty percent of all this open space didn't exist."

They passed a helicopter landing port to their right resting on its own raised platform. It was empty at the moment, but she could smell recently spilled fuel and was going to ask Riley where the aircraft was when there was a *clink*. She looked down just in time to catch a shiny lug nut skidding across the floor before disappearing underneath a machine painted blue and about the size of a car.

They had been walking for a while and didn't look to be any closer to reaching their destination, and she was growing frustrated. That, and her legs were starting to tire, reminding her of just how good she had it back on the *Trident*.

God, how did I get so out of shape?

"You brought me here to talk," she said. "So let's talk."

"We're almost there…"

"No, Riley."

She stopped in the middle of two machines with dials and conduits sticking out of them to both sides of her. One was red and the other was white, and she couldn't even begin to guess what either one did.

Riley stopped five feet in front of her and turned around. "This is the kind of discussion that we should take inside, Lara. Besides, it's cold out here."

"I've never felt more clearheaded."

"It's warmer inside."

"It's warm enough out here," she said, fighting back a grimace as a particularly cold wind whipped through the valley of machinery around them. "Tell me what I'm doing here, Riley. Tell me *now*."

Riley nodded, his blue eyes focusing on her as if he was afraid of missing every reaction on her face in the next few minutes. "I need your boat, Lara."

"I have six of your men on my boat right now that already told me that. So what else do you want from me, Riley?"

He shook his head. "Nothing. Just the boat."

"Why?"

"Don't," he said.

"Don't what?"

His eyes had left her face and gone to her hip because her right hand had slid closer to her holstered sidearm. A year ago the notion that she would reach first for her gun when threatened—or even when she just *felt* threatened—would have terrified her. Now, she did it without even thinking.

"Don't," Riley said again.

"Don't what?"

"Please don't draw your gun."

She didn't know why, but Riley asking her not to do it made her *want* to do it. Again, without her realizing it, her fingers brushed against the grip of her sidearm.

"Lara," Riley said, his eyes returning to hers, "I have a man on the crane, and he's watching us right now."

The crane...

"He can't hear what we're saying, but he can see everything," Riley continued. "If you draw your weapon, he'll shoot."

It's a trick! her mind screamed, but she had to exert every ounce of willpower to keep from turning around and zeroing in on the crane.

"There is no man on the crane," she said. "I looked."

"His name is Peters," Riley said. "Trust me, he's up there. I had to keep him up there, just in case things went sideways. He's my insurance. My *only* insurance. Everyone else is staying out of the way on purpose." He held his hands steady at his sides, the palms facing her as if he wanted her to see he had nothing in them. "I'm not armed, Lara. I can't stop you if you decide to shoot me right now. But Peters will respond if you do that, and he never misses. Never."

He's lying. There is no man on the crane. You looked, remember?

But how easy would it have been to hide someone up there? Very easily, because there were so many metal parts and angles it would be impossible to see every single section of the crane. All a sniper would need was to find a perfect spot, and depending on how long Riley and his people had been here, they could easily have figured that part out a long time ago.

Then again, even if there were someone up there, the distance was too great and the man would be shooting from a high angle. Not to mention all the machinery around her, including the two flanking her right now. There were a lot of reasons why a shooter wouldn't be able to make the shot, even if he "never misses." The odds were all in her favor.

Right?

Maybe…

Lara exhaled a slow breath, but she didn't take her hand away from her hip, though there was now an extra inch of space between her fingers and the Glock. She sneaked a quick look to her left, then her right in case Riley's men were trying to outflank her. She tried to pick up sounds of footsteps behind her, but there was just her slightly racing heartbeat pounding in her ear.

"So talk," she said finally.

"We should do this inside," Riley said.

"No. Out here. Tell me why you need my boat and why in God's name you think I'm going to give it to you."

He nodded reluctantly. "I have people on the *Ocean Star*. Civilians."

"Faith told me you were all civilians."

"Some people are more civilian than others."

"Is that supposed to make sense to me?"

"Maybe. I don't know. This place, this platform, it was an FOB until just a few days ago."

"FO what?"

"FOB. Forward Operating Base. It was used to launch an attack on the mainland very recently. You probably don't know anything about it since you've been out here the entire time."

Is he talking about…Mercer?

Something must have registered on her face, because Riley tilted his head slightly to one side. "Or do you?"

"No," she said.

"I don't believe you."

"I don't give a damn what you believe."

"Fair enough."

"Get to the point."

"I'm trying to."

"Try harder."

He sighed, took a breath, then continued. "I have people I need to transport off the *Ocean Star* and to safety." He looked out toward the ocean in the direction where the *Trident* would have been if not for the wall of metal and tubes in his way. "Your boat showing up out of the blue was a godsend."

"You have boats here. A lot of them."

"I don't have enough, and the ones I do have aren't nearly big enough. If there were still bigger vessels at the ports, I might have risked launching a raid on them, but they're gone. The collaborators sank them a long time ago."

"So you risked boarding the *Trident* with six armed men."

"I had no choice. It was the best and fastest option. I need your boat, Lara."

She shook her head. "You can't have it."

"You don't understand—"

"No, I understand perfectly. You want something I have, and I'm not willing to give it to you. What I do have are six of your men. And they're the only things you're going to get out of this."

"And I want them back," Riley said. "All six of them. They only did what I asked them to. Hart had doubts, but..." He shook his head.

"You should have listened to him."

"I had no choice."

"You already said that."

"It's the truth."

"You're still not getting my boat."

He sighed. "Can I show you something?"

"What can you show me that will make me change my mind?"

"The Lara from the radio would change her mind."

Lara walked toward him—saw his eyes go wide with surprise—and stopped only when she was less than a foot from bumping into his chest. Even though he was taller than her and she had to tilt her head to look him in the eyes, she could feel him wanting to take a step back, but somehow managing to hold his ground.

"Lara," he began, almost stuttering out her name.

She cut him off: "You don't *know* me. If you have any doubts that I've already given orders to shoot your men and throw them overboard and abandon this place when I don't return within the hour, you should wipe it out of your mind right now. You may have heard something I broadcasted on the radio, but you don't know me, or my crew. You don't know what we've been through, or what we've done, or what we've lost. So when I tell you that you don't know a damn thing about me, I want you to take it to heart, Riley, because you don't have a clue what I'm capable of."

"I believe you," he said.

"Good," she said, and glanced down at her watch. "You have thirty minutes left. I suggest you use them wisely."

CHAPTER 13
GABY

THE ONGOING GUN battle between Mercer's men and the collaborators took on a strange ebb and flow—a hellacious five or so minutes of back-and-forth followed by an hour (sometimes two) of long silence where nothing happened.

Danny had gone uncharacteristically silent since their conversation following his return to the room, seemingly content to listen in on the barely-audible chatter coming from the lobby—not that they could really hear anything with the closed door and the sudden spurts of violence beyond the walls.

After he left her, Mason had yet to return. She wondered if he was running around out there with the rest of Danzinger's people, trying to put an end to Mercer's fighters. It was an odd thing to think about, mostly because she had no idea if she cared who won or lost or if she was hoping they might end up killing each other, which would leave just her, Danny, and Nate.

Best-case scenario. Which probably means it won't happen in a million years.

Nate had woken up a couple of times, but the longest he had stayed awake was only a few minutes. That was just enough time for him to see her and smile before drifting off again. She checked his bandages every thirty minutes to make sure he wasn't bleeding again and always had at least one ear open listening for any irregularities in his breathing.

"They gave him sedatives," Danny told her the first time Nate opened his eyes. "I guess they don't want him waking up between now and tonight. Keep him out of their hair."

"Mason said he saved him," she said.

"Did he?" And when she nodded, "You believe him?"

"I don't know." She told him about Mason's claims. "It sounded like Nate."

"He's a good kid."

"Does this mean you're going to go easier on him from now on?"

Danny chuckled. "I didn't say *that*."

She smiled, and spent the next hour or so watching Nate sleep. After everything he had been through, he deserved as much rest as he could get. She wanted nothing more than to pack him into a car and drive to the coast where Lara and the *Trident* would be waiting for them. They could have done that days ago if Mercer's people hadn't begun their crusade against the collaborators.

Mercer.

Was it possible he was the "he" that the blue-eyed ghouls were hunting? No, because it didn't make any sense. She, Nate, and Danny had nothing to do with Mercer, and holding them hostage wasn't going to lure the man here. He couldn't care less if they lived or died, and she would be surprised if he even still remembered them after Larkin. For all he knew, they were already dead and buried underneath what was left of the airfield.

"Whatcha thinking there?" Danny said, his voice breaking through her thoughts.

"What?" she said, looking over at him.

"You look like me when I'm being all thoughtful and whatnot. What's up?"

"You tell me."

"Come again?"

"You're not telling me everything." She let the rest go unsaid but didn't take her eyes away from him.

Danny shrugged. "It's complicated."

"When is it not?"

"Well, this is even more complicated than usual."

"What is it, Danny? What do you know that you aren't telling me?"

"That's the problem, kid; I don't know anything. Not for sure, anyway. At least, nothing that would hold up in court."

"We're not in court. It's just you and me and Nate in here."

"To be fair, Nate's barely here..."

"You know what I mean. So just tell me already."

"I think..." he started, but didn't finish.

She could see that he wanted to say it—this thing that had been spinning around inside his head for the last few days—but for whatever reason, he didn't go through with it. Maybe he couldn't, or he didn't want to.

"Danny," she said.

He shook his head. "It's too crazy."

"*What's* too crazy?" She could feel her patience with him slipping, even if he didn't seem to notice it. "Just tell—"

He held his hand up to shush her just before shouting erupted from outside the door. It came first from inside the hallway next to them, then all the way from the lobby. Pounding footsteps immediately followed, then someone screaming in pain. The *cracks* of gunfire from outside, sounding the closest they had been since the day began.

Gaby stood up and walked to the door, pressing her ear against it. Danny did the same with the wall across from her. She glanced over at him, wondering if he was hearing the same thing, when a loud *boom!* cut through the noise and the door vibrated, along with the walls and floor and ceiling around them.

She took an involuntary step back, but Danny didn't move.

"What was that?" she asked.

"Sounded like an explosion," Danny said.

Gunfire exploded, this time clearly coming from the lobby just beyond the back hallway, the *pop-pop-pop* of automatic rifle fire drowning out every other sound, including more screams and shouting.

"That's not good," Danny said.

"They're inside," she said.

"Or coming in…"

Then, just as fast as it had begun, it stopped; there was just the silence again.

Gaby hurried back to the door and pressed against it and listened, but there wasn't anything loud enough happening out there for her to hear through the slab of wood. She looked down at her bound hands and wondered how far she and Danny could get in their current condition. Of course, it was all a moot point because there was Nate, and he hadn't even opened his eyes through the explosion and gunfire.

A loud *bang!* drew her focus back to the door.

It was a gunshot, and it had come from the lobby. A single, purposeful gunshot.

She exchanged another look with Danny when they heard a second *bang!*

"Shit," Danny whispered. "Get back."

He pushed off the wall and retreated across the room. She did the same, returning to her spot next to Nate, but her butt hadn't touched the floor yet when the door smashed open and a man with an AR-15 stood in the open doorway, pointing the weapon in at them. He saw Danny first, sitting across from him, before swinging his rifle over to her, then back at Danny.

She expected to see Lopez (or someone else who had taken his place at guard duty) lying dead outside the door, but there were no signs of casualties that she could see.

The man was tall and thin, and his face was covered in black and green camo paint. The rest of him matched his face, including thick camo pants and a long-sleeve shirt underneath a tactical vest with slots stuffed with spare magazines. Equally full pouches hung from his narrow hips, including a gun holster.

"Don't even fucking flinch," a gruff voice said from behind the painted face.

Gaby sat perfectly still, and so did Danny. She worried that the loud, crashing door might have woken Nate, but one look at him eased her fears, though it made her wonder what kind of meds the collaborators had given him to make him sleep through all of this.

The gunman saw her eyes going to Nate and said, "He dead?"

"No," she said.

"You sure? He looks dead to me."

"He's just sedated."

"We're on the same side," Danny said, and raised his bound hands slightly off his lap to let the guy see the zip ties.

"Oh yeah?" the guy said, though he sounded doubtful. The fact that he hadn't loosened his grip on his rifle for even a second was proof of that. The weapon was very steady in his hands, which told Gaby all she needed to know about him.

"You're part of Mercer's army, right?" Danny asked.

The man cocked his head, a glint of curiosity showing through the paint. "What do you know about it?"

"We found the flyers. Join us or die, right?"

Not quite right, Gaby thought, realizing what Danny was doing. He already knew this man with the rifle was one of Mercer's killers—everything about him gave that away—and if he was here inside the bank, then that meant the collaborators were dead. (For a very quick moment, the thought of Mason finally getting what he had coming made her heart race with triumph.) Danny was playing on the propaganda flyers they had been finding all over the state, like the one Nate had found earlier yesterday while they were scouting.

But Danny was wrong. It wasn't "join us or die"; it was more like "join us to take back Texas." Or something close. Not that it mattered, and she suspected Danny knew it, too. He just needed to get the man's attention, to sow the seeds of the lie he was already cooking up.

And it seemed to work, because the man relaxed the hand that was clutched tightly around the pistol grip underneath his rifle's barrel. He didn't lower the weapon, though, but it was a good start.

"Close enough," the gunman said, and grinned, showing impossibly white teeth.

Gaby couldn't help but relax a little, even if a part of her didn't believe they were any better off than before. What was that old saying?

Out of the frying pan and into the fire...

BUT MAYBE SHE was worried about nothing because it looked as if Mercer's men were more concerned with the collaborators than they were with her, Danny, and Nate. The man who had found them in the back room called himself Fritz, and he led them to the front of the bank, leaving Nate where he was, but only after Fritz had checked to make sure Nate wasn't playacting.

The lobby was in pieces, and she didn't have to go very far to see the source of the explosion she had heard earlier: Almost one entire side of the bank's front wall was gone, leaving behind a gaping hole in its wake. Brick and mortar had been blasted across the once-wide lobby space, covering a large chunk of the floor. The island counter that had been used for filling out deposit slips had been chipped by gunfire but was somehow still standing, and the same was true for the teller windows at the end of the lobby.

She counted five bodies, all men in black uniforms—Texas collaborators. One of them had the name *Danzinger* stenciled across his tag. The rest were either lying on their stomachs or were buried in rubble along with their names. She didn't see anyone among the dead who was even remotely close to matching Mason's short stature, which made her just a little bit ticked off.

He really is like a goddamn cockroach.

Besides Fritz, there were two others wearing similar clothing, their faces also covered in camo paint in the lobby. One was standing guard next to the hole while the second one sat in a chair with a bent metal leg spooning chunky food from a bag of MRE. Gaby got a whiff of beef ravioli in the air, but she was more concerned about the M4 rifle with the attached grenade launcher leaning next to the man.

A wall versus a grenade launcher. Easy win.

The third man looked up as Fritz led her and Danny across the lobby. "Prisoners?"

"They were like this when I found them," Fritz said.

"So, prisoners."

"They said they're volunteers."

"Volunteers?"

"We saw the flyer," Danny said.

"Flyer?" the man said, confused.

"That shit we've been tossing out of planes since after R-Day," Fritz said.

"Ah, the flyer." The man took a moment to shake some salt from a packet into his bag before going back to work with a plastic spoon. "Names?"

"I'm Danny, she's Gaby," Danny said. "The one sleeping it off inside the back office is Nate."

"Three?" the man said to Fritz.

"Basically two and a half," Fritz said. "Second guy's mostly dead."

"He's just been sedated," Gaby said. "He was shot yesterday."

"How'd that happen?" the obvious leader asked.

Gaby nodded at one of the collaborators. She had never seen the man before and didn't know his name, but one was as good as another right now. "They've been chasing us for a while; finally caught up to us yesterday. Almost killed Nate in the process."

"Why?" the man asked.

"Like we told Fritz here," Danny said, "we left the town we were assigned to so we could sign up. Fight the good fight. Take back Texas. All that good stuff."

"You went AWOL? Is that what you're telling me?"

"AWOL, who-gives-a-shit-wol, whatever you wanna call it. We're not risking our lives for those night-crawling fucks anymore."

Damn, Danny, you almost convinced me *that time.*

But Gaby couldn't decide if the man was convinced or not, and his response was all that mattered. Even with all that gunk over his face, she could tell he was older than Fritz by a few years, and it made sense that in this rankless army of Mercer's that the oldest man probably ended up leading, if just by default. Of course, she could have been entirely off base and the one standing with his back to them, guarding what was left of the wall, was the real leader, even though he hadn't said a peep.

She decided to focus on the man sitting in the chair when she said, "Is it true? What the flyers said?"

"What do they say?" the man asked.

"That you're going to take back Texas. Because that's why we risked everything to leave the town. Tell me it's true," she added, injecting just enough desperation into her voice to be convincing but without overdoing it. Or, at least, she hoped she wasn't overdoing it.

"If it's not, tell us now," Danny said, picking up on where she left off.

"It's true," the man nodded.

Gaby watched the leader slowly finish up his meal and toss the bag to the floor. He pulled out another small packet from his pocket and fished out an oatmeal cookie. Gaby had to stop herself from drooling over the smell.

"We're taking back Texas, and we're always looking for new recruits," the man finally finished.

"Thank God," Gaby said, again putting just enough of the old Gaby—the girly high school Gaby—into her voice to be believable.

Jesus, when did I become such an actress?

"I'm Benford," the man said. "You already met Fritz." He hiked a thumb at the third man in the room. "That's Kip."

Kip tossed a glance over his shoulder and gave them a "what's up" nod. He was much younger than both Benford and Fritz, and despite the paint caking his face couldn't have been older than her.

But then, age was hard to tell these days because everyone grew up so fast. You had to, or you didn't survive.

Benford was smiling at them, white teeth poking through his camo and giving off a slightly sinister vibe. "Unfortunately, we can't just take your word for it, you understand."

"But I have such a trusting face," Danny said.

"You won't get any arguments from me. You get lost in Texas on your way back to California or something?"

"Nah, I'm just naturally sunny."

"I can see that. But like I said, hard to trust people these days, so everyone has to pass a test first."

"I suck at tests. Is it at least multiple choice?"

Benford ignored him and said, "Kip, bring him in."

The kid disappeared through the wall.

"What's going on?" Gaby asked.

"We need to make sure," Fritz said.

"Make sure of what?"

"You'll see," Benford said.

Kip returned, but he wasn't alone. A fourth man with camo on his face—another one of Mercer's—along with Kip was flanking a black-clad figure between them. The man's head was drooping like he didn't have the strength to raise it, and his arms were duct taped behind his back. He was struggling with his footing, forcing Mercer's men to drag and carry him at the same time.

Mason. Please let it be Mason.

The man lifted his head...and it wasn't Mason.

Dammit.

Like the other dead men in the lobby, she had never seen the collaborator before. The part of his uniform where the name tag was supposed to be was missing, along with most of his right sleeve. Blood trickled down his face and thick, bloody clumps scarred both sides of his temple. He looked as if he were in tremendous pain, and she understood why he had so much difficulty walking: His right leg was broken, and blood dripped from both pant legs. When Benford and the others took out the bank wall, they had apparently claimed their share of collateral damage, and this man was one of them.

Kip and the fourth man dropped the collaborator to the floor in front of Benford. The man collapsed on his knees. Despite his weakened state, he somehow managed to stay upright, if just barely, and glanced first at her, then Danny, then around at the other faces in the room. Beyond the blood and bruises, defeat clouded his eyes, but there was a spark of defiance there, too.

Benford drew his sidearm and took out the magazine. Then he pulled back the slide and slid a bullet into it. "One round. Who's it gonna be?"

"Me," Danny said before Gaby could even process what Benford had just asked them.

"What's wrong with the girl?" Benford asked.

"Not a thing," Danny said, "but I talked her into this. The other kid, too."

"Whatever," Benford said, and tossed the gun to Danny. "Make it co—"

Danny caught the gun and shot the collaborator once in the chest before Benford could even finish.

"Well, shit," Benford said, watching the man in black slump to the floor.

Gaby stared at the dead man while Fritz chuckled from somewhere behind her.

"Welcome to the Rebellion," Benford said. "Your first assignment is to drag your old friends into the back office. They're ruining the décor of the place."

"We sticking around?" Fritz asked.

Benford glanced at his watch. "Got plenty of time before nightfall. Maybe we'll get lucky and more of them will show up, give us extra target practice."

THE REBELLION WAS really just four people at the moment—Benford, Fritz, Kip, and the fourth man, Justin. To hear Fritz tell it, they never had any intentions of a prolonged engagement with Danzinger's people, since that went against their mission of hitting and running.

"We kept waiting for them to get reinforcements," Fritz said. He was perched on the island counter, feet swinging back and forth as if he were at the park. "But no one ever came. We were pretty sure they'd at least get a few extra bodies from that buildup in Port Arthur. We put two guys on the road, just in case, to do a little sniping. But nope. We hit them all day, poking at them from every angle, and no one ever showed up. I guess they're stretched thin ever since R-Day. Probably keeping most of their forces in the towns."

"R-Day?" Gaby asked.

"Resistance Day. Our little name for it. Nothing official or anything. He's not a big fan of titles. Or rank, for that matter."

"'He?'" Danny said.

"Mercer," Fritz said. "The Big Cheese."

"Where's he now?"

Fritz shrugged. "He's around."

"You don't know?"

"I know, but you don't need to know."

"I thought we were all friends now. You guys even showed me the secret handshake and everything."

Fritz grinned. "Not yet. But maybe if you keep proving yourself we might show you the secret lair."

"Awesome. Do we get costumes, too?"

"Hey, what you do with your free time is your business."

Danny grinned back at him. "Sweet," he said, and went back to eating from the bag of MRE Mercer's men had given them.

She concentrated on her own bag of Meal Ready-to-Eat, gobbling up the clumps of chicken pesto pasta with the cheap spoon that came with the food. It probably said a lot about how desensitized she had become to how the new world operated that her appetite only increased after dragging the dead bodies into the back room with Danny. She wished she could say she felt sorry for them, but besides Lopez, she didn't know a single person or even their names, and she didn't care enough to read their name tags.

They tried to kill us, and they shot Nate. Screw them.

The MRE tasted a bit bland at first, but a little salt and seasoning from the provided packets lent some life to it. She had pocketed the cookie and beef jerky and saved the coffee grounds for later. The last time she had coffee was on the *Trident*, where they regularly dipped into the reserves they'd brought from Song Island. She thought about Nate and how much he'd enjoy his own calories-heavy bag, but he was still asleep in the back office.

Despite having been "welcomed" to the Rebellion, Benford hadn't given them weapons, and she used the opportunity to try to come up with a scenario where Nate wouldn't be left behind when Benford finally decided it was time to move on, which he would eventually. Right now the only thing keeping them in the bank was Benford wanting to rest his men. They might not have lost anyone in the gunfight, but they had been at it all day and actually looked more tired than her and Danny.

Benford was outside on the sidewalk now with some kind of portable radio set on the hood of a bullet-riddled Jeep. She recognized it as the same one that had chased them yesterday, backed by the technical. The vehicle was damaged, its front windshield smashed and hood badly dented from, she guessed, the same explosion that had taken out the wall. Benford had his M4 with the grenade launcher slung over his back, and he didn't seem all that concerned about standing out in the open, maybe because Justin and Kip were somewhere out there keeping watch while he and Fritz stayed back.

Benford was talking into the radio's microphone and occasionally listening, but she couldn't make out what was being said from inside the building. The radio didn't look like the kind they had been carrying around with them and using to communicate with the *Trident*. Benford's was probably military-issued, while theirs was a civilian model.

"He's like a dog with a bone," Fritz was saying while looking out at Benford. "He knows something's not right about this place. The collaborators have no reason to stake a base all the way out here, and we've seen multiple nests in the bigger buildings. Those things don't normally waste time in a no-nothing place like this, so why are there so many nightcrawlers around?"

"You saw them?" Danny asked.

"Couldn't miss them. They were crammed into every store and building we passed. Had to be hundreds of them in the place. Maybe more..."

"How many did you guys kill?"

"Six in all, counting the one you popped. Why?"

"There were more than six earlier today," Gaby said.

"If there were more, then they weren't here when we hit the bank. And if they're out there, Kip and Justin would have spotted them already." He shrugged. "My guess is they knew they were beaten and took off."

Gaby could picture Mason doing exactly that. The man was an opportunist and a survivor first and foremost. If he thought Danzinger was going to lose, he wouldn't have any hesitation about abandoning them. The only other reason he wasn't one of the dead was if he hadn't been around when the fight got out of hand. She didn't know which explanation she preferred, not that either one did anything to change the results: Mason was still out there, somewhere.

Like a goddamn cockroach that needs to be stepped on.

"Why'd you do that, by the way?" Danny was asking Fritz.

"You mean the bank?" Fritz said. When Danny nodded, "Benford's decision. They had one on the roof and one on the sidewalk outside, but other than that it was like shooting fish in a barrel. Benford had us prodding them all day until he was finally convinced they didn't know what the hell they were doing. It was like they were just satisfied to sit here and wait." He eyed Benford, who looked like he was in the process of wrapping up his radio call outside. "Like I said, dog with a bone. He wants to know why they were here, why no one came to their rescue, and what the nightcrawlers are doing in a place like this."

"Curiosity killed the cat," Danny said, looking out at Benford.

"Yeah, well, don't say that to him," Fritz chuckled.

"Mum's the word."

Gaby drank her bottle of water and dabbed some onto her fingers to clean them against her pants. Like Danny, she knew something Fritz and Benford didn't—the collaborators hadn't abandoned Gallant despite the constant attacks and lack of reinforcements because they *couldn't*. She remembered how Mason had talked about *them* earlier and how unsettled he had looked. He had tried to hide it, but she could see through his façade.

She looked up when Benford came back inside the bank and put the radio away in his pack.

"What did they say?" Fritz asked.

"They don't have any intel about this place," Benford said. He looked and sounded disappointed. "As far as they know, there's nothing important about Gallant, no reason why the enemy didn't want to leave or why there are nightcrawlers all over the place." He looked over at Danny. "What about you? You don't know what they were doing down here?"

"Not a clue," Danny said. "The only reason we're here is because Port Arthur was crawling with soldiers. Your guess is as good as mine why they're messing around this place."

Benford seemed to believe him. Maybe it was the way Danny had told the story—while casually eating his prepackaged food without a care in the world—but even Gaby would have bought the lie if she didn't know better.

"So that's that, then," Fritz said. "We bugging out or what?"

"Short of tearing the place apart?" Benford nodded. "We had our fun. Besides, there's plenty of other targets out there to pick from."

"I can dig that."

Just then, the *crack!* of a gunshot echoed outside, and all four of them dropped to the floor instinctively.

Two more shots followed, then silence.

Gaby glimpsed Danny's bag of MRE skidding across the tiled floor and looked over in time to see him reaching for his hip for a sidearm that didn't exist. He looked over at her and mouthed an exaggerated sigh.

Benford had unclipped a two-way radio from behind his back and hurried over to the hole in the wall. "Justin, Kip," he said into the radio, "give me a sitrep." When they didn't answer, "Justin, Kip. Give me a sitrep, goddammit."

The radio in Benford's hand and the one clipped to Fritz's waist squawked in reply, and a male voice said, "You boys should have left town when you had the chance. This is what happens when you lollygag."

Fuck me, Gaby thought when she recognized the voice.

"Do yourself a favor and let us go in there and collect your guns," Mason said through the radio. "Trust me when I say it's your best option, because you're not going to like what happens when night falls. Nosirree, you are *not*."

Then, because it was Mason and he knew exactly how to get on her nerves:

"Oh, and that hot blonde number who is no doubt listening in on this? Hey, sweetheart, you miss me yet?"

CHAPTER 14
LARA

"THE RIG WAS designed to accommodate about 150 crewmen, but we don't have nearly that many onboard right now," Riley said as he led her off the top platform and into a stairwell, their boots *clanging* off heavy metal stairs as they went down.

She expected to feel claustrophobic as they entered the belly of the structure—like moving around in a submarine—but their path was lit by LED lights, and everything, including the walls, was surprisingly clean. She didn't know why, but she thought a place that was supposed to house oil workers who slaved on heavy machinery for most of the day would be grimier…and smellier.

"Sounds like it should be pretty comfortable with all the extra space," Lara said. "So why are you in such a hurry to abandon it?"

"Comfort isn't the problem."

"So what is?"

"We'll get to that later."

"You keep saying that, but I'm not hearing anything that would make me hand the *Trident* over to you."

"I'm not asking you to hand it over to me, Lara. You just need to let me borrow it for a while."

"I still haven't heard anything that would make me do that, either."

"I haven't gotten to my sales pitch yet," he said as he pushed through a door and they stepped inside a hallway lit by bright natural sunlight.

"Where are we?"

"The crew area, where the workers stay when they're not working."

She found out why the place was so bright when Riley led her past an open door and she looked in at two kids about Vera and Elise's age, propping their chins and arms against an open window on the other side of the room. One of the children, a girl, glanced over and smiled at her, and Lara reflexively smiled back.

"You said you had civilians onboard, not children," she said. "How many?"

"About a dozen in all."

"Why are they here?"

"Because their family is here."

They walked past a couple of closed doors, and Lara thought she could hear voices coming from the other side of both of them.

"Is this what you wanted to show me?" she asked. "Two kids in a room?"

"It's a beginning."

"So there's more."

"I wouldn't be much of a salesman if I didn't have more under my sleeve."

He stopped at another open door, then took a couple of steps out of the way to let her look in.

It was some kind of exercise room, except the equipment had been removed and the space taken over by people. Sunlight streamed inside through windows along the far wall, and she counted at least twenty civilians either standing or sitting around. Some were occupied with card games while others were gathered around a TV watching some kind of movie on a Blu-ray player. A few had staked out private spots to read books. There was conversation, but it was of the hushed variety, as if they were all waiting for something—something bad, or big, or maybe both—to happen. A few of them glanced nervously over at her and Riley.

"Who are they?" she asked. "What are they doing here?"

"Everyone has their own rooms, but I guess they find it easier to all be in the same place," Riley said.

"No. I mean, what are they doing *here*, on the *Ocean Star?*"

"They're part of a support network. Cooks, mechanics—basically the lifeblood of every war effort. They're here because this is an FOB and our job is to keep the war going."

"What war are you talking about?"

Riley was looking at her intently. "I think you know."

He's talking about Mercer's crusade in Texas.

She'd known who Riley was as soon as he began talking about what was happening back in Texas. He was a part of Mercer's army. So were Hart and Faith, and now, the people in this room. She didn't have any doubts anymore, but she couldn't let Riley know that. At least, not until she had squeezed him for every piece of information.

"I don't," she said.

"Are you sure about that?" he asked, not taking his eyes off her.

"I should know what I know, Riley, and I don't know what you're talking about."

He nodded, but there was a ghost of a smile on his lips, as if he had just gotten what he had been waiting (looking?) for. "All right. Let's stick to that story for now." He turned and continued up the hallway. "Come on; I have more to show you."

She looked into the room one more time before following him. "How many people are on the rig?"

"Thirty-two civilians."

"I thought you said you were all civilians."

"Some are more civilian than others."

They turned a corner and passed another large room, this one equipped with flat screens along the walls, but unlike the previous room, none of the TVs in this one were turned on. There was a stack of red chairs in one corner because the space had been converted into living quarters. Instead of civilians, there were a half dozen men and women in assault vests sitting or lying down on spring cots. Everyone wore gun belts, and rifles leaned against their beds or the walls nearby.

They didn't stop at the second room.

"So this is where you're hiding the rest of your Harts," she said.

"I didn't want you to get the wrong idea."

"Which would be what?"

"That I was looking to jump you as soon as you were onboard."

"They're soldiers."

"They're the security force that's supposed to keep the FOB safe."

"How many?"

"Fifteen. I'm responsible for forty-seven lives in all, not counting myself."

"They look a little jumpy."

"Things are a little tense right now," Riley said. "Not just here, but back in Texas, too. Which you don't know anything about."

She smirked at his back but if he heard or saw it, he didn't react.

"There are more FOBs like the *Ocean Star* out there," Riley continued. "Not quite like this one, and staffed differently, but we all serve the same purpose."

"Which is?"

"Keep the war effort alive. Keep the fighting on course. Keep the killing going." He stopped and turned around to look at her. "Mercer."

"Mercer who?"

"Cut the shit, Lara. You know about Mercer," he said. It wasn't a question.

So here it is. The moment of truth.

"No more lies," she said.

"No more lies," he nodded.

"I've heard stories about Mercer, but I've never met him or seen what he's doing out there in person."

"Everything you've heard is true, and it's the reason I need to get these people as far away from the *Ocean Star* as possible."

"I'm listening…"

"We don't want anything to do with the bloodbath that's taking place in Texas right now. That's why I need the *Trident*. It's the only thing big enough to carry everyone here away."

"So you're running, is that it?"

"Yes," Riley said without hesitation. "We're running, Lara. I'm not ashamed of it. It's why I volunteered for this job in the first place, why the people in the other rooms are here, too. Will you help us get as far away from Mercer as possible?"

She didn't answer him, and Riley never took his eyes off her.

"Lara," he said. "Please. I need your help. I'll beg if you want."

"I don't want you to beg."

"What do you want?"

"Tell me everything about Mercer. About this war of his. If you want a prayer of me saying yes, I want to know everything."

"Everything?"

"Everything," she said. "Start at the beginning…"

THEY SAT ACROSS from one another in the *Ocean Star*'s galley—the only two people in the entire place—with chunks of SPAM and fried fish on plastic trays between them. Like life on the *Trident*, Riley's people had no trouble fishing the Gulf of Mexico for a steady diet of fish every day. She took note that the kitchen in the back still had a working refrigerator, which meant Riley had plenty of diesel fuel to waste.

We could definitely use some of that.

"The people here and the ones out there fighting his war right now wouldn't be alive if it weren't for him," Riley said. "He saved our lives. Literally and figuratively. The first few weeks were the hardest, but I'm not telling you anything you don't already know. You were out there, too."

She didn't say anything. The first few weeks of The Purge were not something she liked to dwell on.

May you burn in hell, John Sunday. You and your brothers.

"He knew about the oil rigs," Riley was saying. "He knew about a lot of other things that never occurred to me or most people. I don't know how he knew. It's one of the many mysteries surrounding Mercer. He doesn't talk much about his past, and he doesn't have to. His actions did all the speaking for him." Riley paused and seemed to take a few seconds to search his thoughts. Then, "What you have to understand is, we followed him because we wanted to, because we believed in him. Nothing he did up until what they call R-Day affected that belief. For most of us, anyway."

"What finally changed your mind?"

"The realization that it was happening. The war. It was actually happening. Before, it was just theory. And then…it wasn't."

"You said there are forty-seven people on the *Ocean Star*—forty-eight, counting yourself. How many are out there running around Texas?"

"Over 500," Riley said. "That's not including the people in the other FOBs."

"In all?"

"Almost a thousand."

It sounded like a lot, but even as she turned the number over in her head, she knew it wasn't really. There was a colonel in Colorado who had over 4,000 civilians and military personnel hiding in a bunker called Bayonet Mountain with him at this very moment. Compared to that, "almost a thousand" people wasn't nearly as impressive. Then again, it wasn't as if you needed a lot of warm bodies to drop bombs and shell a helpless town filled with pregnant women and civilians.

"He managed to save that many all by himself?" she asked.

"Not by himself," Riley said. "He started small, with a handful, but the numbers grew and soon they were able to cover more ground, pull more people out of their hiding places. In the beginning, there were just four of them. Mercer and three others. I made five."

"You were there at the planning stages of his war."

Riley shook his head. "It wasn't a war then. Not really. Yes, he talked about it, but he never gave any specifics, and for the longest time it was just this abstract thing he would bring up every once in a while. Mostly it was just people trying to stay alive and help each other do the same. He found out about the silver a long time before we even heard your radio broadcast. But he didn't know about water or UV lights, otherwise we would have used places like the *Ocean Star* a lot earlier." Riley poked unenthusiastically at his food with a plastic spork before continuing. "Eventually we transitioned from survival mode to planning. We'd always been good at searching and loading up on food, supplies, and fuel, but I didn't know what they were really for."

"His war."

Riley nodded. "He's had it on his mind from day one; he just never let us in on any of the details. Back then, we were just glad to be alive and searching for other survivors, and we never knew any better. I guess you could say we were blissfully ignorant and loving it."

"Where did you get the war machines? The planes?"

"The problem isn't finding them; it's training people to use them. We only had one pilot, a former Iraq War airman named Cole. He was able to train two others."

"Why just two?"

"Not everyone can fly a plane, Lara. It's not as easy as climbing into the cockpit and stepping on the gas pedal."

"I guess not."

"We located a unit of Abrams tanks at an Army base. All the ammo we needed was just sitting there for the taking. The tanks are easier to train for—all you really need is a manual and a lot of space—but they have limited range and they're not exactly subtle. From the reports we're getting out of Texas, Mercer's already lost two of his tanks assaulting the towns. The kill squads will eventually do more damage to the collaborators than the war machines as the war goes on."

"Kill squads?"

"Basically hit-and-run teams. They're mostly autonomous, and their job—their only job—is to sow confusion among the enemy ranks, make them think there are more of us out there than there actually are. It's a dangerous job, and the ones running around out there are all volunteers. The hardest of the hardcore Mercer believers."

"Sounds like a bunch of nice guys."

"Not really. Anyway, this is just the beginning. His version of shock and awe. Strike first and fast, before the enemy knows what's happening."

"By indiscriminately killing a lot of innocent people?"

"That part..." He shook his head. "It caught a lot of us by surprise. It's why I'm here. Why everyone's here."

Lara considered that the look in his eyes might have been all for her benefit, but she didn't think so. She hadn't noticed it before, but now that she was sitting across from him and neither one of them had moved for a long time, she saw the bags under his eyes, proof that rest wasn't something Riley was familiar with for a while now.

"Phase one was shock and awe," she said. "What's phase two?"

"Recruitment," Riley said. "Mercer knows he can't keep fighting this with just 500 soldiers, even as well-trained and committed as they are. Guns and ammo aren't the issue. We cleaned up more than one Army depot before all of this. His plan was always to start with Texas, get the Texans behind him, before expanding to the other states. He thinks if he inflicts enough damage, make them fear him enough, that he can convert the collaborators, including all the townspeople that can pick up a gun and fight with him."

"Why now? Why didn't he just wait until he had more men?"

"He said we couldn't, that the longer we waited the more comfortable the townspeople would become with their new life, and it would be harder to convince them. That, and with every FOB we establish, we increase our risk of being discovered. I don't know how much of that was bullshit, honestly."

"What if that doesn't work?" Lara asked. "What if the collaborators won't turn? What if they keep resisting him and he has to kill more and more people?"

Riley pursed his lips. "Then a lot of people are going to die for no reason." He put his spork down and looked intently across the table at her. "Now you know why I have to get my people out of here. I won't let Mercer throw them into the meat grinder. The only option is to run."

"WHAT EXACTLY DOES he want from us again?" Blaine asked.

"To transport his people away from here," Lara said.

"Where is this magical place he wants to take them?" Carly asked.

Lara shook her head. "He hasn't told me yet."

"In case you say no?" Blaine said.

"That would be my guess. I don't blame him. I'd do the same."

The warmth inside the bridge of the *Trident* was a welcome change from the chill of the oil rig and the stuffy air in its hallways. She stood inside the room with Blaine and Carly, the three of them staring out the windshield at the *Ocean Star* seemingly fastened permanently to the Gulf of Mexico. To look at it, she wouldn't have known there were nervous civilians crowding its rooms and hallways or anxious commandos waiting to rebel against the man who saved them.

"I guess he's not entirely dumb," Carly said. "Last night notwithstanding."

"He didn't have a choice," Lara said. "Or he didn't think he did, anyway. He's walking a razor's wire. Playing the loyal soldier to Mercer while committing what amounts to treason behind his back."

"Just from what I hear about this Mercer guy," Blaine said, shaking his head, "I definitely don't wanna end up on his shit list."

"Neither does Riley."

"So what do we get in return for playing chauffeur to his forty-seven people?" Carly asked.

"Forty-eight, including Riley," Lara said. "The most important thing we'll get is fuel, since a dead-in-the-water *Trident* won't exactly help him execute his plans."

"Execute," Carly said. "Nice choice of words, boss lady."

Lara smiled. "Point is, we can fit forty-eight more people onboard. At least temporarily."

"You sure about that?"

"Blaine?" Lara said, looking over at the big man for confirmation.

He nodded. "It'll be a tight squeeze, but it's not impossible. We'll fill up the cabins and open areas, and push comes to shove they can spill outside onto the decks. Lots of space on the aft and bow."

"And hey, a little extra sun never hurt anyone, right?" Carly said.

"They'll also be loading us with supplies, too," Lara said.

"What kind of supplies?"

"Food, water, guns, and ammo. He's agreed to let us have as much food as we can carry in our galley, but I told him he could keep his guns and ammo."

"You can never have too much ammo," Blaine said.

Carly chuckled.

"What's so funny?" Blaine said.

"That sounds like something Will or Danny would say."

Blaine smiled. "Best compliment I've gotten all year."

"Speaking of Danny," Lara said. "Did he radio in yet?"

Carly's face sobered up and Lara got her answer. She glanced at the digital clock on the bridge's dashboard: 9:17 a.m.

"He's late," Carly said. "And not the oh-shit-Aunt-Flow's-late sort of late, either."

"Did you try making contact with him?"

"He's not answering, either. No one is."

"They're probably busy looking for a way down to the shoreline. You know how unpredictable it is out there. If he ran into trouble, he would have let us know yesterday. Did he say anything?"

"No, but…"

"But?"

"I don't know," Carly said. "I got the feeling he wanted to tell me something, but didn't, for whatever reason." She shook her head and put on a brave face. "Of course, when it comes to Danny, I've learned it's not always a wise policy to assume he has more going on upstairs than meets the eye."

Lara reached over and put a hand on Carly's arm and got a pursed smile in return.

"How does transporting Riley's people and waiting to pick up Danny work?" Blaine asked. "What if Danny boy calls while we're en route to wherever Riley wants us to take them?"

"I don't know," Lara said. "But we'll do what we always do—deal with what's in front of us and pivot if something comes up after that."

"So we're definitely doing this?" Carly asked.

"We need their fuel," Lara said. "It won't hurt to restock our galley at the same time."

"I assume this means you think we can trust him," Blaine asked.

"I think so."

"You need to be sure, Lara."

Lara nodded, maybe more to convince herself than Blaine. "Yes, we can trust him."

And she thought, *God, I hope I'm right…*

FAITH, THE GIRL who had been driving her back and forth between the *Ocean Star* and the *Trident*, was coming back to pick her up. This time Lara wouldn't be alone, and stood at the swimming platform at the back of the yacht with Hart at her side and the other five men behind them. They were rubbing their wrists and blinking at the sun like prisoners who hadn't been let out for years instead of less than twenty-four hours.

"You made the right choice," Hart said. "I know it couldn't have been an easy one, but then, you are Lara."

"You figured that out too, huh?" she said.

"After our first talk last night," he nodded. "You sound different in person, but I've heard your voice enough times that it's stuck in a loop inside my head."

She gave him a curious look.

"Some of the guys carry around iPods with your broadcasts on them," Hart said and smiled almost shyly at her. "During a supply run in the early days, one of the groups raided an Apple store. They brought back stacks of those tiny iPods. They're pretty good for loading with music, or in your case, inspirational messages. Doesn't take much power to charge, either, and they last a ridiculously long time."

"Are you telling me there are guys running around out there with iPods loaded with my broadcast?"

"Uh huh."

"That's...disturbing."

"It's hard to explain, but your messages, especially the first one—this stranger speaking to us through the airwaves one night, telling us how to fight back, that there's hope as long as we don't give up..." He shook his head and again looked almost embarrassed. "It had a profound effect on a lot of us, more than you'll ever know."

Lara felt a slight shiver run through her at the thought of Mercer's *(killers)* men flying around in planes bombing civilians or rolling around in tanks shelling pregnant women while listening to and getting inspiration from her messages. The whole thing made her want to vomit, and it was all she could do to concentrate on the approaching vessel instead. Hart must have seen her discomfort, because he let the topic go.

She couldn't be sure, but Faith looked like she was smiling widely as she got closer. The young woman had upgraded to a bigger boat now that she would be driving six extra bodies back to the oil rig instead of just Lara.

"What about Mercer?" she asked Hart.

"What about him?" Hart said.

"When did you figure out he wasn't who he said he was?"

"That's the thing. I can't really say if he ever actually lied to us."

"No?"

Hart scrunched his face in thought, his graying hair rising and falling against the cool wind. "He gave us everything he promised, and in return we gave him our loyalty. It wasn't like he demanded it. We gave it to him willingly."

"You still think you had a choice?"

Hart sighed. "Maybe not. Maybe it was one of those unspoken trade-offs. Whatever it was, I don't think he ever lied to us. He might not have told us everything, but in the early days, as we were preparing for what the younger guys called R-Day, I don't think most of us—or maybe it was just me—fully understood what he was asking us to do."

"Slaughter innocents…"

"Yeah," Hart said quietly, as if that one word drained all of his energy.

One of the five men behind them walked forward and waved at Faith. He was young, with short blond hair, and was beaming as Faith approached them.

James, I presume.

Lara looked past Faith at the *Ocean Star* waiting for them in the near distance. She ended up staring at the towering crane, which looked like a stray limb poking out of the sea. If she stared hard enough, she thought she might have spotted something moving around up there. But of course it could just be the bright sun playing tricks on her eyes.

"Riley told me there was a guy named Peters up there," she said, pointing at the crane.

Hart nodded. "Uh huh."

"He said Peters never misses."

"He doesn't."

"First time for everything."

Hart smiled. "Not with Peters."

CHAPTER 15
GABY

WHATEVER CONFIDENCE BENFORD and Fritz had while they assaulted the bank fizzled when their number was halved, with Kip and Justin likely dead somewhere out there. How else would Mason have gotten his hands on their radio?

Gaby couldn't help but look down at her watch every few minutes. Nightfall came fast in Texas in the winter, and it would be pitch-dark by 5:30 p.m.

And right now...1:46 p.m.

Time flies when you're outgunned.

She looked across the bank lobby at Fritz and Benford crouched at the front of the building. Fritz was peeking out of the hole in the wall while Benford moved from the still-intact front doors to the remaining windows. At some point during his back and forth, he took out his ham radio and spoke into it. He kept his voice low, as if he knew she was eavesdropping, but because of the short distance, she managed to hear snippets of the conversation anyway. Benford did most of the talking and she caught the words *ghouls* and *torch it* before he turned the radio off and slipped it back into his pack.

Gaby exchanged a look with Danny, both their backs against the island counter. They were close enough to see the empty street outside but far enough to stay out of the path of any stray bullets. Hopefully, anyway.

She mouthed at him, *"Did he say 'Torch it?'"*

Danny nodded.

"What did he mean?" she mouthed.

Danny shrugged and she swore he mouthed back, *"Tacos,"* but that couldn't have been right, because it didn't make any sense.

She gave him a questioning look and he grinned, and she thought, *Dammit, Danny, this is no time for one of your stupid jokes.*

She sighed and looked forward at Fritz and Benford. Somewhere beyond the hole between the two men was Mason and who knew how many collaborators. Either he had finally gotten the reinforcements Benford had been waiting for, or Mason had left with enough men to take both Justin and Kip out. Either way, Mason was out there and he had the upper hand, because there was no way for them to leave Gallant First Bank without being shot.

She glanced back at the hallway and at the door on the other side of the dark passageway. What were the chances Mason didn't already have someone waiting in the back alley just in case? The man was an opportunist scumbag and a dozen other unlikeable things, but the one word she would never use to describe him was *stupid.* But just in case Mason did decide to come through there, she and Danny had helped Fritz blockade it with a heavy metal filing cabinet from the manager's office. It had bought them some goodwill, and, hopefully, further convinced Mercer's men that they were on their side.

The silent lull inside the lobby and outside in the rest of Gallant was unbearable. In the aftermath of Mason's mocking radio call, he had gone uncharacteristically quiet. When she looked over at Danny, he was staring at the pile of weapons resting in the corner across from them. Fritz, near the left side of the opening, stood in their way, but he was so focused on what was potentially outside that she wasn't even sure if he remembered they were still in the room with him and Benford.

When Danny looked over at her, she shook her head and mouthed, *"Too risky."*

He nodded, agreeing.

"Any other bright ideas?" she mouthed.

He shook his head, then shrugged before turning back to Benford and Fritz, and said out loud, "Um, guys?"

"What?" Benford said without bothering to look back at them.

"Don't wanna be a downer here, but you are aware that the reason they're not attacking is because they don't have to, right?"

Fritz looked over his shoulder at them. "What's that mean?"

"You know something we don't?" Benford added, also looking back now.

"All those fresh ghoul nests in town that you saw while you were picking your way here," Gaby said. "Remember?"

"Aw, fuck," Fritz said. He shot Benford a quick, worried look. "They're right. We're sitting ducks in here. Those fuckers don't have to come in to get us; if we're still here when it gets dark, they'll be the least of our problems."

"I'm open to suggestions," Benford said.

"The uniforms," Danny said.

"What uniforms?" Fritz said.

"The ones in the office."

"The dead guys?"

"That's them."

"What about them?" Benford said.

"The first thing you learn in the towns is that the ghouls respect the uniform. Hey, men in uniform, who doesn't like them, amirite?" When neither Fritz nor Benford said anything, Danny continued: "Point is, they recognize the uniforms and steer clear. I don't know how or why; they just do."

"He's right," Gaby said, picking up where Danny left off. If they were going to play the collaborator-turned-defectors, she might as well embrace the role, too. "They told us to always keep the uniforms on at night, especially when we're outside the town limits. It's always worked."

"Always?" Fritz said doubtfully.

"Always," Gaby nodded, and thought, *Probably.*

Benford and Fritz exchanged a look, but from their mannerisms she could tell that neither men were convinced.

Danny must have seen it too, because he said, "Don't think of it as wearing a dead man's clothing. Think of it as putting on a dead man's stink to keep back the wolves."

"I got a better idea," Benford said. "The Jeep."

"The Jeep?" Fritz said.

"We get in that Jeep, and we take our chances on the road. Blast our way out of here."

Gaby exchanged her own look with Danny and saw that he was thinking the exact same thing: *"Are these guys serious?"*

When she glanced back, Mercer's men were grinning at each other as if they had just won the lottery. She didn't know why she expected men who were going around Texas killing everything that moved to be open to logic, so it made some kind of warped sense that they would prefer to go out in a blaze of glory.

And our luck just keeps getting better…

"Fuck yeah," Fritz was saying. "We'll drive it right down their throats."

"Can't be too many of them out there," Benford said. He sounded as if he was trying to convince himself and Fritz. "Maybe a half dozen, if that."

"You sure? They did take Kip and Justin…"

"They could have sneaked up on them. We assumed they'd left the city, but what if they didn't? What if they were just hiding out somewhere else in town when we hit the bank?"

"That's possible, I guess."

"We just need to find the key."

"The key?" Fritz said, as if he didn't understand the concept.

"For the Jeep," Benford said, and peeked out at the vehicle in question still parked on the sidewalk outside, so close and yet so, so far away. "It wasn't in the ignition when I was out there earlier."

Danny turned to her, and Gaby saw the spark of something in

his eyes—not mischievous, exactly, but there was *something* there.

Before she could ask him, Danny said to Benford and Fritz, "Whoever was driving it probably pocketed the key when he parked." When the two men looked over, Danny jerked a thumb over his shoulder and at the back hallway. "It might still be there."

"Worth a shot," Benford said to Fritz.

Fritz frowned. "You mean, go through the bodies?"

"Don't be so squeamish. They're already dead."

"That's not helping."

"I'll give you a hand," Danny said.

Fritz got up and jogged, slightly hunched, across the bank.

Danny started to get up, but Fritz pointed the muzzle of his AR at him and said, "You stay here." Then, at her, "You come with me."

"I thought we were besties now," Danny said.

"Not quite." Then, when he saw that Danny hadn't sat back down, *"Sit down."*

Danny did, while Gaby got up and followed Fritz into the back hallway.

As she went, she sneaked a look back and saw Danny watching her. He nodded, as if to say, *"You can do it,"* and she thought, *No I can't, Danny, no I can't,* but she returned his nod anyway, because there were no other options she could see.

Gaby turned around and glimpsed Fritz just before he disappeared through the first door in the back. She followed him and sucked in a breath and steeled herself for what was waiting for her in there. For some reason, dragging them into the room earlier—she could still see the dry bloody trails they'd left behind, leading all the way from the lobby—hadn't affected her at all, but the prospect of seeing them again...

Stop it. You have work to do.

Focus!

Like the manager's office in the back (where Nate was sleeping, blissfully oblivious to everything happening around him), there were no windows in the room, but there was still just enough light to see with once her eyes adjusted to the new environment.

Semidarkness or not, there was no way she wouldn't know about the bodies at the back, because she and Danny had put them there.

"Don't get any ideas," Fritz said as he grabbed one of the dead men and pulled him off the pile to rifle through his pockets.

"What ideas?" she said as she got ahold of a heavy man with a mustache. The *thud!* he made as he landed on the floor made her wince. She'd had a lot of experience with bodies these days, but she still had to fight back against her gag reflex.

"That's a good girl," Fritz said.

She didn't bother responding and instead shoved her hands into the dead man's pockets and rummaged around them. She found a pack of gum and spare 5.56 shells. The man also had random supplies in the pouches around his waist, but the ones designed to carry ammo were already empty, their contents currently sitting in one of the lobby corners right now along with all the weapons. She tossed the useless items and lifted the man up from the floor just enough to go through his back pockets.

"Gaby," Fritz said.

"What?"

"That short for something? Gabrielle?"

"Does it matter?"

"Just making conversation."

"Don't feel like you have to put yourself out."

He chuckled. "Come on; we're on the same side now. Or what, you're taken or something? You and the California surfer?"

"We're just friends."

"Ah," he said, and she thought, *Jesus, is he flirting with me?*

The thought further nauseated her, especially given where they were and what they were doing at the moment. She was still trying to decide how to feel about Fritz's comments when her hand touched cold steel in the dead man's back pocket. She quickly wrapped her fingers around it and pulled her hand out.

"Nothing," Fritz said. He was working so close to her that she could smell his sweat as he reached over and pulled another body toward him, handling the dead man as if he were a (heavy) bag of flour. "You get lucky?"

"No key yet," she said, turning her body slightly so more of her back was to Fritz.

She opened her hand and looked down at the folded pocketknife. The handle was about four inches long, which meant the hidden blade would be around three inches or so.

There is a God.

She had been prepared to do this the hard way, by getting her hands on one of Fritz's weapons—either his sidearm or the knife in a sheath strapped to his left hip. It wouldn't have been easy; Fritz was bigger and stronger, and despite the element of surprise, she would have had to get really, really lucky. There would have been a lot of noise, maybe even a gunshot, and Danny would be at risk.

But what else was new? They were all at risk if they did nothing.

"Maybe it's not here," Fritz was saying. "Wouldn't that be a kick in the balls? Might have to shoot our way out of here on foot. I guess that'll be fun, too."

Fun? That's one way to put it.

"Other guys got into this because they believed in the cause," Fritz continued, oblivious to what she was doing next to him, "but me and Benford? We just like the excitement. Be all you can be, right?"

She pocketed the knife and turned around. "Anything?"

"Zilch." He wrinkled his nose. "And to top it off, they're starting to reek, too."

"We all reek."

He grinned at her. "Some reek less than others."

Jesus, he really is flirting with me.

She managed to force out a smile back at him before turning to the next body. It was heavy, but not too much that she couldn't have dragged it closer with a little straining, and it certainly wasn't heavy enough that she had to make noises as she edged it near her, trying to get it off the two bodies underneath it.

"Jesus, he's a big one," she said between grunts.

"Time to hit the gym," Fritz said.

"Maybe after this."

"Make an appointment. I'm always available for consultation."

"Deal," she said, and grunted again as she pulled at the body.

Fritz got up from the dead man he was searching and moved over and grabbed her man by the arm. Gaby had just enough time to glimpse the collaborator's face—it was the same one that Danny had shot back in the lobby earlier. It might have been the lack of light, but she swore the man looked completely at peace.

"He's not that heavy," Fritz was saying.

"Heavy enough for me," she said.

"I got it," Fritz said, and pulled hard enough that he dumped the body on the floor with a loud *thud*.

While he was pulling, Gaby had taken a step back to give him room to work. At the same time, she slipped her hand into her pocket and took out the folded knife, then thumbed the stud sticking out of the side that allowed users to simply push the knife open with one hand—or more precisely, one thumb.

There was a slight *click* as the blade came out—about three inches worth, with a serrated section—but if Fritz heard it, he didn't react. He stood in front and slightly to the left of her, almost exactly opposite the door behind them, which allowed a stream of pale light to splash across his back. She had no trouble whatsoever finding his neck, portions of it still layered with the face paint he hadn't taken off since she first saw him. Whatever it was he and Benford had covered themselves in, it had stayed in place remarkably well.

Fritz crouched and reached for the dead man's pockets, saying, "You're taking the last two. No fair I have to do all of them. Equal opportunity and all that, right?"

He was chuckling, his back to her, when she jammed the knife into the side of his throat, aiming for the middle while at the same time wrapping her left arm around his head and seeking out his mouth with her palm. He let out a startled grunt and jerked back even as she pushed the knife in further, and his body slammed into her chest and knocked her off balance as they spilled to the floor. As she fell back, all Gaby could think about was locating Fritz's mouth to silence him so he couldn't let out a scream that would alert Benford outside.

A loud *thump!* as she slammed into the floor with Fritz's thrashing body on top of her. There was pain, but she was too busy pulling the knife out of Fritz's neck to properly feel it. An arc of blood spurted across the room, the fresh wetness mingling with the multiple trails of dry blood that smeared the floor from when they had dragged the bodies inside earlier. Fritz's body continued to spaz on top of her as she gave up trying to find his mouth *(Jesus, where the hell is his mouth?)* and instead concentrated on locking her free arm around his throat to keep him from moving around too much as she plunged the knife once, twice, *three times* into his chest.

He continued flailing against her, his much bigger and heavier body making it hard for her to suck in air, even as she heard him letting out a gurgling sound. Warm blood splashed both of her arms, but mostly her left hand as it tightened around his throat in a vise grip. She held him in place even as he struggled, his legs kicking out between hers. The man seemed to never run out of strength, not even when she embedded the knife a fourth time into his chest.

Then finally, mercifully, his entire body went still.

She gasped for a lungful of much-needed air and pushed his body off her, then rolled over onto her side and stared at the darkening wall for the next two, five—ten seconds. Both of her fists and most of her long sleeves were covered in blood, along with her chest and chin. Her clothing clung, damp with Fritz's life force, the fresh stink of death threatening to make her vomit back out the MRE she'd eaten earlier.

Get a hold of yourself!

Danny, remember? He's still in the lobby with Benford!

She pushed up onto her knees and looked back at Fritz just to be sure he was dead. He wasn't moving at all, though his eyes were wide open and staring up at the ceiling. She remembered how he was flirting with her just before she murdered him and could no longer hold back; she bent over to throw up.

But it was a dry heave, and the chicken pesto pasta didn't come up. There was spittle, though, and she swiped at it with the back of her blood-covered palm.

Jesus, what part of her *wasn't* covered in blood?

The sudden realization of voices, coming from the lobby, made her straighten up. She tightened her grip around the knife instinctively.

It was Danny, saying something about a "horse and a bar," though she couldn't make out every word. Maybe it was the ringing in her ears or the sound of her heart hammering against her chest as it tried to catch up to her labored breathing.

Danny was still talking when she shook off the nausea, then tossed the knife and hurried back over to Fritz's body. She pushed it up, ignoring the warmth of his blood against her skin, and tugged the rifle off him, then did the same to the gun in his holster. A black Smith & Wesson automatic, smaller than she would have expected given a man as big as Fritz.

She bypassed the long knife strapped to his left hip and collected all the spare magazines he had on him, including an extra for the pistol, and staggered back up to her feet, feeling much better with the ammo's extra weight on her. She made sure the AR-15's safety was off as she approached the door, listening for clues that Benford might have heard the scuffle with Fritz, but all she could hear was Danny still talking.

Was it just her, or did he seemed to be talking louder than usual? It was almost like he was trying to keep Benford's attention so he wouldn't hear—

Her. Danny was distracting Benford because if anyone could hear what was happening in here with the open door, it would be Danny, who was much closer than Benford.

She smiled to herself.

I love you, Danny. I really, really do.

She wiped her bloody hands on her pant legs so she would have a better grip on her weapons, then leaned out the door and glanced left toward the lobby.

"Oh, come on, that was funny," Danny was saying.

Benford might have grunted, but he didn't take his eyes off the street outside.

"I got another one," Danny said. "It involves girls in bikinis. You like girls in bikinis, don't you, Benford?"

"What I would like is for you to sit there and be quiet," Benford said.

"Oh, you're no fun," Danny said, just as he looked back and saw her, and grinned.

She returned it before slipping the Smith & Wesson out of her front waistband. Danny nodded and began to slowly raise himself up from the floor. Gaby went into a slight crouch, took a breath, and then slid the pistol across the lobby to him.

She had put a lot of muster on it, thinking she needed to in order to clear the space between her and Danny, but it was probably too much and the gun made a *skeeeeeee* noise as it traveled to its destination—

And Benford heard it!

Mercer's man turned around and started to get up, but by then Danny had already snatched the gun off the floor and, still on one knee, twisted and shot Benford twice in the chest. Benford seemed to stumble, as if he had just lost his balance, before sitting back down on the floor with the M4 landing perfectly in his lap.

Gaby hurried out from the back, focusing on the hole in the wall next to Benford's awkwardly sitting form. She half expected Mason's men to use the momentary distraction to attack, but they didn't, and she made it to the front of the bank without having to dodge bullets. She leaned against the wall and peeked out at the street. When she couldn't see another living soul outside, she pulled back behind cover.

"Anything?" Danny asked behind her.

"No," she said.

"Of course not. Why make it easy for me? My luck's not that good."

"What now?"

"Gear up," he said.

Danny slid the Smith & Wesson into his empty holster, then walked over to the pile of weapons in the corner and helped himself to an M4, slung it, and began snatching up magazines from the floor and stuffing them into his barren pouches.

"Grab that 203," he said. "It might come in handy."

Gaby crouched next to Benford, ignored his accusing stare, and picked up his rifle. She poked through his pouches but couldn't find any ammo for the grenade launcher attached to the weapon.

"He must have used up all the grenade rounds," she said.

Danny grunted. "Figures."

She didn't bother taking the spare magazines on Benford. She was already flush with Fritz's, and they were interchangeable with the M4. She slung the rifle and stood up, then stared at the hole again.

The Jeep was still out there on the sidewalk, so tempting and yet so impossible.

"Did you find the key?" Danny asked.

"No, but we didn't look through all the bodies yet."

"Keep an eye out," Danny said, and jogged through the lobby and disappeared into the back room.

Gaby leaned against the wall and this time took her time looking up and down the empty streets of Gallant, Texas. She let out an involuntary sigh as the reassuring warmth of sunlight brushed against her skin.

Something caught her eye as it traveled up the street, whipping past the parked Jeep. She glimpsed a small strip of paper with black lettering on it…it was another one of Mercer's propaganda flyers. She followed the white sheet's progress until it disappeared up the street, then realized she was leaning too far out and pulled herself quickly back inside.

Stupid. If there was a sniper out there, you'd be missing a head right now.

They had to be out there somewhere, close enough to the bank to keep an eye on Mercer's men. The most obvious choice would be the two-story department store directly across from her. The sign above the front doors read "Gallant's Best," and the front exterior was painted red and white with shades of blue. A nod to the American flag, maybe. She squinted but couldn't tell if there were things other than just curtains covering the building's windows. But if Mason's men were in there, the best spots to watch the bank would be either the roof or from behind one of the second-floor windows—

She heard a squawk behind her and glanced back at the two-way radio still clipped to Benford's hip.

"Talk about a curious development," a voice said through the radio.

Mason.

"Does this mean you and Danny boy got the upper hand on Mercer's dickheads?" Mason asked.

She stared at the radio but didn't reach for it.

"What's the matter, kitty cat got your tongue, sweetheart? Don't be shy. If I'd wanted to harm you, I would have done it when you stuck your head out a second ago."

*God*dammit.

"Go on," Mason said. "I won't bite. Much."

She crouched and grabbed Benford's radio but didn't use it.

Mason didn't seem to mind. "I know what you're wondering: How did that handsome devil escape Mercer's boys? Admit it. It's been on your mind ever since you found out I'm still out here kicking and winning it."

She couldn't help herself and finally keyed the radio. "You're confusing me with someone who give a shit."

"She lives!"

"But I'll tell you one sure thing, Mason: Your luck's not going to last forever. One of these days you're going to find yourself in a noose that you can't slip out of."

"Why so serious, sweetheart?"

"I'm not your sweetheart."

"Sweetie, then?"

She looked up as Danny slid quietly across the lobby and pushed up against the wall on the other side of the hole. He looked over at her and shook his head: No key.

"I see Danny boy made it through okay, too," Mason said through the radio.

Danny cocked his head questioningly.

"He can see us," she said. "I don't know where he is, but he can see us right now."

"That sneaky little twat," Danny said. "You're right; I should have plucked out his lying tongue back in Starch."

"I told you."

"Yeah, yeah." Then, "You know, Benford and Fritz weren't completely wrong. We *could* make a run for it."

"What about Nate?"

"Right. Nate..."

"We can't leave him here, Danny. I won't do it."

"There's always Benny..."

"Danny..."

"Kidding!"

The radio squawked and Mason said, "I know what the two of you are discussing right now. 'Should we make a run for it? Surely,' you're saying, 'facing anything out there is better than staying put when it gets dark.'"

"Asshole's kinda psychic, isn't he?" Danny said.

"I don't know about the psychic part, but the asshole part's spot on," Gaby said.

"Just remember," Mason was saying, "I just need the two of you alive. They said nothing about keeping you in one piece. Do keep that in mind."

Gaby looked across at Danny. "Promise me."

He nodded. "We're not going anywhere without Mal Reynolds."

"Who?"

"*Firefly?*"

She shook her head.

"Never mind," Danny said. "Point is, we're not leaving without your boyfriend. And you can take that to the bank. Or, well, since we're already *at* the bank..."

"Thank you," she said, and got up and tossed Danny the two-way radio before dashing into the back of the building.

"What am I supposed to do with this?" Danny asked after her.

"Sweet talk him to death."

"I'll give it a shot, I guess," Danny said.

Gaby slipped inside the manager's office in the back and caught her breath, because where Nate was supposed to be, there was just an empty sleeping bag—

"Gaby," a voice said.

She spun around and found Nate behind her, leaning against the wall while clutching a large book in front of him. His face was pale and covered in sweat, and he didn't look like he could stand at all if not for the wall propping him up.

"Jesus, Nate," she said.

"I heard shooting. What happened? Where are we?" He glanced around the room. "Looks familiar…"

"We're back at the bank," she said, and went to him.

She helped him sit down on the floor, positioning his back against the wall to keep him from toppling over. He flinched with every movement, but just the fact that he was finally awake (and alive) made her overjoyed.

"What's with the book?" she asked.

"My secret weapon," he grinned.

"Looks dangerous."

"I swear it weighs like 500 pounds." He paused for a moment and looked down at his stomach. "By the way, I think I was shot."

"Danny and I dug the bullet out. You don't remember?"

He shook his head. "I don't remember a thing."

"That's okay. What matters is that you're awake and alive."

She stroked his face and leaned forward and kissed him. Tenderly at first, afraid of breaking him, then just a little harder.

"Gaby," he whispered.

She pulled back slightly. "Hmm?"

"You have blood all over you, babe."

"I know."

"Whose is it? Do I want to know?"

"It's not mine or Danny's, and this time it's not yours, and that's all that matters," she said, and kissed him again.

CHAPTER 16
LARA

THE SIGN ON the wall read "Roustabouts 5:00 A.M. sharp" with the "5:00 A.M." in large blocky red letters. She had seen similar signs along the rig, but especially around the living quarters where, she assumed, the "roustabouts" congregated.

"Five a.m.?" Bonnie said, almost whispering. "I don't think I've ever had to wake up at five a.m. even when I was flying around continents doing runway work."

"Must be nice," Lara said, matching Bonnie's pitch.

"Being hot has its privileges, what can I say? You could have passed for a model, you know. What are you, five-seven?"

"Five-five."

"Never mind, then."

"Gee, thanks."

"Just being honest."

They stood in the back of the communications room, watching Riley wearing a headset and standing over a console lined with buttons and monitors while a young woman who had introduced herself as Terry manipulated the controls. The woman, who looked to be in her late thirties with naturally curly hair, seemed to know what she was doing, even though Lara could see her fingers tapping nervously on the table. Lara could only hear snippets of the ongoing conversation, and all of it from the room's side. While Terry was clearly nervous, Riley was calm and his voice remained steady throughout.

"Roger that," Riley was saying into the mic sticking out of his headset. "We'll be ready to receive you by then. *Ocean Star* out."

Riley took off the headset and handed it back to Terry, whose hands were shaking as she took it. "Jesus Christ, Riley. I never want to do that again. I think I'm going to piss my pants."

Riley put a comforting hand on her shoulder and squeezed. "You did good, Terry."

"You think they suspect anything?"

"If they did, then they wouldn't still be on their way here."

"Where are they coming from?" Lara asked.

He looked over. "Texas. We're going to be getting a lot more units coming our way for refueling and resupplying now that the first phase is reaching its end."

"And then back to the war?"

"Some of them. But most will be heading back to The Ranch."

"The Ranch?" Bonnie said.

"That's what the younger guys call it," Riley said. "It's our main base of operations. It's also where Mercer planned all of this and where we built up the forces that're being used in Texas right now."

"So what happens when this unit shows up?" Lara asked.

"We'll pretend like everything's okay and refuel and resupply them and send them on their way."

"Just like that?"

"That's the plan."

Lara exchanged a look with Bonnie.

"What?" Riley said.

"What happens if they don't buy it?" Lara asked.

"They will," Riley said. "We've done this before. Besides, I know the unit that's heading our way right now. One of them is a good friend of mine. I would know if they suspected anything," he added, looking back at Terry when he said it. "We just carry on like business as usual, and everything will be fine."

"You sound pretty certain," Lara said.

"I am."

"What if you're wrong?"

He shook his head. "I'm not."

"HE'S CUTE," BONNIE said.

"Who?" Lara asked.

"Riley. Baby blue eyes."

"Is that what they call them?"

"Tall, broad-shouldered…"

"From what I can tell in the few hours I've been here, he's not taken yet, so feel free to make your move."

"I was thinking more about you."

Lara sighed. "Bonnie, I brought you here to help me do inventory and figure out how much space we'll need to clear on the *Trident* to accommodate Riley's people, and because Carly can't—and won't—leave the bridge until Danny calls in—so don't start with me."

"I'm just saying; you could do worse."

"I don't have to do anything. And my love life—or lack thereof—is not up for debate."

"Sorry," Bonnie said.

The two of them turned a corner and pushed their way into the stairwell. Every step they took produced a loud *clang*, something that used to bother her—anything that made a lot of noise, especially when she was the cause of it, bothered her—but she had become used to it after going up and down the *Ocean Star* all morning.

"Sorry," Bonnie said again. "You're right; it's none of my

business. I'm just worried about you, that's all. We all are."

Again with the "we."

"Tell everyone I'm fine," Lara said.

"I know you are. That's why we trust you with our lives."

Maybe you shouldn't, because I don't know what the hell I'm doing.

"We're behind you," Bonnie said, apparently taking Lara's silence as approval to keep going. "We know every decision you make is because you're looking out for us. Everyone on the boat believes that. We have a lot of faith in you, Lara, and we care about your well-being."

"Like getting me a boyfriend?" she said, and this time smiled at the ex-model.

"Something like that," Bonnie smiled back. "Baby blue eyes, Lara. Baby blues."

"Yeah, yeah," she said as they reached the landing at the top of the stairwell.

The door in front of them was a thick metal airtight structure with a round wheel instead of a traditional lever or knob. Bonnie gripped the wheel and spun it with both hands, then pushed the heavy door open.

They stepped outside and onto a staircase that overlooked the *Ocean Star*'s top deck. Lara tugged at her jacket's collar as they made their way down and over to one of the edges overlooking the western part of the platform. They leaned against a chipped yellow railing with the water sloshing below them while signs around them warned of the importance of hard hats and holding onto the railings at all times.

She had no trouble locating the *Trident* anchored nearby, swaying slightly back and forth against the waves. It was only about a football field's length from them, and if she stared hard enough she could just make out Blaine's outline on the bridge and Carly pacing behind him.

"Carly's going to burn a hole in the bridge's floor," Bonnie said.

"She's worried about Danny," Lara said.

"Hopefully he radios in soon. I'd hate to lose him, Gaby, and Nate."

If we did, it'd be my fault for sending them out there in the first place.

"Yeah, me too," she said instead.

There was a white tube connecting the *Trident* to an old gray refueling ship that was about a quarter of the yacht's size. The vessel had been attached to the other side of the *Ocean Star* when they first approached the rig, so they hadn't seen it before. For a while she wasn't sure if Riley could live up to his promise of fuel, but he'd proven her wrong. The more she learned about the rig's importance to Mercer's war efforts, the easier it was for her to believe that Riley's mutiny was not going to be well-received. The fact that Riley planned on taking the refueling boat with them, along with the inventory and armory, would only add to the insult.

He's risking a lot.

No, that's not true. He's risking everything.

Two men wearing black tactical gear and carrying rifles walked past them. They were part of Riley's security personnel and were back at their stations now that he didn't need to hide them from her anymore. There was also someone on the crane in the background. Lara had seen the man's silhouette every now and then, but never for too long. That would be the oft-mentioned, never-seen Peters.

She unclipped her radio and pressed the transmit lever. "Blaine, come in."

"Blaine here," the big man answered. "Everything good over there?"

"We're on schedule. Faith's taking Bonnie back to you with the first of the supply runs in a few minutes. Depending on how close Mercer's men are from us, there might be one more, at least for now."

"What about the refugees?"

Lara and Bonnie exchanged a grin.

"He's not wrong," Bonnie said. "They are sorta like refugees."

Lara said into the radio, "They'll come over later once Mercer's people are gone. Missing civilians would be a huge tip-off that something's not right on the *Ocean Star*."

"Good point," Blaine said.

"How long before the tank's topped off?"

"Ten more minutes, give or take. Has Riley told you where we're taking him yet? It'd be nice to know now so I can get started figuring out the best route there. It'd also give me something to do other than watch Carly wear out the carpet back here."

"I'll let you know when he tells me. Until then, be on the lookout for Bonnie in a few."

"Roger that," Blaine said.

She put the radio away. "You should get going," she said to Bonnie. "They're probably finished loading the supplies by now."

Bonnie took out a notepad from her back pocket and scanned it. "That'll be the cooking oil. He's giving us half of his stock. Hot *and* generous."

Lara rolled her eyes. "Get going."

"Yes, sir, ma'am, sir," Bonnie said.

She gave Lara a mock salute, then pushed off the railing and headed down the nearby stairs, her boots *clanging* off the steps after her.

"Where did you get that thing, anyway?" a voice asked behind her just before Riley appeared next to her a few seconds later, taking over the spot Bonnie had just vacated.

She knew Riley was only in his early thirties, but he looked so much older than that. It wasn't just the lack of sleep either; there was a heaviness about everything he did and said. In another place, another time, he would be handsome and she might have gotten weak in the knees if they had met in a bar or at a party, but now, watching him staring at the *Trident*, she could only think about the burdens of leadership and the choices he'd made. Not just for him, but for forty-seven other souls.

I wonder if I could make that kind of choice in his shoes?

Will could have. But then, Will could do a lot of things…

"I guess you could say it sort of just showed up when we needed it most," she said.

Riley chuckled.

"Did I say something funny?" she asked.

"The boat showed up when you needed it most, and now it's

here. I needed a way to get my people off the *Ocean Star*, and you showed up. There must be something special about that boat."

Its previous owners would beg to disagree, she thought, but said, "I never asked you how you spotted us in the first place."

"Peters."

"Peters?" she said, and reflexively turned around and glanced up at the crane, though this time she couldn't see anything that looked like a man up there.

"He's got one of those amateur telescopes," Riley said. "It's supposed to be used for astronomy, but he's adapted it for terrestrial surveillance. The damn thing weighed close to twenty pounds and it took forever getting it up there in one piece, not to mention welded into place. He spotted the *Trident* when it was still ten miles away, otherwise we'd never have met."

"Lucky you."

"Lucky us," Riley said.

"Lucky you I didn't give the order to shoot last night."

He smiled. "Definitely lucky me, then."

Neither one of them said anything for a while, and they were content to lean against the railing and let the cold wind whip around them. A fishing boat had already left the *Ocean Star* while they were talking and was now maneuvering toward the back of the yacht, where a couple of figures were waiting for it. Faith and Bonnie would be on that boat along with the first stack of supplies from Riley's inventory.

Finally, she said, "Why an oil rig?"

"Probably the same reason you've been living off the yacht," Riley said. "The *Ocean Star* has the benefit of being isolated. You would have just cruised right past us if I hadn't pulled my idiotic stunt last night."

She smiled and hoped he didn't see it.

"These things were built to withstand time and anything Mother Nature can throw at it," Riley continued. "And while it's not exactly halfway between the Texas shoreline and The Ranch, it's the next best thing."

"You mentioned The Ranch before. Where is it, exactly? Or is that something else I don't need to know yet?"

"Have you ever heard of Black Tide Island?"

"It doesn't ring any bells."

"It's a U.S. government-owned piece of real estate in the middle of the Gulf of Mexico. The military uses it for war games, and it's equipped with a base big enough to have its own accompanying landing strip."

"That's where your planes took off from."

"No. I mean, yes, the planes Mercer's using during R-Day have the range, but the logistics made it impossible, not to mention all the fuel they would burn just getting from point A to point B. The ones they're flying out there were already sitting in Texas air bases, gathering dust. We only used Black Tide to train the pilots."

"You mean people were flying around out here all this time and no one noticed?"

"Like I said, Black Tide is in the middle of nowhere, on purpose. How many other people have you run across before us?"

She thought about the dead body they had fished out of the ocean, then later, the voice on the radio begging her for help but that she had chosen to ignore…

"None," she said.

"It's a big ocean," Riley said. "Anyway, after the pilots were trained, it was just a matter of sneaking them back into Texas with the main force. We already knew where to get everything we needed for the operation. Of course, it took the teams weeks to get the planes working, but Mercer is blessed with men who know their way around machines."

"Blessed," she said, unable and unwilling to hide the derision in her voice. "Not quite the word I'd use to describe what's happening out there right now."

"They're only doing what he asked of them." He leaned closer against the railing, as if he were trying to make himself small. "I'm not proud of any of this, Lara. I wish I could say I was braver, but I wasn't." He looked over his shoulder as the same two guards she had seen earlier passed them by again on their rounds. "When all of this is over, I'll take the blame."

"The blame for what?"

"For not putting a stop to this nightmare before it ever got started. But I didn't. None of us did. We could have done so much more—*I* could have done so much more—but we didn't, and we're going to have to live with that."

She thought about the voice on the radio again, asking for her to make contact, asking for her help...

Lara closed her eyes and counted to five, then opened them again.

"The plan was always to bail once we got out here," Riley was saying, "but my transportation never arrived."

"What happened?"

"At the last minute, Mercer decided to reroute it to help with the war effort. I think he's planning to attack Port Arthur from two sides—land and sea."

"So you needed a replacement transportation, fast."

"Unfortunately, yes."

"What about that refueling ship?"

"It's not exactly designed to haul people around, Lara. And definitely not forty-eight people and all of our supplies."

"How did you convince everyone here to abandon Mercer's war, anyway? That must have been one hell of a discussion."

"It didn't take that much convincing, actually."

"No?"

"As the CO, I was able to handpick everyone here with us right now. So I only took the ones that I knew could be convinced. Most of them are friends, and some are known acquaintances."

"So you only selected people who were already pro-mutiny."

"Exactly."

"Smart."

"One of the few smart things I did, I guess you could say. It took a lot of work and vetting, but I had help."

"Hart."

He nodded. "Hart, Faith, Terry, and a few others. I never told you this, but the *Ocean Star*, in terms of staff, is the smallest FOB out here. It's not because the rig can only accommodate forty-eight people. These were just the ones I could be sure of."

"Are you sure about that?"

He looked over at her. "What do you mean?"

"You said you handpicked everyone here, but how can you be absolutely *sure* everyone sees things the way you do?"

"I don't understand…"

"Fine. You only chose the ones you thought would be the most open to your mutiny. But how can you be absolutely certain every single one of them didn't just say yes when you revealed your plan, not because they agreed with you, but because they had no choice?"

"No choice? Of course they had a choice."

"What if some of them are just going along with you because they're afraid of what will happen if they say no? You said it yourself how difficult it was to do what you're doing because of everything Mercer's done for you. He saved your life. He saved all of your lives. What if not everyone is quite as willing as you to cross the line from having doubts to full-on mutiny?"

Riley didn't say anything for the longest time, and she found it difficult to read his face. Was the notion that he could have miscalculated even registering? Maybe he really didn't understand the possibility that one of the forty-seven people he had brought onboard so they could all escape Mercer's insanity together might not actually want to escape after all.

She felt a little sorry for him for introducing all of these doubts, but she pushed through the guilt *(You're getting really good at that…).* She was getting involved in something that could cost more than just Riley and his people, but also the lives of everyone on the *Trident*, and she'd be damned if she didn't face it head-on.

"I'm assuming you're 100% sure about Hart and the other soldiers," she asked.

He nodded. "I am."

"That leaves the civilians. What are the chances they're just going along with you because they know you have the full backing of the guys with guns? Don't you think in that situation it would be a little intimidating for them to say no? After all, they know you're the one who came up with this idea."

He shook his head. "I didn't pick these names out of a hat, Lara. I looked into the eyes of each and every single one of them when I told them what I was planning. The things Mercer is doing out there in the name of saving humanity…" He shook his head and she could see him growing with confidence. "Trust me, I know every single person on the *Ocean Star* right now, and they all want to wash their hands of this bloodbath."

Lara didn't know if she believed him, but Riley seemed to embrace it as the truth, and she didn't know any of these people—hell, she barely knew Riley—well enough to question his (absolute?) certainty.

"All right," she nodded. "They're your people. I accept that you know them better than me, but I just wanted you to consider the possibility you could be wrong. All it would take is one mistake, Riley, and there's more at stake here than just your people."

"I didn't make any mistakes, Lara. They're all on board. I would stake my life on it. Hell, I *am* staking my life on it."

Famous last words, she thought, but didn't voice her doubt.

Instead, she followed his gaze back out into the ocean, to the *Trident* and the busy activity at its aft.

"I like Hart; he's a good second-in-command," Riley said, "but he doesn't always challenge my decisions. It's nice having someone second-guessing me for once."

"Glad to be of service," she said, and they exchanged a slightly awkward smile.

"I don't know if you've already guessed, but this whole war and leadership thing is new to me. I'm flying by the seat of my pants most of the time, doing my best not to get everyone who depends on me killed."

Join the club.

"How long before Mercer's men arrive?" she asked.

Riley glanced at his watch. "Soon. We'll need to send the *Trident* away so it's not spotted. Five miles in the opposite direction should do it."

"I'll let Blaine know once they finish loading the supplies."

"Hey, Riley," a voice called behind them. "I've been looking all over for you."

"You found me," Riley said, and started to turn. He hadn't gotten fully around when there was a *bang!* and a stream of blood spewed out from behind his back at the same time a bullet *pinged!* off the railing.

Lara spun around as Riley's body sagged to the floor next to her. The only reason he didn't slip right into the water below was because he was clutching the railing with both arms. His face was plastered with a sheen of confusion as he stared at his shooter.

Her mind screamed to *Go for your gun, go for your gun, you idiot!* while the man who had shot Riley took a step toward him and was about to shoot him again. She knew she would never get her pistol out in time to stop him.

So she screamed "Don't!" instead.

The sound of her voice startled the man and he looked over at her, as if seeing her for the first time. She didn't know who he was, but there was nothing strange about that. She hadn't come close to meeting all of Riley's people and could count on one hand the number of faces she would recognize.

He had dark brown eyes partially hidden underneath a dirty baseball cap, and they were focusing in on her even as he swung the gun gripped tightly in his right fist in her direction—

Bang!

The second shot exploded in the air like a crack of thunder at almost the exact same time the man's head, along with the cap perched on top of it, seemed to come apart. He collapsed, gun and body *clanging* against the steel platform floor. The gunshot's echo was still fading across the endless ocean when Lara looked up at the crane and saw a dark figure silhouetted against the sun, and Riley's words rushed back to her:

"His name is Peters. I had to keep him up there, just in case things went sideways. He's my insurance. My only insurance…and he never misses. Never."

She turned back to Riley and found him on the floor, his back resting against the railing while blood pumped out of his right shoulder and dripped down the edge of the rig and into the ocean below. He was staring forward at the lifeless body, a large puddle of brains and skeletal fingers reaching toward him from his would-be assassin.

Lara crouched next to Riley, pulled off her jacket, and draped it over his shoulder, then pressed down hard from both sides. He grunted from the pain but never took his eyes off the dead man.

"Who is he?" she asked.

He wiped at his forehead with a bloodied hand before answering. "Andy. Jesus."

"One of your security guys?"

Riley shook his head. "He's a mechanic. Kept things running. Jesus. I didn't think..." Riley blinked as if he had trouble believing what his eyes were showing him. "I was sure of him. I was so sure of him...."

I guess you weren't sure enough, Lara thought, wondering how many other people were running around the *Ocean Star* right now that weren't quite as all-in with Riley's mutiny as he had proclaimed. Maybe the woman who had served them fish and SPAM in the galley, or the parent of the kid who had waved to her as she walked past their room earlier this morning...

Loud, *clanging* footsteps as people approached them. She looked up as Terry, the woman from the comm room, and two others—including Hart—raced around the maze of machinery and ran to them.

"Oh God, Riley, oh God," Terry said.

The third person was an older man wearing wire-rimmed glasses and civilian clothes. He crouched next to them and reached for the bloody jacket she had pressed against Riley's wound. "What happened?"

"He shot him," she said, nodding at Andy's mostly headless corpse.

"Andy?" Terry said.

"Fuck," Hart said, gritting his teeth.

"You can let go now; I got him," the man with glasses said.

She stood up and backed away as the man and Hart worked to

lessen Riley's bleeding. The older man seemed to know what he was doing, so he was probably a doctor or had experience with gunshots, because he didn't look fazed by Riley's injury. Two more men, both in tactical gear, appeared and hovered over them. The horrified look on their faces told her everything she needed to know: They didn't think this could happen, and the fact that it had left them questioning everything.

After a while, and with so many bodies crowding around Riley, Lara couldn't see him anymore. She walked over to where Andy was instead and stood over his remains.

It was a nice shot. Hell, it was a perfect shot, especially from so high up and at such a drastic angle. She remembered telling herself that there was no way someone up there could hit her all the way down here, that all the odds were in her favor, even as Riley told her not to reach for her gun.

Jesus, that was close.

The radio on her hip squawked and she heard Blaine's anxious voice: "Lara. Lara, come in."

She unclipped the radio and keyed it. "I'm here, Blaine."

"What was that shooting?"

"Long story; I'll explain later."

"But you're okay?"

"I'm okay."

"Thank God." Then, "There's something else. I was going to call you before I heard the shots."

She brushed at a bead of sweat with her hand, forgetting that it was still covered in Riley's blood. "I could really use some good news right about now."

"Danny finally radioed in," Blaine said.

Oh, thank God.

"How is he?" she asked.

"I don't know; Carly's talking to him now. I've never seen her so happy."

"Fill me in later."

"But you're okay?"

"I'm okay," she said.

But Riley might be dead, and if he dies, where does that leave us?
She looked off at the *Trident* sitting where she last saw it.
At least I got him to refuel us first...
"Lara," Terry said as she emerged out of the crowd and walked on wobbly legs over to her.
"Riley?" Lara asked.
They watched as the wall of bodies came apart and the two commandos picked up Riley and, with the man in glasses at their side, carried him off. Hart looked after them, wiping his blood-covered hands on his pant legs.
"Who's the civilian?" Lara asked.
"George," Terry said. "He's our doctor. Or, well, the closest thing we have to one out here. He's actually a veterinarian."
Hart walked over to them. He looked in shock, and she swore he had aged five extra years since she last saw him. "You okay?" he asked her.
She nodded. "What about Riley?"
"George will do the best he can."
"I have a doctor—a real doctor—on the *Trident.*"
"Can you bring him over?"
"Her. And yes. Until then, what happens now?"
"What do you mean?" Terry asked.
"I mean," Lara said, "Mercer's people will be showing up anytime now. Are they going to ask where Riley is if he's not here to meet them?"
Hart and Terry exchanged a look.
"Well?" Lara said. "Are they?"
"Maybe," Hart said.
Lara was annoyed by their uncertainty but managed to temper it down—at least, some of it. "Did the others meet with Riley when they came through here?"
"Yes," Terry said. "I mean, they didn't ask or demand it or anything, but he was always there when they showed up. You know, as the CO."
"What about you?" Lara asked Hart. "Can you take his place?"
Hart was still trying to wipe the blood off his hands when he

looked up at her. "I guess I don't have much of a choice, do I?"

"You're going to have to do better than that."

He didn't answer her.

"Hart," she pressed.

"Yeah," he said. "I can do it."

She wasn't sure if Hart actually believed his own words, but it wasn't like she had any other, better choices at the moment. It was either Hart or…who else was there? Terry? The thirty-something woman who was shaking next to her?

"You're staying, right?" Terry asked her.

The idea that she would leave now—run away, essentially—had never occurred to her until Terry brought it up. She could hear the fear in the older woman's voice, and it bugged her that people who should be telling *her* what to do were always deferring to her instead. There was something very wrong with that.

How did you handle it, Will?

God, I never knew how hard you had to work all the time to keep us alive.

"Yes," Lara said. "We're not going anywhere. I promised Riley I'd take you and the others away from here, and I'm not going to break my word."

She saw the instant relief on Terry's face, and even Hart seemed to stand just a little straighter.

Lara focused on Hart. "What's your plan?"

He shook his head without even thinking about it. "I don't have one."

"None?"

"Riley was the brains of this operation. What about you?"

"Me?"

"I saw you back there on the yacht. Next to Riley, you probably have the most leadership experience. Which, yeah, is sad considering I can probably pass for your dad. But I'm not ashamed to admit it. I'm in over my head here, Lara. I could really use your help."

She took a moment to wipe her hands, still covered in Riley's blood, on her pant legs.

Then: "We're going to proceed like everything's normal.

They're going to show up on schedule and we're going to resupply them, then watch them leave. If something happens that prevents that, then we're going to kill them." She stared at Hart when she added, "You okay with that?"

"Yeah," Hart said.

"You might know some of them. Riley said he knew the ones that were on the way here now."

"I do, too, but that won't keep me from doing what I have to do."

"Good."

"What about me?" Terry asked.

"I need you to get people out here and clean up the blood and"—she looked back at Andy's corpse, left where he had fallen—"the rest of this mess." She glanced up at the crane and shielded her eyes against the sun. "Is he up there? Peters?"

"Only Peters could have made that shot," Hart said.

"Tell him to come down," Lara said. "I want to talk to him before Mercer's men show up…"

CHAPTER 17
GABY

DESPITE THE SUNLIGHT filtering into the lobby through the hole in the wall, she could feel the cold seeping through her jacket and the thermal layers underneath. The weight of the ammo around her waist and Benford's M4 with the now-useless M203 grenade launcher helped to (mostly) keep her mind off what was coming very, very soon.

Tap-tap.

The sounds came from behind her, but she didn't react with alarm. There was only one other person moving around in the bank lobby, and that was Danny, who appeared in the corner of her peripheral vision and settled into a crouch on the other side of the hole in the wall.

"How goes it?" he asked.

"Same-o, same-o."

"That bad, huh?"

She smiled. "How'd it go with you?"

Danny had spent the last ten or so minutes in the back, using

Benford's military ham radio to contact the *Trident* and letting their friends know that they were still alive but weren't going to make it for their pickup today. With her attention focused almost entirely on the city outside the bank, she hadn't been able to hear as much of the conversation as she would have liked.

"As good as can be expected," Danny said.

"That bad, huh?"

"And a bag of chips." Danny leaned his carbine on the floor and made sure his jacket's zipper was all the way up to his neck. "The big news of the day is that they ran across some of Benford's friends out there in the Gulf and were pulled temporarily off course."

"Everyone okay?"

"Lara seems to have it all under control. They finally got refueled and could have come and gotten us if we were somewhere gottenable."

Danny opened a bottle of water that he had scavenged from Benford's pack while looking for the radio and took a drink. When he was done, he tossed it across the opening to her. She caught it and took a few sips as he talked.

"But none of what's happening out there's gonna do us any good in here. Probably a given they have the back alley manned and the whole street locked down. Snipers on the rooftops would also be my guess." He leaned out slightly and peered up at the rooftop ledge of Gallant's Best across the street from them. "That's a pretty big clothing store for such a small town. What do you think they sell in there? Cowboy boots? Belt buckles the size of my head?"

"Why, you looking for a belt buckle the size of your head?"

"Hey, accessories make the man. Besides, it's not the taste in fashion that matters; it's how big it is. Or so I've been told."

She finished and tossed the bottle, with still half left, back to him.

"Too bad we couldn't find the key to that Jeep," Danny said, eyeing the parked vehicle on the sidewalk outside.

"Maybe it's in the glove compartment."

"Don't you think ol' Benford would've checked?"

"Possibly."

"Well, finding out for sure would take anywhere from five to ten seconds. Maybe less if I really haul ass and don't do something stupid like slip when I cross the sidewalk. Alas, that's more than enough time even for these wannabe soldier boys to take their sweet time shooting me in the ass."

"They don't want to kill us, remember?"

"Even if they only tried to wound us, all it'd take is one shitty shot and I'm rolling around on the street, clutching my ass."

"What's the preoccupation with getting shot in the ass?"

"It hurts, kid. It really hurts."

"Are we talking from experience?"

He snorted. "Maybe." Then, still looking out at the Jeep, "Look at it."

"What?"

"The Jeep."

"What about it?"

"It's just sitting there, mocking me."

She smiled. "It's an inanimate object, Danny. It's not mocking you."

"It's definitely mocking me."

"You're just imagining things."

"Hunh." Then, looking across at her, "We all clear on the backup plan?"

She nodded. "Retreat into the manager's office with Nate. Seal the door."

"Nothing quite like a last stand in a podunk town."

"I could think of better things to do with my time."

"Well, sure, if you wanna be a Negative Nancy about it."

"Sorry."

"You're forgiven."

He went suddenly very quiet, his eyes never leaving the streets outside.

"What it is?" she asked.

"When I was hanging up, I told Carly that I loved her, and she cried."

"She misses you."

"I mean, yes, she misses me. Who wouldn't? What I meant was, I think she knew the truth even though I tried to bullshit my way through it. That redhead knows me too well. When I said 'I love you,' she started crying and didn't stop before I signed off."

"I'm sorry, Danny."

"Yeah, me too, kid." He glanced back at the offices. "I think it's time to try on some new clothes."

She nodded, picked up the two collaborator uniforms waiting in a small pile next to her, and jogged across the lobby and into the back hallway. The clothes she was carrying were the least bloody ones she could find among the dead; even so, her stomach churned at the thought of having to wear them. But it had to be done. Even if it didn't work *(It has to work)*, they had to try, because what the hell else were they going to do? The only other option was to give up, and there wasn't a single quitter among them.

Nate was sitting at the back of the office when she entered, a large pile of rifle magazines and bullets scattered between his legs. An M4 leaned against the wall next to him and he was wearing one of the collaborator's gun belts.

He looked up when she stepped inside. "Everything okay?"

She nodded. "Time to get dressed."

He looked at the bundle in her hands and sighed. "You know, you used to have such better taste in clothes."

"I don't like it any more than you do."

He caught one of the uniforms she tossed over and grimaced at the sudden movement *(Shit, I forgot; sorry, Nate)*, then wrinkled his nose at the stench of blood clinging to the fabric.

"Try not to think too much about it," she said.

Nate stuck his finger through one of the bullet holes and wiggled it around. "Look at what I can do, Ma."

She rolled her eyes. "Put it on." Then, "You need help?"

"Nah, I mastered changing clothes when I was ten."

"Ten?"

"I was a late bloomer," Nate said, struggling to stand up.

She wanted desperately to reach over and help him but managed to restrain herself. Nate needed to do it himself; even more importantly, he needed to know that he could. Finally, he was able to stand up on both feet—they were a bit unsteady at first, but that went away after a few seconds—and began undressing.

She gave him as much privacy as possible—which wasn't much since they were in the same room together—while changing into her own pair of blood-stained shirt and slacks.

When he was done, Nate sat gingerly back down and pinched his nose. "Ugh. I thought it'd be easier the second time, but not so much."

He was referring to Starch, when they had used a similar tactic to survive the night. The fact that it had worked then was the only thing giving her any hope at the moment.

If it worked once, it should work again, right?

While working on the buttons of her shirt, she sneaked a quick glance across the room at Nate. He looked so much better since a night ago, and all the rest he'd gotten had definitely helped. He was still shaky on his feet and it would take a while before he was even close to being 100% again, but she felt a lot better knowing that he had survived the worst of his wound.

Now all we have to do is survive everything else they're going to throw at us tonight.

She finished with her shirt by pushing the hem into the waistband. It was a little loose everywhere, but it was the best fit she could find.

"Bandages still okay?" she asked him.

He nodded. "You said Danny stitched me?"

"Uh huh."

"He did a pretty good job. It totally doesn't feel like my guts are about to burst out whatsoever."

"Not funny."

"Too soon?"

"Way too soon," she smiled.

"True, though," he said, picking up a magazine from the floor and thumbing rounds into it.

"How's the inventory look?"

"We have eleven magazines for the rifles and thirteen for the handguns. I separated them by caliber," he added, indicating the smaller individualized sections.

"Nicely done."

"Hey, you give me a job, I'm gonna do it gangbusters or not bother at all."

"I never had any doubt."

She walked over and sat down next to him, placing her rifle on the floor within easy reach.

Nate leaned over and sniffed her. "You stink worse than me."

"I'm pretty sure we stink about the same amount."

"Definitely not."

"Whatever."

He pinched his nose again and said, his voice slightly distorted, "I heard Danny on the radio earlier. How's the *Trident?*"

"Better than us right now." She sensed him watching her intensely and turned to meet his gaze. "What?"

"You're so beautiful."

"My nose hasn't healed right…"

"Doesn't matter."

"The scars on my cheeks…"

"I don't care about scars."

"I'm wearing a dead man's clothes…"

"So am I."

"…and covered in his blood…"

"Ditto."

"I haven't showered in days…"

"You smell wonderful."

She gave him a wry smile. "You're too easily pleased."

"Only when it comes to you," he smiled back.

She leaned over and kissed him. His fingers slipped into her hair, and he tugged her closer. She tried to pull away, not wanting to aggravate his wound, but his mouth was so insistent that she gave up and just enjoyed it because, she told herself, this could very well be the last time they had the chance.

"TICK TOCK. TICK tock, goes the clock."

The sun wasn't completely gone, but it had dipped below the rooftop of Gallant's Best, so she couldn't see it anymore. The street outside the bank had darkened enough that she couldn't tell if the Jeep was brand new or scarred by the same explosion that had taken out a large chunk of the wall.

Her watch ticked to 5:13 p.m.

"Time to check under the beds and in the closet for monsters."

She could barely hear Mason's voice with the two-way handheld radio's volume set to almost its lowest setting. Turning it off completely to silence the man's irritating voice was an option, but Mason talking meant Mason potentially giving away something they could use.

"Hear that?" Mason said. "That's the sound of the real world starting to wake up."

She thought she saw shadows moving behind one of the drawn curtains that covered a window along the department store across the street. Or was that just her imagination? How big was that building anyway? Big enough for a few hundred ghouls to be hiding inside right this moment? Maybe more if they crammed into both floors. And why wouldn't they? The creatures couldn't care less about comfort. That was a human thing, and they were well beyond that now.

"You think he knows?" Gaby asked.

"About the uniforms?" Danny said.

She nodded.

He shrugged. "He hasn't mentioned it yet if he noticed, and that guy runs his mouth more than a fat guy on a treadmill in January."

"I'm surprised you haven't made a run for it yet," Mason was saying through the radio. "If I were a betting man—and I've been known to lay a few shekels here and there on the roulette table— I'd put good money on the Ranger taking his chances before the sun sets. Of course he wouldn't have made it, but he'd have gotten an A for effort."

"Oh, for the love of God, shut him up," Danny said from across the blasted opening in the wall. He was almost completely sitting in shadows, and if not for the white clouds of mist forming as he spoke, she wouldn't know where he was.

Gaby reached down and switched off the radio, then picked it up and clipped it behind her belt. A radio was too valuable to just throw away these days, even if the only person on the other side was Mason.

She glanced down at her watch again: 5:15 p.m.

Christ, where did the last two minutes go?

She searched out Danny in the darkness. "I don't think they're coming."

"Doesn't look that way."

Despite every indication that Mason would stay back until nightfall, they couldn't risk retreating into the backroom until they were absolutely certain. The man was a liar, after all, and couldn't be trusted. But now that the sun had all but vanished and she thought she could feel the floor under her vibrating as...*things* began moving across Gallant...

"Time to boogie," Danny said. He got up and began moving backward across the lobby.

She did the same, anxious to get the hell as far away from the opening as possible. But they didn't rush it and backpedaled one step at a time while keeping their eyes on the wall and the doors and windows in front of them. She turned around only when she saw the island counter passing by to her left and rushed after Danny, past the first office (with the bodies, and Fritz), and toward the manager's room in the back.

"Nate," she called.

He poked his head out of the office, his M4 clutched in his hands. "Okay?"

She nodded. "You got guard duty."

"Gotcha."

Nate stepped out into the hallway and stood guard while she

and Danny went all the way to the back and removed the large metal filing cabinet they had helped Fritz put over the alley entrance earlier. They took it into the office, with Nate retreating into the room after them. They closed the door, then leaned the heavy cabinet against it before pinning it in place with the desk.

It was a decent barricade, and if it was just the black eyes trying to get in, she thought their chances were pretty good the door would hold. But that was the problem. She knew very well it wouldn't just be the black eyes. The blue-eyed ones would also be around tonight, just like they had last night, and that time at the farmhouse in Louisiana…

With the door closed, Gaby could barely make out Danny and Nate standing in the room with her. Danny had unslung Benford's pack and was rummaging through it. A few seconds later there was a double *cracking* sound, and two glow sticks gradually filled the room.

Danny's face, suddenly awash in fluorescent green, grinned at her. "And then God said, 'Let there be awesome green disco lights, and so there was.'"

"Not quite sure that's the line," she smiled back at him.

"Eh, I never was much of a church goin' boy."

"Looks good," Nate said, nodding his approval at their handiwork over the door. "Definitely looks like it could last through the night."

"Winter springs eternal, kids," Danny said.

"You don't think so?"

"If it were just those black-eyed bastards? Yeah. But that's not the case, is it?"

I guess I'm not the only one who remembers.

She looked at her watch, the white neon hand more green than white: 5:20 p.m.

IF THEY THOUGHT Gallant was quiet before, listening to the

excruciating silence from inside a small office in the back of a bank surrounded by four walls and a barricaded door was an entirely new experience.

She sat with Nate at the back, with the door in front and to her right. Danny sat to their left in the corner. No one had said a word since they settled down to wait, and as they listened to what Mason called "the real world" coming awake around them, they continued to maintain the quiet, the anticipation of what all three of them knew was coming *(Anytime now, you bastards)* almost suffocating.

The ghouls were out there by the hundreds, maybe the thousands, so why hadn't they begun assaulting the door yet? Despite straining to hear, she couldn't detect them outside in the hallway or the bank lobby. Which didn't make any damn sense at all. They had to know the three of them were in here. Even the black-eyed creatures, with their limited intelligence *(Dead, not stupid, right, Will?)* could trace the new blood from the streets to the gaping hole in the wall and sniff their trail to the back of the building. And if even by some miracle they couldn't, the presence of the blue eyes would make up for it.

"He'll come for them soon."

"Yes."

"And when he does..."

"We'll end him."

"Finally..."

All of this was for one man. Who the hell were they waiting for?

The question turned over and over in her head and had been since last night. Except now it was so much louder and so much more persistent, with nothing for her to do but listen to the silence as she waited and waited for the creatures to show themselves.

What are you waiting for?

She looked over in Danny's direction, his face covered in the green light from the glow sticks. He had his rifle between his legs, the muzzle pointed up at the roof, and was staring at the door across from him. She couldn't tell if he was lost in his own thoughts or if he was just as mystified by the lack of an attack as she was.

She felt welcome warmth as Nate reached over and found her hand and squeezed. "Can't wait to get our own room on the *Trident*," he said quietly.

"It's going to be loud down there with the engine next door," she said, matching his soft pitch.

"Who cares. That's what earplugs are for. Plus, no one will know what we're doing down there. Know what I mean?"

"Not a clue." She kissed him on the cheek, then pulling back slightly, whispered, "I love you."

"Finally," he whispered back. "I didn't think you would ever say it."

She smiled and kissed him again, then rested her head against his shoulder.

"Tired?" he asked.

She nodded. "You?"

"Like every part of me is about to go all *Scanners*."

"*Scanners?*"

"You know, that movie where the guy's head blows up?"

She shook her head.

"We'll add it to the Netflix queue when we get back to the *Trident*," Nate said.

"Deal."

The office looked different swimming in green, almost surreal somehow. Nate slipped an arm around her, and she wanted to close her eyes and forget about what was going to happen in the next few minutes, or hours. But it was going to happen tonight. The blue eyes hadn't gone through all this trouble to forget about them now.

"He'll come for them soon," one of the creatures had said.

He. Who the hell was *he*?

She allowed herself to close her eyes for a moment even as her ears kept listening for telltale signs that the creatures had finally arrived outside their door, or beyond the walls of the bank, or maybe even above them on the rooftop. Except they weren't in any of those places because there was just *dead silence* all around them.

What in God's name are they waiting for?

She had her eyes partially closed and was concentrating on the warmth of Nate's body against hers when there was a massive *boom!* that tore through the room, so close and immediate that her ears were still ringing even as she struggled to open her eyes and *move, move*, move, *dammit!*

By the time she managed to fully open her eyes, green tendrils of smoke were already starting to fill the room at a dizzying speed. Then Danny was shooting, his face lit up by a staccato effect of green and white and orange as flames stabbed from his M4. He had somehow made it onto his feet before either she or Nate could react and was actually pushing his way into the smoke instead of running away from it like a sensible human being.

Since when does Danny qualify as "sensible?" she thought even as she scrambled to get ahold of her rifle, which she had dropped about the same time the explosion knocked Nate's arm from its place around her body.

She wasn't sure when she lost sight of Danny, but one second he was in front of her and in the next breath he had vanished into the spreading green smoke, and the only thing she could make out was the *pop-pop-pop* of his rifle assaulting her ears as the ringing from the explosion subsided. The M4s they were armed with were only capable of three-round bursts, but Danny was squeezing the trigger so fast that they sounded almost like one continuous full-auto blast.

She finally *(finally!)* got her numbed feet under her and scrambled up, gripping her rifle in one hand and shouting, "Stay here!" back at Nate.

He was coughing and trying not to gag against the smoke, but he somehow still managed to flash her a defiant look as he shook his head. "The hell I am!"

"Nate, please!"

"No!" he shouted back.

Loud crackles of gunfire reached them, coming from *the hole in the wall* that hadn't been there before.

They blasted through from the other room. Jesus Christ!

Nate was already on his feet when she began moving forward.

She could hear him coughing behind her as he followed, and Gaby lifted her rifle as—

A figure stumbled through the jagged opening in front of her. He was wearing black and she glimpsed the shiny lens of his gas mask—

She fired, and the man, moving between rooms, fell awkwardly, landing in the middle of the hole with one part of his body in their room and his legs in the manager's office.

How the hell did he get past Danny?

It was impossible not to inhale the smoke—a combination of disintegrated Sheetrock and explosive powder swarming around the opening—and she started to cough along with Nate even as they kept pushing forward.

Questions swirled around in her head as she forced her legs to move:

Why did the collaborators attack? Why risk an explosion when Mason had strict orders to keep them alive? Or had the "him" that the blue-eyed ghouls were waiting for finally arrived, and their usefulness as bait had finally come to an end?

"Danny!" she shouted as she stepped over the dead man and into the connecting room. There had been a lot of smoke in the other office, but there was even more in here, almost as if the collaborators hadn't properly executed their breach.

The only response to her shouting of Danny's name was the *pop-pop-pop* of automatic gunfire coming from outside the room, through the open door to her right.

"Danny!" she shouted as she stumbled over bodies on the floor.

New bodies, and not the ones they had stacked in the back of the room. These were all black, with gas masks jutting out from their faces like plastic elephant tusks.

"Gaby!" Nate's voice, shouting from behind her. "Wait!"

But she didn't wait. She couldn't. Danny was out there by himself, the continued banging of ferocious back-and-forth of automatic rifle fire forcing her to move faster and *faster*.

"Gaby, wait!"

She ignored Nate's desperate plea and finally made it out the door and into the hallway, ready to see caverns of yellow and white and brown fangs coming at her. She twisted right toward the alley door, but it was still closed and there was just suffocating darkness back there. She turned left toward the lobby—

Pop-pop-pop!

A figure was shooting in the direction of the street while backing up toward her. She couldn't tell what kind of clothes he was wearing—it looked dark, either black or blue, so it could have been Danny or a collaborator uniform. After all, weren't they wearing the same colors right now?

She lifted her rifle and took aim when the man threw a glance over his shoulder. She couldn't see his shadowed face, but there was nothing that looked like a gas mask, and that was the only reason she didn't pull the trigger.

"Back, back!" the figure shouted. *Danny!* "We got incoming, kid! A shit ton of incoming!"

She looked past him and saw that something had swallowed up the hole in the front wall of the bank. No, not something, but some *things*.

Oh, so there they are.

She never believed they would make it through the night without the ghouls finding them. It was simply beyond the realm of possibility, the kind of optimism that only the old Gaby could have fallen prey to. And yet, and yet, she had wanted to believe. God, she had wanted to believe so badly.

But the truth stared her in the face as she took in the forest of pruned black flesh and heard their bones *clacking* as they surged through the opening and poured across the lobby floor like an endless ocean wave.

She turned and ran, and heard Danny's footsteps close on her heels.

"Faster!" he shouted. "Faster!"

Up ahead, Nate had finally found his way out of the door, and his eyes widened at the sight of her and Danny racing back to him.

"Nate, run!" she shouted. "They're inside! They're inside the building!"

She saw the whites of Nate's eyes, and he might have screamed something back at her but she couldn't hear, because at that very moment the floor and the walls and the ceiling began vibrating uncontrollably. She heard the very distinct *clink-clink-clink* of empty brass casings (Danny's, the collaborators, whoever's) that were littering the floor began jumping around like beans.

At first she thought they were being hit by an earthquake, but then she heard it, and the sound sent a spear into the very center of her soul. The first time she was introduced to it was on the road, then again later, outside of Larkin. It was a sound that she would never forget for as long as she lived, whether that be the next few seconds, or minutes, or years from now.

Broooooooooooorrrrttttttttt!

CHAPTER 18
FRANK

HE WAS CLOSE. So close. He could almost *feel* them nearby.

Danny and Gaby.

It was a trap. He knew that without a shred of doubt. Danny, Gaby, and the boy whose name he couldn't remember were being used to lure him to the town of Gallant. They knew he would come, that he would have no choice because the (small) part of him that was still human demanded he come.

They were waiting for him. The blue eyes. And they wouldn't be alone.

He knew all these things, and yet he had come because he had no choice. Simply no choice. Because they had Danny and Gaby, and if there was a shred of humanity left in him, he couldn't ignore it.

They were so close and yet so far away. He wished he could pinpoint their exact location, but there was too much chaos inside his mind as well as outside in the physical world. The universe was breaking apart, death pouring from above, and he caught random flashes of memory from faraway places filled with sand where it was hot and cold and sometimes both at the same time.

Somewhere above him, Mercer's warplane shook the heavens as it returned for another pass.

He didn't know how he had gotten here, but he was sure Danny and Gaby were close even as he concentrated on the two black-clad figures, almost indistinguishable in the pitch-darkness of the floor. They were facing the far wall when he crashed through the window and tucked and rolled and snapped back up to his feet. They turned—fast, but not fast enough—and he saw the whites of their eyes shining through the clear glass of their gas masks.

Collaborators. Traitors.

The one on the left was the first to react, and he had almost fully lifted his rifle when his neck snapped. The second one was slower and dropped his weapon and stumbled back in mortal terror. It didn't save him.

He grabbed the man by the uniform and flung him into the wall with one hand. There was a heavy *crack!* as bones shattered and the *thump!* as the limp body slid unconscious to the floor.

He turned his head at the sound of a few hundred stampeding feet surrounding the building outside. They poured themselves into the first floor below him, and more were coming from up and down the streets.

Moonlight glinted off one of the men's fallen rifles, and he picked it up. It had a name. M-something. And a number. He couldn't remember either details at the moment; not that it mattered, because it would come to him.

It always did, eventually.

The air shifted and the familiar gust of wind swamped the walls of the building, signaling the return of another kind of monster— this one made of metal and fire. The wall in front of him exploded, a tsunami of glass and brick and mortar reaching out at him like spidery tentacles. Shards sliced what remained of the trench coat as he lifted his arms to protect himself and spun at the same time, making himself as small as possible.

Then, a second after its armaments had razed the street outside and everything around it, there was the delayed sound of the plane's roar:

Brooooooooooorrrrttttttttt!

He staggered away from the wall—or what was left of it. Blood dripped from his wounds, long pieces of glass jutting out of flesh, an extended gash across his right cheek, and something the size of his fist protruding from his chest. He picked and pulled at shards both big and small, like annoying wood splinters, the *slurp* of his blood spraying the already-filthy carpet.

Thomp-thomp-thomp!

They had finally made it to the second floor and were now racing through the hallway. In a matter of seconds, they would find the right room and overwhelm him.

"He's inside!" the voices shouted. *"Don't let him escape!"*

He didn't have to break his way through the windows this time, because there weren't any left—or even a wall to stand in his way. There was just a jagged hole, and he charged and leapt and shot free like a bullet through it. The cold night air flooded his hyper senses, the shredded remains of his coat snapping angrily like unwanted limbs behind him.

He sailed through the night air, free of the restraints of gravity, even of human logic, the rifle still clutched in his hands. Maybe he had clung to it as a token of his old self, a reminder of what he once was but could never be again.

As he slashed through the night air like a knife, he glimpsed rubble in the streets below. Vehicles had been reduced to junk, the concrete pavement a shell of its former self. The concentrated fire had left behind severed limbs and decapitated forms, still-intact bodies buried under the upended road. A carpet of *(re?)*death as far as he could see, and yet, miraculously, the buildings around the devastated killing field remained mostly intact. Clearly the sign of a highly skilled pilot at work.

Then he was across and crashing into metal scaffolding that was holding a white sign with letters on it. It buckled and snapped, the grinding of metal like nails on a chalkboard in his ears, so loud that no one could have missed it.

Noises—*pop-pop-pop!*—coursed through the soles of his feet like electricity. Gunfire, coming from the building below him.

Then a new noise—*thump-thump-thump!*—racing wildly.

Heartbeats, also from below.

Human heartbeats.

Had he found them after all? Danny and Gaby and the boy whose name he couldn't remember? Were they below him now, fighting for their lives?

He managed a single step toward the edge when the world quaked as half of Gallant vanished in a ball of fire in the distance. Some kind of bomb. The heat washed across the air, forcing him to turn his shoulders against it. Unnatural warmth made his flesh tingle as the dead and dying filled his head with tortured screams, hundreds of ghouls blinking out of existence as flesh was stripped from bones, which were then pulverized into powder milliseconds later.

He managed to quiet the pained voices in his head, the relentless screams, just as the air above him quivered. He looked up as the creature fell down, smashing him with its fists and driving him to the graveled rooftop floor. Blue eyes glared at him as impossibly long, bony fingers tightened around his throat.

"There you are," it said, even though its lips, inches from his own, didn't move. *"We've been looking for you for so long."*

He smashed the weapon he'd held onto since picking it up from the building across the street into the side of the creature's head. The rifle disintegrated like brittle twigs, but it stunned the ghoul just enough to knock it off him.

He sprang up, realizing too late that the monster wasn't alone.

They surrounded him, blocking his paths of escape.

"We knew you'd come," they said, four voices forming one coherent thought inside his head.

"So predictable."

"...so human."

"Look at him..."

"...clinging to the façade."

"Pathetic."

"Now you're going to die."
"Again."
"But this time..."
"...for good."
"And he'll be pleased..."
"...that we finally ended you."
"...so pleased..."

They attacked as one, and from all four sides simultaneously. They were faster than any of the black eyes could ever hope to be, and stronger. So, so much stronger. He didn't have the element of surprise on his side, and there was no advantage to be had. None.

They went for his arms and legs. He managed to dislodge one, but his attempt to punch through its chest went wrong and he only landed a glancing blow.

His left arm had been grabbed and bent at an impossible angle, and he heard the *crack!* of bone breaking but didn't feel it. Somehow he fell on one knee, then both, and a hand seized his throat before the grip became a forearm pressed against his neck, searching for and finding a hold that refused to yield.

"You shouldn't have come," they said inside his head.
"But we knew you would..."
"...knew you would."
"They'll be the death of you..."
"...again."
"They're only human..."
"They were made for this..."
"...destined..."
"They're chattel..."
"...meat..."
"...storage..."
"Let it go."
"Stop fighting."
"Why are you still fighting?"
"You have no idea how long..."
"...he's been planning this..."
"It's all part of the plan."

"Accept it."
"Accept it!"

He somehow ended up staring at the sky. It was a strangely bright night, and the wind was cool against his flesh. He closed his mind from the pain as two of them pulled at his arms while a third, behind him, put pressure on his head until his neck was straining and he could feel the muscles stretching beyond their limits, hear the tendons tearing one by one, by one…

"It's over," they said.
"This is how it ends."
"She wasted her life to turn you…"
"…such a mistake…"
"…remedied, now…"
"Thank her when you see her again."

He refused to think of her. She was gone. Dead *(again)*. Outside a gas station somewhere unimportant. Ironic that his last breaths would also happen on the rooftop of a building somewhere unimportant.

But he didn't give in. It wasn't in his nature.

"Still fighting," they said.
"Give in…"
"…this is the end…"
"…inevitable."
"It's all part of the plan…"
"His plan…"
"…give in!"

Lara, he thought, his mind's eye filling with memories of her. Images and sounds and sensations that he had held onto even though doing so weakened him and kept him unsure and hesitant. But he couldn't let go because it was her. It was Lara. The natural and crystal blue of her eyes, always so full of life even at her lowest moments. The smooth touch of her skin and the warmth of her breath against his neck as they lay together.

The best nights of his life.

The best days.

Because she was there.

Lara.

Lara…

I've failed you.

Again.

Forgive me.

Forgive me…

Then something strange—a sudden uptick in the cold followed by the loud scream of metal piercing air.

Then something heavy falling from the sky.

Plummeting faster, faster, *faster.*

"No," they said inside his head. *"No!"*

Yes, he thought, and closed his eyes as the heat of the expanding blast absorbed the buildings around him and the solid rooftop under him disintegrated and he tumbled, out of control, into a black void as his skin burned and peeled and screams from a hundred—a *thousand*—creatures filled his mind in a tsunami of pain and horror and, oddly enough, sweet release…

BLUE EYES PEERED at him, but the shape was all wrong. *Everything* about it was wrong. It wasn't thin enough and the smell coming off it was sweaty, dirty, and greasy, but not the chaos of cold and heat coexisting. Warm air flowed forth as it breathed in and out with some difficulty, the weapon clutched in one hand and draped over its knee almost *too* casually.

"Man, talk about dropping in without calling first," it said.

No, not an *it*.

A *he*.

"Good thing we were in the other room when you showed up. Of course, you guys made a real mess, but I'll let that one slide since I don't think it was you that dropped the bomb. Or da bomb, as the kids say. On the plus side, you also buried all the corpses we had piling up in here, so thanks for that. They were becoming a real eyesore."

It was a man and his voice was…familiar.

"It wasn't easy, you know. I was *this* close to putting a bullet in your head and calling it a day," the man said, pinching his forefinger and thumb together. "That trench coat—or what's left of it—saved your life. Where do you do your shopping anyway, and do you get a discount if the stuff is only thirty—excuse me, I meant, ten—percent intact?"

The part of him that still recognized pain had shut down. It was an automatic response by his mind to spare the rest of him so he could keep functioning. He couldn't turn his head, but he could sense the other blue eyes around him. Two of them. Except there was no cold or warmth coming from their skins, and their accusing voices had quieted inside his head.

They were gone. Dead. *(Again?)*

Thick, coagulated black blood covered the parts of his body that he was still able to retrieve sensations from. He was gashed and bleeding, even in the areas that he couldn't see, and partially buried in rubble from the stomach down. Only the top half of him had been spared the crushing weight of the building as it came tumbling down after the concussive force of the blast took apart its roof. Massive blocks of concrete made a prisoner out of him, and he was certain his arms were no longer connected to his pulverized shoulder joints. His legs…no, he would have to turn the pain receptors back on to find out what had happened to them.

He couldn't turn his head because it was twisted to one side, his chin resting against a drooping shoulder. The muscles and tendons along his neck had been severed, pulled until they snapped.

He was hurt. Badly.

The man crouched in front of him was gesturing with the gun. "Bullet to the head. Kind of a gyp, don't you think? You're faster, stronger, all kinds of crazy comic book supervillain shit, but all it takes is one little ol' bullet to the ol' noggin and you're kaput. Doesn't even have to be silver."

He was alive. Why was he still alive? Because the man had chosen not to end him, even though he could with a simple *(so simple)* pull of the trigger. A slight pressure and it would be over, along with all the nights of stalking Mabry, finding his weaknesses, looking for the perfect angle to attack.

"In case you were wondering, yes, it looks like you've seen better days," the man said. "I'd say you look like shit, but that would be an insult to poop everywhere."

The man had mischievous blue eyes, and blond hair matted with dirt and sweat stuck to his forehead. Streaks of dried blood stretched from his right temple to his chin and curved around cracked lips. There was blood in the air. A lot of it. Old and fresh. The man was bleeding from multiple wounds. Painful, but not life-threatening. At least, not anymore. Medical ointment tingled his nostrils.

They were inside a partially darkened room, half of it lit by streams of moonlight invading from the gaping holes above them where the roof used to be. He reached out with his mind, but his range was limited in his current condition. It turned out he didn't have to go very far after all.

There. They were outside the building. Immediately outside. Tens of hundreds, possibly thousands. They could sense his presence in return. Not just him, but the other blue-eyed ghouls, too. The two lifeless ones buried with him, and somewhere out there, two more. Not dead, but close. Dying.

The black eyes would not come in. They were confused and *scared*.

The man was still looking at him, the sparks of curiosity evident in his eyes. "You know, don't you? They were out there beating on the door until you and your pals started dancing around up on the roof. Then they retreated back into the street. Not that I'm complaining, mind you."

He didn't answer. He wanted to, but when he sent the command, his mouth wouldn't move and no sounds came out, not even the hiss that he despised so much.

"Ah, sorry about that," the man said. "Forgot to tell you, but you don't really have lips anymore. Or a mouth, for that matter. I guess you're going to have to grow them back, huh? *Can* you grow them back?"

He blinked, and the man actually smiled.

"She wanted me to shoot you in the head," the man said. "We've had a recent history of not shooting people when we should have, so I don't blame her. But I had to know." He leaned in closer. "Can you hear me in there? Blink twice for *yes* and, well, I guess you wouldn't blink if you can't understand me, right?"

The man stared at him, and there was a slight uptick in his heartbeat. He was anxious.

So he blinked once, then a second time.

"So you can hear me. Hot damn!" He rocked back on his feet. "What number am I thinking of?" A chuckle. "Just joshin' ya, buddy. Or am I? You guys are psychic, right?"

He didn't blink.

"No?"

He remained still, eyes fixed on the man's beaten and bruised face.

"Just a bit?"

The man sat down on the floor, the gun in his hand still draped nonchalantly over one bent knee. He could smell the fresh gunpowder in the air. All it would take was a shot to the head, just like with the other two dead blue eyes.

"You were there, in Starch," the man said.

Starch? Yes, he remembered. It was a town not far from here, and of some significance to him. Or was it? His mind was stuck between trying to battle the pain and digging deep for memories that were slippery to the touch.

Starch. Yes.

He blinked twice.

"What about outside of Larkin? In the airfield hangar? Did you have something to do with that, too?"

Airfield? Hangar? He didn't recall a Larkin. But then his recollection was unreliable at the moment in his fugue state.

"No?"

No? Yes? He wasn't sure. With parts of his mind shut down to prevent the pain overload, it was hard to concentrate. There was a way to remember, but it would hurt. It would hurt a lot.

"What are you doing?" Was that concern in the man's voice? "Pain's finally pulling into the station, huh? And here I thought you guys didn't feel pain anymore. I guess it's true what they say—you do learn something new every day."

Yes. Pain. A lot of it. And there was going to be more as he released the clamps that kept them at bay and his body began to burn. It started as small sensations, like tiny flickers of fire being lit before growing in intensity and beginning to flood the rest of him one brutal inch by brutal inch.

But at the same time the fog began to lift and memories returned, and while he still had great difficulty sifting through them and recognizing what he was looking at, it became easier with every passing second.

"Hey, you going to die on me or what? Um, again?"

The events of tonight returned.

Then last night.

All the way back to a fortnight.

No, too far.

Back, back…

The pain. God, the pain…

Yes, Larkin. The airfield. The hangar. In the room…

The pain!

He blinked twice.

The man raised both eyebrows. "Well, slap me on the ass and call me Sally." Then, leaning forward again, "Who the fuck *are* you, buddy? *What* are you?"

He didn't answer. He couldn't. He knew who he was, but he had no voice and no ability to respond in any meaningful way. So he remained silent even as flames roared through him like lightning, scorching everything in their path. It was unlike anything he had experienced since the transformation, and he hoped never to face it again.

Slowly, very slowly, he attempted to push them down, shutting off the pain receptors one by one by one…

"I guess that was a stupid question," the man said. "You not having a mouth to answer with and all."

No mouth. No lips. Or tongue. Could he regenerate a tongue? Maybe. He would find out soon enough.

"Do you know me?" the man asked, his blue eyes watching him intently as if they could look into his soul.

Soul? Did he even have a soul anymore—

Wait. What did the man ask?

"Do you know me?"

Yes. He knew him.

Didn't he?

Yes, it was in there somewhere, hidden in the deeper recesses of his mind. He had refused to let them go in all the weeks and months since she changed him. It was buried deep and stored at the very bottom where everything important resided. He didn't go to them often because they were dangerous. Remembering the past, remembering *her*, was dangerous.

But he dug through them now. Searching, searching…

There.

He blinked twice.

"You know my name."

He remained still.

"You know me, but you don't remember my name?"

Two blinks.

"I don't know if I should be insulted by that. I'm guessing I should, just a little."

Crunching sounds before a second figure appeared behind the first. The newcomer was tall and slim. Despite the blood and sweat and dirt, the natural smell of a woman clung to her skin. Where had she come from?

"Are you done with it?" she asked. There was something in her voice—traces of fear and anger and…disgust? "Just put it out of its misery. Do they even still feel pain?"

"Apparently they do," the man said.

"Shoot it and get it over with."

"He knows me."

"What?"

"He knows me," the man repeated. "He was at Larkin. And

Starch."

"The one at Larkin looks nothing like this one. It had black eyes, remember?"

"I know, but it says it was there. And I believe it."

"You *believe* it? Danny, for God's sake, *look at it.*"

Danny.

The name was like precious cargo rising to the top of his mind after being buried in the ocean for a millennia. He grasped desperately for it and held on, afraid it would slip out of his reach. It was important, this name.

Danny.

"Sua Sponte."

"Rangers lead the way."

"Not yet," the human named Danny said. "I don't know what'll happen if I shoot it."

"It'll die," the woman said. Her name eluded him, but it was familiar, and down there somewhere, too.

Danny…

"Yes, it will," Danny said, and turned to look at her, "but I don't know what that'll do to all the party people standing outside our walls right now."

The woman shot a quick, nervous glance across the room. He didn't know what she was looking at.

"I'm more concerned with our lack of a full roof at the moment," Danny said, pointing at the open holes in the ceiling above him.

"You think they'll come in if it dies?"

"I don't know. That's the point."

"So what, then?"

Danny looked back at him and tilted his head slightly to one side, as if trying to mirror his unwitting pose.

"Danny," the woman (girl?) said. "What are you going to do with it? We can't just leave it there. What if it digs itself out?"

"I don't think it can."

"You sure about that?"

"Mostly sure."

"Have you been…talking to it?"

"Yes and no. It's been mostly a one-way conversation with a few blinks thrown in. Might be worth waiting for it to grow its mouth back so we can have a proper tête-à-tête."

"Can it…do that?"

"I have no idea what it can or can't do. That's one reason I haven't sent him to the big Blue Yonder yet. Maybe we can learn something from him. If that's even possible; I don't want to just throw the opportunity out the window."

"'Him?'"

"What?"

"You just called *it* 'him,' Danny."

"Did I?"

"Yeah…"

"Well, technically I'm not wrong. It was a him, once upon a time."

"But not anymore."

"That boat would seem to have sailed a while ago, yup."

The girl shivered in the darkness. "Are you just going to sit here all night and talk to it?"

"That's the general idea. You should go keep Natmillian company. I'll shout if I need a hand."

The girl turned to leave, but not before looking back at him one last time. Then she was gone and he heard whispers, followed by the presence of a third heartbeat somewhere outside the room that he hadn't noticed earlier because of his weakened state.

Danny had moved closer while he wasn't paying attention and was now peering at him. There was a new intensity in his eyes as he stared, as if he was searching for something important.

What was he looking for? More importantly, what did he expect to find? What was there left *to* be found? What if all Danny saw was a lifeless corpse that refused to die, with an empty black hole where a soul used to be—

"Jesus Christ," Danny said, his voice barely rising above a whisper.

Then, as if he was afraid to say the word out loud:

"Will?"

BOOK THREE
SHOOT THE MESSENGER

CHAPTER 19
KEO

ONCE IN THE boat and on their way, Keo paid attention to his surroundings for the first ten or so minutes, but after a while his mind started to wander. After all, there were only so many identical stretches of ocean you could stare at until it got old real fast, which in Keo's case was around the twenty-or-so-minute mark.

Instead, he spent his time observing Erin, Troy, and the other four in the boat with him. The only time they stopped was to pour gas into the boat's tank from the generous supply they had brought with them. Keo couldn't begin to guess where they were headed, though he'd never thought of The Ranch as being out in the middle of the Gulf of Mexico. Just the name alone had him envisioning fields of grass and grazing cattle and possibly a horse or two. But no, they were definitely heading farther and farther out to sea.

Maybe The Ranch was a submarine or a ship. Maybe even one of the many Navy destroyers or aircraft carriers that no one had seen since The Purge. What about an adrift oil tanker being commanded by a one-eyed maniac? The possible identity of The Ranch became more elaborate as the sights *(What sights?)* around him remained the same and boredom set in again.

Keo sat at the stern of the offshore vessel with his hands and legs duct taped, empty red gasoline cans tapping against his boots as the boat moved against the waves. They had restrained his legs only after he had climbed onboard, as if he could escape with his hands bound. He wasn't even sure he could swim if he fell overboard. How long could he tread water before he succumbed to fatigue and drowned? He was a good swimmer, but he wasn't *that* good.

The good news was that he had stopped bleeding and no longer needed a wad of paper stuffed up his nostrils. His exposed forehead and nose had gone mostly numb from the chill of the winds plastering him nonstop. He would have liked a painkiller or two to dull the remaining pain, but that wasn't one of the options offered up by his captors. Which was to say, they didn't offer up any options whatsoever.

Troy and Erin sat on both sides of him on raised chairs, while the unnamed two that had come with him from Texas sat on a bench at the front. No one had said a word since they cast off, and the only noise was the wind roaring in Keo's face. Although they had been traveling for some time, it didn't look as if they had made any progress. Of course, that could have just been because the damn scenery never seemed to change.

Eventually the never-ending blur of ocean and nothingness took their toll, and Keo stopped fighting the boredom and closed his eyes, only to wake up with a start when a hand pushed at his shoulder. He opened his eyes to the sight of Erin leaning in front of him with what almost looked like a smile.

"What?" he said, shouting over the wind to be heard.

"First and last warning," she shouted back. "You nod off and fall overboard, and we're not stopping to fish you out. Without your arms and legs, I'm guessing you'll sink right to the bottom."

"Unless the sharks mistake you for snacks first," Troy said.

"Might be the most merciful thing. I hear drowning sucks."

"Sharks, huh?" Keo said.

"It's an ocean, numbnuts. There are sharks and a lot of other things out here you don't wanna come face-to-face with."

Keo stared at Troy for a moment, wondering if the man actually believed that or if this was just a bad attempt at intimidation. He decided it might have been a little of the former and a lot of the latter.

Troy grinned, proving him correct. "Just fucking with you, Bruce."

"Bruce?" Keo said.

"He thinks you're Chinese," Erin said. "Bruce Lee?"

"I've been mistaken for worse."

"Like what?" Troy asked.

"A guy named Fred who I used to know back in the day."

"What's so bad about Fred?"

"That's what Fred asked himself every day."

Troy gave him a puzzled look.

Erin flashed Keo another almost smile. "Give him a minute. Troy can be slow on the uptake sometimes."

"Fuck off," Troy said, and turned back into the wind.

Keo took a second to scan his surroundings in case things had changed since he last had his eyes open. He shouldn't have bothered. There was still just water—lots and lots of water—shimmering underneath the afternoon sun.

"Almost there," Erin said, as if reading his mind.

"The Ranch?" Keo asked.

"Not yet."

"So, what's 'there?'"

"You'll find out when we get there."

Keo looked ahead, and he didn't see anything but an empty horizon and an endless field of blue water. "I don't see anything…"

"It's out there."

"And what's going to happen when we get there? Are you going to kill me, Erin?"

"That's not my call."

"Whose call is it?"

"You'll find out."

"When we get there."

She nodded. "That's right."

Keo sat back and checked to make sure his jacket's zipper was done all the way up to his neck. It might have been his imagination, but he swore it had gotten a lot colder since he was last awake.

"I don't think Troy likes me," he shouted to Erin.

This time she came so close to a smile that Keo decided to go ahead and call it one anyway, as she said, "Whatever gave you that idea?"

IT WAS AN oil rig in the middle of the Gulf of Mexico.

Keo had to admit, of all the possible locations for The Ranch he had considered, an oil rig had never occurred to him. Though, as he stared at the gray concrete foundations and yellow stripes crisscrossing the platforms, he thought it made perfect sense. It was isolated and surrounded by water, and even if it ever came under attack by collaborators, you wouldn't need that many people to defend it. In fact, he counted at least a half dozen locations where snipers could hold off an assault force by inflicting enough damage to dissuade them. The crane sticking out of the side of the massive structure was one of those places.

Keo looked over at Erin. "The Ranch?"

"No. Just the 'there' before the real 'there,'" Erin said. "It's called the *Ocean Star*, and it's just a waypoint station." She kicked at one of the empty cans near his feet. "We need to refuel."

"So *not* The Ranch."

"I guess you're not as dumb as you look," Troy said.

"A lot of people would disagree."

"I bet."

"Give it a rest," Erin said. "You two sound like an old married couple."

"I call groom," Keo said.

Erin ignored him and climbed off her raised chair and walked the short distance to the center, where the two men who had picked them up stood at the helm. The rushing wind prevented Keo from hearing what they were saying, not that he needed to know to get the gist of it. They were going to dock underneath the oil rig.

"City on the sea," Erin said as she walked back to him. "That's what they call these things. They'll be here long after we're gone. Of course, by then the birds will have taken over. At least that way they won't be a total blight on nature."

Keo glanced up at a flock of birds flashing by overhead, making a straight line for the metal structure in the near distance.

"How many of these do you guys have out here?" he asked Erin.

"Need-to-know," Erin said.

"That's why I asked. I need to know."

She smirked and grabbed her things off the floor and slung her pack while Troy did the same on Keo's other side. Neither one looked nearly as impressed as he had been with the rig's continually growing size, which told him they had been here before. Likewise for the four in front of him as they guided the boat under the *Ocean Star* and prepared to dock.

"Am I going up there, too?" Keo asked.

"Unless you'd rather wait for us down here," Erin said.

"The weather's nice, and maybe I can borrow a fishing pole, get us some chow while you guys go do your thing up there."

"Kind of you, but I'm going to have to insist you come up with us. Don't worry; they have a brig where we'll stow you while we go about our business."

"Okay, but when we run out of food, remember I offered."

"I'll keep that in mind," Erin said.

THEY HAD TO free his legs so he could move on his own power up the stairs, his footsteps, along with Erin in front of him and Troy behind him, *clanging* with every step. A variety of birds perched along the railings of the structure watched them pass by, seemingly oblivious to human presence. For every one that was awake, he saw two or three that were asleep.

"Who's up for bird soup tonight?" Keo asked.

"Do you ever shut up?" Erin, walking a few steps in front of him, asked.

"Can't help it. I tend to talk a lot when I'm being led to an interrogation and possibly death."

"It doesn't have to be that way."

"No?"

"You could always join us."

"I would if you told me who or what you people are."

"Because you don't already know," she said, and though he couldn't see her face, he imagined her smirking when she said it.

"I get the feeling you don't believe me, Erin."

"Whatever gave you that idea?"

"Man's intuition."

"I've never heard of that one before."

"It's like woman's intuition, except manlier."

"Ah," she said, and turned a corner and kept ascending.

"What are the chances I'm going to survive The Ranch?" Keo asked, following her around the bend in the stairs.

He was surprised Troy hadn't intruded on his back-and-forth with Erin yet. As far as he could tell, the man was still back there, close enough that Keo considered spinning around and going for his gun. Worst-case scenario, they'd both go over the railing and into the water, which would undoubtedly spell death for him with his hands still tied. Then again, what did he have to lose?

"That depends on what you say," Erin was saying in front of him.

"I don't know anything," Keo said.

"I didn't say you did. I said it's going to depend on what you *say* when you're presented with the questions."

"Well, at least the truth is on my side."

"Right," Erin said. "You just keep clinging to that, Keo."

A man appeared above them—forties, broad-shouldered, with grays in his hair. He wore the same black uniform and tactical vest as the two that had helped them dock below the rig. Keo looked for a name tag but didn't see one on the newcomer, either.

"Welcome back," the man said, extending a hand to Erin.

She shook it. "Thanks, Hart. Where's Riley?"

"He came down with a cold," the man named Hart said. "Stuck in bed, so I'm running the show until he gets back up on his feet."

"He okay?"

"It's a cold. He'll get over it."

"You guys have a doctor onboard, right?"

"George. He's a vet."

"Same difference," Troy said, piping up for the first time.

Hart gave a slightly weird smile. "Yeah. George's come in real handy lately."

The older man stepped aside to let them up onto the highest deck of the oil rig. The wind picked up noticeably, and the first thing Keo observed as soon as he climbed up was just how bright it was up here, with nothing but open skies above him.

He expected to see people around, but there were only a couple of men with slung rifles standing guard along the edge of the platform to his left. One of them was leaning against a chipped railing and the other one was absently chewing something. They wore the same attire as Hart, which weren't uniforms exactly, but close enough. Both guards looked oblivious to their arrival.

Machinery outnumbered people on the top deck, with the derrick sticking out from the center in front of them and the even taller crane lording over everything. Keo stared at the towering structure for a moment, trying to spy the lookouts he knew had to be up there. After all, you didn't take over a place like this and not make use of its best assets.

"You returning to The Ranch?" Hart was asking Erin as he led them across the platform.

"For now," Erin said. "All the teams will be returning one by one, so you're going to be pretty busy for a while. Richards and José are downstairs refueling; when they're done, they'll be heading back to shore to pick up more people. That means I'm going to need one of your boats to continue on."

"Sure, no problem. How are you for supplies?"

"We'll fill up what we need, but it shouldn't be too much. What about you?"

"The pantry's fully stocked, so no worries. How's the war going out there?"

"It's…going."

"Is that good or bad?" Hart asked.

"I guess it depends on your perspective," Erin said.

Hart glanced back at her, apparently not quite sure how to take her response. Keo shared his confusion.

"I guess it depends on your perspective"? Keo thought.

"Casualties?" Hart asked.

"Maybe more than we'd like," Erin said, and looked over her shoulder at Keo. "You wanna add something?"

"I'm just a tourist," Keo said. "I don't know anything."

"Who is he, anyway?" Hart asked. "Why is he tied up?"

Erin turned back to Hart. "The better question is, where is everyone?"

"Huh?" Hart said.

"The last time I was here, there were kids running around. Where are all the civilian workers, Hart? Don't tell me they all caught a cold, too."

She stopped suddenly, and Keo had to do the same or he would have bumped into her. Erin's right hand drifted uncomfortably close to her holstered sidearm while behind Keo, he heard Troy shuffling his feet and the sound of a safety being *clicked* off.

Uh oh.

Hart, realizing that the party had stopped, did too, and turned around.

"Well?" Erin said. "Where are all the civilians, Hart?"

The older man looked past Erin and at Keo. No, not at him,

but at Troy standing over Keo's left shoulder. Unlike Erin, whose rifle was slung over her back, Keo knew for a fact that Troy had his cradled in front of him the entire time they'd walked up the stairs.

"They're inside," Hart said, shifting his eyes back to Erin. "There's no work to be done out here right now."

"You sound a little nervous, Hart," Erin said. "Why are you so nervous?"

"I'm not."

"Bullshit," Troy said behind Keo. "You're definitely nervous."

Hart shook his head and attempted a smile, but it came out so badly that Keo thought, *And things were going so well, too.*

"You're being paranoid," Hart said. "Relax. There's nothing going on. Just calm *down.*"

Hart was still talking when Keo glimpsed black-clad figures moving in the corner of his left eye. It was the same two guards that had greeted them when they first stepped onto the platform. Keo hadn't noticed before, but the men had been shadowing them this entire time while keeping their distance. They were now moving toward them, and one of them had begun to unsling his rifle.

Oh man, here we go!

Before Keo could do or say anything, things went from bad to *absolutely fucked* when two shots exploded behind him *(Goddammit, Troy, you fucker)* and the guard reaching for his rifle stumbled and fell as his partner scrambled to get his own rifle free. The guy was simultaneously too slow and in too much of a hurry, and it was like watching a bad comedy routine as he fumbled with the deadly weapon.

Keo waited for Troy to finish the poor sap off when something slammed into him from the front and knocked him backward. He grunted when his back crashed into the hard steel floor and pain stabbed through him, but it was nothing compared to the heavy weight of another person landing, then moving frantically on top of him.

Who the hell? he thought when a third shot rang out and a body collapsed in a pile next to him.

It was Troy, his rifle somehow still clutched in his hands. Blood gushed out of a hole in his chest where the bullet had exited after it had punched through the back of his throat. The chances were pretty good poor Troy was dead before he even hit the deck.

Keo didn't have a lot of time to think about Troy's last seconds of life because the weight on top of him suddenly lifted and he could breathe (and move) again. It was Erin *(?)*, and she had rolled off him and scrambled to her knees as two more men in tactical vests appeared out from behind the machines and surrounded her, their rifles pointing at her head.

"Don't shoot!" someone shouted.

It was Hart, who for some reason was on the floor too, and was slowly picking himself up. What was Hart doing off his feet in the first place?

It took about two seconds for Keo to gather the evidence and play the scenario out in his head: The body that had knocked him down was Erin's, and someone had to have done the same to her. That someone was Hart, who had barreled into Erin and drove her into him.

"Don't fucking shoot!" Hart shouted. He lifted one open palm toward the sky—no, not the sky, but at the towering crane.

I knew there was a sniper up there.

But sniper or not, it didn't stop Erin from wrapping her fingers around her holstered sidearm. Keo thought about rolling away and getting out of the line of fire, but that might just end up drawing attention to himself. And right now, he didn't want to make any sudden moves, especially since the two newcomers and the third remaining guard had their rifles pointed at Erin, and all three looked a little nervous.

Oh, who was he kidding? They looked a *lot* nervous.

Keo sat very still on one knee and barely breathed. He had never felt so vulnerable in his life—unarmed and with his hands bound in front of him, and Troy's blood, bright under the sun, oozing along the ridges in the floor around him.

What to do, what to do?

"Erin, don't," Hart was saying. He was clearly trying his very best to stay calm but was only partially (if Keo was being generous) successful. "Take your hand away from your gun, Erin. Don't draw that sidearm!"

It was bad enough Keo was helpless and trapped in the midst of a situation that was borderline FUBAR. He also didn't have a clue what was happening, and that might have been the more aggravating part.

Wasn't the *Ocean Star* a part of Mercer's group? Didn't Erin say they were coming here to refuel and resupply before continuing on to The Ranch, wherever the hell that place turned out to be? Both she and Troy hadn't looked nervous at all as they approached the rig, clear signs that they didn't see *this* coming, either.

Man, I'm so confused right now.

"Erin!" Hart said—he was almost shouting now for some reason. "Don't do it! Riley wouldn't want you to do this!"

"Riley?" Erin said, and though Keo couldn't see her face because he was behind her, he could hear the confusion in her voice. "Is he dead?"

"No," Hart said. "But he's been shot."

"Shot? By who?"

"It's a long story," Hart began to say, when Keo thought, *Fuck me*, because he could see Erin's fingers tightening around the gun and saw the slight hitch in her elbow as she began to draw the weapon.

He slammed into her from behind, catching her almost in the small of her back with his shoulder, and knocked her off her knees and threw her back onto the deck. Her hands had abandoned the gun in order to stop her fall and Keo spilled on top of her, hearing her scream as his weight drove her chest-first into the steel floor.

He felt like laughing—wasn't this what had just happened to him?

One good turn deserves another, pal!

He rolled off Erin's back and scrambled to his knees but didn't get any farther because the muzzle of a rifle was pointing right in his face from just a foot away. Worse than that, the eye looking at him from behind the iron sight of the weapon was blinking so rapidly Keo was afraid it might explode at any second.

Keo stared back at the man and said, stretching the words out as far as they would go, *"Don't...pull...that...trigger."*

The man kept blinking and a bead of sweat dripped down his forehead despite the cold wind. But he didn't shoot.

"Jesus Christ," Hart said from behind him. When Keo looked over his shoulder at the older man, he said, "You almost got yourself killed, you dumb bastard."

"Yeah, well, it was either that or let her draw," Keo said.

Hart turned to Erin as two of his men pulled her up from the deck. Her face was flushed red and she blew hair out of her face while they twisted her arms behind her back and zip-tied them.

She looked away from Hart and at Keo and actually snarled at him. "I'm going to fucking kill you."

"Hey, I saved your life," Keo said.

"What?"

"I saved your life."

"You were saving your own hide!"

"You say tomato, I say potato. Same difference."

"I should have let Troy throw you overboard like he wanted to."

Keo glanced back at Troy's lifeless corpse.

Jesus, what a shot.

He turned back to Erin. "Troy and I were best friends; he'd never do that. But let's not get bogged down with the past, huh? We're both alive, and that's all that counts."

"Who the hell are you, anyway?" Hart said, staring at Keo.

"Keo."

"Kay?"

"Keo."

"What, like the car?"

Keo grinned. "I've been called worse."

CHAPTER 20
LARA

"SMALL WORLD," KEO said when he saw her walking through the door.

"Getting smaller all the time," she said. "What happened to your face?"

"Ran into a tree."

"Why didn't you go around it?"

"It was a very big tree."

"I'd ask if you've ever been in a jail cell before, but I think I already know the answer."

He grinned at her from the back of the *Ocean Star*'s brig. Except for the still-fresh bruising around his nose and forehead, he didn't look any worse than the last time she had seen him on the beach outside of Sunport. She was surprised, though, that the woman sitting on the bench next to him wasn't Jordan. There were four other men inside the cell with Keo and the woman, but none of them looked familiar, either.

She looked back at Keo. "Wanna tell me what you're doing

here? Besides causing trouble, I mean?"

Keo got up and walked the short distance over, then leaned against the metal bars in front of her. "You know me. Always popping up where you least expect me."

"Where's—"

He shook his head before she could say Jordan's name.

"Bad?" she finished instead.

The grim look on his face was the only answer she needed. Before she could ask any other stupid questions, he said, "I know what I'm doing here—well, sort of—but what are *you* doing here? I was told this was enemy territory, but here you are, not even in shackles."

"Long story," she said.

"Ah, one of those."

"When is it never one of those?" She glanced back at one of Riley's men standing guard at the door behind her. "He's a friend."

The man took out a key and walked over. "Back," he said to Mercer's men. When they had all retreated to the back, the guard opened the cell door with one hand, the other resting on his holstered sidearm.

Keo stepped outside and the man quickly slammed the door shut, locking it again.

"Free at last, free at last," Keo said. He looked back into the cell at the woman. "Sorry about Troy."

The woman glared at him but didn't reply. Not that she had to. Those eyes pretty much said everything she was thinking.

"Her name's Erin, and she's one of Mercer's top guys," Hart had said while briefing her on what had happened on the platform earlier. "She and Riley were there in the beginning with Mercer. Only Rhett and Benford have been with him longer."

"Is that why you were trying so hard to keep Peters from shooting her?" Lara had asked.

"Riley and I know her from way back. There was a time when he actually considered bringing her with us, but she'd gone to Texas before he could make the offer."

Lara looked in at Erin now. Except for the glare she had shot in

Keo's direction, Lara couldn't really read anything else of note on Erin's face. She didn't look angry, exactly, but she wasn't fine with her current circumstance, either.

"Riley knows her longer than anyone," Hart had said. "He really thought she might have come with us if he'd gotten the chance to sell her on the idea."

Riley thought he knew Andy, too, and how did that turn out?

The woman must have sensed her staring, because she looked away from Keo and over at her.

They exchanged a long, silent look before Lara turned back to Keo. "Come on; let's get you cleaned up."

"Are you saying I stink?" Keo asked.

"Are you saying you don't?"

He sniffed himself, then shrugged. "Fair enough."

She led him to the door, then out into the corridor. Lights perched along the edges of the oil rig had turned on automatically at dusk and were now visible through the small windows along the walls.

"How's everyone on the tugboat doing?" Keo asked. He was rubbing his wrists as he walked beside her.

"Complicated," she said. "But we're dealing with it. Wanna tell me what you were doing with Erin and the others?"

"As soon as you tell me how you got so chummy with these guys. As far as I know, they're both Mercer's crew. Only…not, apparently."

She told him about Riley, about his attempt to hijack the *Trident* last night, then his plans to detach himself from Mercer's war and, finally, their agreement.

"He dead?" Keo asked when she was done.

"He's in sickbay with Zoe now. Hart's also there. He wants to talk to you."

"You trust him?"

"He's in over his head, but he's willing to listen. What happened earlier with Erin was my idea; he was just going along with it."

"No. I meant Riley. You trust him?"

"He hasn't lied to me yet."

"As far as you know."

She nodded. "As far as I know. But he hasn't done anything to make me believe he can't be trusted. In fact, he's probably a little *too* trusting for my liking."

"The getting shot by his own people thing."

"Uh huh."

"That's gotta sting." Then, "Where is the *Trident*, anyway? I didn't see it when we were pulling in."

"It's docked on the other side of the *Ocean Star* and out of view."

"Smart."

"We have our moments."

They walked in silence for a moment, before Keo said, "Should I even ask if the Ranger made it back yet?"

She shook her head and sighed. "It's complicated…"

"YOU WANNA DO what?" Hart asked.

"Kill Mercer," Keo said.

"Why the hell would you want to do that?" Hart said. Lara couldn't tell if he was against the idea or just confused by it.

"It's personal," Keo said.

Lara stood between the two men near the door, listening to them going back and forth inside the oil rig's sickbay while watching Zoe check on Riley's vitals across the room. Both Hart and Keo were talking in low voices—or, at least, they had started that way. If Zoe was bothered by the conversation as it grew in volume, she didn't stop adjusting the IV drip connected to Riley's arm to let it be known. Riley was heavily sedated and hadn't woken since they brought him inside the room hours ago.

"Was that what you were doing out there when you got caught?" Hart asked. "Sneaking around, trying to find Mercer?"

"Something like that," Keo said. "I didn't know where he was or even what he looked like, so I had to take more chances than I would have liked."

"How was getting captured going to help you?"

Keo shrugged. "It wasn't my first choice, but it worked out. Erin was taking me to him for interrogation."

"Where?"

"The Ranch."

"You know about that?"

"It's been a topic of multiple conversations I've had with your fellow Mercerians."

"'Mercerians,'" Hart grunted. Lara couldn't tell if he liked the word or found it insulting. Maybe a little of both. "Why didn't they just shoot you on the spot?"

"Only Erin can answer that," Keo said. "She's the only reason I'm still alive now."

"Hunh," Hart said.

"That mean something to you?"

Hart glanced over at her, and Lara could tell he was replaying their last conversation about Erin and Riley. "Maybe," Hart said.

"Tell Keo what you told me," Lara said.

Hart nodded and repeated what he had told her about Riley and Erin, how Riley had almost recruited her, but she left for Texas first. Keo listened silently, processing the new information without interrupting.

"The Ranch is an island called Black Tide," Lara said when Hart was finished. "That's where they were taking you."

"So that's where Mercer will be," Keo said. "Which leaves the obvious question: How do I get there?"

"Reaching Black Tide isn't the problem," Hart said. "I can give you the coordinates, and you could get there by boat with enough fuel reserves."

"What's the security like?"

"That's the good news…"

"Good, I like good news."

"Right now, Black Tide is at its most vulnerable. You won't find a better time to assault the place. With the war in full swing, there won't be enough men left to watch every inch of the place, so you could easily sneak onto it at night."

"So I could just swim ashore with no one the wiser?"

Hart shrugged. "Theoretically."

"I'm a very good swimmer."

"It's true," Lara said. "Keo is half dolphin."

"So about that boat and a map…" Keo said.

"You have your pick of boats; we won't be needing them anyway, thanks to the *Trident*," Hart said. "You can fill it with as much gas and reserves as you need to reach the island. Getting back, well, that's your problem, because we're not going to be here when you come back. That's assuming you make it out of there alive."

"You let me worry about that."

"Can I ask why?" Hart said, looking curiously at Keo.

"Why what?"

"Mercer. Why, and what do you hope to achieve by killing him?"

"Some assholes just need killing," Keo said. "Your Mister Mercer is one such asshole."

"JORDAN," LARA SAID.

Keo nodded and leaned against the railing at the top of the stairs, with the submarine door into the oil rig closed behind them.

"He killed her?" Lara asked.

"Not with his own hands, but he may as well have."

"This war of his…"

"Yeah."

"I'm sorry, Keo. I know you two were close." She paused for a moment, searching for the right words. "I really liked her, even though we only met for a short time."

"She was easy to like."

"When did it happen?"

"After Sunport. We were on our way to T18."

"And Gillian?"

"I don't know. We—I never made it to her."

Keo went quiet and they spent the next few minutes staring silently at the sunless horizon, at the black-and-blue of the ocean *sloshing* under the full moon. Even the wind seemed to have settled down, and she didn't have to zip her jacket all the way up unlike the last time she was out here. She focused on the *Trident*, anchored nearby with just enough of its lights turned on to give its position away.

"What are you going to do after you kill Mercer?" she finally asked.

"I don't know," Keo said. "I haven't thought that far ahead."

I was afraid of that.

"We could use another able body on the *Trident*," she said.

"You got Hart and the other guy."

"Riley hasn't told me where I'm supposed to take them. If we don't like it there, it wouldn't make sense to stay. This alliance of ours might be very short-lived."

"Does Hart know the location?"

"I think so, but he won't tell me without Riley's permission."

"Loyal to the end, huh?"

"Loyalty's a hard thing to find these days."

"And there's the kind that convinces you dropping bombs on pregnant women is perfectly A-OK."

"I didn't say it was always a good thing."

She glanced over at him. There was a single light bulb over the door behind her, and it cast a halo around them. She wished she were looking at the face of someone who expected to come back from his "mission" alive, but she knew better.

"I could really use you back on the *Trident* with me, Keo," she said.

"My greatness precedes me," he smiled, though it wasn't nearly as convincing as his usual smiles.

"It's well deserved."

"I knew you secretly liked me."

"Don't be an ass."

He chuckled. "Just sayin'."

"Come with us."

"You mean after I finish with Mercer."

She shook her head and turned around to look at him. "No. I don't mean that at all."

"What do you mean?"

"Forget Mercer. Come back to the *Trident* with me instead."

"I can't."

"Why not?"

"Because *I can't*."

"At least tell me you're hoping to also stop this war by killing him."

"I could, but it'd be a lie." He looked off at the darkness around the oil rig and gritted his teeth. "There's nothing noble about this, Lara. There isn't a grand plan. There's just me and him."

"You just want to kill him, is that it?"

"Yes."

"That's it."

"That's it."

"Jesus, Keo."

"Yeah…"

She turned away and leaned back against the railing. "Danny's probably dead," she said quietly.

"What?" Keo said, looking over at her for the first time since they stepped outside. "I thought you said he was just having a problem getting back. That's a hell of a long way from 'probably dead,' Lara."

"Carly hasn't stopped crying since he radioed in hours ago. She doesn't think he's going to make it."

"Jesus. What did he say?"

"It wasn't what he said; it's what he didn't say."

"What about the girl and her boyfriend?"

"They're with Danny. If he doesn't make it, I don't think they have much of a chance on their own."

Keo let out a loud, frustrated sigh and laid his forehead against the chipped railing for a moment before lifting it back up, and Lara thought, *Goddammit, girl, you are one manipulative bitch, aren't you?*

"You're putting me in a tough spot," he said.

"I'm asking you to live."

"What makes you think I don't want to live?"

"Cut the crap, Keo. Don't insult me by lying."

He shook his head. "I don't know what you want me to say."

"Say yes to coming back with me and forgetting about Mercer."

"I can't do that. Jordan's dead because of him."

"I'm sorry about Jordan, but there are other people still alive who care for you. Like Carrie. She's been waiting for you."

"You told her I was here?"

"Not yet."

"Good. Keep it that way."

"Why don't you want her to know?"

"I won't be staying long anyway. Plus, I've never been very good at good-byes."

"What about Bonnie?"

"What about her?"

"She likes you, too."

"I don't blame her. I'm fucking handsome, and there's not exactly a lot to choose from these days."

Lara couldn't help herself and laughed softly.

"What's so funny?" he asked, feigning hurt.

"Nothing," she said, and shook her head.

"Besides, you're a tough kid."

"I'm twenty-six going on forty-six."

"Don't be so hard on yourself. You don't look a day over thirty-six."

"I feel it. Every imaginary day of it."

She sucked in a deep, cool breath and looked over at the *Trident* nearby. It wasn't late enough that everyone would be asleep already, so most of the crew were probably gathered in the galley over a late-night dinner and maybe a board game. In her wildest dreams *(nightmares?)* she would never imagine so many people putting their lives in her hands. And why should they? She was a twenty-something civilian with no military training. What the hell did she know about leading people?

Nothing. Not a damn thing. That was always your job, Will.

"If Danny's gone, we're going to need you even more," she finally said. "I can't keep doing this by myself. It's too much."

"You seemed to be doing all right to me. Look, you've even adopted an oil rig."

"Just the people on it…"

"You stuck your neck out for strangers."

"They had something I needed…"

"Now who's bullshitting who?"

The girl's voice on the radio flashed across her mind again, begging for her help…

"Maybe you're right," she said. "Maybe I'm just trying to make up for some bad decisions. So what's your excuse?"

"I'm just tired."

"Tired of what?"

"Tired of fucking everything up that I touch. I'm tired of trying, Lara."

"We're all tired," she said. "I'm tired. Carly's tired. Danny, Gaby, Riley, Hart… We're all tired, Keo. But we push on, because we don't give up. You know who gives up?"

He didn't say anything.

"Assholes," she said.

He smiled. "Assholes, huh?"

"Don't be an asshole, Keo. If you won't stay with us, if you won't come back to the *Trident* with me, at least promise me you're not going out there just to get yourself killed. Tell me you'll at least *try* to make it back, and mean it."

"What if I can't?"

"You can. You just have to make the choice."

"Okay," he said.

"Okay, what?"

"I'll do my best. How's that?"

She nodded. "Good enough."

"Tough oil rig," he said.

She reached over and put her hand over his. He pursed his lips and stared off at the darkness and didn't say anything.

"I'm sorry about Jordan," she said after a while.

"Yeah, me too," he said softly.

CHAPTER 21
KEO

A YOUNG BLOND twenty-something named James led Keo to the *Ocean Star*'s armory, which took them through the civilian area. Kids peeked out of open doors as they walked through the hallway, and Keo saw people packing up their belongings inside rooms.

"Looks like everyone's ready to go," Keo said.

"Never thought it'd happen," James said. "When Riley asked us to join him, I was pretty sure we'd all end up dying out here."

"That's the spirit, kid."

James grinned nervously at him. "You have no idea how crazy all of this is."

"Oh, I think I know a little bit."

"Maybe, but you weren't there in the early days, back when it was just us and Mercer. He saved our lives. If it weren't for him, we wouldn't be here. And now we're betraying him…" He shook his head. "I don't expect you to understand."

I don't need to understand, kid. I just need a clean shot.

"So make me understand," Keo said. "Why is everyone leaving

if all of you owe Mercer so much?"

"Because of Texas. What's happening over there." James actually winced. "I want to have kids one day. Even after everything that's happened, I want to be a dad and raise a family, and I can't do that if I'm a part of what's going on out there."

Kinda late to be jumping ship, isn't it, pal? he thought, but of course didn't say it out loud. Whatever he thought of James or Hart or the rest of Riley's people, Keo had to admit, it took some guts to go against Mercer.

"Looks like you guys are going to make it out of here just fine," Keo said.

"I hope so," James said, "because sooner or later someone's going to figure out what's really happening. No one wants what happened this afternoon to happen again." James gave him a forced grin. "It's kind of being a chicken shit, I know, just running away…"

"Hey, nothing wrong with running. Done plenty of it myself."

"The thing is, it's better than shooting it out with people we've been spending the last year of our lives with. A lot of them are still our friends. I get why they're out there following Mercer. Most of them lost everything, and this is all they have."

"What about you? What did you lose?" Keo asked as they turned a corner.

Apparently they had also left the civilian population behind, because the hallway was almost empty and the only sounds were their footsteps.

"Friends and family, like everyone else," James said. "But I was one of the lucky few; I found someone in all this mess. She's the one who introduced me to Riley, got us here. Faith."

"Not a lot of that going around these days."

"No, I mean, her name's Faith."

"Ah." Then, "What changed her mind?"

"I guess it was me. I was one of the people Mercer sent out there to scout the state. That's how we mapped out the towns for attacks. We knew where they were, got a good idea of their sizes, and even the best attacking options. Me and a lot of other people spent a lot of time out there hiding and reconning."

"You saw the pregnant women."

James nodded. "They were one of the first things we noticed. We snapped a lot of pictures, and they were in a lot of them. And that was it."

"What was it?"

"Faith saw them. The pictures. Everyone did. But it didn't really register until we got closer to R-Day. When the teams started leaving Black Tide Island one by one, it got real real fast. We couldn't avoid it anymore."

"So you joined Riley's crew."

"Basically."

They turned another corner and walked in silence for a while. Keo was thinking the hallway was never going to end until it finally did.

"Here we are," James said.

"Here?"

"What, you expected Fort Knox?"

"I guess not," he said.

Keo exchanged a brief nod with the two guys in tactical vests cradling rifles and standing guard in front of a door. There was nothing to indicate there was an armory behind them. The guards stepped aside, and James stuck a key into a padlock and pulled the door open. Keo followed the young man inside.

The armory was a converted storage closet and wasn't mind-blowingly impressive, but it had a decent selection and there was a lot of everything, more than enough to arm everyone on the rig (including the kids) five to six times over. He wasn't too surprised by the surplus since guns were easy to find if you knew where to look, and Mercer struck him as the type who would know.

A light bulb flickered on above him while Keo looked over his choices. Racks along the walls held automatic rifles and shotguns and shelves housed handguns and ammo while spare gun belts hung from hooks.

"This everything?" Keo asked.

"What, you want more?" James said.

"I was hoping for a little variety."

"Like what?"

"You don't happen to have an MP5SD lying around, would you?"

"I don't even know what that is."

"Heckler & Koch submachine gun."

"Uh, no. What you see is what you get. Sorry."

"Beggars can't be choosers, I guess," Keo said, and grabbed a Sig Sauer P250 and an M4 off the rack. "Silver bullets?"

"For what?"

"Ghouls."

James shook his head. "Not here. Would be nice, though, right?"

"But you know about them?"

"Of course we do. We found out even before Lara sent out her first broadcast. Mercer figured it out."

"So why don't you have silver bullets?"

"Dude, we're in the middle of the ocean. What do we need silver bullets for all the way out here?"

Because you might not always be in the middle of the ocean, Keo thought, but decided arguing with James was pointless and turned his attention back to the rifle instead. "This thing come with any accessories?"

"What are you thinking?"

"Maybe something that goes boom, for instance."

"Hold that thought." James crouched next to one of the shelves and rummaged through the ammo cans and boxes before straightening up with something in his hand. "This do?"

Keo took the M203, a grenade launcher that could be attached to the bottom of his carbine. "I need you to do something else for me…"

"You want a bazooka, too?"

"If you got it. If not, just tell Hart I need to speak to him."

"What about?"

"Erin," Keo said.

HE SHOWERED IN one of the unused crew quarters and didn't bother to look at himself in the fogged-up mirror when he walked past it. The long scar along his cheek tingled after the hot spray, but his nose and most of his face felt better even though he was pretty sure he looked like a big red mess of bruises.

At least you're still alive, pal. That means you can still pop Mercer. If you're lucky, you'll be able to do that with the M203 from a distance.

Lucky, he thought, and couldn't help but smile to himself. After all he had been through, just thinking that he might get lucky was almost worth a long laugh.

He had black clothes laid out on the small bed, with the rifle he'd taken from the armory leaning against the wall nearby. Keo hadn't loaded up on weapons because more guns and ammo weren't going to help him get on Black Tide any easier. Once he accessed the island, he could always acquire more firepower if he needed it.

He had put on the black cargo pants and was pulling on a T-shirt when someone knocked on his door.

"Yeah?" he called.

"It's me," a voice said.

"Give me a minute."

"I'll wait outside."

Keo grabbed the gun belt and slipped it on, then picked up the Sig Sauer P250 from the chair nearby and holstered it. He shoved his feet into fresh new socks and boots and left the rifle behind.

At the door, he looked out at James, waiting outside. "Hart's ready for you," the younger man said.

"What about Erin?"

"She's waiting, too."

Keo nodded and closed the door behind him, then followed James for the second time through the oil rig's long hallways.

"You think she'll do it?" James asked.

"I won't know until I ask," Keo said. "How well do you know her?"

"There were a lot of people on Black Tide, and we never really crossed paths because of our jobs. Also, she's higher up than me."

"I thought you guys don't use ranks."

"You don't need ranks to know who's out of your league. The people Mercer trusts the most he puts in positions of leadership."

"Like Riley?"

"I guess even Mercer makes mistakes."

I'm counting on that.

They entered into the stairwell and made their way up, footsteps *clanging* against the metal steps.

"You're really going to do it, huh?" James asked. "Kill Mercer."

"That's the plan."

"It won't be easy."

"Nothing ever is."

James pushed through another metal door and led Keo out of the stairwell and into another brightly lit hallway.

"It's going to be tough," James said. "Getting on Black Tide is one thing, but getting to Mercer… That's not going to be easy."

"That seems to be the going consensus."

"When I told Faith about what you were planning, she wanted to know if you were crazy."

"What did you tell her?"

"That I wasn't sure."

Keo grinned.

As they walked some more, he could sense the kid was holding something back, so he said, "What is it?"

James hesitated, but finally said, "Truth is, I don't know whether to wish you good luck or not. I mean, what we're doing here, we're betraying Mercer's trust, I know, throwing everything he did for us right back in his face, but still…"

"He saved your life," Keo said.

"Yeah, he did. Faith's, too. Everyone's. If it weren't for him in the early days, we wouldn't be here. We owe him everything. In a lot of ways, he's a good man. Maybe even a great man."

"Those pregnant civilians he's murdering out there would disagree with you."

"I know, I know. Believe me, I know. We all know, that's why we're here." The young man shook his head. "Having said all that, I still don't know whether to wish you good luck or not. Sorry."

"Don't sweat it, kid."

"I'm twenty-three," James said.

"Good for you," Keo said.

"I SHOULD HAVE let Troy killed you," Erin said.

Keo smiled at her. "You said that already."

"It bears repeating."

"Why don't you say it one more time so we can put it to bed?"

"I should have let Troy killed you."

"Happy?"

"No."

"It'll have to do." Keo looked over at Hart, standing on the other side of the open door. "Can we have some alone time?"

"You sure?" the older man asked. He looked exhausted, and sweat matted his hair to his forehead.

"I'm sure," Keo nodded.

Hart glanced at Erin, sitting on a chair in the middle of the room. Her hands were zip tied at the wrists, but her legs were free. She ignored Hart and concentrated on Keo, and he saw the curiosity in her eyes. She didn't know what was happening, but she wasn't afraid, either.

"James will be outside," Hart said before closing the door behind Keo.

Keo leaned against the wall next to the door and didn't say anything. Erin watched him back intently, maybe trying to read his face for clues.

Finally, he said, "They told me you and Riley were part of Mercer's original Four Horsemen."

"They said that, huh?"

"You and Riley and some guys named Benford and Rhett. At the beginning, they said, there were just the four of you, and you built this army and helped Mercer collect everything he would need to launch this war of his."

"People here talk too much."

"James, the kid standing guard outside, said Mercer's plans didn't feel real until the day the teams started leaving the island. Then he couldn't ignore it anymore. The people in the towns, the pregnant women..."

Erin kept quiet.

"Riley told Hart he considered trying to convince Rhett, but he didn't because he couldn't be one-hundred percent sure."

"Apparently, Riley's one-hundred percent sure isn't so sure after all," Erin said.

"You heard about the shooting, huh?"

"Like I said, the people on this rig talk too much."

"But Riley was pretty sure he could convince you, but before he got the chance, you had already left for Texas."

"Is that what he said?"

"That's what he told Hart. Was he right?"

"Riley hasn't been right about a lot of things."

"I don't think he was entirely wrong."

"No?"

"You know why I think that?"

"Do share."

"Because you didn't let Troy kill me," Keo said. "I think you're done with it."

"With what?"

"Everything happening in Texas right now. You saw what's happening out there up close, and you're done with it. Men, women, and children being slaughtered just so Mercer could send a message to the collaborators. Maybe, once upon a time, you thought you could do it, go along with his plan. After all, he saved your life. Saved all of your lives, or so everyone keeps telling me. But when you saw the bodies, smelled the charred flesh... The battlefield is never the same in person. It changes you."

She didn't say anything for the longest time, and Keo didn't push her. He watched her instead, observing the way her shoulders tightened, the way she sat straighter as he talked, and could almost time to the exact second when her eyes drifted; he knew she was reliving what she had seen out there. Keo could always tell when the man next to him had lost his nerve; it usually happened long after the bullets stopped flying and they were beyond the battlefield.

He saw the doubts in Erin's eyes now. They were clear as day. Maybe they had always been there, but it had never clicked for him because he didn't know to look for them.

Better late than never.

"It's done," she said, meeting his eyes again—except this time the hardness was gone. "I was a part of it. Maybe not the ones dropping the bombs or commanding the tanks, but I did my part. I can't take any of it back. I can't make it unhappen."

"What did you do, exactly?"

"I was in charge of Support in one of the FOBs. After we abandoned it, I moved over to coordinating the kill teams outside of Lochlyn."

"You were heading back to Black Tide Island even before I showed up."

"The first phase of the operation is ending. By tomorrow morning there'll be a lot more people moving through here on their way back to The Ranch."

"You told Hart this?"

"I don't have to. He already knows." Then she narrowed her eyes at him. "So what am I doing here, Keo? What's your deal?"

"My deal is that I'm going to Black Tide Island to kill Mercer."

"Oh, is that all?" She half-rolled her eyes at him and sat back in the chair. "Hell, if that's all you wanted, you should have just let me take you to him."

"That was the plan. I had nothing to do with what happened on the *Ocean Star* this afternoon."

"No? You knew that woman in the brig…"

"That had nothing to do with this afternoon. I didn't know she was going to be here. I would have been happy with letting you take me to Mercer. It would have saved me a lot of trouble."

She seemed to think about it for a moment before nodding. "I believe you."

"You should. It's the truth."

"You'll forgive me if I don't instantly believe everything that comes out of your mouth."

"That's understandable. But now that I have the upper hand, we can both agree I don't have any reasons to lie to you."

"Don't you?"

"No."

"Then what do you want from me? All of this"—she looked around the room—"even Hart's little interrogation, was clearly designed for you and I to have this conversation. You took me out of the brig on purpose so the others wouldn't hear. So what do you want from me, Keo? I'm tired, it's been a long day, so please get to the fucking point already."

He smiled and nodded. "I want you to finish what you started: Take me to Black Tide Island."

"You don't need me for that. Hart could tell you where it is."

"I've been told that getting there is the easy part. I might even be able to land in one piece by myself. But all of this would go so much easier—increase my chances of success—if I had someone to help me with the locals. Basically, a guide that everyone knows and respects. One of Mercer's trusted lieutenants, say. You know someone like that?"

She smirked. "I guess you're not as dumb as you look."

"I keep telling people that." Then, "Are you in?"

"You want me to help you kill Mercer. Is that the 'in' you're talking about?"

"That's exactly it."

"Why?"

"Because he needs killing."

"No, not that. Why would *I* help you?"

"Because you want to stop what's happening out there and what will keep happening if he keeps his war going. More towns filled with more people whose only crime is that they can't fight like us. And because you know that Mercer's phase two is going to be much, much worse." He paused to let his words sink in before continuing. "Tell me, Erin, how much sleep have you gotten since all of this started?"

She didn't answer him, but she didn't have to. He'd had no trouble seeing the bags under her eyes when he first met her, and now, with the bright ceiling lights in the room, they were even more noticeable. If she had gotten more than a few hours sleep a day all this week, he would be very surprised.

"Enough to get by," she said.

"Bullshit."

"You don't know anything about me, Keo."

"I know what people have told me about you, and I know that keeping me alive after Lochlyn was a stupid decision, but you reasoned your way into it because you didn't want more blood on your hands. I told a shitty lie and you went along with it, not because you believed me, but because you just didn't want one more death on your ledger."

"Fuck you," she said.

"Maybe later," Keo said. "Right now, you need to take me to Black Tide and get me on that island in one piece so I can do what you and Riley should have done but were too much of a fucking coward to do."

She clenched her teeth and stared defiantly back at him. If her hands weren't bound and she had a gun, he wasn't sure if he would still be alive right now.

"This is your chance to fix your mistake," he continued. "You won't be able to bring back all the lives that've already been lost, but you can prevent new ones from being snuffed out. Get me on Black Tide Island, and I'll do the rest."

Slowly, very slowly, her jaw relaxed, as did the rest of her body. "Can you do it?"

"Yes," he said without hesitation.

"It won't be easy."

"So everyone keeps telling me."

"And what happens if you succeed? You think it'll stop all of this?"

"Yes," he answered, again without hesitation. "From everything I've heard about the man, he's almost single-handedly driving this by the force of his personality. Without him, it would grind to a halt—at least temporarily. But that might be enough time for people like Riley, like James and Hart, to finally feel safe enough to speak up. As long as Mercer's running the show, they'll never speak up. It's too dangerous, and it's not just their necks on the line. Everyone has friends and loved ones to think about."

Shit, you almost convinced yourself that time, pal!

Keo didn't know if he actually believed what he had just told Erin, but he wasn't going to voice that doubt, and he was hoping it didn't show on his face.

"He has loyalists," Erin said. "They'll keep fighting even after he's gone."

"Commanders don't keep a war going, Erin. Foot soldiers do. Civilians like the ones on the *Ocean Star* do. Without them, the machine can't keep going."

Keo picked up another chair from a corner and walked over, then sat down in front of her. Only a few feet separated them, and he caught her eyes sneaking over to his holstered sidearm as he took out a knife and sliced the zip ties from her hands. When he put the knife away and looked up, her eyes had returned to his face while she rubbed her wrists.

He leaned forward, and if she wanted to, she could have reached over and snatched his pistol out of its holster.

Except she didn't.

Not yet, anyway.

"I need a guide," Keo said. "You know the place. I don't. And I can't afford to still be running around looking for Mercer when the sun comes up. So I need you, Erin. Are you in or out?"

Her stare never wavered from his face. "You're either insane or delusional if you think you can pull this off, even with my help."

"Are those my only two choices?"

"Or suicidal."

"How about none of the above?"

He smiled at her then leaned in even closer. She would have

absolutely no trouble grabbing his gun now.

Except she still didn't.

"Help me end this madness," Keo said. "Only one more person needs to die. You know deep down that I'm right, that this is the only course of action left. There's no other way."

"On one condition…"

"Name it."

"Promise me you'll do everything possible to keep the body count to a minimum."

"I'll do the best I can."

"*Promise* me."

"I'll keep the body count to a minimum," Keo nodded.

She sat back in her chair and let out a long sigh, as if the weight of the world had just been lifted from her shoulders. "When do we leave?"

He stood up. "Have you eaten yet?"

"Not since this morning."

He picked the chair back up and returned it to the corner. "We'll get something to eat first, then shove off at midnight. It'll be a nice moonlit boat ride in the dark. Might even be romantic, if you play your cards right."

"You would like that, wouldn't you?"

"I'm single, you're single…"

"In your dreams."

"Oh, trust me, we've done more than just a moonlit boat ride in my dreams."

She smirked. Then, as he turned to the door, "Hey."

Keo stopped and looked back.

"On a scale of one to ten," she said, "how certain were you I wasn't going to take your gun and shoot you just now?"

He didn't answer. Instead, he drew the Sig Sauer and tossed it to her.

She caught the gun easily, and by the startled look on her face, he guessed she figured it out pretty fast.

"It's not loaded," Erin said, weighing the gun in one hand.

"Not as dumb as I look, remember?"

She sighed and tossed him back the gun. "Dick."

"Not the worst thing I've been called tonight," Keo said as he holstered the gun.

"You said you needed to get this done before morning."

He nodded.

"So tell me you have a good plan to make that happen," Erin said. "Tell me that this isn't a spray-and-pray suicide run."

"I have *a* plan," Keo said. "Whether it's a *good* plan… Well, I guess we'll find out, won't we?"

CHAPTER 22
GABY

"BACK AT STARCH," Danny said. "It was the same one. I couldn't put my finger on it before, but I always knew there was something different about that one. It just took me a little time to figure it out."

"Danny, its eyes look just like all the other blue eyes," Gaby said. "How can you tell it apart from the ones that attacked us last night?"

"Trust me on this, kid. It's him."

"What if you're wrong?"

"I'm not."

"But what *if?*"

Danny shook his head. "I'm not. And I need you to trust that I'm not."

She didn't answer him, because she didn't know how. She was afraid of what would come out if she opened her mouth. Instead, she stared at him across the semidarkness of the hallway and said nothing. Danny was bleeding from a number of cuts along his temple and arms, and despite the stink of smoke, sweat, and blood clinging to every inch of him—and her and Nate, and the entire building, for that matter—he was still in one piece.

Danny was looking at her, but not *at* her. He was staring at—and through—the closed door behind her. On the other side was the creature that had literally fallen into their laps when the back section of the bank's roof caved in from the blast. It had been some kind of bomb, and if it had detonated any closer they would all be dead right now instead of just dirty and smelly and bleeding from small cuts.

"Torch it," Benford had said into the radio. Whoever he had been talking to hadn't managed to set the town on fire, which she was grateful for, but if the First Gallant Bank was any indication, the lone warplane had left plenty of wreckage behind outside their walls. Thank God there had just been the one plane. If there had been more, with extra munitions available to drop…

She glanced out the hallway at Nate, just to make sure he was still there. He was crouched next to the counter in the lobby and only had eyes for the large pile of rubble that had inadvertently covered up the hole put in the front wall by Benford's grenade launcher. Slabs of partially intact concrete jutted out of the chaos, the big and small pieces awash in the blue of the moonlight that pooled inside the bank through the large, jagged opening where that section of the roof used to be. Rooftop gravel carpeted almost the entire length of the lobby, with most of it concentrated near the front.

Gaby was just glad she couldn't see the street outside, because that meant whoever (whatever) was out there couldn't see in, either. Not that she had any delusions a pile of brick and mortar and concrete was going to keep back the creatures if they wanted to come in. All it would take was a short climb and they would be inside.

Except they didn't climb over, or do anything to show themselves.

But they were out there. She knew that without having to hear or see them, even if she thought she could *smell* their stench coming in through the multiple holes that pockmarked the bank's ceiling. It was also a lot colder now, and she clutched her jacket to her chest while making sure her rifle remained within reach.

She looked back at Danny still staring past her. "What are you going to do with it, Danny?"

He shook his head and didn't answer right away. She could tell by his expression it was a question he had been asking himself all night.

"If it is Will—" Gaby said, but stopped herself short. Then, "If it *was* Will, then it would explain a lot."

"Why it told me to put on the uniform in Starch," Danny said.

She nodded. "I don't suppose he told you how he knew that would work?"

"No lips, remember?"

"Right. No lips. You think he can grow them back? The black eyes never could. When they lose something, it seems to be gone for good."

"He's not one of them."

The question is, what is *he?*

"If that *is* Will," she said, "how do you think he did it? How did he save us at the hangar without actually being there?"

"I've been thinking about that…"

"And?"

"Willie boy always thought the creatures had a kind of hive-like mind, always connected somehow. He thinks that's how they know where to swarm when they discover survivors, or how the blue eyes control them." He tapped his temple. "Think of it like a network of bloodsucking, well, bloodsuckers."

"Like what, the Internet?"

"Yeah," Danny said. "Some kind of ESPN shit."

"You mean ESP."

"Uh huh. The Worldwide Leader in Bloodsucking."

Gaby managed a smile. There wasn't an inch of her that wasn't sore and dirty (and smelly, even if that part was harder to confirm), but the upside was that they were all alive. Still wearing bloody dead men's clothes, yes, but alive nonetheless, and right now that was all that mattered and all she wanted to concentrate on.

After a while, she said, "If it is Will, do you think he was the one the other blue eyes were trying to lure here? Were they using us to get to him?"

Danny, she saw, was grinning stupidly at her.

"What's so funny?" she asked, annoyed.

"You said *he*, not *it*."

"I did?"

"Uh huh. More than once."

She sighed. "Give me a break. I'm doing my best to wrap my head around all of this, but it's not easy. I feel like my head is spinning and I don't know which direction is up or down."

Danny chuckled. "Now you know how I've been feeling since Starch."

"WHAT DID DANNY say?" Nate asked when she crouched next to him beside the island counter, about five feet from where the pool of moonlight ended in front of them.

"He's not sure yet," she said, readying her M4 across her knees even though there was nothing to shoot at (*Jinx!*).

She looked out at the opening where the wall used to meet the ceiling, but there was now just a gaping hole staring out at the moon above them. With so much bright moonlight, it was easy to make out the footprints plastered across the lobby floor, so many that they overlapped each other many times over. When they were retreating, the creatures had taken the bodies of Benford and the dead collaborators that had been assaulting the bank with them.

Wouldn't want to waste a single drop of that precious blood, right, boys?

The silence inside and outside the bank hung over them like a physical thing, a blanket that could drop at any second and smother them underneath it. The thought made her nervous and Gaby clutched the rifle tighter, if just to give her hands something to do.

"What about you? You really think it's him?" Nate asked. He

glanced briefly backward at the manager's office.

"Danny seems to think it is."

"He would know, right?"

"What do you mean?"

"How long have they known one another? If anyone would recognize Will, even under all that, it would be Danny. Who knows him better?"

She nodded. "Once you've been in combat with someone, survived the end of the world side-by-side with them... That kind of connection is hard to come by."

"Like us?"

"We still have a long way to go."

"But we'll get there."

"Maybe, if we can get out of this town alive first."

"Eh, I don't know, it's not that bad. Bullet holes and destroyed buildings notwithstanding, I think it'd make for a pretty good summer vacation spot."

She smirked. "You're doing Danny now, is that it?"

"You know what they say, 'If you can't beat 'em...'"

"Become as annoying as them?" she finished for him.

"How'd you know?"

"I've been around Danny too long." Her legs were tiring, and she finally gave in and sat down on the floor, but only after brushing small chunks of rooftop gravel away. "How's your side?"

"Hurts, just like everything else."

Pain lets you know you're still alive. Right, Lara?

"I was expecting fire," Gaby said.

"From the bombing?"

She nodded.

"I guess there isn't anything left in Gallant that's flammable," Nate said. "Or, at least, not enough to start and maintain a fire. We're lucky that Warthog only had two bombs to drop."

"Yeah, lucky," she said quietly. Then, "We have to get back. The *Trident*. Whatever it takes, we have to get back."

"We will. Just a few more hours, and it'll be sunup. Then we'll go home."

He put an arm around her, and Gaby leaned against his shoulder, welcoming the warmth of his body to help fight back the cold that swamped the lobby. She wondered if she would ever be able to enjoy moments like these without guns within reach or undead things moving outside her walls. Were those things even possible anymore?

"I was thinking…" Nate said quietly.

"What?"

"That thing in the office. If it really is Will…"

"It's a big if…"

"I know, but if it really is Will, then it changes everything, doesn't it?"

"How?"

"He saved our lives at Larkin, then again in Starch. He did that, Gaby. He didn't have to, but he did. The question is: Why?"

Why? I've been asking that question all night, and I'm no closer to the answer.

"If he's still Will, what else can he do?" Nate continued, though now Gaby wasn't sure if he was even talking to her anymore or just speaking his thoughts out loud. "What does he know? How long has he been out here? What has he been doing?"

"We think the blue eyes were trying to lure him here, using us as bait."

"There," Nate said.

"What?"

"He knows something, Gaby," he said, unable to hide the excitement in his voice. "Get it?"

"No…"

"Think about it," Nate said. "If they're this desperate to stop him, if they're going through all this trouble just to bring him here, he must know something they don't want us to know. The question is: What?"

SHE FELL ASLEEP with Nate's voice in her head, asking her "Why?" and "What?" over and over again, and opened her heavy eyelids back up to the sight of Danny hovering over her.

"You catching a little nap there, little girl?" he said, grinning down at her.

"Oh, God," she said, and hurried up to her feet, the sound of loose gravel *crunching* under her boots. "Nate…"

She didn't have to look far to see him leaning against the counter where she last saw him, his head lolled slightly forward. He was snoring softly yet somehow still clutching the rifle resting across his lap.

She shook off as much sleep as she could and picked up her rifle from the floor, feeling simultaneously embarrassed and angry with herself. "I'm sorry, Danny. I must be more tired than I thought."

"Don't beat yourself up over it, Tex," Danny said. "No harm, no foul."

She snapped a quick look at the front wall across the lobby, at the undisturbed barricade and the pools of moonlight coming in from the openings above. Still dark, and nothing had come in while she was asleep.

Stupid. So stupid.

"I'm sorry, Danny," she said again.

"Stop apologizing," he said. "Nothing happened. Everything's hunky dory." He took out a bottle of water and handed it to her. "Partially my fault. I was too preoccupied in the office, didn't think to check up on you lovebirds until now."

She chased away more of the grogginess with the water before handing the bottle back to him. "Any progress?"

"If you call the fact that we had a nice, long chat progress, then yes."

"He's talking now?"

"Lips grew back."

"So they can regenerate flesh."

"One second he's mouthless, the next he's making sounds. Or hissing, anyway. Musto presto, new lips-for-you-to."

"What did he—it—whatever—say?"

Danny sat down and she did the same, her eyes wandering back to the front wall again.

"It's him. One hundred and twenty-two percent," Danny said. "He knew things I never told anyone. About me, about us."

"Like what?"

"Afghanistan. SWAT. This really hot blonde who I picked up at a bar and was convinced I was going to marry, only to find out— Well, you don't need to know all the details. Point is, he knew things that only Willie boy would know."

"What if you're wrong?"

"I'm not."

"But what *if*."

"We already went over this, kid. You just have to trust me. I'm not wrong."

"You're that sure?"

He nodded. "Sure as sure can be. Surest, if you will."

"That's pretty sure."

"You're damn straight."

She managed a half-smile. "What is he doing right now?"

"Recuperating. He took a pretty solid beating before he dropped in on us. It was apparently quite the death match on the rooftop, with attempted quartering and such. Real serious shit."

"So he's really hurt."

"On a scale of Ouch and FUBAR, he's about plus ten beyond FUBAR."

"That doesn't sound good."

"Nope. That's why I dug him out of the rubble to help him heal faster."

She must have gasped out loud, because Danny chortled and looked barely able to contain himself.

"Relax," he said. "It's free, and as you can see, I'm still in one piece and adorable."

"You should have waited for us."

"To do what?"

"I don't know; watch over you in case it tried something?"

"It didn't."

"But it *could* have."

"But it *didn't*," Danny said. "It's Willie boy. He's skinnier—okay, he's basically skin and bones—and he's seen better days hairwise. But you have to admit, he looks pretty snazzy in that trench coat."

"That's a trench coat?"

"Well, it was, about a few million pieces ago."

"Why was it—he—wearing a trench coat?"

Danny shrugged. "Fashion sense?"

She sighed and shook her head with exasperation, not sure if she was angry with Danny or unable to wrap her mind around the fact that there was a loose blue-eyed ghoul behind her right now, with nothing between her and it *(him?)* but a single door. She had seen what they could do back at the farmhouse and last night. How fast and strong and so goddamn hard to kill they were unless you got them in the head, and that was so, so much easier said than done.

"Did he tell you how it happened?" she asked.

"He said it was Kate's doing."

"His Kate?"

"One and only. That night, after we ran the gauntlet from the farmhouse…"

She nodded. How many times had she relived that day? Too many to count.

"She got to him, then," Gaby said.

"Yeah," Danny nodded.

He didn't add anything else and she had difficulty finding the right words, so the two of them sat in silence and listened to Nate snoring lightly next to them while staring at the barricaded wall. She knew Danny was thinking the exact same thing that she was: That day after the farmhouse, when they lost Will to the roadblock…

After what seemed like hours, though it was probably just a few minutes, she said, "So what now?"

"We wait until sunup, then go home," Danny said.

"What about him?"

"He had a pretty interesting story to tell me. Once a Ranger, always a Ranger, as the saying goes. New Willie has been reconning the enemy, gathering intelligence. Apparently he's made himself such a nuisance that the enemy cooked up this little scheme and stalked us all the way from Starch just to use us as bait to lure him here."

She looked over at Danny. "So does he? Know something they don't want us to know?"

Danny grinned back at her, his blue eyes glinting with mischief—or maybe that was just the moonlight reflecting off them.

"Well?" she said. "Does it—him—*Will* know something or not?"

"I guess you could say that," Danny said. "Does knowing a way to save the human race count?"

CHAPTER 23
KEO

"THIS FEELS FAMILIAR," Erin shouted about two hours into the trip.

She stood behind the helm of the twenty-footer, the balaclava that covered almost her entire face except for her eyes playing tricks with her voice. If he were sitting anywhere on the fast-moving vessel besides a few feet in front of her on a narrow bench, he might not have heard a single word she said.

He pulled his balaclava down slightly to shout back: "Yeah, but this time I'm not in any danger of getting tossed overboard."

"Oh, I wouldn't say that."

He grinned and pulled the mask back up, leaving the cold wind to smack against the exposed parts of his face.

The offshore boat they were moving in had a T-top, but the canopy was missing. Even so, it was the best and fastest vessel Hart had to offer. If anyone were around to see them, they would spot a long, white object slicing at fast speeds across the wide-open Gulf of Mexico. There was absolutely nothing else around them, the

Ocean Star having faded into the distance *(Probably for good)* a long time ago.

Keo was looking forward when Erin appeared next to him and said, "Move over."

"The fuck?" he said, glancing over his shoulder at the empty helm.

"Relax; it's on cruise control," Erin said, laughing behind her ski mask.

"I didn't know this thing had cruise control," he said, scooting over on the bench to give her space.

Erin sat down with a heavy sigh. "The girl told me about it before she gave me the keys."

The girl was Faith, James's girlfriend. The two made for a nice-looking couple, and Keo found himself wishing them well as he and Erin set off. He was, though, resigned to the realization that he would never find out how they did, because chances were very good he wasn't going to ever see them again. Not them or Lara or anyone else on the *Trident*, for that matter.

There you go again being Captain Optimism, pal.

Next to him, Erin closed her eyes and leaned her head against the fiberglass helm. "You know what's funny?"

"Johnny Carson?"

She ignored him, said, "Despite everything I know, I would have found a way to justify it—what's happening out there, what we're doing. It wouldn't have been easy, and some days would be harder than others, but I think I would have pushed on anyway, lying to myself. And every day the lies would eat at me more and more. It was already bad even before I met you."

"What would have happened then? When you couldn't handle it anymore?"

"I don't know. I guess I'll never know now, but probably nothing good."

"So you're saying I was your savior?"

"Don't flatter yourself."

"Sounded like it…"

"What I'm saying is, I think I would have kept on going to the bitter end, and I wouldn't have been the only one. When I see what Riley's doing back at the *Ocean Star*, it just reminds me what cowards the rest of us are. At least he's doing something."

"From what I hear, his plans wouldn't have gotten very far if Lara and the *Trident* hadn't shown up."

"Maybe, but he's at least doing *something*. Unlike us. We would have kept telling ourselves about all the things Mercer did for us to justify our cowardice." She paused for a brief moment before continuing. "Even though we saw the collaborators as enemies, we told ourselves we were doing it for their own good, that we were ultimately saving them. We knew all about the pregnancies, the daily bloodletting. We scouted them months in advance of the attacks."

"James told me."

"We knew what was going to happen. What the body count was going to look like. You don't throw planes and tanks into the mix and not know."

She went silent and stared forward, and Keo couldn't tell what she was looking at—or maybe what she was looking *for*. For all he knew, she could have been staring past the open seas and into the past, wondering how things might have changed if she had acted.

So that's what guilt looks like on someone else.

"I should have stopped him," Erin said. "God, we had so many chances."

"We?"

"Those of us who had doubts. When I think back, I know it wasn't just me."

"Like Riley."

She nodded. "I always knew he wasn't comfortable with the plan. I could see it on his face, in his eyes whenever we met with Mercer to discuss strategy. He was always so quiet, especially compared to the others."

"Who else was in the inner circle with Mercer?"

"There was me, Riley, Benford, and Rhett. We were the first four. Later, he added others. Bellamy, Jerkins…"

"And you all had doubts?"

"Not all of us. But it wasn't just Riley and me, I know that. I don't know, maybe in some naïve way we—*I*—were hoping Mercer would move past it. He talked about it on and off, but it just never seemed real until a few months before R-Day officially started." She sat back and sighed. "We're civilians, Keo. We're not like you, bred for this sort of thing. We trusted in Mercer. Trusted in him implicitly."

"That's what manipulators do," Keo said. "They prey on your loyalty."

"Maybe. I don't know. I just know how hard it was on my own in the early days. When he found me, living became more than just surviving. It became *living* again."

"Was that before or after he brought you to Black Tide?"

"Before."

"How did he know about the island in the first place?"

"He never said, but he's ex-Army, so that probably has something to do with it. I would never think to look for weapons at an Army base. I wouldn't even know where to find one off the top of my head. Do you?"

"Ran across some guys who did the same thing in Louisiana."

"Friend or foe?"

Keo pulled up his balaclava and tapped the scar that ran down the side of his face.

"So that's what happened there," Erin said. "What became of them?"

"There was shooting and bad words," he said. "I don't play well with ex-Army types. Wannabe joke-spouting ex-Army comedians are the exception."

"Good to know."

Keo pulled the mask back down over his face and stared at the nothingness in front of them. "Don't take this the wrong way, but you sure we're going in the right direction? Because it's been a couple of hours, and I still don't see anything that even looks like an island out there."

"It's a secret U.S. military base, Keo. They're not going to make it easy to find. With an ocean this big, you'd have to be either super lucky—or unlucky, depending on how you want to look at it—to just stumble across Black Tide by accident."

"So what you're saying is, yes, we're going in the right direction."

"Yes, we're going in the right direction."

"Okay. Just wanted to make sure."

"So I've been spilling my guts, and I noticed you haven't reciprocated."

"What were you hoping to hear?"

"What happened?"

"What happened what?" he asked, even though he knew damn well what she was referring to.

"You know what," Erin said. "You're not going there to stop this war by killing Mercer. It's personal. I can see it on your face when you talk about him. So what happened? What did Mercer do to you?"

"One of your teams killed a friend of mine. I tracked them back to Lochlyn."

"You thought he would be there?"

"I was hoping he'd be there."

"What about Davis and Butch? The iPod?"

"I shot Butch and took Davis for questioning."

"Is he dead? Davis?"

"I don't know."

She looked over at him. "Don't lie to me, Keo."

"I'm not lying to you. He was still alive when we parted company. I don't know what happened to him after that. I had other things to worry about."

"Is that the truth?"

"Yes."

She turned away.

"You knew them?" Keo asked.

"Of course I knew them. They were part of my unit."

"Davis?"

"He was a good friend," she said, and didn't say anything else.

"HOW DOES AN island that small make it through all the tropical storms and hurricanes that whip across the Gulf of Mexico every year?" Keo asked.

"Simple but tough Army engineering would be my guess," Erin said. "In all the time we've been here, we've survived over a dozen storms the likes of which I've never experienced before. It was terrifying the first few times, but after a while you get used to it, and now you just hunker down until it passes. The place is incredibly sound, and it's been designed to be used and reused. That includes the airfield, the surrounding woods, and the beaches. I wouldn't be surprised if braving storms was part of the curriculum."

They sat on the same bench at the front of the twenty-footer, staring at the first light he had seen since they left the *Ocean Star*. It wasn't even that bright, but against the vast emptiness of the sea and the night, it might as well be a lighthouse beacon. With the single engine that had been propelling them for the last few hours turned off, the world was once again dead silent, with just the *sloshing* of the currents under and around them.

Keo scanned the island from side to side, noting where it began and ended now that his eyes had adjusted to the darkness. It was about two kilometers long, but he couldn't tell from his current distance how much of it was covered in vegetation, though there didn't seem to be a lot of trees. Or, at least, nothing tall enough to stand out against the dark canvas that surrounded the place like a black glove.

"Two kilometers?" he asked.

"Just a bit longer than a mile," Erin said.

"How wide?"

"Maybe a quarter mile. There's a landing strip that runs through the middle. The main facilities are joined into one contiguous structure, and it's ringed by woods and beaches. The first few weeks after we arrived, we were always stepping on empty shell casings that had been left behind. We're looking at the back of the island now. Boats usually dock on the other side where there are piers and slips. This side is pretty much used for beaching exercises. But since we're coming from the *Ocean Star*, it makes sense for us to land here."

"Where there's less security."

"Exactly."

"Hart said the place was primarily used for war games."

She nodded. "There were stacks of files and old maps detailing various scenarios they had run through this place in the past. I don't think they spent a lot of time here though, probably as long as it took them to complete whatever games they had in mind. It's a durable place, but it's not exactly cozy."

"So, shitty accommodations?"

"I guess soldiers don't need more than a cot and a pillow."

"You guys didn't find any of them when you showed up?"

"Soldiers? No. It was empty. No ghouls, either."

"Lucky you."

"Not luck. Mercer knew it would be empty. That's why he brought us here."

Keo sneaked a look at her, sitting next to him. There was something about the way she had said Mercer's name. He had noticed it twice now: there was a reverence to it, the kind of respect that made him question if she could be trusted when the chips were down and his hide was on the line. Maybe he had made a mistake deciding to trust someone who, less than a day ago, had threatened to kill him more times than he could count.

"You good with this?" he asked.

She looked back at him and saw the way he was eyeing her. She pursed her lips into a forced smile. "No. Not at all."

"What does that—"

"I mean, I'm not good with what we're about to do," she interrupted, "but yeah, I'm good with *this* this." She faced forward again. "It has to be done. If he's gone, there's a chance we can pull the others back and stop this war and save lives."

"Whose lives?"

"Theirs, ours, all of us."

Keo nodded. He didn't want to tell her that the chances of that actually happening were low, that even with Mercer gone there were probably going to be true believers determined to carry on the fight in their dead commander's memory, or something equally ill-conceived.

But right now Erin didn't need to know about his doubts. He couldn't afford for her to start having second *(third?)* thoughts. God knew this was going to be tough enough without having to worry about her, too.

"How are we going to do this?" he asked.

"There's nothing special about it. I already radioed ahead when we were on the *Ocean Star* and told them we were coming. They're expecting us"—she glanced at her watch—"about now."

"That's the whole procedure? Call ahead and then show up?"

"It's not *Get Smart,* Keo. There are no hidden doors or passwords to go through. If you found the island, then you were meant to be here."

"What about defenses?"

"There are guards along the beaches and around the main facility, but that's about it in terms of potential trouble spots. Everyone who can fight is either in Texas or on their way back."

"Will they care it's only the two of us showing up?"

"The guys I made contact with on the radio will, but they won't be on the beach waiting for us. The guards who will be won't know any different."

He nodded and looked up at the sky. Pitch dark, but it wouldn't stay that way for very long. Not that he needed a lot of time, but darkness was always better for wet work. There wouldn't be nearly as many people standing guard, and those who were would be staving off fatigue and sleep. In his experience, even the most capable soldier wasn't at his full alertness in the early morning hours. Best-case? The people here would be used to long, peaceful night sleeps, which would give him even more room to work.

Worst case? Everything blows up in his face, and he was dead before morning.

Either/or.

"All right," he said, slipping the balaclava back down over his face. "Let's get you home."

THERE WERE TWO of them—men, from the way they stood and the shape of their outlines—and they were waiting on the beach as Erin cut the engine a second time and let the currents push them forward. Keo could make out night-vision goggles over the guards' faces, which meant they had seen him crouched at the bow of the offshore vessel even better than he could see them.

He glanced back at Erin. "Is this going to work?"

She didn't answer right away, but the obvious concern on her face, lit by the dashboard lights, didn't exactly give him confidence.

"Yeah, sure," she said finally.

"You don't sound very convincing, Erin," he said, just barely suppressing a laugh. Because what else could he do in this situation but laugh?

"It'll work," she said. She followed that up with a nod, though he wasn't sure if that was for his benefit or hers. Then again, given the way she was staring at the two guards waiting for them (likely armed to the teeth), he could probably figure out the answer.

Keo turned back around to face the beach. He had his rifle slung behind him and still wore his gun belt because it wouldn't make sense for a Mercer man to return "home" unarmed. Judging by the relaxed posture of the two, it was the right move. The guards stood watching, but he didn't see anything about their forms to indicate they were anxious or alert, and they certainly weren't holding the rifles dangling in front of them with anything even close to resembling menace.

So far, so good.

"We won't be the first one to come back," Erin said behind him. "They'll be used to this by now. The fact that there are just two of us may raise some questions later, but not from these two.

If your plan works, this will be all over by the time enough people have woken up to start asking those questions."

They were less than twenty meters from the sand when one of the guards waved, while the second one turned his head to look up the beach as if he found something more interesting up there. That was exactly the reaction Keo was hoping for, and seeing it did more to convince him than Erin's assurance had a few moments ago.

Keo returned the wave and stood up as the surf carried them closer. He jumped off the boat as soon as he felt the fiberglass hull sliding against soft sand and landed knee-high in freezing cold water.

The guard laughed, night-vision goggle perched on top of his forehead. "Nice jump, Geronimo."

There wasn't a lot of light on the beach, at least nothing like he was used to back on Song Island in the old days. The guards were clearly relying mostly on moonlight and their gear to see with, and the closest light emanated from an LED lantern hanging off a tree about thirty meters behind them. It wasn't nearly enough to reveal the entire stretch of beach, which made Keo think he could have swam to shore just fine under the cover of darkness.

Keo grinned back at the soldier. "Hey, I almost had it."

"Almost only counts in horseshoes and grenades, dude," the man said.

"Tell me about it," Keo said, and turned around and grabbed the boat's V-shaped bow and pulled it in.

The guard helped with the other side, but the second one was more concerned about not getting caught in the waves that were washing ashore than lending a hand. As Keo and the Good Samaritan pulled the boat up, Erin walked to the front and picked up the line from the floor.

Keo backpedaled up the beach, his soaked boots *squishing* under him. Erin tossed him the line, and Keo pulled the boat further in. The guard was too busy talking to Erin and the other guy had wandered off.

Definitely so far, so good.

There was a metal spike to which Keo tied the boat's line. It wasn't exactly a sophisticated docking system, but then they were landing on the backside of the island.

"Just you two?" the guard was asking Erin behind him.

"Just us," Erin said.

"How's the war going? We don't get a lot of information. Heard it was going well, though."

"Yeah, we're bulldozing through the collaborators," Erin said. "Pretty soon there'll just be the monsters to deal with."

"That's when all the silver bullets come in, right?"

Erin nodded. "That's right."

"Can't wait for that. I'm tired of playing security guard over here."

"Don't worry; you'll get your chance soon enough."

"Looking forward to it," the man said.

As he was tightening the rope around the spike, Keo took a moment to scan the rest of the island. There wasn't much in the way of defenses that he could see except for the two guards he had already met, though Keo did glimpse two more figures farther up the beach to his right. Still, four people weren't nearly enough to cover the entire two-kilometer span of the island on this side, but maybe there were more people than he could see with the naked eye. Either that, or Mercer really was stretched thin. Which, if true, meant the man was definitely putting all his eggs on the collaborators turning on their ghoul masters and bulking up his ranks.

Good luck with that, pal.

Erin had walked over to join him, and she handed him his pack and asked, "You ready?"

He nodded and said in a low voice so the closest guard didn't hear, "You good?"

"Yes," she said, louder than he would have liked. "Let's go; I wanna grab some shut-eye before sunup."

That last part, he guessed, was for the guard's benefit.

Keo followed her up the beach, sliding the pack's strap over his left shoulder only in order to keep his right arm free. The M4 with the grenade launcher thumped reassuringly against his back, within easy reach. When he looked back at the water, the guy who had helped him pull the boat up had already returned his NVD over his eyes and was walking off to join his buddy.

"What about the boat?" Keo asked.

"Someone will take care of it later," Erin said.

They waded through knee-high grass in a field on the other side of the beach. It was easy to pick up the signs that Uncle Sam had been here and had chopped down a lot of the scenery, leaving a mostly unobstructed view of the place. Keo spied the roofs of buildings jutting out of the ground in the distance, and though he expected to see planes taking off and landing, the only sounds came from the crickets in the woods and birds in the trees around him.

"What that guy said about silver bullets," Keo said.

"What about it?" Erin asked.

"I can understand why people on the *Ocean Star* weren't equipped with them, but what about the teams in the fields? The ones in Texas right now?"

"Mercer's orders."

"Why?"

"Their job is to strike at the collaborators, not fight ghouls. If they had silver ammo, they'd be tempted to do the very thing he told them not to do. This way, they're forced to stay on course. Hide at night, fight in the day. And you don't need silver bullets to do that."

Four guys in a tank apparently didn't get that message.

"That's a pretty hardcore way to ensure your soldiers do exactly what you tell them," Keo said. "And all the kill teams went along with it?"

"A lot of them protested—I was one of them. But he stuck to his guns and we found ways to be okay with it, like we always do. I heard rumors that some of the teams stole silver bullets from the armory and took them with them. But I never actually met any that did."

"The funny thing is, I agree with him."

Erin looked over, surprised. "You do?"

"Not his no-silver policy even if you die because of it part. That's just stupid. But on the not engaging the ghouls part, yeah, I get that. It's pointless."

She nodded. "He said it was a losing battle. There are so many of them, killing a hundred here, a thousand there wouldn't even make a dent in their number. He said we'd just use up all the silver ammo we spent so much time and sweat making. He wanted to save it for emergencies, but mostly for when we finally took the fight directly to the monsters. That's why we still have people out there whose only job is to collect silver."

"He's playing the long game."

"Always. From day one, his goal was to first take away the ghoul's greatest resource—cut their supply line, as he put it."

"Humans."

"He'll kill as many as he needs to get them to turn on their masters."

"What if he ends up killing everyone instead?"

"That's why I'm here on Black Tide with you, Keo. To make sure that doesn't happen." She ground her teeth together, and he heard the conviction in her voice for the very first time when she added, "There has to be a better way to take the planet back. There *has* to be."

Maybe there was and maybe there wasn't, but Keo wasn't too concerned with the answer at the moment. Right here and now, he could only concentrate on one thing:

Find Mercer. Kill Mercer.

He replayed the look on Jordan's face as she bled out in his arms next to the highway; the oddly contented smile she gave him as he held her, forever frozen in his mind's eye. Days later, and he still didn't know how he felt about her, but he knew that he liked her and knew exactly how he felt about watching her die.

Somewhere on the other side of the field they were moving through, lights shone from a series of blocky gray buildings. Mercer would be in one of those right now, oblivious to what was coming for him.

Keo glanced down at his watch.
3:36 a.m.
He smiled.
The hour of the wolf…

CHAPTER 24
LARA

WHEN RILEY OPENED his eyes, the first thing he said was, "Andy shot me."

Lara nodded. "Yes, he did."

"Then someone shot him…"

"Peters."

"I told you he never misses."

"So I've been told," Lara smiled.

Riley closed his eyes for a brief few seconds, then opened them again. "You're still here. How long has it been?"

"I am, and it's past midnight. You've been heavily sedated. I'm surprised you're already talking."

He squinted. "Feels like an elephant's sitting on me."

"But you're alive."

"Yeah, there's that." Riley looked pale and in pain, but his voice was surprisingly stronger than it should have been for a man who had been shot very recently. "I had a dream…"

"What was it about?"

"The *Ocean Star* was sinking."

"Sounds more like a nightmare."

"I guess it was." He peeked down at his bandaged side. "Andy shot me," he said again.

"How much do you remember?"

"I remember that it hurt like hell." He sighed and looked up at the ceiling. "It's quiet. Why is it so quiet?"

"It's one in the morning, Riley."

"No wonder it's so quiet." He turned his head to look at her. "Is everything…okay?"

"You mean has Mercer sent anyone to attack the *Ocean Star* yet?"

He nodded.

She shook her head. "Not yet."

"Thank God." Then, "Did I almost die or something?"

"No," Lara said, and sat back in her chair while trying to decide how much to tell him.

They were the only two people in sickbay at the moment, and except for Riley's slightly labored breathing, it was as if the world outside didn't exist beyond the thick walls. Zoe had returned to the *Trident* a few hours ago, satisfied that Riley was in good hands with the rig's vet/doctor, George, taking over. Like everyone onboard the yacht, Zoe had a lot of work ahead of her.

"Hart took charge after you went down," Lara said.

"Where is he now?"

"Overseeing the transports."

"Transports?"

"We're shuttling your people to my boat."

"In the middle of the night?" he asked, eyebrows rising in either curiosity or alarm, she couldn't really tell.

"We didn't think it was prudent to wait any longer, in case more of Mercer's men showed up on their way back to Black Tide."

"Something happened, didn't it? Besides Andy shooting me. What else happened while I was out?"

"Erin's group came through. Hart did the best he could in your place, but they didn't buy it. Something about the lack of civilians on the top deck spooked them."

"Erin noticed," Riley said. It wasn't a question.

Lara nodded. "According to Hart, yes."

"Is she…?"

"No. But you did lose a man, and someone named Troy was killed by Peters."

"But Erin's alive?"

"Yes," she said, noticing the relief on his face. "It was bad, but it wasn't nearly as bad as it could have been."

"Who was it? My guy."

"I don't know his name. You'll have to ask Hart."

"Was it a man or a woman?"

"Does it matter?"

"Yes." He ran his hands over his face. "I brought them here, Lara. They're my responsibility. Every single one of them. Even Andy…"

The burden of leadership, Will. How did you ever shoulder it for so long? I've been at this for only a few months, and I already feel a million years old.

"Hart handled it," she said. "He's not a bad second-in-command."

"He'd rather be fishing," Riley said, and smiled. "You wouldn't believe how hard it was to convince him to lead the mission to your boat."

"It's a good thing you did. If someone else were in charge, that night might have gone differently. We might not be having this talk right now."

Riley nodded and scooted up to a sitting position, stuffing pillows between him and the wall. He grimaced the entire time but kept at it until it was done. She resisted the instinct to lend him a hand, mostly for his ego's sake.

After finally settling back down, he said, "How's it going? Moving everyone over to the *Trident*?"

"It's going," Lara said. "Everyone's been very cooperative. We should be done by sunup, if not before then. I'm having Hart transfer the rest of the supplies over at the same time on different boats, but they're going to take much longer than the people.

Everyone's handling the move surprisingly well. You could even say enthusiastically."

"Must be the idea of cruising around in that sweet ride of yours," Riley said, looking over at the sickbay's only window, not that he could see anything but darkness on the other side. "Is there a reason you're doing this now?"

"Between the time Andy shot you and now, we've already gotten five radio calls from Mercer's people in Texas. The first group is supposed to be here by ten in the morning. There'll be more by midday."

"They're moving much faster than I expected…"

"Is that good or bad?"

"For the war effort, it's good," Riley said. "But not for the people caught in the middle. If they're already starting to return to Black Tide en masse, it means they're having a lot of success in Texas."

I wonder how Mercer measures "success." Maybe in body bags.

"Thank you," Riley said, looking back at her. "I mean it, Lara. You could have bailed, but you didn't." He smiled, and it was probably a little too smug for her liking. "I knew *the* Lara wouldn't back out of the deal."

She frowned. "Please stop calling me that."

"Don't freak out," Riley said, and she thought, *Too late*, "but some of my guys are carrying around iPods with your messages in a loop on them."

Lara sighed. "I know. Hart told me."

"I know it's not something you're comfortable with, but your messages gave a lot of people hope. To a lot of us, you're not just Lara, you're *the* Lara. You're famous."

"Glad to be wanted, I guess," she said. Then, hoping Riley would take the hint and move on, "Maybe it's time you filled me in on where I'm taking your people."

"I guess I should tell you, since we're in this together now."

"I think so."

"Have you ever heard of the Bengal Islands?" he asked.

Lara smiled. "I might have heard a thing or two about it."

"Don't tell me…"

"Yeah."

He broke out into a big, stupid grin. "Maybe I was right the first time."

"About what?"

"This."

"What is 'this?'"

"Fate. You showing up just when we needed you the most. It's got to be fate, Lara."

"I don't believe in fate," she said, and thought, *At least, not anymore. Not after Will didn't come back to me.*

"I do," he said.

"Then you're a fool."

"I've been called worse. I know what Mercer's going to be calling me when he learns about what I've done."

"You think he'll come after you?"

"I don't know."

"You haven't thought about it?"

"I guess I never got that far," he said, and seemed to drift off.

He looked as if he was thinking very seriously about her question when there was a squawk and she heard Maddie's voice coming through the radio hanging off her left hip.

"Lara, come in."

She unclipped the radio, but said to Riley first, "She's one of my people."

He nodded, though she wondered if he actually heard her. He looked gone, as if he was still trying to come up with an answer to her question.

She felt like giving him some space and stood up and walked over to the window, where she keyed the radio. "I'm here, Maddie."

"Uh, there might be a little problem," Maddie said. "Well, maybe a possible complication."

Riley, hearing that, glanced over.

"What kind of 'complication?'" she said into the radio.

"Hart was doing a head count of the *Ocean Star* folks, and he thinks we might be, uh, missing a few, uh, heads."

"Be more specific, Maddie."

"Hart says a couple of the civilians are missing."

Riley sat up straighter. It was a mistake, and he grimaced with pain from the sudden movement.

"Did he check the entire boat?" Lara said into the radio.

"Twice," Maddie said. "All the civilians should have been on the *Trident* by now. The only ones that should still be on the *Ocean Star* with you are a few of Hart's soldiers."

"There's an armory," Riley said.

"I know; I had Hart put guards on it after you were shot," she said. "The guns were the first things I had your people move over to the *Trident*. I know I said I didn't need them before, but I didn't see any point in leaving them behind when we go."

"I think that's a good idea," he nodded.

"What are the chances some of the civilians might have snuck weapons onboard? Like Andy?"

"Pretty good. It wasn't like we searched everyone. Or anyone, for that matter. There was no reason to."

"Lara?" Maddie said through the radio.

"I'm here," she answered. "Where is Hart now?"

"Doing a third head count."

"That's a waste of time," Riley said. "They must have stayed onboard while you guys were shuttling people over. It wouldn't make sense for them to go along only to sneak back here."

Lara nodded, then walked over to the door and pushed the lock into place.

"Why did you do that?" Riley asked from behind her.

"Just in case," she said and walked back to him. Then, into the radio: "Maddie, you said all the civilians except two are onboard?"

"That's what Hart says," Maddie said.

"I want you to pull anchor and take the yacht farther out."

"How much farther?"

"At least another half mile."

"Should I ask why?"

"Just in case."

"Gotcha. But you know we're not done with the supplies, right?"

"Doesn't matter. We can finish it later. Right now, I want you to put some distance between the yacht and the platform."

"What about you?"

"When you see Hart again, tell him to radio me on this frequency and we'll coordinate what to do next. Your job right now—your *only* job—is to take care of the *Trident* and everyone onboard, understand?"

"Roger that," Maddie said.

"Why the second 'just in case?'" Riley asked when she put the radio away.

"Because I don't know what those two missing crewmen will do. Best-case scenario is they'll hide until we leave."

"And the worst-case?"

"They use whatever guns they snuck onboard and finish what Andy started. And maybe they won't stop with you. Maybe they'll decide no one should be able to leave, either."

Riley shook his head. "If you think they'll blow up the *Trident* with all those people onboard, it's not going to happen. They wouldn't do that. I know everyone who served onboard the *Ocean Star*. None of them are capable of something that heinous."

"You thought you knew Andy, too."

He flinched. "Below the belt, Lara."

"But true," she said, and stared back at him.

"Goddammit, I know you're right." He swung his legs over the side of the bed and leaned forward to gather his strength, even though those movements probably cost him more unnecessary pain. "I messed up," he added quietly.

"Think of it this way," she said, "you're three out of forty-six. These days, if you're batting over .500, I'd say you're coming up ahead."

He made an effort to smile, but she could tell he was far from convinced.

"THEY WERE IN the comm room," Hart said when Lara opened the sickbay door for him. "But they took off long before we showed up."

"What were they doing in there?" Riley asked from his bed.

"I don't know, but they didn't go in there for their health, I'm guessing."

"Who was it?"

"Ezekiel and Lang."

Lara looked back at Riley. "Anything special about them?"

Riley shook his head. "Nothing that I can think of. Ezekiel's one of the mechanics and Lang helped out in the galley."

"A mechanic and a cook?"

"Basically."

Lara turned back to Hart. "Any ideas where they're hiding now?"

"Not a clue," Hart said. "It's a big place with a lot of nooks and crannies to hole up. Frankly, if they are hiding and waiting for us to leave, I'm not sure we should even bother looking for them."

"I agree," Lara said.

Riley nodded. He had looked stronger when he first woke up, but the last hour had drained some of that strength, and just sitting on the bed seemed to take a lot out of him. "The only thing to be concerned about is that they might have called for help. Given us away."

"What's the status on the supplies?" Lara asked Hart.

"About sixty percent are already onboard the *Trident*," Hart said.

"The essentials first?"

"Just like you said."

"Then that's going to have to be enough."

"You mean leave the rest behind?"

She nodded.

"That's too much to abandon," Riley said behind her. "We might need everything we can get when we reach the Bengal Islands."

"I'm thinking about your people, Riley," Lara said. "There's a lot of space between the storage area and the top deck. A lot of rooms and doors and corners. Right now we don't know if Ezekiel and Jones plan on doing anything. If they even have just one gun between them…"

Riley shook his head. He clearly didn't like it, but he said anyway, "You're right. It's not worth risking one more man to this war." Then to Hart, "We'll leave the rest behind, like she said."

"You're going to have to help him topside," Lara said to Hart.

Hart nodded and glanced back at two men in black tactical gear, weapons out, standing guard behind the open sickbay door. "Phil, give me a hand."

One of the men turned around and stepped inside.

Hart walked over to Riley. "It's going to hurt."

Riley gritted his teeth. "I'll try to keep the crying to a minimum."

Hart chuckled, then with Phil, they flanked Riley and helped him up to his feet. Riley's face turned red almost right away with the strain.

"We'll have to move slow," Lara said. "And give me that," she added, reaching for Hart's rifle.

"I'd ask if you knew how to use one, but that would be a stupid question, wouldn't it?" Hart said.

She gave him a wry look.

"What about the prisoners in the brig below us?" Hart asked. "We never talked about what we were going to do with them."

"They're Lang and Ezekiel's problem now," Lara said.

Hart and Riley exchanged a look, but neither one protested.

She walked on ahead of them, stepped outside in the hallway, and stopped next to the remaining sentry. "What's your name?"

"Jolly, ma'am," the man *(boy)* said. He may or may not have been out of his teens—and if he was, then it was just barely—though he was at least a foot taller than her and big around the chest and shoulders.

"Jolly?" she smiled.

"It's a nickname, ma'am," Jolly said, and actually blushed.

"I'm Lara."

"I know, ma'am."

"You can stop calling me *ma'am*. I'm not that old."

"Sorry, ma—Lara."

"Better," she said, then nodded up the hallway. "We're going to lead them upside and to the boat, okay, Jolly?"

"Gotcha, Lara."

"Good," she said. "Let's go."

"THEY MIGHT HAVE called for help. Given us away," Riley had said.

Lara thought it was a pretty good bet the missing crewmen had done exactly both those things. Why else would they go through the effort of using the comm room? They would know it was empty, with Terry and the others already onboard the *Trident*.

So the question was: Who did they call for help and give Riley's plans away to?

The only thing that kept her from panicking even just a little was the knowledge that they weren't going to be here to wait and find out. She felt a flush of pride at having convinced Hart to start moving his people over to the *Trident* sooner than he had expected. Not that Hart had really put up much resistance. She hated to admit it, but the older man was somewhat of a pushover.

They made it to the top platform without any problems, even though Lara kept expecting Ezekiel and Lang to pop out from behind every corner they approached. Judging by his awkward steps and bunched shoulders, so did Jolly, who seemed to be alternating between moving beside her and just slightly ahead of her. The young man was, she realized after a while, purposefully making sure he was always first to reach the potentially dangerous points so she wouldn't have to.

Who says chivalry is dead? she thought, smiling to herself.

They made slow but steady progress, with Hart and Phil trailing behind with Riley between them. She didn't rush them because they could afford to take their time. Sunup was still far off, and Faith was waiting on the docks below. Two more men were standing guard when they emerged out of the submarine door at the top of the entrance, and the suddenly bigger party moved through the windy top deck.

As well as things were going, Lara kept waiting for the gunshots that never came. Wherever Ezekiel and Lang had escaped to, all signs were pointing to the two men being determined not to reveal themselves. Which was fine with her, and frankly, more than she could have hoped for.

Glancing to her left off the platform, she could see the lights of the *Trident* standing out against the suffocating blackness of the ocean, still maintaining its safe distance from them.

Lara unclipped her radio and keyed it. "Maddie, we're on our way now."

"Roger that," Maddie answered. "Any trouble?"

"So far, so good. We'll see you soon."

"Sarah's keeping a pot of coffee hot for you."

"You guys have coffee?" Jolly asked as they rounded a hulking piece of machinery that had conduits sticking out of its sides. Predictably, Jolly had casually hurried ahead before falling back beside her when they were safely around it.

She fought back a smile and said, "Don't you?"

"No, ma'am. I mean, Lara."

"The place we were at before had boxes of them. We had to leave most of it behind when we left, but fortunately we brought enough to last for a while."

"I'd love some coffee. Black. How do you take yours?"

"Same."

"Awesome," Jolly said.

Awesome? Lara thought, not quite sure if she was amused because Jolly was so easily impressed or because he sounded very much like a crushing teenage boy. He reminded her a bit of how Benny was around Gaby, though taller and less awkward.

A radio squawked behind her and she heard Hart's voice.

"Status."

"You guys are in the clear," a male voice answered through Hart's radio. "No one's followed you outside."

"All right. Chain the door and catch up to us."

"On our way," the voice said.

It was another "just in case" plan, though this time Riley had come up with it. If Ezekiel and Lang were indeed hiding below deck, chain-locking the main entrance would keep them pinned inside so they couldn't come out to freely take potshots at them or the *Trident*. The last thing she needed right now was someone armed with a grenade launcher lobbying rounds at the yacht. It was a small chance, but she'd rather it be zero instead.

By the time Riley's other two men caught up to them, they were already moving down the stairs at the edge of the platform. Yet another one of Riley's men stood below them, waiting with a flashlight.

"Lara?" Jolly said as they went down.

"Yes?" she said.

"Don't take this the wrong way…"

Oh God, I already don't like where this is going.

"But I just wanted to say it's cool finally meeting you," Jolly said.

Okay, not so bad, she thought, and said, "Likewise, Jolly."

"Anyways," the young man continued, "I thought you might get a kick out of knowing that me and some of the other guys carry around iPods with your messages on them."

"Oh yeah?" she said, fighting back the cringe from showing on her face.

"It's just the same two broadcasts you put out," Jolly said. "But—and again, don't take this the wrong way—but sometimes I pretend you're saying something else."

Oh God, someone shoot me now.

"Nothing bad," Jolly quickly added. "Just stuff like the weather and traffic reports."

She was so relieved that she didn't even try to fight back the short laugh. "Traffic reports?"

He grinned, pearly white teeth showing, but if he was slightly embarrassed or blushing again, she couldn't tell in the semidarkness of the stairs. "You know, like you were doing the newscast? Just to give some variety to the messages and all. Nothing perverted or anything. I hope that's okay."

"That's fine, Jolly," she said, and made an effort to smile at him.

"Thanks," he said, before quickly hurrying down the stairs ahead of her just before another turn came up.

"Told you," Riley said behind her. He wasn't even trying to suppress a chuckle. "*The* Lara."

"Shut up, Riley," she said.

THEY LOADED RILEY onboard Faith's boat first, settling him down on the front bench, then climbed in after him. Faith powered up the engine and maneuvered them into the water, Riley's people at the stern standing guard with weapons ready and eyes watching the *Ocean Star* for signs of Ezekiel and Lang.

But neither men showed up, and before long Faith made another turn and they were on an intercept course with the *Trident*.

When they had put enough space between them and the oil rig, Lara sat down on the bench next to Riley while Hart and the others remained standing around them. She looked back one last time at the lights blinking on the edges of the massive platform as it began succumbing to the blackness.

"How long will the lights last?" she asked.

"Until the generators run out of fuel," Riley said. "A day, tops."

"Communications?"

"Nothing runs without diesel, and we're taking most of that with us."

He was referring to the refueling ship, which at the moment was anchored on the other side of the *Trident*. They would bring the second vessel with them as insurance. It was going to slow them down, but speed wasn't going to be an issue once they cleared the area, regardless of what Mercer did in response to Riley's mutiny tomorrow. She didn't think they would need the old boat anytime soon, but the Bengal Islands were a long way off and they had a detour or two ahead of them.

"Who do you think they radioed?" she asked.

"The comm room can reach anyone, including Black Tide," Riley said. "If I were them, that's where I'd direct everything. Texas right now is too unpredictable, and they probably knew they wouldn't get much assistance from there."

"If that's true, then Mercer already knows about the mutiny."

Riley nodded but didn't say anything.

"I asked before what he would do when he found out," Lara said. "Did you come up with an answer yet?"

"I don't know what he'll do," Riley said. "I really don't."

"Maybe he won't get the chance to do anything," Hart said. He was standing next to them, one hand on the railing to steady himself as they moved across the slightly bumpy water. "If Keo gets the job done, I mean."

She nodded, though she didn't really like to think about Keo succeeding, because it meant he wasn't coming back. She remembered watching him leaving with Erin and thinking that she was never going to see him again.

"Who's Keo?" Riley asked.

Lara told him about Keo and him leaving with Erin.

"Are you surprised she's helping him?" Lara asked him.

There was almost a ghost of a smile on his lips when he said, "Not at all."

"What do you think?" Hart asked.

"About what?" Riley said.

"He means Keo killing Mercer," Lara said. "Is that going to stop the war?"

Riley took a moment to think about it. She couldn't tell if it was such a foreign concept that he was having trouble grasping the question or if he really was running through all the scenarios before answering.

"Maybe," he finally said. "There are a lot of people who'll throw down their guns, but there's also a lot who won't."

"What about Rhett?" Hart asked.

"I think he'll argue for stopping the bombings, definitely. Bellamy, Jerkins, and Taylor might feel differently."

"But there *is* a chance," Lara said.

He nodded. "If your friend can kill Mercer, then yes, there's a chance." He looked over at her. "Can he do it?"

"Keo's very good."

"But can he *do* it?"

"Yes," she said. "If anyone can do it, it's Keo."

Even if it kills him, she thought, but didn't say that part out loud.

CHAPTER 25
KEO

HE DIDN'T KNOW if he should be pleased, disturbed, or slightly annoyed at how easy it was to move around the main building. As with the beach, there weren't nearly enough people left behind on the island to post on every corner or watch every hallway, and accessing the facility was a simple matter of checking in at the guard station, where Erin did most of the talking; she was, after all, one of Mercer's easily recognized lieutenants, and that came with a lot of respect.

Once Keo separated from Erin on their way to the communal living quarters for the non-married people, he simply followed the numbers on the walls, which also happened to have helpful arrows pointing the way toward his destination. There wasn't a single soul in sight to question, much less stop him. There wasn't even an occasional soldier for him to worry about getting past; everyone who wasn't sound asleep was already outside standing guard.

"Technically he should be sleeping in the communal area because he's single, but I guess even he couldn't bring himself to justify that," Erin had said before they went their separate ways. "It's part of the role he's playing. I recognize that now."

"The Everyman," Keo had said.

"Yes."

"What about guards?"

"What you see is what you get. The rest will be coming back later today or the days after. Like you said, you'll have to get it done before the sun comes up or it's going to get a hell of a lot harder."

"No pressure."

"I'm serious, Keo," she had said, stopping at a door marked *Quarters* and fixing him with a hard stare that was meant to deliver just how serious she was. Then, lowering her voice slightly to an almost whisper, "You were right to come here now, in the middle of the night. Everyone is either asleep or dead on their feet. What did you call it?"

"The hour of the wolf."

She snapped a quick look past him and up the hallway. "Sooner or later, someone's going to ask who you are. Mercer's going to want an after-action report, and I'm going to have to explain what happened to Troy and the others. You understand?"

"Relax," Keo had said. "This isn't my first rodeo."

"We have to stop him, Keo. I should have done it months ago when I had the chance, but I didn't. That's on me, and I'm going to have to live with the consequences for the rest of my life. So please, stop him. Do what I and Riley and everyone else couldn't bring ourselves to do. *End this.*"

Keo had nodded. "I will."

He was thinking of Jordan bleeding to death in his arms when he finally located the room he had been looking for, in the exact part of the building where Erin had told him he'd find it. There were no guards posted outside, or anywhere in this or the previous three hallways he had walked through, and when Keo tried the lever, it moved without resistance.

Too easy. Way too easy.

He put his hand on the Sig Sauer P250 and looked left, then right, then left again. He stood perfectly still and listened for sounds of running feet, shouting voices, and safeties being clicked off. *Some* indication that his trip from the singles living quarters to Mercer's room had not gone completely unnoticed.

But there was nothing.

There would be dead silence if not for the hum of lights above him and the vibrations from generators in the background. No one was coming, rushing around the corners, or converging on his position so he couldn't enter this room and take the life of the man on the other side.

Way, way *too easy.*

It had to be a trick. Maybe Erin had gotten some of the details wrong, or gotten the hallways mixed up. After all, except for the numbers marking each door, they all looked the same in the last four hallways he had walked down.

"Are you sure?" he had asked her.

"506," she had said for the second time.

"What if he moved?"

"He wouldn't."

"What *if* he did?"

"Why would he? He's been in that room since we got to the island. He was there when we left for the mainland, and he'll be there after returning."

He was staring at the number now.

506.

It had to be a trick, because this was too easy. *It was just too goddamn easy.*

He sighed, thought, *Fuck it*, and pushed the door open and slipped inside, palming and drawing the Sig in one smooth motion as he did so.

Once inside, he stood perfectly still, mostly because he couldn't see a damn thing. After moving around in the brightly lit corridors the last five minutes, it took Keo a while for his eyes to adjust to near darkness. When he could finally make out gray floors, walls, and the shape of a small (much too small for someone of his position) cot at the back of the room, Keo searched out and found the light switch on the wall behind him and flicked it into the on position.

In the second or two after the light bulb *buzzed* to life, Keo glimpsed the room's Spartan design in a glance.

It was essentially a big concrete box—nothing fancy or very big, but perfect for a grunt who needed a place—any place—to rest. There was nothing comfortable about it, but he'd been in worse places during jobs. Besides the cot at the far side, there was a flimsy-looking nightstand in the corner to his right with a canteen and a two-way radio sitting on top of it. A complete wardrobe was folded over the back of a wooden chair at the foot of the bed, with a pair of polished boots next to it. There was a closet carved out of the wall with just enough space for a dozen or so articles of clothing to dangle from hangers. A gun belt hung from a hook next to the bed with a pistol in the holster, but there wasn't a rifle anywhere in the room that he could see.

The springs on the bed *creaked* as the body on top of it moved suddenly, and Keo found himself wishing the pistol in his hand had a hammer so he could do the oh-so-dramatic *click!* like in the movies. He briefly thought about jerking back the gun's slide to achieve the same drama, but that would have just ejected a perfectly good bullet.

Instead, he had to make do with holding the gun at waist level and aiming forward at the figure sitting up in front of him, whipping a wool blanket sideways. From the looks of it, the man had fallen asleep while still wearing his uniform—the familiar tan color topped with a black collar and the white sun emblems stitched along the sides.

The man swung his legs off the cot and stared across the narrow space at Keo while trying to blink sleep from his eyes. After what seemed like forever, he finally said, "Are you sure you have the right room, son?"

Keo nodded. "Pretty sure."

"How can you be so sure?"

"I have an inside man."

"Ah."

Keo didn't know why he didn't just pull the trigger right then and there. The man wasn't even armed, so it would be like shooting fish in a barrel.

So do it and get it over with. That's what you came here to do, isn't it? So get it over with already. Maybe you can still catch up to Lara and the Trident *afterward...*

Except he didn't. Not yet.

The truth was, the whole thing threw him for a loop and Keo had to readjust on the fly. It wasn't how he had pictured any of this going down at all, not even close. It didn't help that the man in front of him looked nothing like how Keo had imagined him. For one thing, he was missing horns and hooves and a tail with a long pointy arrow at the end. His skin was more tanned than it was a shade of devil red, and he leaned more toward *grandfatherly* than *mass murderer* or *war criminal*.

The man was in his fifties, with brown hair that looked almost blond against the slightly yellow ceiling light, and looked fit enough to be dangerous. In so many ways, Keo was reminded of Pollard, another ex-military officer who had made Keo's life difficult. Just thinking about the other man made the scar along the side of Keo's face tingle.

He didn't need to see the name *Mercer* stenciled across the man's shirt to know who he was pointing a gun at. He was in the right room, all right; there was no question about that. Keo could read every line on the grizzled face, and even heavy with sleep there was intelligence and a certain *(madness?)* something about the eyes. Keo imagined the cogs spinning behind the worry lines that crisscrossed the man's forehead, processing information and coming up with and discarding scenarios, even as the man gazed back at him.

"I don't recognize you," Mercer finally said.

"You know everyone on the island?" Keo asked.

"Yes." He stared at the gun in Keo's hand for a brief second, then perhaps deciding there was nothing he could do about it, refocused on Keo's face. "At least tell me your name, son."

I'm not your fucking son, asshole, Keo thought but didn't say. Even the slightest bit of annoyance might give Mercer something to use against him.

He willed himself to stay calm before answering, "Keo."

"Interesting name."

"It gets me free drinks in the bars."

"Does it really?"

"Nah."

If Mercer was the least bit amused by that, it didn't show on his face. "So what's this all about, Keo?"

"Oh, I think you know."

He sighed tiredly. "Maybe if you gave me some hints. Then again, it is the middle of the night, and I'm not exactly at my best."

"Your mom ever told you never to sleep in your clothes?"

"Yes, but sleep is a precious commodity these days. You take it when it comes." He paused, then, "I give up."

"Already?"

"I'm very tired. Why don't you just tell me why there's a stranger with a gun pointed at me in my own quarters, and we'll move on from there."

"I'll give you a hint," Keo said, and pulled a piece of paper out of his back pocket and crumpled it into a ball before tossing it over.

Mercer caught it and opened it before taking a few seconds to straighten the sheet over one knee, then looked down at it. Keo thought the man might have been stalling for time, but he dismissed it. Mercer was simply letting him know that he would not be rushed, even with a gun pointed at him.

"I hear Texas frowns on littering," Keo said. "They even have an official motto and everything."

Mercer ignored him and laid the piece of paper on the cot next to him before looking back at Keo. "I take it you're not here to enlist."

"'Fraid not, boss." Keo gestured with the Sig Sauer. "But I am here to join the bullets in this gun with your brain."

Mercer's mouth curved into a slight smile.

"Her name was Jordan," Keo said.

"Was it?" Mercer said.

"Your men killed her. She died in my arms."

"She was a collaborator."

"No."

"No?"

"No. She was fighting them. We both were."

"Then I'm sorry."

"Are you?"

"Yes," Mercer said. "But mistakes happen in war."

"Collateral damage?"

"That's right." He narrowed his eyes at Keo. "I can tell you know a thing or two about that. But you're not a soldier."

"You sure about that?"

"Yes. I can always tell just by looking at someone if they're ex-military. It's in their eyes, on their face, even in the way they stand or hold a gun. You know the Army, but you were never one of us. My guess is, someone you knew was. A parent, maybe. Or siblings. You grew up around the Army and maybe that's why you steered clear of it, though in many ways you simply joined another Army, one with less strict…guidelines."

"Keep going…"

"You're a man of violence, with a long history of blood on his hands."

"You got all that just from looking at me, huh?"

"I'm a fast study. And I've always been good at reading people."

"What else do you see?"

"I don't know how you got in here, but you don't expect to leave alive. Not that you're too worried about it. In fact, you've already accepted that things will end here for you, so long as you can take me with you."

"Not bad."

Mercer shrugged. "I have my moments."

"You should go on the road. Become a carnie."

"Not quite the future I had in mind," Mercer said, and stood up.

Keo watched the older man walk the short distance to the canteen sitting on the nightstand. He passed the gun belt hanging on the wall but never looked at it. Mercer opened the cap and took a slow, purposeful drink.

"So this is personal," Mercer said, lowering the canteen and brushing his lips with the back of a shirt sleeve. "Simple bloodthirsty revenge?"

"Revenge gets a bad rap. Don't knock it till you've tried it."

"I'd rather waste my energy on more productive things."

Mercer spun the lid back into place before returning to the cot, passing the gun hanging off the wall a second time and sitting back down in almost the exact same spot. The springs creaked under him, the only other noise in the room besides the hum of the single light bulb, the generators in the background, and the sounds of their breathing.

"You want to ask me something," Mercer said. It wasn't a question.

"What makes you say that?"

"You haven't shot me yet, so I assumed you have something else on your mind other than just killing me. Please, do go ahead. I'll answer, if I'm able."

"Aren't you the giving kind."

"I wouldn't want you to leave this room feeling unfulfilled. After all, we both know you're not going to get off the island alive."

"You've said that already."

"Because it's true."

"I don't know, I'm pretty good at this," he said, gesturing with the Sig again.

"Oh, I don't have any doubts whatsoever about that, Keo. I know you're an old hand at this."

Keo stared at the man. He could see now why people like Erin, Gregson, and even Hart would view Mercer as some kind of potential savior. The man was unsettlingly calm, even with a gun pointed at him. Mercer wasn't the very least bit scared. He didn't even seem slightly disturbed by what was happening, as if this was a regular occurrence for him.

So shoot him and get it over with. What the hell are you waiting for?

Because I have to know. I have to know…

"Are you crazy?" Keo asked.

The older man gave Keo a wry (disappointed?) look, as if to say, *"That's it? That's all you could come up with?"*

"No," Mercer said.

"You must be crazy."

"Why 'must' I be?"

"What you did in Texas, what you're planning on doing next."

"Someone has to do something. It might as well be us. I don't take any of this lightly, but—"

"Someone has to do it," Keo finished for him.

Mercer nodded. "Yes. Someone had to do it."

"What happened, did you lose someone? Is that why you've gone cuckoo for Cocoa Puffs?"

"Not at all."

"You didn't lose anyone?"

"We've all lost someone. Even you have, I'm sure. But that's not anything new. It's the cycle of life. We're born and we die, and others are born and take our place. It's how nature works. But there's nothing natural about what's happening in those towns. Man was not born to be enslaved at birth, Keo. We were not created to provide sustenance for monsters that shouldn't exist. It's unnatural."

"Some would say what you're doing is unnatural."

"They'd be wrong. I'm trying to bring back the natural order of things. Fate saw fit to appoint that role to me, but I never asked for it."

"Fate?"

"Fate. Destiny. God. Whatever you want to call what's behind this."

"There's nothing behind this."

"Of course there is. Just because you can't grasp it, or see or feel it, doesn't mean it doesn't exist."

"So God's telling you to do this?"

"Would it make you feel better to think of me as some Bible-thumping nutcase, Keo?"

"Are you?"

"I believe there's something out there desperately trying to balance the universe. Maybe I'm a part of it; maybe I'm just playing a very minor role. And maybe it sent you here to kill me, to end my command. If that's the case, then so be it."

"So you actually think you can win this war by dropping bombs on towns full of kids, old men, and pregnant women?"

"Is it really that farfetched?"

"Have you been out there? Have you seen how many of them there are? All you're doing is killing a whole lot of people when there aren't that many of us still left to begin with. You'll never be able to do enough with the limited resources you have. All you're doing is giving the nightcrawlers minor headaches. This crusade of yours will never expand past Texas."

"Headaches can grow into tumors."

"Good one, but it's still bullshit. You don't even have enough men right now to cover half of Texas, and you expect to take the entire state? What about the other forty-nine? Mexico? Canada? However many you think are in Texas, there are millions—*billions*—more out there."

Mercer smiled.

"What's so funny?" Keo asked.

"You seemed to be under the impression I haven't considered all the possibilities. I have. Every single one."

"And yet here you are, fighting an impossible war."

"This was never going to end overnight. This is the fight of our lifetime, Keo. And when we're gone, our children and their children's children will still be fighting it. There isn't any easy way out. No quick victories. The only other option is surrender. Become slaves. I'd rather die on my feet than on my knees."

"Nice speech. Is that what you used to convince the others?"

"I didn't need to convince them. They always understood what was at stake."

Not all of them, Keo thought, and said, "Your own people are already turning on you."

"Just because you've given up doesn't mean the rest of us will too, Keo."

"You'll never be able to hold everyone together when more of your people start coming back home with stories about dead pregnant women and children. You're massacring civilians, you crazy bastard."

Mercer frowned. It was the first real emotion the man had surrendered, and Keo felt a rush of triumph.

"And you're here to murder me for... What was her name?" Mercer asked.

"Jordan."

"Jordan," Mercer repeated.

"I don't like the way you say her name."

"No?"

"I don't want you to say her name again."

"You're losing your composure, Keo."

"Fuck my composure, and fuck you," Keo said, and lifted the gun and pointed it at Mercer, wishing again that the P250 had a hammer for him to dramatically cock back and hear that *clicking!* sound, but he had to be satisfied with the resigned look on Mercer's face.

The man wasn't afraid—if he was even capable of that particular emotion. No. That wasn't fear staring back at Keo; it was a man who was at peace with his decisions.

He's either insane, or he just doesn't give a fuck.

"Shoot true," Mercer said. "You don't have a suppressor on the weapon, so the first shot will alert the base and the guards on duty. You'll want to be out of this room and running as soon as I drop. Given my lack of resources at the moment, my guess is you'll make it almost to the front doors, but no farther."

"There's a rear exit close by. I plan to take it."

"Your inside man."

"Uh huh."

"He or she would have also told you about the sentries in the fields. Even if you managed to elude them, you'd never access the boat yards alone."

"What makes you think I'll be alone?"

"An extra gun or two won't help you very much." Mercer shrugged. "But that's all a moot point, since I'll be dead anyway."

"You're not even going to pretend to beg for mercy?"

"Everyone dies, Keo. If fate dictates that I die here, tonight, then so be it. The war will go on. Better men than I will assume leadership roles."

"Your true believers."

"No, just loyal men who understand what I'm trying to accomplish."

"Well, in that case, I might just have to stick around and kill them, too."

"Ambitious."

"What the hell, I could always use a hobby. Life's boring these days without a little Internet porn to pass the time with."

Keo lined up his shot.

"One thing," Mercer said.

"Changed your mind about begging?"

"Not at all. I was just going to ask: You don't know anyone important onboard the *Trident*, do you?"

Keo jerked his forefinger off the Sig Sauer's trigger and glared at Mercer. "What the hell are you talking about?"

"We were alerted to Riley's mutiny a few hours ago. Not everyone on the *Ocean Star* is a traitor. There is still a patriot or two onboard."

*Sonofa*bitch, Keo thought, but he forced himself to smile back at Mercer and said, "What makes you think any of this matters to me?"

"Because you didn't just know where to find Black Tide, you also made it onto the island without anyone stopping you. That means your inside man has to be one of Riley's people. And because you're not one of my mine—I would remember a face like yours, especially that scar—that only leaves you as a member of the *Trident*, the group that Riley struck a deal with. Am I close?"

Close enough.

"What did you do?" Keo asked.

"I dispatched one of our warplanes to intercept them. The pilot has a full tank of fuel and his orders are simple: Find the *Trident* and sink it. The good news for you is that we haven't heard back from him yet, which means his mission is still ongoing."

"It's a big ocean."

"It's not big enough to hide from a plane flying at high altitude and equipped with infrared. Not to mention plenty of fuel to search and our very own inside man to tell us which direction they went. All those warm bodies crammed into one moving boat, out there in the middle of a black sea… You really think they're going to be able to slip by unnoticed?"

Keo ground his teeth together and glared at the man. "You're willing to murder your own people just to stop them from leaving your crusade?"

"Not at all," Mercer said. His face remained stony, his voice even. "I have no idea Riley and the others are onboard the *Trident*. As far as I know, the yacht is full of enemies—strangers. Sinking it, and unfortunately killing every soul on board, was a terrible accident. Or, at least, that's what I'm going to tell my people, and that's exactly what they'll believe, because I've never lied to them before."

Keo curled his finger back around the pistol's trigger. It would be so easy. One quick pull and Mercer would no longer exist. Keo could already smell the gunpowder, see the viscera on the concrete wall behind the man's head, the spray of brain matter that would splash the cot's bedsheets…

Do it. Do it!

What are you waiting for? Do it!

"Call the plane back," Keo said.

"I can, but not from in here," Mercer said. "And not with you pointing that gun at me."

"I thought you were ready to die."

"I am, but I'm not interested in becoming a martyr. There's still too much work left to do. Texas was always just the beginning, and I plan on seeing it through to the very end—or as far as I can take it before my time is up."

"The very bitter end?"

"Hopefully it won't be too bitter."

"There are a lot of innocent people onboard the *Trident*. A lot of them once believed in you."

"Casualties of war."

"You'd sacrifice them…"

"It wouldn't be a sacrifice, but it would be a tragedy. I don't know Riley and the others are on that yacht, remember?"

Keo squinted his eyes. If Mercer was feeling triumphant, it didn't show on his face.

"Where?" Keo asked.

"The Comm Room," Mercer said, and stood up. "After you give me your gun. This is the only way it's going to work. The *Trident* and all the lives onboard it are in your hands. That's a hefty responsibility. I know a thing or two about that."

The gun was suddenly very heavy against Keo's palm, the trigger more resistant than usual against his finger.

He thought of the *Trident*.

No, not the boat itself, but the people on it.

Lara. Carly. Carrie. Bonnie. The big Mexican and the small Texan. The girl who Lara had adopted and Carly's little sister. But most of all, he thought of Lara on the *Ocean Star*, telling him not to be an asshole and to at least try to survive Black Tide Island.

"Clock's ticking," Mercer said. "Make your choice, son."

"I'm not your fucking son," Keo said through gritted teeth.

Mercer didn't react at all, but he didn't sit back down, either.

"I'll make you a deal," Keo said.

"I'm listening…"

"Let the *Trident* go. Tonight. Tomorrow. Just let them go. Don't look for them again."

"And in return?"

I'm sorry, Jordan, he thought, and said, "I don't put a bullet between your eyes. I step out of this door and we never see each other again."

"I need more than that."

"I'm all out of candy."

"You might not care about Riley's people, but what about your friends?" Mercer asked.

Keo didn't say anything.

"The only thing left is to ask yourself one question," Mercer said. He held out his hand with the palm up. "How much of your friends' lives are you willing to sacrifice to claim my one?"

CHAPTER 26
LARA

"THERE," LARA SAID, pointing at the heavily marked map spread out on the table inside her cabin. "The Bengal Islands."

Riley nodded. "That's the one. Or ones, to be more specific."

"And you know what's there?"

"On the islands?"

She nodded.

"Are you talking about potential survivors?" Riley asked.

"No," she said, watching him closely across the table.

He was probably leaning too heavily against the wooden edge and putting more of his weight on it than he might normally have if he wasn't a little drowsy from the meds. Zoe still didn't want him moving around on his own power even with the crutches, but Riley was right when he said he couldn't stay bedridden forever, and not with his people crowded onboard the *Trident*. This was one of those times when they needed to see him, if just to be reassured they hadn't made the biggest mistake of their lives.

"You know what the islands are mostly used for, right?" she

asked him. "Who goes there? And why?"

"It's a haven for criminals," Riley nodded.

"So you know."

"You sound surprised."

"I guess I am, a little."

"I was an auditor before all of this. I spent a lot of time freelancing for the U.S. government, looking for places where people hid their money when they thought Uncle Sam had taken enough of it." He gave her a wry smile. "I know how *I* know, but how does a third-year medical student know about the Islands' reputation?"

"Keo told me about it."

"Him again. Too bad I never got the chance to meet the guy, though Hart had some good things to say. Was he a soldier or something?"

"Honestly, I don't know what Keo used to be before all of this."

"You never asked him?"

"He's never been all that anxious to talk about it." She shrugged. "Besides, what happened before doesn't have anything to do with now. And right now, he's a good friend and someone I wish had come with us."

"Instead he's going after Mercer."

"He has his reasons."

"A lot of people have reasons to want Mercer dead."

"He's done some bad things. They've hung men for less."

Riley nodded, then, "So what else did you want to talk to me about?"

"Your soldiers. How good are they?"

"I wouldn't really call them soldiers."

"So what are they really?"

"They're trained, don't get me wrong, but they didn't volunteer to run around Texas creating chaos for a reason. They're not killers. Aside from skirmishes here and there before R-Day, they haven't really been in prolonged conflicts. At least, not the kind of gun battles that we might encounter if the aforementioned criminal elements are still hanging around the Islands when we get there."

"But you trust them to stand up in a firefight?"

Riley seemed to think about it for a moment before nodding—though not quite with enough confidence for her liking. "I don't think they'll run from a fight, if that's what you mean."

That's not what I meant at all, but I guess it's good enough…for now.

"What about your people?" he asked.

"We've been surviving out here for the better part of a year. We're not going to run from anything."

"You guys have been through a lot."

"We have."

"Lost a lot…"

"Everyone's lost someone, Riley."

For a moment, his eyes drifted away, as if some long-buried memory was rushing back to him. She knew what it was because she had seen that expression on a lot of faces these days, including her own when she stared in the mirror. She didn't want to ask him who he'd lost, because eventually the question would get turned back to her.

"And you're okay with us not going straight to the Islands?" she asked him.

Riley nodded. "In your position, I'd do the same thing. Besides, the Islands aren't going anywhere. They'll still be there waiting for us when we reach them tomorrow or next week or next month."

That's what I keep telling myself, and maybe that's why we never seem to get there.

"When do you expect them to radio in?" Riley asked.

"As soon as they're able."

"It'll be nice to have an Army Ranger around."

"What about those kill teams Mercer has running around Texas?"

"They're mostly civilians, though Benford was in the National Guard. I'm not sure how long ago, though. He and a couple of ex-Army guys did most of the arms training back in the early days."

"I take it you didn't have a lot of weapons training while auditing for the U.S. government?"

"You took it correctly. The first time I ever picked up a weapon was after all of this happened. It was a huge learning curve."

Lara felt like laughing. If Riley only knew the things she'd had to do, how much she'd had to change since the world ended. They were things no one had ever taught her—not her parents or any of those long and hard years in school. Sometimes when she thought about what she'd been through, she had a difficult time understanding how she was even still alive.

Adapt or perish, right, Will?

"I have a question for you," she said, looking across at Riley.

"Sure."

"What if Keo succeeds?"

"I don't understand…"

"Would you go back?"

"Where?"

"Black Tide Island."

"Go back, after what I did?"

She nodded. "Think about it: How many other people like Erin are out there running around killing for Mercer right now? How many of them are exactly like her in that they just need someone or something to get them to do the right thing? Mercer's death could be that catalyst."

"Go back to Black Tide Island," Riley said quietly.

"You could make a difference."

"How?"

"If Mercer's dead, there'll be a power vacuum. Someone will have to step in and assume command of all those people, all those guns." Lara let that sink in before continuing. "I'm willing to bet there are more people like you and Erin than you think."

"There are," he nodded. "But why would any of them listen to me? After what I did?"

"Maybe they'll listen to you *because* of what you did."

He stared at her, confused.

"You did what many of them, including Erin, couldn't—you finally said no to Mercer," Lara said. "You disobeyed him at great risk. How many of them wanted to, but were too afraid? Maybe that's why they'll listen to you."

"Or maybe they'll just shoot me as soon as I step onto the island."

Lara gave him a wry smile. "Or that."

He chuckled. "That's not very reassuring, Lara."

"Sorry. Anyway, I was just thinking out loud."

"Your friend would have to succeed first for any of this thinking out loud to matter," Riley said.

He was looking at her, but not really *at* her. She could tell that she had planted a seed in his head and it had taken root.

"There's that," she nodded, remembering the last time she saw Keo, and their last conversation on the *Ocean Star*.

"Don't be an asshole, Keo," she had told him. *"If you won't stay with us, if you won't come back to the* Trident *with me, at least promise me you're not going out there just to get yourself killed. Tell me you'll at least try to make it back, and mean it."*

"What if I can't?" he had answered.

"You can. You just have to make the choice."

"I'll do my best," he had finally relented.

Do your best, Keo, she thought now. *You better do your goddamnest best, or I'm going to find you and kick your ass.*

"HOW GOES IT?" Maddie asked when Lara stepped onto the bridge.

"You tell me," she said.

"We're on course. The question is: How long do we wait for them?"

"As long as it takes."

"Does Riley know that?"

"He knows."

"And he was good with it?"

"I didn't give him a choice."

"That's my girl," Maddie said.

The small Texan was planted behind the helm where Blaine usually was and looked just as comfortable, even if she didn't quite fill out the room the way Blaine did. If it were anyone else but Maddie guiding them across the endless expanse of the Gulf of Mexico right now, Lara might have been worried, but next to Blaine, there was no one else who knew more about the *Trident*.

"Any word from them yet?" Lara asked after a while.

Maddie glanced at the dashboard. "Nothing yet, but we're not expecting them so soon, right?"

"No…"

"You worried?"

"I'm always worried."

"I mean, more worried than usual?"

"No. They know better than to do something stupid while it's still dark out there." She leaned toward the wraparound front windshield, as if she could see her friends out there, hiding among the thick blackness that covered the ocean. "They should be hanging out in the water right now, far from land, waiting for sunup to go ashore."

"Still feels weird with everyone separated like this."

"You want me to ask someone to keep you company?"

"No, I'm good," Maddie said. "I've been spelling Blaine all this time, so I'm used to being all by my lonesome up here. Anyway, I like it; gives me time to reflect."

"On what?"

"Life and other stuff."

"Sounds deep."

"Oh yeah, it gives me headaches, too."

"Did you ever come up with something insightful? I could use a little good advice right about now."

"Just keep doing what you're doing, boss lady."

That's what I was afraid you'd say.

"That's it?" Lara said.

"You're doing all right in my book. Anyone who says differently doesn't know what they're talking about."

"I guess I'll take that. Thanks."

"No prob."

"Any complaints so far about Riley's people crowding the boat?"

"No one's said anything to me yet. Besides, it's nice to have more people around. Was starting to get tired of staring at Blaine's ugly mug all the time. There's a couple of cute guys in the bunch, too."

"I'm sure Blaine will appreciate hearing that."

"Eh, he knows he's ugly. God knows why Sarah doesn't think so."

Her radio—and Maddie's, perched on the dashboard—squawked, and they both heard Benny's voice. He sounded noticeably anxious as he said, "Lara, come in, please."

Lara keyed her two-way. "What's up, Benny?"

"I'm at the back of the upper deck right now and saw something that... Well, I'm not sure. I could use a second pair of eyes."

"I'm on my way." Lara glanced at Maddie. "You sure you don't want some company up here? How about one of those cute guys?"

"Maybe you can ask Hart to come up here."

"Hart's old enough to be your father."

"What can I say, I like 'em gray," Maddie smiled. "They know how to appreciate a woman."

"I'll see what I can do."

She hurried out of the bridge and through the hallway, then across the upper deck. She could already hear the din of people moving around and talking in nervous but excited voices from the entertainment area beyond the narrow corridor. She walked through the group of people, exchanging nods with a few of the men, though she didn't spot Hart anywhere.

To keep any one area of the yacht from becoming too congested with bodies, they had spread out Riley's people across all three decks, with the majority in the lower and main floors. The *Trident* wasn't the *Ocean Star* and it didn't have the space to accommodate all forty-something of Riley's people comfortably, but everyone seemed to be making the best of the situation as far as she could tell.

But she had to keep reminding herself they were just a few hours into their arrangement. It was going to take time—maybe a few days—before restlessness set in and people began to notice the lack of freedom to move around. When that happened, she was going to need Riley and Hart to help her deal with it. The good news was that she was sure she could rely on both of them.

Lara maneuvered her way to the back of the floor and pushed out of the door and found Benny bracing against the railing, peering up at the sky with binoculars. There wasn't a whole lot of moonlight tonight, and all she could see with the naked eye was a darkened sea of nothing, which was appropriate since it correctly mirrored the ocean around them at the moment.

"Benny," she said, closing the door behind her.

He lowered the binoculars and looked over his shoulder. "I don't know for sure, but there was something up there."

"What was it?"

"It looked like…"

"What was it, Benny?"

"I thought it might have been a plane, but…"

"But what?"

"It's gone."

"When did you first see it?" she asked, taking the binoculars from him.

"About five minutes ago," Benny said. "Then it just disappeared. It looked like a black dot up there, but it's so dark it's hard to be sure."

She wanted to ask the teenager if he might have imagined it, but she didn't want to undermine his already fragile confidence. Lara peered through the binoculars instead. It was equipped with night-vision and rendered the world in a sea of green. There were barely any clouds above them, but she spotted a few in the distance.

She scanned left, then right, but there was nothing up there.

"I don't see anything," she said, and turned around in case whatever the "something" Benny had seen (or thought he had seen) was now behind them.

"False alarm, I guess," Benny said. "Maybe I'm just a little paranoid?"

"You okay?"

"Maybe it's all the new people on the boat. Feels weird having so many people suddenly around."

"I know how you feel."

"Yeah?"

She looked back at him and nodded. "We've been out here by ourselves for so long. Suddenly adding a bunch of new faces can be disconcerting."

"That must be it."

"Don't worry about it," she said and handed the glasses back to him. "I'd rather you stay a little paranoid than sleep on the job. I need everyone as alert as possible until we're in the clear, which won't be for a while."

"We're not leaving the others behind, are we?" he asked, though she knew what he really wanted to say was, *We're not going to leave before we pick Gaby up, are we?*

"We're not leaving anyone behind," she said, and thought, *Not again. Never, ever again.* She smiled at the young man and gave him a pat on the shoulder, feeling more than a little weird doing it since they weren't *that* far apart in age. "I promise."

He looked relieved and went back to scanning the horizon. Lara watched him for a moment, feeling as sorry for Benny as she did for herself when she finally accepted that Will wasn't coming back, that he was gone for good.

At least Gaby's still around to be seen, Benny. So there's that.

Lara didn't have the urge to face the crowd inside the floor again so soon, so she walked over to the side railing. She hadn't taken more than a couple of steps when a speck of something black and nearly indistinguishable against the darkened sky flickered across her vision. It might have been completely invisible if it hadn't been moving across a stream of white clouds when she looked up.

"Benny," she said. "Binoculars!"

He must have heard the urgency in her voice (she was pretty

sure she might have screamed) and quickly shoved the glasses into her extended hand. Lara held them up and focused on the clouds, but the object was gone. Or was it?

"What is it?" Benny asked. "Did you see something?"

"Give me a second."

She tried to picture where the object had been when she last saw it, then attempted to track its trajectory from left to right—

There!

"Oh, dammit," she whispered.

"What is it?" Benny said behind her. "What do you see, Lara?"

It wasn't actually black, she realized now that she was able to focus on it for more than a few seconds—maybe more of a grayer color, possibly even white, against the dark sky backdrop.

"Lara?" Benny said. "What is it? What do you see?"

She kept moving along the deck in order to keep it in view, and when she saw what it was in the process of doing, her heart might have stopped beating entirely.

It was a plane, and it was turning back toward them…

CHAPTER 27
KEO

KEO WAS USED to having guns pointed at him. Two guns, three guns. Four? Why not. It could be fifty, for all he cared, because all it took was one guy and one shot to do the job.

Of course, Mercer's men didn't see it that way, and there were already two of them in the hallway when he began marching their leader from his quarters to the Comm Room on the other side of the main building. Just his luck the men would turn the corner as soon as he stepped out of the room with Mercer.

It took a lot of effort to make sure the men never got behind him, and each time one of them drifted too far back, Keo had to stop and pull Mercer against him, with his back against the wall, and order them back in front of him. He thought about using the M4 he still had slung, but while the firepower was a major plus, the weapon's length made it untenable for quick close-quarter action. Even so, he was tempted to lob a grenade round or two to wake the whole place up, maybe give Erin a heads up that the shit had, indeed, hit the fan.

Two guns became four when they rounded the second corner, because the first two had radioed for reinforcements. Keo recalled the two new arrivals *(Two more makes four, unless my math is off)* as being the same two from the front doors when he first entered the facility with Erin. Four later became five when they took the final turn, because there was another man standing outside the Comm Room.

There would probably have been more if the island wasn't already pressed for bodies and if Mercer hadn't ordered the rest to stay at their positions.

"Send them away," Keo said as they approached the Comm Room.

"No," Mercer said.

"You do remember that I have a gun pointed at your head, right?"

"And the answer's still no."

"You're pushing your luck, pal."

"So are you."

So what else is new, Keo thought as he backed his way to the door, reached over and found the lever, then pushed it down. With Mercer between him and the soldiers as a shield, he bent slightly at the knees and turned his head and peeked into the room, noticing a lone figure sitting on the far side, oblivious to what was happening outside in the hallway.

Keo tightened his grip around Mercer's arm and backtracked into the Comm Room, then moved quickly over to the wall where he once again put Mercer between him and the soldiers as they rushed inside after him. It took a while, but the woman sitting in front of the row of communications gear finally sensed that someone else—a *lot* of someone elses—were in the room with her and turned around. Keo saw why she was so clueless when she did—she was wearing a headset with thick earpieces.

The woman shot up from her chair and stared wide-eyed at Keo and Mercer, then (hands shaking) removed her headset and said, "Sir, what's going on?"

"It's fine, Jane," Mercer said in that impossibly calm voice of his. "Please sit back down."

But Jane remained a statue, seemingly incapable of moving.

"It's all right," Mercer said, and nodded.

His calmness had an effect on Jane and she finally sat back down, then oddly rested her hands in her lap like she was back in school. Unlike Mercer and the men pointing their weapons at Keo, her uniform collar was white.

The room wasn't particularly large, and with all the electronics equipment hugging the back wall, it didn't leave a lot of space for Keo and Mercer and all five soldiers to breathe. It was suddenly so quiet that Keo thought he could hear all eight heartbeats beating at the same time, but that might have just been his and Mercer's. Or his, anyway, because he swore Mercer was as relaxed as any man could be with a gun jammed up his chin.

Guy's got the emotions of a robot.

"Send them out," Keo said.

He kept his head hidden behind Mercer's, leaning out only far enough to see just in case one of the soldiers decided to risk a shot from close-range.

"We already went over this," Mercer said. "That's not going to happen."

"Look around you, pal. You really think six people with guns drawn in a room this small is a good idea? All it takes is one Nervous Nelly and we're all dead."

Mercer didn't take long to think about it, and maybe the sight of his men fidgeting nervously in front of him sealed the deal. "Not all of them," he said.

"Three," Keo said.

"Two."

"Deal."

Mercer nodded at two of the men—the first two that had intercepted them on the way over here. "You and you. Wait outside."

The men pulled up their rifles and backed away without a word before slipping outside the open door. They weren't even trying to hide their relief as they left.

"Sir," Jane said, her voice trembling slightly. "What's happening?"

"Everything's fine, Jane," Mercer said. "Has Cole radioed in yet?"

"Ten minutes ago, sir."

"Contact him for me, please."

"Yes, sir," Jane said and swiveled around in her chair, though she glanced back at Keo and Mercer one more time before getting to work. "Cole, this is Black Tide Island. Please come in. Cole, this is Black Tide Island. Please come in."

"Relax," Keo said to the three men in front of him.

The three didn't respond. At least, not verbally. One of them shuffled his feet (*Olsen* was scribbled across his name tag) and another (Travis) wrinkled his nose like he had an annoying itch he couldn't get to. The third man, the biggest of the bunch, didn't move a muscle, and dark brown eyes remained laser focused on Keo. *Jasper* was stenciled across one side of his chest.

"Tell your men to relax, Mercer," Keo said.

"Relax, men," Mercer said. "Everything is under control."

Jane turned around and slipped off her headset again. "Sir, I have Cole on the radio."

"Put him on the speakers," Keo said.

Jane looked to Mercer for approval, and he nodded. She hit a switch and Keo heard a deep male voice coming through the walls around him: "Waiting for further instructions, Black Tide."

"The microphone, Jane," Mercer said, holding out his hand.

Jane picked up the mic and walked the short distance over.

"She can go, too," Keo said.

"Agreed," Mercer said, and nodded at Jane.

Like the other two, Jane didn't argue and hurried past them and out the door, moving as fast as her feet would carry her.

Everyone's getting out alive except me. Just my luck.

"Just the five of us, boys," Keo said, forcing his best devil-may-care smile at the three soldiers standing across from him. "You guys fans of the show *Full House?*"

No response.

"Guess not," Keo said.

Mercer had pressed the transmit button on the microphone and was saying into it, "Cole, this is Mercer. Come in."

"Yes sir, I read you loud and clear," the pilot answered. "Didn't think you'd still be awake, sir."

"Neither did I."

"This isn't a fucking date," Keo said. "Get to the fucking point."

"What's your situation, Cole?" Mercer said into the microphone.

"Spotted that white whale I was looking for," Cole said.

White whale? Keo thought, then, *Right. The* Trident. *Clever, jackass.*

"Can't tell how many people are onboard," the pilot continued, his voice coming loud and clear through the speakers along the walls. "It's currently heading southwest."

"Southwest?" Mercer said.

"Looks like it might be angling back toward the Texas shore."

"Interesting," Mercer said, but he hadn't keyed the mic when he said that last part, so Keo assumed it was meant for him. "Why are they heading back to Texas?"

Good question, Keo thought, but he said, "Tell him to back off and return to the island."

"I can't do that."

Keo jammed the gun harder against Mercer's chin, and the man grunted. Travis and Olsen reflexively took a single step forward, fingers tightening around their weapons' triggers. Jasper, on the other hand, remained where he was.

Mercer held up a hand. "It's all right, men. Back up."

Travis and Olsen obeyed instantly, stepping back until they were standing side-by-side with Jasper again. The big man had never taken his eyes off Keo, and his rifle hadn't wavered even an inch.

Keo turned his focus back on Mercer, but not before slipping just a little bit farther behind his human shield. "Tell the pilot to back off *now*."

"And I told you, I can't do that," Mercer said. "You know how this has to work, Keo. Your life for the *Trident*. There is no other way this can end. I told you there was going to be a price to pay."

"What guarantees do I have that you'll keep your word?"

"You have just that. My word."

"I don't trust the word of a madman."

"Says the man who snuck onto an island with the sole purpose of murdering someone he's never met."

"You don't have to have met someone to know they need killing."

"You've done it before, I take it."

"More times than you can count, pal."

"I don't know, Keo; I can count pretty high."

"Sir?" Cole said through the speakers. "What are your orders?"

"Good question," Mercer said. "What are my orders, Keo? Or let's put it this way: If Cole doesn't get any response from me in the next few minutes, will he follow through with my initial orders or completely disregard them and return home? Before you answer, keep in mind that he doesn't know who is onboard the *Trident* at this moment. As far as he's concerned, it's an enemy boat, and I've already given him authority to shoot it out of the water."

Keo listened to Mercer's heartbeat—not hard to do with the man pressed up tightly against him, their bodies touching back to front—and waited to hear the slight increase. Except there was none. It was perfectly *flatlined*. If Mercer was even a little bit anxious or scared, Keo couldn't detect it, which was a hell of a feat because he was almost certain he could hear one of the soldiers in front of him actually hyperventilating.

"Sir," Cole said through the speakers, sounding slightly concerned by the lack of response, "do I proceed with the initial orders?"

"The man is getting anxious, Keo," Mercer said. "What should I tell him?"

"Tell him to turn back," Keo said.

"Give me one good reason why I should."

Lara, Keo thought as he let the gun swivel against his trigger finger until the muzzle was pointed away from Mercer. He released his grip on the older man and Mercer stepped forward, then calmly turned around and took the Sig Sauer before removing the M4 slung over Keo's back.

The soldiers in the room with them relaxed and lowered their weapons slightly, but not entirely.

"The pilot," Keo said. "Turn him around."

Mercer put Keo's handgun into his front waistband and handed the carbine over to Jasper, then keyed the microphone. "Cole, turn around and come back to the island."

"Sir?" Cole said, confused.

"Mission's over. Come home."

"Roger that, sir."

"So I was right," Mercer said, this time to Keo. "You're part of the *Trident*'s crew."

"Would you have let him do it?" Keo asked.

Mercer didn't answer him right away. Instead, he walked over to the row of communications gear and put the microphone back down in its reserved slot, then calmly swiped at a small film of dust on one of the screens.

Finally, he looked back at Keo and said, "It's hard to make an omelet without breaking a few eggs."

"Collateral damage," Keo said.

"Collateral damage," Mercer nodded.

"And now?"

"And now, nothing. If Riley wants to take his people and leave, then good riddance. I need men and women who are dedicated to the cause. Bringing them back would just infect the others."

"You're going to let them go. Just like that."

"I'll keep my word. I'm not going to pursue them. But if they should cross my path again, then that goes beyond the perimeters of our agreement, do you agree?"

Keo nodded. "I do."

"Good." Mercer looked over at his soldiers. "It's been a long night, and we're all tired. Take Keo to the beach and shoot him in the head and give him to the ocean." He focused on Jasper when he added, "I want it to be fast and painless."

"Yes, sir," Jasper nodded back.

Olsen and Travis grabbed Keo from behind while Jasper drew his sidearm and held it at his side.

"A bullet to the head, huh?" Keo said to Mercer.

"You surrendered your mission to save your friends," Mercer said. "I respect a man with that kind of conviction."

"That makes one of us."

Mercer ignored the insult and nodded at his men then turned around, effectively dismissing all four of them.

"You can't win," Keo said. "You'll just end up killing a lot of people, but you'll never be able to win. Not this way."

"We'll see," Mercer said without bothering to turn around.

Olsen and Travis tightened their hold around Keo's arms, and one of them (maybe Olsen) grunted, "Come on, man, make it easy. It's over."

"Who's fighting?" Keo said, and relaxed his arms against their grips.

He caught the two of them exchanging a surprised, then suspicious glance when he didn't fight back. He could have told them he had no intentions of resisting, that he had already decided there was no point. It wasn't like he had any places to escape to even if he could get out of the Comm Room in one piece. There were two more waiting outside (and the unarmed woman), and as soon as someone fired a shot, the entire island would be on high alert. Not just the ones already awake, but *everyone*.

Besides, Mercer had, against all odds (because Keo was ninety percent sure the man was lying through his teeth) kept his word and let the *Trident* go. And if he was to be believed, he would continue doing so unless some bad stroke of luck had Lara and the others crossing his path again.

In many ways (maybe in all the ways that mattered), the night hadn't ended so badly after all. Sure, he'd come here to kill Mercer and avenge Jordan and failed at both, but he had ended up saving Lara and the others onboard the *Trident* instead. They were his friends. He'd spent a lot of time with them, long enough to know that he liked them. So, in terms of accomplishments, he had to admit he was definitely coming out ahead.

He must have been smiling as they led him to the door, because Olsen, to his right, said, "You look pleased with yourself."

"Going for a swim, boys. I've always loved the water," Keo said, and smiled even wider.

"Guy's crazy," Travis said from his left.

"Keep him moving," Jasper said, his footsteps heavy behind them—

Bang! Bang!

Gunshots. Two of them, coming one after another, and less than a second apart.

Then someone screamed. A woman. Followed by footsteps fading fast.

Keo couldn't see how Jasper reacted behind him, but he saw Olsen releasing his arm as the man scrambled for his rifle while Travis was less decisive and continued clinging to Keo. Even as Keo tried to figure out what was happening, the words *Drop! Drop! Drop!* flashed across his mind.

He did exactly that, letting both legs turn to jelly and dropping like a sinking rock. In the process, he dragged Travis down with him. His knees had just slammed into the floor, sending stabs of pain through him, when a familiar figure appeared in the open doorway in front of him.

Erin.

She had a gun in one hand, and if she saw him she didn't give any indication of it. Instead, she fired again, the gunshot a thunderous *boom!* in the small communications room. She had fired high, which meant she wasn't aiming at him, so it was either Olsen to his right or Jasper somewhere behind him. Keo hoped it was Jasper because he had a feeling the big man was going to be the hardest one to take down.

Two shots responded from behind him and from such close proximity that they might as well be nukes going off, and Keo wondered if he might not have gone deaf as a result. In front of him, Erin seemed to take a staggering step back before collapsing, having made it only a couple of steps into the room, while her gun fell out of her numbed right hand and clattered to the floor.

But it wasn't Erin's falling gun or Erin herself that Keo found himself staring at. No, it was the instantly recognizable oblong-shaped green object rolling out of her left palm when the back of her hand slapped the floor and the fingers unfurled and—

Uh oh, Keo thought as he spun at the waist while a pair of hands tried desperately to keep his left arm in place. Travis, unwilling to let go despite everything happening around them. But Travis wasn't fast or strong enough, and Keo twisted free and turned around and looked up at—

Jasper, staring back at him, even as he started to lower the Smith & Wesson in his right hand to aim at Keo's head, when someone shouted, *"Grenade!"*

The shout froze Jasper in place—at least, for just a second—but it was enough time for Keo to launch himself and grab Jasper's arm and jerk back down with everything he had. The loud *crack!* as Jasper's arm snapped at the elbow was only drowned out by Jasper's screams, but Keo was beyond caring. He wrested the gun out of the man's suddenly pliant hand and spun back to the door.

Travis was on the ground, staring wide-eyed at the grenade that had rolled out of Erin's left hand. Except Travis didn't see what Keo had spotted earlier—*the pin was still intact*. Erin might have come here with the intention of taking all of them *(Mercer)* out with the grenade if she couldn't do it with the pistol, but somewhere between shooting the two outside and stepping into the Comm Room, she had never armed the frag device.

But Travis didn't know that and kept trying to get up, draw his gun, and keep his balance at the same time, and failing at all three. Next to Travis, Olsen lay on his back on the floor with blood pumping out of his chest.

Keo was still taking stock of the action behind him (a second? Half a second, if that?) when a fist landed against the back of his head. But the blow, while catching him by surprise, wasn't nearly as strong as it could have been if it had been delivered by someone who didn't have a broken arm and was relying on his weak hand. Still, it staggered Keo just enough while Jasper followed, useless right hand dangling at his side like a stump while his left cocked back for another strike—

Keo shot the man in the stomach at almost point-blank range. At the exact same time, he glimpsed Mercer in the back of the room taking aim with the Sig Sauer he had taken from Keo earlier.

"Keo!" Mercer shouted.

Fuck you! Keo wanted to shout back, but he was too busy ducking as Mercer fired and Jasper's body twitched against the impact above him.

He grabbed the big man by the shirt collar and hid in front of him, using him as a shield the way he had done Mercer earlier. Except Jasper was much heavier (and dead?), and it took all of Keo's strength to keep him propped up on his feet. Keo stuck his gun between Jasper's side and left arm and squeezed off two rounds in Mercer's direction.

The first shot missed completely and hit a radio receiver, but the second struck Mercer in the left thigh and the man stumbled, his gun hand wavering for just a heartbeat before he raised it again and fired a second time, then a third—

Keo shoved his shoulder into Jasper's limp body and ran it forward, using the man as a moving battering ram. He only caught a blur of Mercer before he had crossed the remaining space between them and slammed the soldier into his superior and knocked all three of them down like stray bowling pins. It would have been comical if Keo weren't so close to death that all he could think was *move, move, move!*

Luckily for Keo, he ended up on top of Jasper, whose back had collided with Mercer and now pinned the man to the floor under them. Mercer glared up at him, but his gun was somewhere trapped underneath Jasper's heavier body, along with his entire right arm. For the very first time since he met the man, Keo saw real concern flashing across Mercer's face.

So he is a real boy after all!

Keo might have laughed out loud if he wasn't too busy checking on Travis, who had finally managed to gather enough of his senses (and had realized the grenade wasn't live) to stand up and turn around.

He shot Travis in the hip—it was his best angle while still perched on top of the unmoving Jasper—as the soldier was turning, gun in his hand. Travis let out a startled grunt and dropped the pistol, then stumbled to the door and leaned against it while grabbing at his wound. He still had his rifle slung over his shoulder, but he might not have remembered as he hobbled outside into the hallway.

He's got the right idea, Keo thought as he looked back at Mercer, still struggling underneath Jasper. The only thing Keo cared about was that the older man's right hand—and the gun in it—was still absent.

He could already hear pounding footsteps behind him coming from outside the Comm Room. In a minute—maybe half that time, but even that was being overly generous—there would be enough guns here to keep him from doing what he needed to do, what he had come here to do in the first place.

After all the struggling hadn't done him any good, Mercer finally ceased all movement and seemed to lie back and stare up at Keo. "Don't," he said.

"Don't what?" Keo said.

"The war," Mercer said. "Someone has to do it. If not me, then who?"

"Fuck your war," Keo said, and shot Mercer between the eyes.

He was rewarded with a fresh coat of red paint on the floor.

CHAPTER 28
GABY

"COME OUT, COME out, wherever you are."

She hated the sound of his voice and the stupid cavalier attitude he was trying to project through the radio. She would have turned the two-way off if she could, but there was no upside to that and plenty of downside. As long as he was talking, he was giving her valuable information even if he didn't know it. She couldn't decide if he was stupid or if he just didn't care.

"We can play this game forever. I got all the time in the world, sweetheart. Don't know about you, though."

I'm not your sweetheart, asshole.

She would have said it out loud if she weren't afraid he might hear the pain in her voice. At least this way he didn't know if she was even still alive, and that, hopefully, would deter him from coming in because she wasn't entirely certain she could take Mason and however many men he had out there with him if they did.

She had to be satisfied with peering out from behind the corner of the large countertop because the last time she poked her head up over it, someone nearly took it off with a bullet that was still lodged somewhere in the wall behind her. She looked past the broken curtain glass wall that separated the diner and the empty street beyond. There were no signs of a shooter out there, not that they would have made it that easy for her to spot them, because they were definitely out there somewhere.

The diner was a placed called "Tobey"-something; the rest of the name was buried with the debris that covered large sections of the streets outside. And this was one of the few parts of Gallant that was still (mostly) intact. The rest, particularly around the middle section, was almost complete rubble. She hadn't realized the full extent of damage Mercer's warplane had inflicted on the abandoned town until she, Danny, and Nate stepped out of what was left of the bank and into the morning sunlight.

The carnage was everywhere they looked. Shards in big chunks and small pebble sizes had carpeted everything, and walking over them was like trying to tiptoe through one of those mailing foam bubble wraps where every step produced a sharp *crunching* noise. Despite all that, Tobey-whatever was strangely in one piece—or its interior, anyway, which was why she had stopped to search it for supplies, and maybe a forgotten bottle of water or two.

"Now you're just being rude, Gaby." Mason again, his annoying voice still coming through the radio sitting on the floor behind her. He was either having the best time of his life or he wanted her to think so. "If you're waiting for your boy toys to come to the rescue, you're gonna have a long wait ahead of you, sweetheart. They got problems of their own right now."

As if on cue, a series of *pop-pop-pop* cracked across the Gallant morning skyline. They originated from her left, farther up the street…which was the direction where she had last seen Danny and Nate.

"Speaking of the devils," Mason said.

She pulled her head back and scooted away from the counter until she was leaning against the back wall with the kitchen window above her. She was still facing the street, even though she couldn't see very much of it. She laid her rifle across her knees and opened the pouch around her waist and pulled out the field first-aid kit.

There was a hole in her left shoulder, the bullet that had caused it wedged somewhere just under the clavicle. The shot had come from across the street and sailed undeterred through the already-broken front windows. Sooner or later, she was going to have to dig the bullet out. Or have someone do it for her, more likely. Either way, it was going to hurt even more than it was hurting now, and it was hurting now plenty.

She gritted her teeth and fought back a scream the entire time she treated the wound, the silence around her only broken by the *pop-pop-pop* of automatic rifle fire continuing to roll back and forth from up the street. Danny and Nate were out there, either together or separately, and making their way toward her. She could tell from the way the gunshots continued to get closer with each new volley. More importantly, she knew they wouldn't abandon her, just as she would never abandon either one of them.

Gaby swallowed the pain and didn't stop working until she was done. She breathed in a deep breath and blinked away the tears, then tossed the remains of the kit and picked her rifle back up and crawled to the other side of the counter, toward the blasted front doors. To get to the other end, she had to maneuver around the fresh trail of her own blood. There was surprisingly very little, which she guessed was a good thing.

"Gaby, you still there?" Mason was saying through the radio behind her. For all she knew, he could have been talking this entire time, but she just hadn't noticed because she was so focused on treating the wound. "I'm starting to think you don't like me. After all we've been through. Remember Louisiana? Those were good times, huh?" Then, almost as an afterthought, "Remember Josh?"

She ignored him *(The past is the past. Concentrate on the now!)* and kept going until she reached her destination and looked out from behind the counter. She scanned the street and the buildings on the other side.

A thrift shop and a donut place were flanked by a couple of storefronts whose signs had come down last night, their windows blown out and contents scattered. Mason and whoever else was out there with him had to be in one of those places, she was sure of it. How else could they have seen her going into the diner earlier, and then later, taken that second shot at her?

"That kid," Mason was saying, undeterred by her silence, "I swear he had it bad for you. Even when he had you locked up in that town, he was convinced you'd see the light. You know teenagers in love, runaway hormones and all that good stuff." Mason paused for a moment before continuing. "I guess he was wrong."

She wasn't sure if he was trying to goad her into answering or if he really was just reminiscing. And he had to know that the longer he toyed with her, the more time he was giving Danny and Nate to reach her. Or was that the point, she wondered, even as the *pop-pop-pop* continued unabated outside, getting closer…

Is that it? Is he using me as bait to lure Danny and Nate here?

That, more than anything, pissed her off. Gaby had stopped thinking of herself as a damsel-in-distress a long time ago, and to be used as one now…

She leaned against the counter and rested for a moment. The crawling from one side to the other had tired her out more than she wanted to admit. Her shoulder continued to throb underneath the bandage, as if the entire arm was going to fall off at any moment.

Maybe that would have been best; maybe the pain wouldn't be so unbearable if the arm just plopped right off…

NO!

She opened her eyes.

When had she closed them?

She blinked against the sweat and wiped dirt from her face, then painfully picked herself up from the floor and searched frantically for—there, her rifle. She grabbed it with her good hand.

How long had she been out? Worse, she had laid her head

down on the floor just beyond the edge of the counter's protection, and it was a miracle Mason or whoever was out there with him hadn't spotted her and ended everything right then.

Stupid. Don't ever do something stupid like that again!

She pulled farther back from the edge and sat up, using the wall as support, and tried to calm down her breathing. Her left shoulder pulsed with every breath she took, and the pain was still as awful as anything she had experienced. What she wouldn't do for some painkillers, or maybe just a little bit of morphine. They still had some from when they treated Nate—

Wait, something's wrong.

She didn't know what it was—what grabbed her and refused to let go—for the first couple of seconds, but then it came to her.

It was quiet around her.

The shooting had stopped!

Glancing down at her watch did her no good because she had no frame of reference. They had climbed out of the rubble around the bank as soon as the sun washed over the town, and it had taken her maybe an hour to walk the length of the street, maneuvering around the destruction, all the while looking for danger. No one had wanted to separate, but they had no choice. They weren't going to get anywhere on foot with their cargo.

They needed a vehicle. A *working* vehicle. And that meant spreading out to cover as much ground as possible. It was a calculated risk, especially with Nate still hobbling around moving almost entirely on pain meds.

"Gaby?" Mason's voice again, coming from the other side of the counter. She looked over at the radio, still sitting where she had left it. "I feel like I'm talking to myself here. Won't you say something?"

He doesn't know.

She could hear it in his voice: Mason had no idea she had lost consciousness for…however long it had been. Maybe it was just a few seconds, after all, because he sounded more bored than anything.

"It's not too late, you know," Mason said. "With Mercer's

people out there, we can always use more volunteers. You'd fit right in, and you can count on me to keep quiet about what you've been up to out here. We'll just pretend it never happened. Clean hands and all that. What do you say?" When she didn't respond, "I bet all the boys would go crazy trying to get into your—Uh, I mean, be all friendly like with you."

This time she didn't stop herself from crawling back down the length of the counter and snatching up the radio and keying it. "That ship sailed when you tried to kill me, you piece of shit."

"She lives!" Mason laughed. "Sorry about that. I thought you were someone else."

"Fuck you."

"Okay, okay, I admit it, I knew it was you. Can you blame me? These last few days have been a real pain for both of us."

"Go to hell," she said, and lowered the radio back to the floor. Just holding it to her lips was tiring, and with her useless left arm it meant she had to rely on her right, and she preferred to be holding the M4 instead.

"That's not very ladylike, is it?"

She lifted the radio back up with some effort. "Fuck off."

"You kiss Nate with that mouth?"

"I do more than that."

Mason laughed again. It was loud and booming, and she tilted her head to see if she could hear it outside the diner, but she couldn't. Wherever he was, he was well hidden enough that his voice didn't travel. At least she had the satisfaction of knowing that with everything reduced to rubble around her, he couldn't have been all that comfortable out there.

"By the way, you hear that?" Mason asked. When she didn't respond, he said, "Shooting's stopped. You know what that means, don't you? The rescue has, alas, been canceled. You're all by yourself, Gaby. There's just you and me now. Somehow, I always knew it'd end up this way."

She glanced to her left, where all the shooting had come from before the silence. What were the chances Mason was telling the truth, that Danny and Nate had been stopped on their way to her?

No. He's lying. That's what he does. He lies.

She looked back at the radio. Mason was in a mood to talk, so who was she to keep him from flapping his gums? The more attention he paid to her, the less he was looking for Danny and Nate, because she didn't believe for a second they were both dead, and death was the only thing that was going to keep them from coming to her.

She picked the radio up. "Last night…"

"What about it?" Mason said.

"You attacked us."

"So?"

"You weren't supposed to do that. But you did."

"That's what's on your mind? Now? With Danny and Nate dead, and you in that diner all by your little lonesome, surrounded by my guys?"

She ignored him and said, "Why did you attack last night?"

"Because I could," Mason said. "Because the person our mutual friends were luring to Gallant had arrived, and they gave me the go-ahead to finish you off. I know, I could have sat back and let the little beasts finish the job without ever having to get my hands dirty, but I really wanted the satisfaction of shooting Danny in the face. It must be the Army Ranger thing. I don't have a lot of ambitions in life—survival's always been the number-one goal—but to take out a Ranger… Well, I couldn't resist."

Danny's going to love hearing that…because he's not dead.

God, please, don't be dead, Danny. Don't be dead.

"I met your friend, you know," Mason said.

Friend?

"Will," Mason said. "The other Ranger. Back in Louisiana, outside of Dunbar. That was me. I put that together. Well, most of it. See, we've been connected for a while now, only you never knew it." He chuckled, clearly satisfied with himself. "You don't know how many times I wanted to let that slip while you were dragging me around Texas."

"You were there…"

"Not just there. I was the one who handed him over to them.

To her."

Her?

Gaby stared at the radio, not quite sure what she was feeling. Anger? Hatred? Guilt?

There had always been a large hole in her knowledge about what had happened to Will that day and the days after. The not knowing had affected Lara the most as she waited for him, but it hadn't been easy on her and Danny either because they were the last two to see him alive, and it weighed heavily on them that they had left him out there, alone.

Maybe, she thought, that was why it was so hard for her to believe that the *thing* from last night was Will, because admitting it was also accepting that Will hadn't managed a miraculous escape, a fairy tale she continued to cling to all the way up to last night. In so many ways, accepting that the blue-eyed creature that had shadowed them from Larkin and Starch and now Gallant was, in fact, a transformed Will was the same as coming face-to-face with her failure.

"Hey, you still there?" Mason was saying. "You didn't fall asleep on me, did you?"

She didn't bother answering him. Her shoulder hurt and her left arm had grown three (five?) times its normal weight, and it was difficult just to lift it an inch off the dirty diner floor. Besides, Mason's voice was starting to give her a headache.

"Sweetheart?"

Don't call me sweetheart, you sonofabitch, she thought, but didn't have the strength to say into the radio.

"I guess this is goodbye—"

She was so numb and tired and ready to just close her eyes and go to sleep that she almost didn't react when a hellacious series of gunfire crackled through the radio and cut Mason off in mid-sentence. At first Gaby thought it was all taking place on Mason's side of the radio, but no, she could actually hear it outside in the street, too.

Crunch! as something broke underneath a heavy boot to her left.

Gaby turned her head—at this point it was the easiest part of her to move without sending jolts of pain through her body—as a man in a black uniform stepped out from a back hallway. The man had frozen in place when his boot came down on a piece of fallen plaster, the *crunch* that she had heard earlier. He was cradling a rifle and looking forward, searching for (her) something when she saw him.

Almost as if in slow motion, the man turned his head in her direction, and for the briefest of heartbeats they stared silently across the length of the counter at one another. The gunfire from across the street continued, but neither one of them heard it at the moment. For a second—maybe two—there were just the two of them in Tobey-something, staring at one another, both shocked to see the other there.

Mason?

No, not Mason.

She hadn't needed to see his face to know the man wasn't Mason because he was too tall and too skinny. He was holding his rifle in front of his chest, the muzzle pointed slightly forward and down, so when he reacted he had to lift the weapon and turn at the same time. She didn't have to do anything because her M4 was already flat in her lap, the muzzle pointed right at him.

She simply squeezed the trigger and the carbine jumped slightly without the benefit of a second hand to steady it, but she unleashed enough rounds—and, more importantly, in the right direction—that the man screamed as bullets chopped into his legs just around the kneecaps. Many more rounds missed him and slammed into the far wall—and he collapsed to the debris-strewn floor, his body jerking uncontrollably the entire way down.

Gaby didn't stop firing until she had emptied the entire magazine. She quickly pulled out a fresh mag from her pouch with her good hand and reloaded the rifle, her eyes glued on the twitching form the entire time. The collaborator had landed on his back with both legs still attached, but enough blood had gushed out of his destroyed limbs that they blanketed the area under and around him in no time. A thick stream was already flowing in her direction, and Gaby found herself fascinated by it even as she jerked back the charging handle, doing the whole thing without having to look down at the rifle once.

She couldn't see the dead man's head or face because of the angle he had landed, but she could hear him gulping for air just fine. Because of the way his hands were positioned, she had no fears that he was going to reach for the fallen rifle or his holstered sidearm anytime soon.

"Did you get her?" a voice asked. It was Mason, and it was coming from another two-way, this one still clipped to the *(dying)* dead man's waist. Mason sounded out of breath, as if he had been running. "Carter, did you get her?"

No, Carter didn't get me, you shit.

Gaby scanned the diner while doing her very best to ignore the new stabs of pain that seemed to be coming from everywhere. If one of Mason's goons had managed to sneak into the building unnoticed, a second—even a third—could have done the exact same thing.

So where were they? Because she was ready. Or she was as ready as she was going to be, anyway.

After about five seconds without an answer from Carter, the radio on the floor next to her squawked, and Mason said, "I guess it's true what they say: If you want something done, you have to do it yourself." He sighed, sounding exasperated but resigned. "Maybe next time, sweetheart. Until then, don't forget me, huh?"

Go to hell, she thought. *Go to hell…*

───── ─────

SOMETIME BETWEEN WHEN Mason signed off and she was telling him to go to hell while staring at the unmoving body at the other end of the counter, she closed her eyes and didn't open them again until a voice said, "Hey-o, what have we here?"

She snapped awake and turned her head because *the voice had come from right next to her—*

"Relax, it's me," Danny said.

She let out a relieved sigh and forced her finger off the trigger. "Jesus, Danny..."

"No, just Danny, but you're not the first person to confuse me with a higher power."

He was crouched next to her, looking past her at the dead body on the other end. She choked back tears at the sight of him. She didn't know how he was still alive or how he had gotten here, and she didn't care, either.

"You made a hell of a mess there, kid," Danny was saying. "Remind me never to invite you to Danny's Game Nights in the future."

"I'd kick your ass," she said.

"Oh, I have no doubt," he said, and grinned at her through a face full of scratches and bandages. Gaby didn't even want to think about what kind of work Zoe was going to have to do on all three of them when they made it back to the *Trident*.

All three of us...

"Nate?" she said, almost too afraid to see the response on his face.

Except he smirked, which was a good sign.

"Limping around somewhere outside, but otherwise still in one piece," Danny said. "Well, mostly. I had to leave him behind so I could take care of the dudes hiding in the donut shop."

"What happened?"

"There were guys. I killed them. No big whoop."

"Did you get him? Mason?"

Danny shook his head. "Sneaky little bugger must've snuck out before I showed up and ventilated the place."

"He's really good at that..."

"His luck's going to run out sooner or later."

"Hopefully sooner..."

Danny nodded when suddenly he jerked his head toward the street and lifted his M4 from the floor.

"What is it?" she asked, because she hadn't heard anything.

"Cars," Danny said.

"I don't hear—"

"Stay here," he said before she could finish.

"Danny, wait—"

But he was already on his feet and rounding the counter.

She sighed and tried to get up, but the pain was too much and she had to sit back down. With the carbine still across her lap, she waited to hear gunshots, but there was just the silence and...

She gave up and closed her eyes.

"HEY," NATE SAID as he hovered over her.

"Hey," she said, smiling up at him. "You're alive."

"I am. And you are, too. You did a pretty good job with that shoulder. Good thing you've had a lot of experience lately."

"You really okay?"

"Stop worrying about me."

"I can't help it."

He smiled. "Okay, if you insist."

He reached down and stroked her cheek, and she leaned against the familiar and welcoming feel of his hand as she tried to figure out where she was.

She was lying down, she knew that much, but where? It wasn't the diner's hard-tiled floor under her, but it wasn't quite a mattress, either. Maybe one of the booths? It was definitely something soft, and she never wanted to get up.

"It's a van," Nate said, seeing the look on her face.

"A van?"

"They found it near the shoreline. I don't think they had any idea how handy it's going to be, with you and the chest and all."

"They?"

"I've been called worse," a familiar voice said.

Gaby turned her head and saw Carly leaning over the front passenger seat of the vehicle. She had a ball cap on, long red hair spilling out along the sides, and she had a contagious grin on her face as she looked back at Gaby and Nate.

"And yes, in case you were wondering, I was totally eavesdropping on all the lovey-dovey talk," Carly said.

"Thank God you're here," Gaby said. "I'm getting so sick and tired of staring at these two guys all the time."

"You're just saying that because I brought a van to pick you up."

"Yeah, that too."

"Now that we're all caught up, what's in the chest?"

"The chest?"

"*The* chest," Nate said. "Remember?"

Oh. Right. The chest.

It was an old-fashioned wooden treasure hope chest, to be specific. They had found it in an antique shop next to the bank. The building had almost completely collapsed in on itself from the bombing, but the chest, all thirty-by-eighteen-by-twenty inches of it, stood out from the destruction anyway, heavily chipped by falling debris but intact. They had covered up all the edges where even the littlest bit of sunlight could possibly penetrate with duct tape and ended up using three full rolls just to be absolutely certain.

"So what's in the chest?" Carly asked again, looking from Nate to Gaby.

"You didn't ask Danny?" Nate said.

"He wouldn't tell me. Kept saying it was a surprise."

"Oh, it's a surprise, all right."

Carly sighed. "See, this is why I could only get Blaine and Bonnie to come with me to rescue you guys. Because you guys suck. Even Lara turned me down."

"Liar," Danny said as he leaned into the front passenger-side door and kissed Carly.

She wrapped her arms around his neck and pulled him in tight. After a while, Gaby wondered if the two of them even remembered that she and Nate were still back here doing their best not to notice, which was difficult since they were just a few feet away.

After a while, Nate cleared his throat. "Come on, guys, do you really have to do that in front of us? It's kinda gross."

Danny stopped sucking face with Carly just long enough to grunt out, "Shaddup, Nate-o-meter."

"Yeah, shaddup," Carly said before dragging Danny's mouth back onto hers.

Nate sighed and looked back at Gaby. "It's going to be a long car ride."

"We're going home?" she asked.

"Bonnie already radioed the *Trident*. They'll be waiting for us at the shoreline, and this time they're not going anywhere until we're back onboard. Lara's supposed to be sending some people to meet us halfway as insurance."

"People? We have 'people' now?"

Nate shrugged. "She didn't elaborate, but apparently a lot's happened on their end while we've been running around out here."

"More surprises," Gaby said. Then she smiled up at Nate again. "What the hell. I like surprises…"

EPILOGUE

"WE TOOK A vote," the man with the bald head and red facial hair said three seconds after he entered the room and sat down on the chair, facing Keo from the other side of the iron bars. Keo liked a man who got right to the point.

"Pray tell," Keo said.

He didn't bother getting up from the stained cot in the back of the cell or making any effort to open both eyes. One was enough to see the newcomer. Sunlight streamed in through the room's only high window, but it was still closed and therefore didn't do anything to clear up the stale air. The irony sucked—he was sitting on an island with an abundance of fresh air, but he couldn't breathe in a single speck of it.

"Half voted to shoot you and toss you into the ocean," the man said. "The other half wants to make it slow and painful."

"I'll take choice number three."

"There is no choice number three."

"I demand a recount."

The man frowned. "You're not taking this very seriously."

"This is totally my serious face."

"Your life is on the line."

"Yeah? So what. Same shit, different day."

The man smirked. "Interesting life you must lead."

"You have no idea. I should write a book."

"What would you call it?"

"Keo's Life of High Adventure and Shitty Luck."

"Doesn't sound like such a great life, after all."

"Depends on how you look at it," Keo said.

The man smelled of fried fish, something Keo hadn't had the pleasure of enjoying the last three days. At least they had fed him something, even if he couldn't tell what that "something" was. But food was food, even if it did come in clumpy white liquid form on a heavily chipped and peeling cafeteria tray. They hadn't bothered to give him any utensils—not even the cheap, flimsy kind—so Keo's fingers were still sticky with this morning's rations.

"I'll tell you some stories if you tell me how the war's going," Keo said.

"We're pulling most of our people back earlier than planned," the man said.

That was surprising—not that they were pulling people back, but that the man was actually answering his question. Normally Keo couldn't get a single word out of his guards, and the last four people who had come to see him hadn't offered very much in terms of information, never mind what was happening beyond the island's beaches.

"We're not sure how to proceed without Mercer," the man continued. "He was the engine that drove the revolution. Without him…" Baldy shook his head. "We're at a crossroads, Mr. Keo."

"Just Keo. Mr. Keo was the guy I pretended to be back in college in order to get some cheap tail."

The man chuckled. It even sounded genuine.

"You got a name?" Keo asked.

"Rhett," the man said.

"Nice to meet you, Rhett."

"Can't say the same, unfortunately."

"Understandable. I did murder your boss."

"Yes, you did."

"So why am I still alive, Rhett?"

"Erin."

"Erin?" Keo said, remembering his last image of her lying on the floor inside the Comm Room.

"We've been trying to figure out for the last three days why she did what she did," Rhett said. "She was one of us. More than that, she was one of Mercer's chosen few. And for her to do what she did... That's why you're still alive."

There was sadness in Rhett's face, the look of someone mourning more than just a colleague, but a friend...and maybe something more?

"Were the two of you involved?" Keo asked.

Rhett smiled but shook his head. "No. She wasn't interested."

"You ever heard of Rogaine?"

"No. I mean, she wasn't interested in *men*."

"Ah."

"You didn't know?"

"I never asked."

"Not that that has anything to do with anything," Rhett shrugged. "Anyway, we've spent the last three days gathering information, talking to people—everyone she knew, and who thought they knew her. We were at a dead end until we found this." He reached into his back pocket and took out a piece of folded paper. "One of her friends found it. It was wedged under her pillow, which is why she didn't see it until this morning when she was changing the covers."

"What is it?"

"A note from Erin." He opened it but didn't show the contents to Keo. "It explains why she did what she did and what she was hoping to accomplish by it."

"I'm not in there, am I?"

"No. She didn't even mention you once."

"Given my luck with women, that figures."

"It's about Mercer. And the war. Or, as she calls it in the letter, 'Mercer's bloody crusade.'"

"What else does it say?"

"The rest is meant for her friend."

"Come on, Rhett, have a heart. I haven't had much entertainment in here waiting for you guys to make up your minds."

Rhett folded the paper and put it back into his pocket. "Suddenly it made sense why she did what she did. It's something that a lot of us have thought about, but it took Erin's sacrifice to finally bring it into the light."

"The townspeople," Keo said. It wasn't a question.

"Yes," Rhett nodded. "The townspeople."

"None of that explains why I'm still alive. Mind you, not that I'm complaining, but being all alone in here day after day makes a guy think, and my head hurts."

"We know you came to the island with Erin. What we don't know is how much of a partnership the two of you had."

"Assuming we had one, how does that work out for me?"

"I don't know. I guess it would depend on how we ultimately decide to judge what Erin did."

"So how's it looking?"

"Fifty-fifty."

"Eh, I've had worse odds."

Rhett nodded. "If I were you, that would be my play, too. I don't see any other option, given that you blew Mercer's brains all over the Comm Room."

"In my defense, I wanted to blow his brains all over his private quarters. We just ended up in Comm."

"In any case, I don't know what's going to happen to you, Keo. For better or worse, right now you're nowhere near our top priority."

"Daebak."

"What?"

"Just glad not to be number one with a bullet, is all."

"No promises." Rhett stood up and returned the chair to the corner. "Like I said, we're at a crossroads. With Mercer gone, we don't know how to proceed. Half of us wants to abandon the war effort, and the other half wants to finish it in Mercer's memory."

"Which half wants to kill me slowly and painfully?"

Rhett grinned. "Both halves want to kill you, remember?"

"Yeah, but I'm not a fan of the whole 'slowly and painfully' part."

"Who is?" Rhett walked to the door. "Sit tight, Keo. No one's going to kill you yet, slowly or painfully, until we decide where to go from here."

Keo finally stood up and walked to the cell bars. "Hey, Rhett."

Rhett stopped at the door and looked back.

"Do I at least get a phone call?" Keo asked. "Even a condemned man on death row gets a last wish."

"No one has phones anymore, Keo."

"One radio call, then."

"And who would you radio?" He added quickly, "If I were to grant you your wish, hypothetically speaking."

"A friend," Keo said. "She happens to be a hell of a lot smarter than me—but that's not saying much—so maybe she can help you out with your little problem, too."

"What problem would that be?"

"You got an army, but you don't know what do with it." He leaned against the bar and held Rhett's gaze. "Tell me, why did you go along with Mercer's plan in the first place? You had to know it wasn't going to mean dick in the larger scheme of things. Deep down, what was the reason? The *real* reason?"

"I wanted to fight back," Rhett said without hesitation. "After everything they took from us—our loved ones, our friends, our city, our fucking planet—I wanted to strike back at the fuckers, and I didn't know how. Mercer gave me a way."

"See, the thing about sitting here all by my lonesome night after night is that it leaves you time to think."

"And a headache, right?" Rhett grinned.

"Yeah, that too. Anyway, it occurred to me that I might know a guy who knows a way you can still do that—strike back at the ghouls—without that whole murdering innocent civilians part. And I bet this army of yours would come in real handy in making that happen."

"A guy? You said you wanted to contact a 'she' earlier."

"I can't find the guy, but she can."

Rhett stared at him but didn't say anything. Keo couldn't tell if the man was trying to decide if getting him a radio was worthwhile or how best to dispose of his body. Given how bad he was at reading people, it was probably a coin flip.

"Erin told me she should have stopped Mercer a long time ago," Keo said. "It was her one big regret—that she let all of this happen. Mercer's dead, but the damage is done. His way was never going to work. You have to know that."

Rhett remained silent, but he didn't turn and leave, either.

"I'm offering you another way," Keo said. "A real path to victory. You interested?"

Rhett began walking back toward him. "I'm listening…"

"Good," Keo said. "First things first: Get me that radio. Second thing: Can someone open that fucking window already? I'm choking on my own BO in here…"

Made in the USA
Middletown, DE
18 April 2017